Vying FOR THE *Viscount*

Books by Kristi Ann Hunter

HAWTHORNE HOUSE

A Lady of Esteem: A HAWTHORNE HOUSE Novella

A Noble Masquerade

An Elegant Façade

An Uncommon Courtship

An Inconvenient Beauty

HAVEN MANOR

A Search for Refuge: A HAVEN MANOR Novella

A Defense of Honor

Legacy of Love: A HAVEN MANOR Novella from The Christmas Heirloom Novella Collection

A Return of Devotion

A Pursuit of Home

HEARTS ON THE HEATH

Vying for the Viscount

HEARTS *on the* HEATH

Vying
FOR THE
Viscount

KRISTI ANN HUNTER

BETHANYHOUSE
a division of Baker Publishing Group
Minneapolis, Minnesota

© 2020 by Kristi L. Hunter

Published by Bethany House Publishers
11400 Hampshire Avenue South
Bloomington, Minnesota 55438
www.bethanyhouse.com

Bethany House Publishers is a division of
Baker Publishing Group, Grand Rapids, Michigan

Printed in the United States of America

Library of Congress Cataloging-in-Publication Data
Names: Hunter, Kristi Ann, author.
Title: Vying for the viscount / Kristi Ann Hunter.
Description: Minneapolis, Minnesota : Bethany House Publishers, [2020] | Series:
    Hearts on the heath
Identifiers: LCCN 2019056904 | ISBN 9780764235252 (trade paperback) | ISBN
    9780764236372 (cloth) | ISBN 9781493425181 (ebook)
Subjects: GSAFD: Love stories.
Classification: LCC PS3608.U5935 V95 2020 | DDC 813/.6—dc23
LC record available at https://lccn.loc.gov/2019056904

Scripture quotations are from the King James Version of the Bible.

This is a work of fiction. Names, characters, incidents, and dialogues are products of the author's imagination and are not to be construed as real. Any resemblance to actual events or persons, living or dead, is entirely coincidental.

Cover design by LOOK Design Studio
Cover photography by Aimee Christenson

Author represented by Natasha Kern Literary Agency

20 21 22 23 24 25 26   7 6 5 4 3 2 1

To the One who knows my future
Psalm 139:15–16

And to Jacob, for always helping me find
the missing piece of my plans.

Prologue

MADRAS, INDIA
MARCH 1817

There were many things Hudson thought he should feel, given that this was the moment he'd anticipated and prepared for his entire life, but instead of satisfaction, excitement, or even fear, all he felt was ready. Before him was the ship that would carry him to a new life. It wasn't grand or remarkable. It was simply there, ready to do its job, just like he was.

Over the past month, there had been other sensations. Momentary grief. Guilt that the grief hadn't been greater at learning of the death of a grandfather he'd never really known. Frustration that said grandfather had encouraged Hudson to stay in India instead of coming to England while the old man was still alive.

Anger at himself for listening to the man he didn't know instead of his own instincts.

Worry over what would happen given the fact that the letter he'd received meant the estate, land, tenants, stable, and horses he'd inherited had already been under the care of stewards and managers for six months and would remain that way for at least another six as he traveled.

It hadn't taken long, though, for all those feelings to fade under the weight of the fact that finally—*finally*—he was going to step into the life he'd been waiting twenty-eight years to live.

As the firstborn son of the firstborn son of the sixth Viscount Stildon, Hudson had always known his destiny. Assuming, of course, that he managed to stay alive and fulfill it.

Hiding away in India had been enough to protect Hudson from the schemes of a crazed uncle who wanted the title for himself, but it had meant exposure to other dangers. Such as the fever that had taken his mother's life when he was twelve. And the snake that had bitten and killed his father ten years later.

Now what had once seemed nothing but a vague dream was reality. Hudson was the viscount.

It was a day he'd awaited with equal parts anticipation and dread. No longer a vulnerable child, he could take his rightful place in England. He'd been raised with all the education and experience his father said he would need.

He liked India, but he had never belonged there, never had anything he felt was his own. Perhaps in a few short months, when he stepped foot on the soil of his father's birth, he would know what it was to feel acceptance.

There was nothing in India he was loath to leave behind, nothing that would make him wish to return.

In fact, all he was taking with him was contained in three chests: two large ones he wouldn't see again until the ship docked in England and one smaller one to be stored in his cabin, along with a travel cabinet that he'd been assured was a necessity for any man about to spend six months at sea.

Hudson had never been to sea, but he had roared across the plains on a galloping horse, the wind in his hair and his knees tightly gripping an unsteady seat. It was likely to be rather the same.

All he had to do was survive another six months of waiting and he would finally be home.

SOMEWHERE ON THE COAST OF AFRICA
MONTHS LATER

He didn't know where he was, when it was, or even who he was anymore. His only certainty was that he didn't want to get back on that boat.

Of course, being off the boat wasn't much better. Despite the fact that he *knew* he was standing solidly on the ground at a port he'd forgotten the name of as soon as the captain had said it, his entire world remained unsettled.

The first time they'd stopped to take on water and supplies, Hudson had lunged for the gangplank, hoping that the shoreline would provide some relief from a middle that churned more than the water the ship cut through.

Then, as now, steady ground had provided only a modicum of relief. He was able to eat more than a few swallows at a time, and he'd been able to fill his nose with a scent other than fish and salt. Oh, how he missed being able to take a deep breath and enjoy the aroma of grass, leather, and horse.

At the second port, he'd tried staying on the ship, hoping to maintain what little adjustment he'd been able to make to the vessel's constant motion, but the heaving of a boat at dock was even worse than it had been at sea.

So this third time around, he'd gotten off. He'd focused on getting in a few hearty meals and having his shirts laundered, since he frequently sweated through them as he tossed about on his small bed in moaning misery.

Sleep was elusive, as lying down only made the room spin, so he was forced to spend his one evening ashore trying to sleep in a chair, but at least he'd strengthened his resolve enough to make it to the next port.

One port at a time and eventually, with the Lord's blessing, he'd make it to England.

The thud of quick footfalls pounded down the dock behind

Hudson, and he barely had the presence of mind to brace himself before the runner grazed his side. With a spin that sent a pounding pain spiraling through his brain and down his spine, Hudson kept himself and the boy from dropping into the water.

"Ho, there," Hudson said, searching his throbbing brain for a name. The boy and the rest of his family were taking the same ship, along with their Indian caretaker, or *ayah*, but he hadn't spent a great deal of time with them or any of the other handful of passengers, as he'd been too busy clinging to his bed.

"It's a bit too far to swim to England. Better we take the ship instead." He pulled them both from the edge, looking around for someone—anyone—to take responsibility for the lad.

The little boy, who looked the very spit of Hudson when he'd been nine or ten, grinned, seemingly unconcerned about the fact that he was alone on a dock in a strange country. "I wonder what England is like."

"You and me both," Hudson murmured.

Everything he'd seen on this journey, when he managed to peel open his eyes, had looked more foreign than he had anticipated. How much different would England be?

For the past twenty-eight years, the country had been nothing more than a blob on the globe, a faraway land that starred in all his father's stories and preparations for the future. He glanced around the port. Would that blob look and sound this strange when they got there in a few very long months?

Another visual search revealed no panicked caretaker. Should he escort the boy to the ship? Was the rest of the family aboard already, assuming the boy was among them? If Jesus' parents could leave Him behind in a synagogue, it had to be feasible for the parents of a normal human boy to misplace him.

Probably prudent to stay where he was, especially since that meant another few moments in which his world only seemed to roll about. What did one do with a boy when one could barely think straight enough to remember one's own name, much less someone else's?

His inadvertent companion clutched a finely carved wooden horse in his arms. Hudson might not know anything about boys, but he knew God's most graceful creatures very well. He pointed at the carved animal. "Do you like horses?"

The boy nodded vigorously. "Papa bought it for me in the market. He says one day I'll have a horse just like this and I'll ride him through the park. I think I'll name him Chicken."

Hudson was still trying to come to grips with the strange name for an equine as the boy barreled on, the jumbled mess of words making it evident that he was as fascinated by horses as Hudson was. Even if he didn't yet know how to properly name one.

"Henry!" cried a female with a thick Tamil accent a few minutes later. An Indian woman rushed across the docks, two younger children in tow. She muttered under her breath about young boys with more excitement than sense, and Hudson bit his lip to smother the grin.

"Ayah, look! Papa bought me a horse." The boy proudly held his carving aloft, abandoning Hudson as if they hadn't been in the middle of a discussion about the shapes of muzzles on different breeds of horses.

A finely dressed man and woman walked up behind the harried ayah. The woman's mouth was pressed into a tight, thin line, while the man looked somewhat unsure of how to feel as he gave Hudson a nod. "Thank you for watching out for my son, Lord Stildon."

So Hudson had formally met them at some point, then. Like England, the title had been little more than a mark on paper for most of his life. It was familiar enough that he knew to answer to it, but hearing it aloud still gave him pause.

The man—a Mr. Martin, Hudson believed, though not with enough conviction to use the name—smiled indulgently down at the boy. "He's off to school, you know."

No, Hudson didn't know. Or rather, he *knew* but had never experienced. As a boy, he'd been forced to watch as his friends departed on one boat after another, bound for England and education, his friendships destined to become nothing more than a few dwindling letters.

Mr. Martin didn't seem to notice Hudson's frown. Instead, the father set a heavy hand on his son's shoulder and laughed. "Can't have a proper Englishman growing up in India without decent schooling."

Hudson rather hoped one could turn out to be a proper Englishman without an English school, but he didn't say as much. The tutors his father had hired had been competent fellows, and Hudson would put his brain up against anyone's.

The proper Englishman part was still to be determined.

"Which school?" Hudson asked because he knew how to be polite.

"Eton, just like his father." The man's chest expanded with pride.

"Of course," Hudson said. His father had gone to Eton. So had his grandfather. The best Hudson could say was that one of his tutors had taught there for a few years.

Mercifully, the captain called for them to come aboard, and Hudson allowed the family to go up in front of him in the hopes that the uncomfortable conversation went with them.

His luck, it would seem, hadn't been packed in his sparse trunks, because Mr. Martin fell back from his family to walk alongside Hudson. "What brought you to India?"

"I was born there."

The man chuckled. "And you came back? Even though ships disagree with you so?"

That assumption was far simpler than explaining he was only just now traveling to see his motherland, so Hudson didn't bother correcting the other man. "I was helping my father build up horse racing in Madras."

12

In truth, leaving the horses behind had been the most difficult part of his departure. With both his mother and father dead, Hudson had made the horses his life. Only the knowledge that a stable full of sweet goers was supposedly waiting for him in England made it doable.

"Where will you go once we dock?"

"Suffolk." Though he'd had to look the place up in a book of maps, the vast green Heath was easy enough to picture, as India held several such beautiful areas. It was the grassy plain being dotted with hundreds upon hundreds of some of the finest horses in the world that Hudson couldn't quite imagine.

Assuming, of course, that everything awaiting him hadn't fallen to ruin in the yearlong absence of a proper owner. Had his grandfather taken the time to ensure there was something for his grandson to come home to? What if Hudson was traveling halfway across the world with the hope of finally belonging somewhere only to end up alone and aimless?

That new consideration made it almost impossible for him to tread up the gangplank and endure more weeks and months of utter torture.

Wood bit into his fingers as his grip tightened on the railing, and he narrowed his gaze on the shrinking docks as the ship went into motion. Piece by piece, building by building, the land faded away.

Was Hudson's life doing the same thing, abandoning him to an unsteady journey to an invisible destination? Little by little, he'd learned that life would eventually take away anything outside of himself.

His childhood friends had left India behind, heading to Eton or Harrow, like the young boy from the dock, but Hudson had still had his family. After his mother's death, he'd still had his father. Then he'd been left with the solace of horses and his reputation and abilities around the stables.

Now, Hudson had nothing but a chest of clothing that was

ill-suited to his final destination and the obligation his father had
drilled into him since birth.

Father always said life was better around the next corner, but
Hudson had never found anything but disappointment. His faith
had grown more than a little thin.

He swallowed hard, searching himself for the strength to believe
that this time, this change, would be the one that finally completed
him, that finally gave him a settled peace of belonging. There was
a God in heaven, and even though He hadn't answered any of
Hudson's other pleas, surely He would answer this one.

If He didn't, Hudson wasn't sure which corner to turn next.

One

The problem with life was that one's plans could be up-ended by the multitude of other living creatures in the world—both human and equine. The all-too-recognizable and equally unwelcome jerk of her horse nearly sent Miss Bianca Snowley tumbling to the ground. So much for a long, hard ride across the Heath to blow her problems out of her mind. She'd simply have to find that sense of peace elsewhere this morning.

With a sigh, she pulled the horse to a stop, kicked free of the stirrup, and dismounted, wincing as her foot landed on uneven ground and sent a shot of pain up her leg. She shook it out and gave the horse a reassuring pat on the neck before looping her arm through the reins.

Owen, the groom who'd been riding with her, circled his horse, Apollo, around to where she was standing. The tall former race-horse with a deep, rich chestnut coat snuffled in protest.

"I'm well, Owen," Bianca said as she set about adjusting her riding skirt for walking. "I'm afraid Atalanta isn't going anywhere but back to the stable, though."

"We'll return immediately," the groom said, shifting his weight to prepare to dismount.

Bianca stopped him with a look. It was well known that the groom tended to avoid tasks whenever possible, but would he truly wish to give up a ride on Apollo, a beast that possessed enough power to win four of the ten races he ran a few years ago?

Of course not. Nor could Bianca allow him to make such a sacrifice for something as silly as perceived propriety. Besides, Apollo had barely managed to do more than fill his lungs with fresh air. He deserved a good long run. "We have not even reached the edge of Hawksworth's pastures, Owen. There is no reason for both of us to miss a charge across the Heath."

The groom frowned. "You mean to return alone, miss?"

If she couldn't free her thoughts in the wind created by a running horse, she could at least enjoy a solitary walk with a beautiful horse at her side. It was the next best thing. "I promise to go straight back to the stable and remain there until someone returns. It's empty but for horses right now, and I rather think I'll enjoy their company."

He didn't look happy about it, but Apollo, despite being excruciatingly well trained, was starting to fidget. There was a limited window of time in which the Heath would be open for horses to run this morning, which was why all the grooms were out exercising the animals at the same time.

"Apollo needs to run, Owen." Since it was a statement that couldn't be argued, Bianca took Atalanta's reins and started the short walk back to the stable.

"I'm waiting until you top the hill," the groom grumbled.

"If that makes you feel better," she called over her shoulder.

She rubbed a hand over her mount's soft nose and received a jarring nudge to the shoulder in return. "If that is your version of an apology, I accept."

After one last reassuring pat to the horse's cream-colored neck, Bianca resumed walking, though she put a bit of space between herself and the horse in case the animal tried to apologize again. "Don't worry, we'll be taking that saddle off and seeing what's wrong with you in a few short minutes. Hopefully it's nothing but a pebble in your shoe."

The horse nudged her shoulder once more, drawing a low chuckle from Bianca as she opened the gate and led the horse into the stable yard.

She kept a tight hold on the horse's reins, even though she expected the mare was already intent on returning to the stable. Part of the beauty of horses was their unpredictability. Of course, part of their appeal was the ability to control that volatility. She'd long ago recognized that she liked the power of having a huge animal listen to her and depend upon her.

The affection from the beasts was pleasant, too, even if it was actually a hunt for the treat they could smell in her pocket.

A masculine laugh joined hers on the air, making Bianca's feet come to a halt. There was a man in the stable. The stable that was supposed to be empty. She and Owen had been the last ones to depart fifteen minutes ago, and the household servants never ventured out to the horses.

It was possible Mr. Whitworth, the stable manager, had decided to come by today, but he would know all the grooms would be out this morning. Besides, Bianca could count on one hand the number of times she'd heard the man so much as snicker.

So, who was in the stable?

Bianca's blood surged so hard through her veins that her fingers shook as she secured Atalanta's reins to the fence that bordered the drive to the grand estate house. Was it a horse thief? A neighboring stable owner hoping to convince Mr. Whitworth to make some sort of business agreement? What if the disturbing man who had tried to take the horses after Lord Stildon died had returned?

All the moisture in her mouth turned to dust as she crossed the drive with careful steps. The loose stone shifted under her feet but didn't make much noise as long as she stayed balanced on her toes.

She was probably being an empty-headed ninny about this entire thing. Surely Mr. Whitworth's tall, broad form was going to come into view and they'd both be able to laugh about her overactive imagination while she took care of Atalanta.

But if it *was* a thief, she would . . . she would . . . well, in all honesty, if he was after a saddle or two she'd simply let him be. She was female, after all, and while she considered herself to be quite the sportswoman, she wasn't going to claim any unusual bravery or warrior-like talents. No one could be allowed to harm the horses, though.

The door to the stable had been left open to allow fresh air to circulate into the building, so Bianca crept along the wall and peered around the edge. Despite the abundance of windows, the interior was far dimmer than the exterior, and her eyes took several moments to distinguish which shadowy shapes were supposed to be there and which weren't.

As the man came into focus, it was abundantly clear he numbered among the very out-of-place items.

Rumpled and showing signs of road dust on his boots, the man stood at Hestia's stall. The box stall door was open, and the dark brown thoroughbred was nibbling at the carrot extended toward her in one of the man's hands. The other hand held a coil of rope.

The man was attempting to steal away with Hestia.

The man—or whoever had hired him—was clever. Hestia had never run all that well, but her children were another story. She was the best mare the stable had, though currently she wasn't carrying a future champion. If someone else managed to get their hands on her and hide her away, he could benefit from the theft without the horse ever showing up at the racecourse.

Bianca couldn't let that happen. She pulled back and flattened herself against the stable wall, her breathing speeding up to match the pounding of her pulse. If Hestia left the stable with that man, they'd never see her again.

A quick glance around revealed a complete lack of anything resembling a potential weapon. In fact, it showed a complete lack of anything at all. The front of Hawksworth stable was always kept neat, tidy, and professional. Who knew they should leave a pitchfork lying about for such an occasion as this? She'd left her riding crop tied to Atalanta's saddle, so her only options were whatever was on her person. She could not waste a moment. The man was already coaxing Hestia out of her stall.

It took a bit of tugging, and she almost fell twice, but Bianca managed to pull off her riding boot without making more noise than someone would expect from horses shifting about in their stalls. While far from a proper weapon, the heel was sturdy, and the length of the footwear gave her something to grip. It would have to do.

Hestia was depending upon Bianca and her boot.

After one more deep, steadying breath, Bianca hid the boot behind her back and entered the stable. Her gasp of pretend shock would surely have made Shakespeare cry, but it was the best she could muster. She spoke in a rush to keep the man from dwelling on the fakeness of her opening. "What do you think you're doing?"

The man paused in the middle of looping his rope around Hestia's neck. "I beg your pardon?"

Ha! As if she would pardon a horse thief, even if she could. "I asked what you thought you were doing."

Fortunately, the thick fabric of her habit disguised any trembling of her weak knees. This man could not be allowed to think she was intimidated—though she was—or that she didn't know how to actually get rid of him—though she didn't. He had to believe her a threat to his well-being if he continued with his task.

"I'm taking this horse for a walk." The man turned a questioning look to her. "What are you doing?"

So much for the hope that her mere presence would make him run. The boot it was going to have to be.

"I'm stopping you from stealing that horse." She charged forward, swinging her boot around to the front so she could hold it like a club. Hopefully the heel that was hard enough to make a horse mind its rider was substantial enough to do damage when it connected with a human.

She swung the footwear to and fro, hitting as much of the stall wall and door as the man, but it had the desired effect of getting him to step away from the horse.

"Who—what—I say now—" The man couldn't quite manage a sentence as he tried to shield himself from her swinging boot.

Confidence gaining with every inch that Bianca managed to drive the man back, she started to yell. "Get out of here," she said, embracing the idea of being Hestia's avenger. The boot nearly jerked from her hand as it solidly connected with the man's shoulder, but Bianca held on and swung it again, aiming for his midsection this time. "Tell whoever sent you"—*swing*—"that no one"—*swing*—"steals"—*swing*—"from Hawksworth stables."

"I'm not—" A grunt cut off the man's sentence as the boot glanced off the back of his shoulder. He reached out, grasped the boot, and tugged, pulling Bianca into frighteningly close proximity. Close enough that he could grab her up and abscond with her, if he so chose.

Bianca brought her other boot—the one still on her foot—into play and kicked toward him. Her aim was a bit better with a kick than a swing, but she wasn't going to be bragging about either as she kicked wildly into the air as often as she connected with his shin.

Finally, the man shoved her away and stumbled out the door. He stood on the drive, blinking at her for several moments, until Bianca started swinging her boot and screaming as she ran at him once more. She gave one more mighty swing and nearly turned herself around as the man ducked out of the way. He jerked back two steps, then turned and ran.

Bianca retreated to the stable, breath rushing in and out of her lungs at an alarming rate, and allowed an enormous smile to split her face. She'd done it! She'd saved the horse.

Unless the man wasn't alone. What if he had companions nearby and he'd only run to get help, someone to hold her off while they stole away with Hestia?

No. Bianca would not allow that to happen. She would stand her ground.

With one eye on the door, Bianca limped over to Hestia's stall and gave the horse a strong pat on the neck as she secured her back into her stall. Then she paced awkwardly, boot held at the ready. The man might return, but he would not find these beautiful animals unprotected.

She gave an anxious glance outside as she passed the open door. The boot was all well and good, but it wouldn't hurt to send up a prayer that one of the grooms would return soon. In the meantime, it might behoove her to find a better weapon.

Two

Suffolk was as beautiful as his father had claimed, and the estate and stable were even grander than his grandfather had described in his letters, but no one had warned Hudson that the area was inhabited by crazed women.

Hudson rubbed his hands over his face and leaned against the rock wall, the jagged surface of the artfully cut stones digging into his back as surely as the woman's bootheel had tried to implant itself in his head. He'd felt more than a little foolish running away, but what else was he to do? Hit her? Grab her?

Pushing off from the wall, he arranged a stack of crates so he could climb up and see through the thin windows that lined the back side of the stable. His ears were still ringing from the echoes of the woman's shrill screams, but he needed to make sure that his instinctive belief that she meant no harm to the horses was correct.

She paced up and down the wide, clean aisle peering into empty stalls and giving a pat or two to the inhabitants of the non-empty ones. Her face was indistinguishable due to distance and the wave of the glass, but the stiffness of her body was easily recognizable. He rather doubted she was ready to listen to reason, should he make a reappearance.

A stall divider blocked his view momentarily, but then the woman returned, boot back on her foot and pitchfork in hand.

Definitely not prepared to listen to reason.

Who was she?

She didn't live here at the house. Despite the fact that most of the servants had already been in bed when he arrived late the night before, he was certain the few he'd been greeted by would have let him know if the house held any other occupants. According to the solicitor, there were no close female relatives, unless one counted the woman his uncle had married in Ireland a decade prior, or the daughter they'd had three years after that.

Hudson tilted his head and considered the pacing, obviously angry woman. He wasn't familiar enough with English ladies to guess his attacker's age, but even a horse could see she was well beyond the age of seven. The wife, then? Not unless she had held her years with remarkable grace. Despite viewing the woman's countenance through the blur of a swinging boot, he was certain she had been young.

She'd thought he was a horse thief. The idea inspired both humor and concern. The servants in the house hadn't been expecting him last night, either. In fact, everyone he'd encountered seemed surprised to learn he was the new viscount. Hadn't his grandfather prepared them?

The solicitor in London, who'd taken nearly two days to convey all the pertinent information to Hudson, had been evasive about the prior titleholder. It seemed the man had held back more than an invitation from his letters.

Eventually, she stopped pacing and leaned the pitchfork against the wall. After looking out the door in several directions, she departed. Moments later she was back, leading a horse.

Was this the one she'd arrived on? Had she thought Hudson was a horse thief because she was one? Surely she didn't think to trade horses. While the beast she was leading was certainly a fine animal, the only thing it had in common with the glorious racehorse was both seemed to be in possession of four working legs. No one but a blind man could confuse a dun with a dark bay, even if they didn't know the difference between a thoroughbred and a pleasure horse of indeterminate breed.

She didn't approach the racehorses, though. Instead, she unsaddled the cream-colored horse and led it into one of the empty stalls. Without any apparent hesitation, she set about doing the work expected of the grooms—brushing down the horse, seeing to its hooves, filling the water bucket.

Hudson had been in and around stables his entire life, and never had he seen anything like it. Surely the dark green riding habit and tall, round hat with its towering feather plume wasn't the normal attire for working women. Nor did he want to consider whether or not the man his grandfather had left in charge of the stable was hiring women as grooms to begin with.

A breeze ruffled the sleeve of his thin linen shirt, sending a shiver across Hudson's shoulders. He'd been in such a rush to see if the stable he'd inherited was as fine as the prior viscount had claimed that he'd simply thrown on the same shirt and trousers he'd traveled in the day before and made his way to the stables. Between the lack of proper outer garments and the dirt and wrinkles, it was little wonder the woman had confused him for a man with criminal intent.

He shivered again and rubbed a hand roughly over his arm as he climbed down from his perch on the stacked crates. Why did it have to be so cold here? He'd been chilled for the few days he'd spent in London when the sky was grey and the sun little more than a suggestion, but today was bright and sunny. Shouldn't that mean it would be hot enough to make a man sweat? Apparently not in England.

There was nothing he could do about the weather, but he had to decide what to do about the woman. It was obvious she meant no harm to the horses, so there was no need to chase her off until he knew who she was. His curiosity urged him to circle the building and confront her immediately, but she still had that pitchfork within easy reach.

Another breeze wafted through his lightweight shirt, and he trudged along the back wall of the building with a sigh. Even if the woman gave him time to introduce himself, she wouldn't believe his story, given his current state. He wouldn't even believe him. First, he would take care of his appearance, then he would deal with the woman.

Hopefully, donning all the proper layers would make him warm enough, even if the fabrics were more suited to India's warm days than England's brisk air. He'd have to see to acquiring new clothing soon. He should probably hire a valet before that, though. Perhaps leaving all his staff behind in India hadn't been the wisest decision, but he couldn't see uprooting his servants from their lives simply to accompany him onto a boat. He certainly couldn't see any of them being any great help in England, where they would likely be even more baffled than he was.

A maid squealed and jumped out of the way when Hudson burst in the back of the house, slamming the heavy wood door into the wall in frustration.

Hudson gave her a nod but kept walking, ignoring her wide-eyed stare as she took in his disheveled appearance. He took four wrong turns, then went up three levels and down two before finding the correct passage to the wing of bedchambers and private parlors.

Whoever had thought a round house would be ideal had obviously never lived in one. It was impossible to know where one was going when all the corridors curved. Fortunately, the private living quarters wing was somewhat normal. At least it was a rectangle.

A manservant stood near the end of the corridor, and Hudson requested a bath be prepared. Such a task likely wasn't in the man's duties, but surely he'd know how to accommodate such a request. Thus far Hudson had met a total of three servants—no, five, if one counted the screeching maid and the lurking footman. Only the butler had been a position Hudson recognized. He'd told the man to have the house presented later this morning, since he hadn't wanted to delay seeing the horses.

He should make his appearance respectable before he met anyone else. It wouldn't do to keep scaring the servants, or to have them think he constantly wallowed about in travel dust.

Two more wrong door attempts preceded his finally locating his bedchambers. All he'd cared about when he finally got in the night before was finding a horizontal surface that didn't move. He'd even told the terrified scullery maid to leave his trunks in the front hall until the other servants woke. The trunks had been gone when he passed through on his way to the stables, so he had to assume they'd been delivered here, but they weren't in the bedchamber itself.

Other doors lined the room, though, and presumably one would reveal his clean clothing. He knew which portal led to the washroom and, obviously, the one he used to enter and exit, but that still left three doors unaccounted for.

The first went to a small office of sorts. On one of his wrong-turn wanderings this morning, he'd seen a large library and an elaborate study. Perhaps his grandfather had used that one for impressing guests? Whether or not Hudson wanted to maintain two studies remained to be seen. It was the least of his concerns at the moment.

Opening the second door revealed a short, narrow passage. This certainly wasn't the way to his dressing room, but where did it go? It was too dim and narrow for a servant's corridor, but the decor was nonexistent, so it wasn't meant to be seen or lingered in. He stepped into it, squinting his eyes to look into the shadows.

Light from his bedchamber was enough to guide him to the door at the other end of the short corridor. Opening it revealed another bedroom, presumably waiting for a new mistress for the home.

Hudson slammed the door. Yes, choosing a wife was something he needed to see to—and soon, since he was now the only person standing between his uncle and the title he'd wanted all those years ago. But would a wife make settling into a new country easier or more difficult?

The Englishmen in India had seemed to allow their wives to guide their social connections, while they focused on more practical, business-related ones. Hudson would, of course, have to eventually learn how to mingle among other English, but his first priority was establishing himself in the local racing populace.

As only one door remained unopened, he was unsurprised to find his dressing room behind it. His travel chest sat against one wall, and the large trunk of clothing lay open, though it was only partially unpacked. One full change of riding clothes had been prepared and laid out, which was all Hudson needed anyway. He could hardly wear more than one outfit at a time.

Muffled movements indicated the arrival of his bathwater, and Hudson took a deep breath and held it before blowing it out slowly. He could do this. His father had raised him for this, hadn't he? It didn't matter that all Hudson had was head knowledge and very little actual experience. He was a smart man. He could do this. It was a new country and a new stable, but truly, how difficult could it be?

Three

His optimism lasted for an entire hour.

After bathing and dressing, Hudson requested that the butler have the staff present themselves to their new employer. Walking the line of servants whose roles he didn't know or understand had made his head spin.

Fortunately, his stomach was no longer churning, and he was looking forward to a meal for the first time in months. The breakfast he'd then been presented had been so dreadfully bland that his swallowing of it was something of a miracle. The best that could be said for it was that it stayed where he put it.

Now that his stomach wasn't rumbling and he was clean and properly dressed, people might believe he owned the place. It was time once again to brave the stables.

When it took him two tries to find the long, curving corridor that connected the main house to the stable, his confidence began to waver.

No screaming female greeted him as he slowly opened the door at the end of the passage. There was, however, a man.

He looked to be a bit taller than Hudson and of similar coloring, though his clothing was nearly all dark, a stark contrast to Hudson's light golds and greys.

"The new Lord Stildon, I presume?" the other man asked, turning away from the horse he'd been looking over.

Hudson nodded. "And you are?"

"Your stable manager. My name is Aaron Whitworth." He inclined his head in greeting. "I am illegitimate."

What on earth was Hudson supposed to say to that? He'd of course met several well-to-do men of less-than-respectable birth—India was rather full of them—but he'd been taught that such things were never discussed, even if everyone knew about it. His mouth opened and then snapped shut before opening again. A response was obviously required, but what should it be? "I, er—" He cleared his throat and tried again. "I am Hudson, Viscount Stildon. I, um, am not illegitimate."

Mr. Whitworth tilted his head back and let out a short but authentic laugh before looking at Hudson with a smile. "I should think not. Quite difficult to inherit a title if you are."

"Impossible, actually," Hudson said as he made his way farther into the stable. "Do you always introduce yourself that way?"

The other man gave a bit of a shrug. "It's become a bit of a habit, I'm afraid, though I don't usually do so professionally. It slipped out in this case, though I have to admit it prevents the uncomfortableness that occurs later when the truth comes out."

"I see." In truth, he didn't, or rather he understood but still didn't know what to say about it. He glanced around the stable and then back to Mr. Whitworth. "Are you a good stable manager?"

He cocked his head to the side, and his dark eyebrows rose. "The best around."

It was said with such calm surety that Hudson was inclined to believe him. Besides, he had no reason to question his grandfather, at least not when it came to the stable. He'd seemed a very knowledgeable and competent horseman in their letters.

His skills as a grandfather, however, were entirely suspect.

Hudson inclined his head toward Mr. Whitworth. "Well, then, if you are as good as you say you are, I don't see where the, er, matter of your birth has any bearing." He gestured around the stables. "It's not like any of the horses are legitimate, either."

There was complete silence, and then Mr. Whitworth was laughing again. When he stopped, his smile was wider, more natural. "I believe we're going to get on well, my lord. Welcome to Newmarket."

Hudson's shoulders loosened, and he resisted the urge to roll them about and relieve more of the abated tension. "Do you live here on the estate?"

Mr. Whitworth's eyebrows lifted a bit. "No. I also manage another stable here in Newmarket. I have a cottage nearer to there. Normally I'm only in Newmarket part of the year. But I've had to spend more time here since your grandfather hired me."

The way the manager was talking, it was as if he expected Hudson to know about him and his situation. And why wouldn't he expect such a thing? It was logical to assume that his grandfather had informed his heir about major developments.

Only he hadn't, and at some point Hudson was going to have to trust someone enough to tell them that. If he stumbled along with everyone assuming he knew more than he did, what sort of errors might he make?

It didn't sit well with him to trust a man whose mettle he'd yet to test, but Mr. Whitworth's introduction had been frank and honest. He would also be the man most likely to see Hudson's blunders up close. If anyone was in a position to subtly guide Hudson without anyone else being the wiser, it was this man.

Hudson walked over to a stall to examine—or at least appear to be examining—one of the horses. "How long ago did Grandfather hire you?"

"About a year and a half ago." Mr. Whitworth joined Hudson and leaned a shoulder against the stall wall. "I've known him a while, of course, since I've run horses against him over the years.

When it became apparent his illness was going to progress more rapidly than anyone could have guessed, he offered me the position. I, well, I couldn't tell him no. He was a dying man and had no idea how long it would take for you to get here."

Hudson jerked his attention from the chestnut carriage horse and met the slight accusation in Mr. Whitworth's eyes. "He was ill? He didn't tell me."

The note about the prior viscount's death had been vague, but Hudson had assumed that something sudden had taken him, like an accident or a lung disease. Instead, it would seem the man had sent two, if not three, letters, well aware that his end was imminent, and still he'd encouraged, in fact demanded, Hudson to stay in India.

Mr. Whitworth said nothing, as there was no good response to such an admission, but some of the hardness eased from his features.

After a tense moment, the manager ran a hand along the back of his neck. "Have you met the horses yet?" He pushed away from the wall and moved toward the box stalls on the other end of the aisle. "Some of them are out in the pasture, but there are a few in here."

Hudson followed, anxious for more than the glimpse he'd managed to get earlier. Would Mr. Whitworth know who the woman was? She looked comfortable enough in the stable to be a frequent visitor. The question was whether or not Hudson wanted to admit he'd been beaten with her boot during their first encounter. For the moment he would focus on the horses. "Where are the youngest ones?"

Mr. Whitworth shifted his weight and gave Hudson a long look before opening the stall door of the horse Hudson had been attempting to guide out earlier. "You don't have any little ones right now. There's a gap in your stock. Lord Stildon's will left provisions for me to keep training the existing horses and enter races, but I never had the authority to arrange breeding. He held on to that right to the end, and the solicitor wouldn't release funds after he died. We had two foals shortly after his death, but unless you do something soon, you're going to have a two-year gap in your racers instead of only one."

Hudson's jaw dropped. A two-year gap? Had his grandfather wanted Hudson to fail? Why would the man go to such lengths to make Hudson appear the fool? He was going to have to do something soon to establish a solid reputation.

The question was *what*.

Mr. Whitworth led Hudson into the stall and gave the reddish-brown mare a pat on the neck. "This is Hestia. Two of our best winners are from her. We've high hopes for any foal she produces."

"I was in the stables with this horse for a few moments earlier this morning. I encountered a spot of trouble that might arise again."

Dark eyebrows lowered in concern as Mr. Whitworth turned from the horse. "Was there a man here?"

"Er, no. A woman."

Concern cleared, and a glimmer of amusement followed. "I'm afraid I'm not well versed in that area. Any advice I'd give would be the headless leading the blind."

It took Hudson a moment to gather the other man's meaning, and then hot embarrassment crawled up his neck. "It wasn't that sort of trouble. It was just that the trouble came in the form of a woman."

"It usually does," the manager murmured.

Hudson slid his eyes closed. Could he make more of a muck of this? Monkeys in the marketplace were more graceful than he was being at the moment. He was simply going to have to explain the incident and hope Mr. Whitworth knew who the woman was. "A woman accused me of trying to steal one of the horses. She proceeded to attack me until it seemed prudent to step away." Or run with his arms covering his head, but that distinction didn't really pertain to the moment. "I watched her from the window for a while to see if *she* was of a mind to steal the horses, but all she did was pace the stable for twenty minutes."

"She *attacked* you? With what?"

What did it matter what she'd attacked him with? Shouldn't Mr. Whitworth be far more concerned with the trespasser who had laid claim to the stable? Shouldn't they be trying to determine if she'd been here before? "Er, well, she attacked me with her riding boot, but I think the graver matter here is that the stable was left vulnerable to such a trespasser."

"Did she have brown hair and a ridiculous cluster of green feathers on her hat?"

"Yes," Hudson said, his trepidation growing along with a sense of reassurance, as the woman was at least known to the other man. "You've encountered her before?"

"Oh yes." The manager nodded, a slight tilt to one side of his mouth. "I had to convince Mr. Knight—he's your head groom—that it wasn't prudent to hire her. We let her exercise some of the pleasure horses and help around the stable, but I drew the line at allowing her to ride the thoroughbreds, stay overnight, or participate in the birthings."

Hudson's mouth gaped open a bit. Of all the scenarios he'd contemplated, that wasn't one of them. "But who is she?"

"Her name is Miss Bianca Snowley." Mr. Whitworth slipped a harness and lead rope onto the mare. As he led the horse out, he sent Hudson a wide grin. "She's your neighbor."

His neighbor. Meaning a well-born young lady had been scraping horse hooves in his stable. Did all of Newmarket know she did that? Would that reflect poorly on him that he allowed such a practice to occur? He had, of course, been known to care for the horses in the stable in India on occasion, but that wasn't the same. Or at least it seemed like it wouldn't be.

Were things more different in England than he'd thought?

His mind was soon taken with the more pressing concern of

learning about the stable. He met the horses and the grooms, was informed of the normal schedule for the day, and saw the collection of prestigious races his stable had won. Yes, it would seem that what his grandfather had left behind was every bit as spectacular as he had claimed.

Now it was up to Hudson to keep it that way and make it even better.

His stomach grumbled, reminding him that breakfast had been a rather unsatisfying venture. It was far too early for dinner, but his stomach was determined to make up for the many months in which he could only eat small bits of horrible ship fare. Not that what he'd eaten this morning had been much better.

Andrew, the groom who had stumbled out of the stable the night before with a sleepy smile to see to the carriage that had delivered him from a nearby inn, shot that smile Hudson's way once more. "There's a tavern on the edge of town. Got the best beef stew in the county."

"Too many carrots," grumbled Roger, another of the grooms. His mouth seemed as perpetually stuck in a frown as Andrew's seemed inclined to smile.

Hudson hadn't eaten a great deal of carrots in his life, but he was certainly open to trying them. And if they had a distinct enough flavor for someone to think there were too many in a dish, well, at least it was better than the bowl of gruel and plain roll he'd been given this morning.

The housekeeper had assured him that the meal quality would improve after there had been opportunity to send someone out for better ingredients. He supposed he couldn't really blame his staff for that since they hadn't known he was coming, but the idea that anyone ate such flavorless mush for a meal was disturbing.

Mr. Whitworth cleared his throat. "I'm sure *Lord* Stildon can do better than the local tavern, gentlemen. Why don't you saddle up Hades for him?"

The grooms gave a swift nod and set about the task. Mr. Whitworth turned to Hudson. "Newmarket is on the other side of the Heath. We can't ride across it right now because it's closed to all but trainers, but you can see it from the road. I'll take you by the yard where your current racers are training. From there you can have your choice of where to eat in town."

If Mr. Whitworth said anything after that, Hudson missed it. The exquisite, all-black horse the grooms led out of the stall at the far end of the stable captured all his attention. Every line, every twitch, was perfection.

He'd encountered a few horses that were finer in his lifetime, but unlike those, this one was his. As he mounted the steed and patted his sleek, dark coat, a sense of calm eased the tightness lingering in his chest. Finally, everything he did was going to have an impact on his own future. He was going to carve out his own niche in this world, and he was going to get there on the back of this horse.

Four

The pot of tea sitting on the dressing table had gone cold by the time Bianca poured herself a cup and gulped it down. It eased the parched sides of her throat even if it offended her tongue, but more important, the chill of the brew meant that she was most definitely behind schedule.

Owen and Miles had been the first grooms to return to the stable from exercising the horses, and while both men were meticulous in their care of the animals, they were not the ones she wanted to report the intruder to. She'd delayed her departure as much as she could, obviously more than she should have, given the state of the tea.

Every Tuesday and Saturday it was delivered to her rooms at precisely ten o'clock, which was when she should start getting dressed for the day and preparing to receive visitors. Most of the time, she and her stepmother simply resided in the same house, but two years ago, Mrs. Snowley had insisted that Bianca start being available to callers twice a week.

Mostly because it looked bad to have the younger sister taking visits while the older hadn't yet faded away into abject spinsterhood.

Bianca threw her plumed riding hat on the dressing table, along with the pins that had secured it in place, and started tugging at the fastenings of her riding habit as she crossed to the dressing room. Dorothy, the lady's maid Bianca shared with her younger sister, wouldn't be able to assist Bianca until Marianne was completely ready.

Life had been so much simpler before Marianne entered society.

Bianca had enjoyed three blessed years of freedom, attending only the parties and assemblies she wanted to, sitting for callers when visits had been arranged prior, and running about Newmarket as she wished. But when Marianne came out, Mrs. Snowley decided to have more of a say in Bianca's life as well.

It was dashed inconvenient.

It wasn't that Bianca didn't want to marry; it was simply that she hadn't found anyone worth marrying. What was the point of getting away from her stepmother if she disliked her husband?

Of course, at four and twenty it might be time to adjust her standards. She discarded the habit onto a wooden chair in the corner and picked up the dress that had been prepared and laid out for her. In stark contrast to her practical dark green riding habit, the pink silk with pale blue trim was lovely and delicate, but she was fairly certain she'd seen Marianne dressed in pink when she'd stepped into the room to let Dorothy know she'd returned.

Both of them in the same color was not a good thing.

A light knock preceded Dorothy's rushed entrance into the bedchamber. Bianca frowned in her direction. "Is Marianne in pink?"

Twin splashes of red spread across the maid's cheeks. "Yes, miss. The blue one has a tear in it, and the only other presentable gown was pink."

Bianca groaned. She knew—everyone knew—that it was best if Bianca gave Mrs. Snowley as few reasons as possible to compare the two girls. In her mind, Marianne would always come out superior. She was, after all, Mrs. Snowley's actual child, whereas nothing could acquit Bianca of the sin of being a living memorial to Mr. Snowley's first wife.

Two other dresses hung on hooks near the pink dress. Bianca reached for a pale green one and shook it out. A few wrinkles marred the skirt, but that shouldn't be very noticeable once she was seated.

"I think this one will do."

Dorothy's mouth puckered as if she were being forced to eat lemons, and her arm shook a bit as she extended it to take the dress from Bianca. "If you wish, miss."

Bianca set about removing her riding boots as Dorothy did her best to smooth the skirt across the nearby bed. "We both know"—Bianca paused to give her riding boot a mighty pull—"that I'll be blamed for any and all faults in my appearance, including wrinkles."

"I know, miss, but—"

"I'm not wearing pink if Marianne is wearing pink." Bianca's boots thudded against the wall, adding a sort of definitive firmness to her sentence.

The maid sighed. "Yes, miss."

Twenty minutes later, Bianca was moving toward the stairs, giving her skirt one more shake and tucking away an errant curl that she'd been too impatient to allow Dorothy to affix properly. She was already ten minutes late to the drawing room. Any further delay would have the woman suggesting Bianca's trips to Hawksworth's stables be reduced.

While Bianca was certain her father wouldn't agree, he did have an irritating tendency to follow his wife when it came to the raising of their daughters, simply to keep the peace.

"Good morning," Bianca said cheerfully as she joined the other women in the drawing room. No callers had arrived yet, fortunately, but that didn't stop Mrs. Snowley from pinching the corners of her mouth together in disapproval.

"Whatever have you done with your hair?" Mrs. Snowley sneered as she poured Bianca a cup of tea.

"I thought perhaps if I secured it as a windblown look, it would remain the way I left it," Bianca said as she accepted the cup of darkly steeped, bitter tea without sugar or milk. Just the way she hated it.

Mrs. Snowley pressed her lips together in a tight frown. Bianca merely smiled. She'd long ago learned that if her responses were sufficiently ridiculous then her stepmother couldn't come up with an intelligent rejoinder, and she refused to speak unless she believed she sounded brilliant.

Marianne held no such compunction. "Do you truly think that would work? Won't your hat still smash it down?"

Bianca tried to look like she was thinking over her half sister's statement. She'd never quite decided if Marianne was as simple as she seemed, or if that was her way of manipulating people. Until she knew for sure, she tried to err on the side of kindness. "Probably. Perhaps I'll simply maintain my chignon from now on."

If possible, Mrs. Snowley's look grew darker. She preferred a certain level of elaborate decoration both in her house and on herself, but Bianca was only willing to endure so much frippery. "We have guests coming for dinner Monday evening," Mrs. Snowley said with forced brightness.

Bianca blinked. Monday? They never had company to the house on Mondays. She wasn't going to ask, though, she absolutely wasn't. She did not want to show any sort of interest in anything Mrs. Snowley was planning. Every time she did, her stepmother either took great glee in the event being something Bianca would hate, or she managed to find a way to postpone or cancel it. It was much safer to simply drink tea and eat biscuits.

To that end, Bianca selected a treat from the tray and took a large bite. If her mouth was full, even her stepmother couldn't expect her to talk.

"Who's coming?" Marianne asked. Bianca's curiosity blessed the girl.

"Mr. Octavius Mead and his son, Theophilus."

Satisfaction practically dripped from the words, and Bianca refused to look at the older woman to see it stamped across her features. The prospect of spending an evening in the company of Mr. Theophilus Mead was appalling. It didn't matter that his father was a particular friend of her father's, Bianca would never like the man. There were many rumors about the way he treated his horses, and every one of them appeared to be true, as far as Bianca was concerned.

It was a shame, really. He was relatively handsome, personable, and a decent rider. While Bianca's main goal was to find a husband with adequate stables and enough leniency to allow her to work with the horses, she had to admit it would be nice if he also wasn't an utter bore. Personality did not win out over mistreatment of horses, though.

Bianca took a bite of biscuit and uncouthly followed it with another large swallow of tea, allowing the sweetness of the food to balance out the bitterness of the drink. As she swallowed and sank her teeth into the biscuit once more, she silently imagined the crunch was Mr. Mead's shin being kicked by the horse he'd been whipping mercilessly in his impromptu race against Lord Davers last week.

"I've told Dorothy to give you extra attention that evening, Bianca. I expect you to cooperate."

The biscuit lodged momentarily in Bianca's throat before sliding painfully the remainder of the way down. She croaked out, "What?"

Mrs. Snowley frowned again. "It's past time you marry. You cannot live on my and your father's charity forever."

Taking care of one's family wasn't truly charity, but debating that would avoid the true point.

"I have every intention of marrying." Bianca took a swallow of bitter tea.

"Unless you plan on marrying a groom from Hawksworth, I don't know how you think you'll find an appropriate match. Mr. Mead is ideal, and I'm putting myself out a great deal to have guests on a Monday evening. I expect you to make the most of the opportunity."

Bianca gaped at her stepmother, trying to form an adequate answer, but she didn't have one. The truth was, she didn't do what other women did to secure husbands. She'd always assumed that because she wanted something different in a husband, her method of finding one would be different.

What if it wasn't? Was she too late?

Mrs. Snowley had said her piece about Bianca's participation in the upcoming dinner and so changed the subject to what Marianne should wear to entertain their guests and which dishes should be served at the dinner.

Bianca selected another biscuit and nibbled at it.

She liked dresses and she enjoyed her food, but of much more concern to her was that her stepmother had dropped any hint of subtlety in her attempt to get Bianca to marry.

Given that even Bianca had considered she should increase her attempts at finding a husband, she couldn't argue Mrs. Snowley's point. She could, however, dread the measures her stepmother would go to accomplish the goal.

It was likely that every conversation for the rest of the morning would include the same rehashing of clothing and food choices and more than one veiled, or perhaps not so hidden, barb at Bianca's increasing age and decreasing marriage chances.

Unless, of course, someone arrived with a distracting *on dit*. Wouldn't that be nice? Someone with actual news to discuss, even if it was only news about who would be attending that night's assembly.

Bianca had never wanted to hear a bit of gossip more in her life.

The first callers, Miss Wainbright and her mother, entered the room with such bright faces it was obvious they knew something more luscious than whether or not there would be waltzing at the evening festivities. Bianca sat up a little straighter, as did Marianne and Mrs. Snowley.

Their skirts hadn't even settled on the edge of the settee before Miss Wainbright was speaking. "Have you heard?" Of course they hadn't heard. If they had, one could lay bets on Mrs. Snowley speaking about it first.

Miss Wainbright folded her hands into her lap as if she expected to be crowned queen at any moment. "The new Lord Stildon has arrived."

The biscuits Bianca had eaten earlier turned into lead in her gut. The new Lord Stildon had been nothing but speculation for so long that she'd begun to think the man didn't exist.

Bianca set her cup down to bury her suddenly shaky fingers in her skirt. Surely the man she'd seen that morning in the stables wasn't the new viscount.

Dear God, please don't let that have been him.

It wasn't exactly a fair prayer, but Bianca didn't much care at the moment. If the fear curling through her gut proved true, she was going to have to come up with an amazing apology.

Marianne eased forward to perch on the edge of her seat. "When did he arrive?"

"Late last night. Word is that he arrived on a late stage but wouldn't spend the night at the inn and hired a man to take him on to Hawksworth, despite the dark hour."

"Was he alone?" Mrs. Snowley asked.

Mrs. Wainbright nodded in the exact same manner as her daughter. "Completely alone. He's young too."

"He's quite handsome," Marianne added.

Bianca frowned at her sister. The girl hadn't even known the man existed until two minutes ago. "By whose account?"

Marianne flipped a hand through the air. "Oh, everyone's."

"He's a young viscount, Bianca," Mrs. Snowley said firmly. "Why shouldn't he be handsome?"

As the Wainbright women murmured agreement, Bianca wondered if the whole lot had gone mad. Did they not remember the baron who had attended last year's races who looked like his face had been stomped on by a horse? Or was a baron too lowly a title to overcome a less-than-desirable physical appearance? Or had the baron's happily wedded status decreased his handsomeness potential?

Still, these women hadn't even met the viscount yet.

Bianca rather hoped she hadn't met him either, though if she had, Marianne was going to be proven right. Despite his bedraggled appearance and seemingly nefarious purposes, the man hadn't been bad to look at, objectively speaking.

"You should send over a maid to buy an egg." Mrs. Wainbright leaned toward Mrs. Snowley. "Have her see if she can catch a glimpse of him."

"At the very least she could ask about him," Marianne said thoughtfully.

"Didn't Miss Snowley go riding there this morning? Did you see anyone new?" Miss Wainbright shifted her entire body to face Bianca, gripping her hands together in anticipation.

What should Bianca say? That she *had* seen a man but that she'd beaten him with her boot? The fit of vapors Mrs. Snowley was likely to have from such an admission almost made it worth giving, but Bianca held her tongue. If that had been the viscount, she was in enough trouble as it was.

Of course, if it hadn't been the viscount, then she had bought herself a great advantage. Should the new viscount be pleasant and unattached, was it possible she could marry into the very stable she dreamed about and measured every other stable against?

As soon as the idea lodged into her head, she had to wonder if that wasn't exactly what she'd been waiting for the past few years. Though the idea felt somewhat mercenary, Bianca had to admit being the mistress of Hawksworth was an incredibly appealing dream.

A dream she'd likely already crushed. There was little chance that the same day a new, unknown viscount came to town was the same day an inept horse thief descended as well.

Her heart raced, and she took a deep breath to calm herself. "I'm afraid it was straight to the stable and back, as usual. I don't venture up to the house."

"Perhaps you should start." Mrs. Wainbright turned her attention to the biscuit selection, now that the important information had been delivered.

"Or you could take Marianne with you next time."

Bianca narrowed her gaze at her stepmother. There was something very uncomfortable about the gleam in the other woman's eyes.

Now was not the time to argue, however. It was much safer for her if the conversation lingered on speculation about the new viscount. "Do you think he'll come to the assembly tonight?"

The other women jumped at such a notion, and once more the discussion turned to clothing as they speculated over what the unmarried ladies in the group should wear—or rather, what Marianne and Miss Wainbright should wear. As long as Bianca wasn't dressed in a way that brought shame to her family, Mrs. Snowley wouldn't give her one bit of extra attention.

Bianca ignored the idle chatter, but her mind was on a similar course. If the new Lord Stildon did make an appearance tonight, she needed to be ready to apologize. What was the appropriate outfit for a woman to wear when she groveled?

Five

I
f his own stables had been a marvel, the training yards were a revelation. So was the reaction of the people milling about.

"So, you're the mysterious heir we've been waiting on?" A man with a head of messy dark curls who'd been introduced as Lord Davers sneered as he took in Hudson's loose-fitting, lightweight clothing. "Your father was Lord Stildon's elder son, you say?"

"Yes," Hudson confirmed, wondering once more what his grandfather had been thinking.

"What do you intend to do with Hawksworth?" another man asked as he leaned on a fence and watched a trainer work with a horse in the distance.

Do with it? Hudson darted a glance toward Mr. Whitworth, but the man had stepped away from the group to lurk in a corner shadow. There wouldn't be any assistance from that direction. "I intend to live there."

The men around him chuckled, but it didn't ease the tension Hudson was sensing. "Do you intend to let Whitworth have his way there? The Earl of Trenting does that. The man can't be bothered to learn his own horses."

"I know horses."

The looks that came his way ranged from disbelieving to indifferent. "We'll see." Lord Davers knocked his boot against the fence post to dislodge a bit of dirt before taking a step toward Hudson and lowering his head, as if to speak a confidence despite their public position. "Piece of advice? Be careful around Whitworth. The man knows his horses, but he sometimes forgets his place. Unless you're seeing to the horses or checking on the trainer, being seen with him, well, makes us wonder about this title you've mysteriously inherited."

Though the other two men had clearly overheard Lord Davers's less-than-subtle words, they said nothing as the dark-haired man walked away and instead turned their talk to horses. Twice, Hudson inserted his own thoughts and knowledge into the conversation, and while the men accepted his presence and participation, neither sought it.

Eventually the entire situation became unbearable and Hudson walked away, moving toward the corner where Mr. Whitworth leaned.

"I need a tailor," Hudson announced. "One that will adjust an existing order for the right price so I can have at least one set of new clothing now."

One of Mr. Whitworth's eyebrows winged upward. "Is this for any particular occasion?"

Hudson nodded. "A social event. The first one I can procure access to that has most of the local horsemen in attendance. Is there a club? A dinner?"

From what he'd seen of the men who traveled to the Indian racecourses, horsemen the world over were the same. They were a cozy group and didn't welcome outsiders until they'd proven they belonged. He'd forgotten that, given that he'd never been on the outside before, but he wasn't going to let those men, or even one man, question his parentage or his ability to run a stable.

Mr. Whitworth rubbed a hand over the back of his neck. "There's an assembly tonight. It's public. Anyone can attend for the price of a subscription."

"I'll do that, then."

The manager opened his mouth, then snapped it shut and shook his head. "If you're going to the assembly, you're definitely going to need new clothes."

SOMEHOW, DESPITE THE strange clothing he'd put on to leave his strange house and make his way into a strange town, Hudson had expected the event he was attending to feel familiar. After all, it was a small gathering of like-minded individuals of a similar class, wasn't it? How different could it be from the ones he'd attended in India?

As it turned out, it could be as different as an elephant was from a horse.

Colors swirled about the scene before him. That part looked familiar, as he'd seen many an item of colorful clothing growing up. He'd even seen that colorful clothing draped over many female forms. What he hadn't experienced was the lighter, delicate feminine tones mingling with the deeper male voices in a variety of conversations that created a general rumble through the room.

He tugged at the cuff of his jacket and shrugged his shoulders, uncomfortable despite the fact that he could find no fault in the tailor who'd rushed to alter a proper suit of evening clothes he'd been preparing for another order. The thick fabric lay across Hudson's shoulders exactly as it should, but that didn't make it feel any less stiff and cumbersome.

At least it did make him somewhat warmer.

The lack of chill seeping into his bones didn't help his current situation any, though. If asked before this moment, he would have sworn his father had taught him everything necessary about being a gentleman. There had been tutors, dinners, opportunities to have veiled business conversations over a friendly game of cards.

But none of that had prepared him for the scene before him. What if all the women were like the one from this morning? Would they pepper him with dancing slippers as soon as they recognized he was a newcomer? Probably not, but they might when they saw he hadn't the first idea how to establish himself in mixed company. It certainly wasn't going to lay anyone's concerns about his ineptitude to rest.

He moved his gaze around the room, tracing one face and then another, seeing one stranger after another, and then he came to the undeniable conclusion that this had been a mistake.

A small burst of laughter rose above the general rumble, and the craving for personal interaction swelled through him, filling every space that wasn't eaten up by fear that he should have waited.

Fortunately, most errors could be corrected by removing oneself from the problem and trying again. He would simply slip out the way he'd come and try to insinuate himself into his new society in a smaller way tomorrow. In the future, he would avoid assemblies, now that he knew what they were.

Part of him wanted to blame Mr. Whitworth for not explaining that an assembly was . . . well . . . this, but the man likely had no idea Hudson had never seen a gathering such as this. It seemed part of Hudson's acclimation difficulty was going to be in not knowing what he didn't know.

With a shake of his head, he turned on his heel. Simply putting the entire cacophony to his back eased the tension in his chest. Yes. Tomorrow he would try again.

"You don't want to do that."

Hudson jerked his head around to see a young lady standing between two windows. There was no candle on the wall above her, so the moonlight streamed in the two windows and created a small pocket of shadow that she was well ensconced in. Only the outline of her could be seen, the paleness of her dress and her skin creating a lighter patch within the shadow.

The boldness of the woman to address him first and without introduction reminded Hudson of his morning encounter in the stable. Clearly his father and tutors had been out of touch with the modern English woman. Perhaps women had been quiet and biddable when those men had been younger, but obviously something had changed over the years.

Hudson took a small step in the woman's direction, trying to make out her features. "I don't want to do what?"

"Leave." She nodded toward the people filling the main area of the assembly room. "Someone has noticed you, I'm sure. If you leave now, they'll think you've cut them. You can't leave until midnight."

Hudson's eyebrows shot up. No one had given him such an order since his father had passed. Suggestions, yes, even strong encouragements, but no one had commanded him in years. "I can't?"

"Not without an excuse that somehow involves death or dismemberment, preferably your own."

How was he to respond to that? It was such a ridiculous notion that he couldn't quite credit it. "On what authority should I accept your assessment? You don't know me, and you seem to have a significant connection to them." He tilted his head toward the more populated side of the room.

Her laugh was light as her head dropped forward and a bit of moonlight caught the dark curls piled on top of her head. "If I were to scream like a banshee and throw my shoe at your head, I'm sure you would be able to place me. That might draw a bit of unwanted attention, though."

Hudson couldn't help giving a smile and brief laugh of his own. "Ah." He took a step closer to the figure in the shadows, and a few more details became visible. The dress was a light shade of green, and the dark curls were framing a face he could now recognize, though the expression was considerably more self-deprecating than accusing now. "You now intend to keep me captive instead of running me off?"

"It isn't a punishment, I assure you. It's an apology of sorts."

"You mean you don't think I was stealing the horses?"

She sighed. "A bit hard to steal something you already own."

One statement was all it took for Hudson to once more feel at a loss. Having people know who he was without any sort of proper introduction left him feeling somewhat exposed and vulnerable. "Confinement seems a strange way of making amends."

"If you leave now, they'll all think you want nothing to do with them, and they will reciprocate in kind. Not once will it occur to them that they frighten you to bits."

He opened his mouth to object to her assessment of the situation, but truth was truth. Were he to deny it, he'd seem as high in the instep as she said they'd accuse him of being.

"If you don't mind," she continued, "do turn away a bit. It looks like you're conversing with a wall instead of merely standing by one, and I don't wish to have my favorite hiding place revealed."

Though being so rude as to turn his back to a woman went against everything he'd been taught, he shifted to face the crowd. "Is that better?"

"Much."

Everyone still seemed to be ignoring him, but the woman behind him had been confident that wasn't the case. He had no choice but to take her word on it. That didn't mean he was ready to venture into their ranks and experience their more direct scrutiny.

He cleared his throat. "I am assuming that someone over there is aware that you arrived here tonight. Aren't you afraid they'll think you've committed the unpardonable sin of departing before midnight?"

"Oh, I'll come out once the dancing starts. Until then, I'd rather avoid . . . certain people."

Every prayer and plea to the Lord that Hudson had ever heard or considered sliced through his mind on its way heavenward. There was going to be dancing? Would it be considered rude if he took her shadowy hiding spot once she abandoned it? "How does one go about avoiding people without damaging their reputation?"

"Stay on the dance floor as much as possible," she said with a light laugh. "That's what I do."

That was one tactic that would make him look more of a buffoon instead of less. He was probably better off having them think he walked about with his nose in the air. At least then there was a chance their dislike would still contain respect. He hadn't a clue how to dance. Attempting to do so would likely cost him all chances of gaining anyone's good opinion. "Are there other options?"

"There's a cardroom to the right. It's small, and within an hour it will smell like a barn on fire from all the candles and the men. If you stay in there all night, most of your conversation will be with older gentlemen."

Her tone made it sound as pleasant as mucking out three-day-old straw, but Hudson rather thought he could manage an evening of it. "I'll take that under advisement."

Her laughter was a bit louder this time and accompanied by a snort of derision. "Do you really intend to sit among the grouchy husbands who couldn't convince their wives to stay home tonight?"

"It would seem I have no other options."

"You hate dancing that much?"

Was hating dancing better than not knowing how to do it? Probably, but Hudson's mind was far too jumbled to maintain even the mildest of lies. "I wouldn't know. I've never done it."

"You've never danced?" Astonishment was clear in her voice. "Where have you been hiding? You know, two hundred years ago people would be saying you were some sort of magically created being. Fortunately, we're now more modern than that and simply question the legitimacy of your claim."

Hudson sighed. What he wouldn't give for one hour to ask his father and grandfather what they'd been thinking. Apparently India hadn't been safe enough. The only way to protect Hudson had been hiding his very existence.

"No one knew about you, you know," the woman continued,

"until your grandfather's solicitors informed all the estate and stable workers to carry on as they were until the heir arrived. One year later, here you are."

Hudson winced. She was only stating plainly what he'd managed to piece together earlier that day, but it seemed worse hearing it instead of assuming it.

It also killed any idea he had that his uncle wasn't as bad as his father had claimed.

He cleared his throat. "As I grew up in India, well aware of the existence of my grandfather and England, I can't speak to the fact that the reciprocal is not true."

She huffed out another short laugh. "You sound like my brother, spouting off fancy words when he comes home from school, trying to look educated and important. The accent gives you away, though. India explains that."

He hadn't noticed that his speech was any different from the others around him. Of course, he hadn't interacted with that many people. Still, the last thing he wanted was her—or anyone else's—scrutiny.

She moved to stand beside him, giving him a chance to take in her features without shadow or obscuring boot swings. Brown hair, brown eyes, straight nose. She looked like the few other women he'd met from England, but she certainly didn't behave like them. "Are you no longer afraid of being seen?"

"The dancing is going to start soon."

"Is there a great deal of that expected tonight?"

"Is there a . . . India must be a truly foreign place. Dancing is all there is tonight. Well, aside from the cardroom and the spinsters in the corner. It's certainly the main entertainment." The woman looked over at the musicians. "All the dances tonight are to be called. Mr. Pierre isn't including the waltz until next week's assembly. As long as you go to the end of the line, you'll have plenty of time to observe the movements before having to execute them yourself."

"As accommodating as that sounds, I have no idea what you mean." He should hold his tongue, or at least not be quite so curt. She was trying to help, to apologize, as she'd said earlier. Not knowing how to accept her generosity was almost as frustrating as not knowing what to do in the first place.

Her mouth pulled to the side as she considered him for a moment.

"Leave it to me," she said with a sigh. "You go find Mr. Pierre and introduce yourself. After tonight he'll expect you to pay the subscription fee, but your newness and title should appease him for one evening. Then ask him to introduce you to me and ask me to dance the first set with you."

She started to turn, but Hudson reached out an arm to stop her. "What are you going to do?"

"If I take the time to explain that, we'll lose our opportunity." She nodded toward a cluster of men. "Now, go. Mr. Pierre is over there in the green vest."

She slipped around the edges of the conversing groups of people with the ease of someone who felt as comfortable in this atmosphere as they did in their own home. Did he trust her?

Did he have a choice?

True, she'd tried to knock his head in with a boot, but it had been with noble intentions. If one considered her motives, the encounter had been honorable and courageous. He'd rather have such a person on his side than against him.

Since a cramped, smoky, smelly cardroom sounded much too close to the confines of the ship he vowed never to set foot on again, he resettled his thick, encumbering jacket and went off in search of Mr. Pierre.

He'd foolishly thought that coming to England would ease all the discomfort that had plagued him for years, but thus far being here had only given him more questions. Since a full life wasn't simply going to come to him, he was going to have to go out and get it.

Six

Every woman knew that some apologies required more than simple words to be authentic, though perhaps Bianca understood this more than most.

How many times had she heard her stepmother apologize under the stern look of her father, only to have nothing change? The older woman still forgot to tell Bianca about social invitations, scheduled trips to the modiste for times when Bianca was already busy, and insisted that the girls' shared lady's maid, Dorothy, attend to Marianne the moment she wished, even if Bianca was in the middle of getting dressed.

Mrs. Snowley's apologies had meant nothing, but Lord Stildon would have no such cause to doubt Bianca's. Attacking a man in his own stable was a rather significant offense, but she was certain that she genuinely could make amends.

Perhaps she could even make those amends in such a way that left him feeling beholden to her. Only hours ago she'd come to the conclusion that marriage would solve all her problems, and here was her chance to gain the attention of an extremely eligible bachelor. He seemed kind, and he obviously had a sense of humor. Did she really need more than that?

She took a deep breath and looked around the room. This evening needed to go well if she was going to consider a life with the man and his horses. All she needed now was a plan. Given the look of clear terror on Lord Stildon's face a few moments ago, it needed to be a really good plan.

Taking out the ticket she'd been given upon entering the room, she ran a thumb across the number engraved upon it. Eight. How many ladies had taken tickets when they entered? Not that it mattered. Eight had as much chance of being drawn from the bowl as any other number.

If she prevented that, though, she'd be able to ensure that she and Lord Stildon were situated at the bottom of the set. If the man couldn't learn the pattern by the time the dance worked its way down to them, there wasn't much else she could do.

A string quartet sat in the corner of the room, preparing their instruments for the night's festivities. A bowl sat near the foot of the violinist.

Perfect.

She plastered a grin onto her face that she hoped appeared somewhat abashed and aimed it at the violinist as she reached for the bowl.

"Don't mind me," she whispered as she rummaged through the tickets, searching out the one that matched hers. "I'm feeling rather shy tonight." Once she found the number eight, she held it up next to her ticket so the musician would know she wasn't sabotaging any other woman's evening, and then tucked both tickets away into the small reticule dangling from her wrist.

As this was hardly the first time the man had played for one of Mr. Pierre's assemblies, she could hardly blame him for appearing shocked as she sidled away. Shyness had never been a problem for her. As she'd told Lord Stildon, she survived these evenings by spending the entire time on the dance floor. Dancing all night was exhausting, but not half so much as listening to Mrs. Snowley contrive to find Marianne an exemplary match while simultaneously telling Bianca everything she was doing wrong.

If it weren't so uncomfortable, her stepmother's talent might be impressive.

Bianca wove her way through the people, keeping her eyes down so as not to invite conversation. She needed to situate herself in a reasonable position for Lord Stildon to request an introduction, or her removal of herself from leading the first dance would have been for naught.

She didn't have much time, since dancing always started promptly at half past eight and pairs would soon begin to form, but moving about the room turned out to be quite easy since everyone was staring in Lord Stildon's direction.

And the man had thought he could simply slip away unnoticed. Bianca chuckled to herself as she found a good position. A stranger could hardly enter the town, much less the assembly hall, without being noticed. Did he have any idea that he'd already been the topic of a day's worth of gossip?

Probably not, but he would soon. There was little chance he could get through this evening without knowing that everyone in here was speculating as to his identity, his authenticity, and his intentions.

He turned from speaking to Mr. Pierre and locked eyes with her. She offered him an encouraging nod. The half smile he returned caused the three girls behind Bianca to emit tiny gasps.

Unless someone could drag up something to illegitimatize or demonize the man, he was going to have quite a reputation about town. The mothers and daughters would make sure of it.

Assuming, of course, that Bianca could get him through this night without any undue embarrassment.

Mr. Pierre strutted toward her with Lord Stildon at his side and a large smile on his face. Handsome, mysterious bachelors were good for assembly subscriptions. Titled ones were especially beneficial.

"Miss Snowley," Mr. Pierre said in a quiet, gentle voice that indicated his delight hadn't affected his discretion, "may I present to you Lord Stildon?"

Bianca curtsied and tried to appear solemn and honored by the man's attentions, but all she wanted to do was laugh. The situation was amusing enough, but Lord Stildon's own attempt at solemnity pushed the entire business into the realm of hilarity. Both of them were exuding far more gravitas than the situation required.

"Good evening, my lord." Bianca dipped her head in Lord Stildon's direction.

"The honor is mine." Lord Stildon bowed in response. "I wonder, if you are not yet engaged, would you stand up with me for the first dance?"

How had he known exactly what to say? If it came about that he wasn't as helpless as he'd seemed, she would throw him to the wolves.

Without him knowing, of course. She didn't want to ruin her apology.

"Of course, my lord." Bianca narrowed her eyes as she attempted to further assess the man. She should know better than to assume surface impressions were always accurate. Still, she rested her hand on his proffered elbow. "If it wouldn't be an imposition"—my, weren't they being all that was polite?—"may we take a short round by the refreshment table first? I was on my way for a cup of punch."

"As you wish." He guided her, or rather appeared to guide her, as she was the one who tugged him along to the table in the corner.

"Did I get it right?" he whispered as she sipped the cup of punch. "I overheard another gentleman asking someone to dance as Mr. Pierre led me over, so I copied the words."

Clever and observant, but not a liar. That was good. She wouldn't want to marry a liar. "Yes, perfect."

"What do we do now?" He shifted his weight and darted a

nervous glance toward the large gathering of people. "I confess to a bit of confusion at asking you to stand up with me when we're already on our feet."

"Later the women waiting to dance will be in chairs." Bianca watched the clock in the corner, trying to time the completion of her punch perfectly. More than half the room was watching her, and she couldn't make her plan obvious. "For now, though, we wait. We need to allow everyone else to line up first, then we take the spot at the end."

"Should I get punch as well?"

"Only if you're desperately thirsty. It's not exactly pleasant fare."

A glimmer of humor dispelled some of the tension from his gaze as his mouth tipped up into a small smile. "Then I appreciate your sacrifice all the more."

"As you should." She grimaced. "Although I do rather owe you after this morning."

"Think nothing of it." He shrugged, and the tension returned as he looked at the crowd from the corner of his eye. "If I hadn't wanted an adventure, I'd have stayed in India."

Something about the statement felt wrong, but she hardly knew the man well enough to know if he was prevaricating or not. Perhaps it was simply the irony of the statement that felt jarring. "Usually young men hie off to India to find adventure and escape the doldrums of England."

"I suppose it all depends upon one's perspective," Lord Stildon murmured.

"The dancing shall now commence." Mr. Pierre picked up the bowl Bianca had recently rummaged through and shuffled the tokens around before selecting one. With grand ceremony, he held the ticket up to read the number. "Our first dance will be led by the lady holding ticket number four."

Movement rolled through the room as Miss Gibson took her

spot at the front. Bianca sipped her punch, watching the other couples line up according to their respective numbers. If she waited until the last minute, they'd be required to stand at the bottom.

With a nod, she set her cup aside and took Lord Stildon's arm again. "Now we join them. All you have to do is watch the pattern as it comes down the line."

They slid into place at the end of the dance configuration just as the music began. The intense look on his face as he studied the dancers made her grin. As the pattern came closer and closer to them, his countenance grew darkly determined.

"This is supposed to be fun," Bianca whispered as she took his hand and they circled around another couple. "You might want to cease looking like you intend to stomp upon everyone's feet. At least, I assume your intention is quite the opposite, as I am in evening slippers and not riding boots tonight."

His face relaxed a fraction as he moved through the next step, though his gaze remained sharp. During a slight pause when they stood side by side, he leaned over to whisper, "Do I do this with you all evening, then?"

"Not unless you wish to declare our engagement at the end of the assembly." Bianca almost immediately regretted such a quip. She might have been secretly contemplating marrying the man, but she hadn't intended to jokingly offer herself up to him.

That didn't stop a small part of her from being slightly offended by the look of alarm that dashed across his face, even as another part of her found it humorous.

She cleared her throat before continuing. "Seek out the attentions of whichever woman led the dance. She'll move to the bottom every time."

They fell silent as they continued through the pattern, moving their way up the line. It wasn't until they were on their way back down the set that he leaned down to speak into her ear once more. "Do you come to my stables often?"

"Nearly every day." His introduction of an entirely new topic of discussion indicated a certain level of comfort with the dance pattern. The pride she felt over that was uncalled for, given she'd done nothing but put him in a position to learn.

He gave a low hum of acknowledgment as the dance took them in separate directions. Through the rest of the set she waited for him to say more, to tell her she wasn't welcome, to question her persistent presence, to . . . well, anything. Instead, he simply continued with the dance.

He stumbled a bit once, trying to move in the wrong direction. Bianca managed to swing him around before he could disrupt the pattern too much, but still he said nothing.

Once their set was complete, he bowed and gave her another smile. "Until we meet again, Miss Snowley."

It was as close to permission as she was likely to get, and relief had her excusing herself from the next set instead of finding another partner. As she sipped another glass of atrocious punch, she watched Lord Stildon navigate an introduction to Miss Gibson, once more looking stiff and slightly terrified.

Her new neighbor might be excessively confusing, but at least he wasn't cutting her off from his horses.

"The two of you barely spoke a word through that entire set. Is it your intention to impress him with demure silence? I do hope you realize there are several young ladies more accomplished at such a demeanor than you are."

The sour punch, made all the worse by the undesirable company, left Bianca's mouth feeling tight and dry. Still, she took another sip as she turned to acknowledge her stepmother.

Experience told her that silence was her best option, but that didn't mean she couldn't imagine dumping the remainder of the punch over the top of the older woman's head. What would orgeat do to the elaborate grey-blond curls?

"I promised your father to help you along this year," Mrs.

Snowley continued with a sigh. "If Marianne manages to settle down before you, he'll think it all my doing."

Considering Mrs. Snowley hadn't given a single thought to Bianca's marriage prospects until halfway through Marianne's first Season, the idea wasn't entirely without merit. Bianca preferred to think that her lack of marital status had more to do with her own discernment.

It didn't matter that her discernment had more to do with an eligible man's stables than his prospects. Every girl had her criteria.

As her stepmother droned on, Bianca was more and more hopeful that Lord Stildon was going to prove of acceptable enough character that she could finally have a man to set her cap for.

IF IT WEREN'T for the fact that returning to India would require him to set foot on a boat, Hudson would chuck the entire business of his estate back into the hands of the solicitor. This time, though, there wouldn't be any hope to sustain him through the horrible months onboard the ship. Instead he'd have to suffer the anguish of knowing he'd failed, along with the turmoil caused by the waves.

Staying here, even though it wasn't going as he'd thought it would, was the better of the two prospects. It had been foolish, perhaps, to think because he'd been raised with the notion that England was his true home then merely being here would relieve him of that disjointed feeling of not belonging. Disappointment that things were simply foreign in a different way solidified his determination to make himself a place here.

After two hours of following Miss Snowley's instructions, Hudson's feet hurt and his resolve was cracking. He'd managed not to embarrass himself too much, but his cheeks ached from his attempts to appear a genial, happy fellow.

To make matters worse, it seemed that everyone in attendance only knew how to have three conversations. While that had the benefit of allowing him to know what he should say, it also numbed his mind. After all this dancing, he knew that the weather had been fine today but might not be tomorrow and that poor Judson Hughes had gotten drunk and managed to get himself stuck in his horse's feed trough. Everyone also wanted to know if Lady Rebecca intended to make an appearance since having her debut Season in London in the spring.

Hudson didn't know who Judson Hughes was and could only guess at the identity of Lady Rebecca, but he'd still probably mumble about them as he fell asleep tonight.

He'd caught enough words here and there to know a fourth conversation was bubbling about the room, but as he was the topic, no one was making him privy to the details.

Given what he'd heard at the training grounds earlier, that might be a polite blessing.

Despite the relative success, or at least the relative lack of failure, there was a pounding pain beginning to roll up the back of his head. The prospect of more dancing and more numbing conversation made the pain pound harder, so he excused himself and went in search of the cardroom Miss Snowley had mentioned earlier. The smell was indeed awful, but it was blessedly free of females and even more welcomingly free of dancing.

He'd received so many speculative glances in the past few hours that he barely acknowledged the new ones aimed his direction as he observed the tables to ensure that here, at least, all would be familiar.

After a brief introduction, he joined a game and settled in to an activity that he was finally confident he could do.

Conversation in the cardroom was somewhat more varied than what he'd heard while dancing. Familiar business discussions joined in with the swish of cards sliding across the table and the clink of money joining the pile in the middle, and soon the pain in Hudson's neck and shoulders abated. Even if he didn't know the names or the horses being discussed, he knew the rhythm of these conversations.

After a couple of hands, his companions started to test him, to allow him into the edges of their exchanges in order to take measure of his character and knowledge. There was an edge of hostility, though not as severe as he'd experienced at the training yard, even though at least one of those men was in attendance.

These were the men he'd spent his life waiting to join, preparing to do business with. What could he do to win the respect of the stable owners, gentry, and other area aristocrats?

"Gliddon said he's offering up Hezekiah for stud this year," an older gentleman said as he pulled out a tin of snuff. If Hudson had heard the man's name earlier, he'd long since forgotten it. "One lucky bidder only, though."

"His price is far too steep for me," a younger man said.

Another man, Mr. Theophilus Mead, snorted and dealt out the cards. "He might as well declare it part of Lady Rebecca's dowry and be done with it."

"Now that would be a prize," Lord Davers said before scooping up his cards and flaring them out. "Lady Rebecca for a wife and a near-guaranteed champion in the stable."

Men who'd been playing cards at the next table wandered over to join the conversation. A balding man with tufts of grey hair over his ears frowned. "You think he'll make that a requirement? That the man be ready and able to marry *and* worthy of a horse from Hezekiah's line?"

"He's a fool if he doesn't at least consider it," the old man who'd started the conversation said. "Hezekiah is a mighty enticement. He'll at least hold on to the option until Lady Rebecca is settled."

Mr. Mead shook his head. "Lady Rebecca has breeding, beauty, and a connection to the Earl of Gliddon and his stable. Along with her dowry and what she's set to inherit when Lord Gliddon passes on, she hardly needs further decoration."

"Do you intend to throw your hat in the ring, then?"

"Without a title, he doesn't stand a chance," Lord Davers said with a smirk before throwing his marker into the center of the table.

"One thing is certain," one of the men surrounding the table said. "Every racing aristocrat with an eligible son is going to be descending on Newmarket soon in the hope of winning the prize—be it lady, stallion, or both."

Hudson gave his cards enough attention to avoid any sort of significant loss, but his mind was circling around this new information. He'd needed a plan to impress these men, a way to prove to all of them that he was someone to be respected in the area of horse racing, and they'd all but handed him the way to do it.

He had a stable and a title, and though he hadn't thought it his main priority yet, he was in need of a socially capable wife.

Only one question remained. Who was Lady Rebecca?

Seven

The past year had shown Hudson just how much he didn't know about himself, but a few areas of confidence remained. He knew horses, he was fairly certain he still knew cricket, and he knew how to adapt. Life in India changed so often there was no choice but to adapt.

Saturday's sun had yet to make an appearance in the Sunday sky as Hudson rose from his bed. He opened the doors that led from his room to a small balcony and stepped into the brisk predawn air.

The feel of the air, the smells, even the sounds were unfamiliar. What had he expected? That everything English would feel comfortable and natural just because he'd been raised to think of this as where he belonged?

Yes, some part of him had. It was a childish thought that had lingered in his mind as he reached adulthood, and it wasn't until now, with the idea spectacularly disproven, that he realized how much he'd clung to it.

He took a deep breath and reminded himself that he was the same capable, knowledgeable man he'd been in India, where he'd had to adapt to the frequently changing town and culture. The only difference was that instead of one or two things changing, everything had changed.

When the chill seeping through the Indian *banyan* he used as a dressing robe grew too cutting for him, he returned to the house and went to the small study off the bedchamber.

Everything in this room was simple, chosen for efficient practicality instead of impression. He lowered himself into the large chair behind the desk and ran his hands along the well-worn arms.

Was this where his grandfather had sat when he read Hudson's letters? Was this where he'd answered them? What activities were so private, so personal that they necessitated a second study?

Hudson began opening drawers, surprised to find several legal documents, including a copy of the quarter-end financial statements of the estates and stables. He had already seen detailed day-to-day books lined up on the shelves of the main study. Why keep a second set of books?

Another drawer revealed stacks of letters, bound together by twine. He removed a bundle and released the tie.

His father's familiar handwriting strode across the page.

The date was a year before Hudson's mother had succumbed to fever, and the contents were about Hudson. Specifically about whether he should return to England for school.

> *If my younger brother's actions are as unpredictable as you say, then I cannot, in good conscience, send my son home for school. I will allow you to choose tutors, if that makes you feel better, but an uneducated heir is better than a dead one.*

Hudson grinned at his father's words. He'd never believed in being vague about something that could be stated plainly.

Many of the letters discussed Hudson and his upbringing—far more than he would have expected. He flipped through them, truly understanding for the first time the extent to which his life had been planned.

Lines he'd heard his father utter time and again appeared in several of the letters. There was something steadying and comforting about seeing the words here in England. It was a connection between his new life and his old.

My living in India has not weakened my appreciation for God and England. They are my true home. Madras is but a temporary residency, a necessity in order to ensure the line continues as it should.

How many times had Hudson heard something similar? How many times had he been told that he shouldn't become attached, that one day he would be where he belonged, that home was a land on the other side of the globe?

The tone of the letters changed somewhat after the death of Hudson's mother. All discussion of Hudson coming to England ceased, though Hudson had no way of knowing if that was because his grandfather stopped asking or because his father ignored the requests.

In fact, Hudson wasn't mentioned much at all. More and more of the content turned to the work his father had poured himself into during the last few years of his life.

I believe the work I am doing with the local horsemen is something God brought me here to do. It may be a strange destiny to some, but I can see the improvements and changes daily.

Hudson tossed the letter back into the drawer. God might have placed his father in India with a purpose, but as far as Hudson had seen, that was the last time God had intervened in the man's life.

Or perhaps it was merely Hudson's life the deity didn't feel a need to interfere in. The lack didn't make Hudson angry—after all, he was more than capable of seeing to his own life—but he sometimes had difficulty reconciling the belief that God loved him with the fact that God had left him to deal with his problems on his own.

Which might be why Hudson was sitting in his house instead of venturing into town to attend church. Everything he'd thought he knew about life was crumbling under the weight of reality. He wasn't sure his fragile faith could hold up under a similar attack.

In the next drawer down, Hudson found another set of letters written in an even more familiar hand—his own. He shifted those in childish scrawl out of the way, suddenly anxious to remember when he'd been confident and sure of the man he would become.

> *I negotiated the sale of a horse today. Father assures me that I am learning all the necessary skills for being an accomplished viscount. Some of the ways Father taught me to do business seem strange here, but he assures me that is how it is done in England.*
>
> *When I come home, I will make you proud.*

Hudson's loose-fitting robe suddenly felt a little too tight. His experience over the last few months, even the last few days, proved how ill-prepared he was for life in England.

The last letter he'd sent was sitting in the drawer unopened. Had his grandfather even seen it, or had someone else taken care of it? Had a servant slid it into this drawer with a sense of unease, wondering if and when Hudson planned to make an appearance?

He broke the seal and glanced over the words.

> *Surely India is no longer necessary for my protection. I am an adult now, no longer prone to the accidents of youth. An accident here would be far easier to explain away than one in England.*
>
> *I am eager to start my life there. I yearn to be the man I was born to be. When I get there, I know everything will fit together as it should. My thoughts and mannerisms are those of an Englishman. My heart is that of British aristocracy.*
>
> *India may have been Father's destiny, but mine is England.*

Hudson threw the paper down, glaring at it as he wished he could glare at the foolish man he'd been when he wrote it.

If he could answer that letter, what would he say?

You are not as prepared as you think.

This may be your destiny, but you will not slide into it with the comfort of a well-worn riding boot.

There is a fine line between confidence and arrogance, and you crossed it long ago.

Hudson sighed. All of those statements were fitting.

Last night had thrown him into a whirlwind of unfamiliarity that he'd had to endure in order to maintain his reputation. He'd managed to blunder through well enough, but to continue in such a state was unacceptable.

He'd been waiting twenty-eight years for this moment, and it hadn't lived up to even his weakest expectations. Perhaps it was he who hadn't managed to meet those expectations.

It was exhausting to realize the one hope he'd held on to since childhood wasn't going to happen easily. He was going to have to work for it, demand that life make a space for him. Just the thought made him tired.

Hadn't there been times when God told His prophets to go to bed and everything would be better in the morning? Perhaps that would work for him. Not that he could spend the whole day in bed, but maybe he didn't have to solve all his problems today. Perhaps today, it would be enough to simply breathe and consider the fact that he was finally in England.

As HE SAT before a low flickering fire on Sunday night, the setting sun streaming over his shoulders, he realized that the situation wasn't as horrid as it had seemed yesterday, and he didn't feel as tired at the thought of carving out his own destiny.

Finally all the work he did, all the decisions he made, would have effects that he could hold on to. Now he could craft whatever future he wanted instead of simply living in limbo in the one his father and grandfather had apparently argued over for years.

Since he was a child, he'd wanted an esteemed stable of his own, a line of champion racehorses, and the respect of his peers. He'd been told all of that would be his when he came to England, and he had to believe that he could still have it, even if it hadn't fallen into his hands as soon as he'd disembarked.

If Mr. Whitworth was to be believed, Hudson had a prime mare in his stable. Matching his mare with the stallion everyone was admiring last evening would win him instant respect from the other racing gentlemen.

And if it came with a quality wife and social success at the same time? Well, a single solution to all his problems might be enough for him to believe God was interested in having a hand in his life after all.

BIANCA HAD STOOD before many a stranger in her lifetime. Never before had that stranger inhabited her own mirror. There was no denying that the image in front of her bore little to no resemblance to her normal Monday morning look.

Artful curls fell on either side of her face, framing carefully pinched cheeks and skin brushed over with a bit of powder. Her best riding habit had been enhanced with a length of lace at the neckline, and her hat sat at a jaunty angle instead of its normal, practical positioning.

Aside from the frown marring the perfectly adorned features, the picture was rather beautiful.

During the entire dressing process, Dorothy had glanced frequently in the mirror, assessing Bianca. She couldn't blame the maid. Until now, she'd been too impatient to sit for curls unless it was visiting day or there were evening entertainments. Lace had been saved for special occasions, and hats had been for keeping her hair contained and the sun out of her eyes.

Was she truly changing all of that for a chance to catch the viscount's eye? Yes, marriage would gain her confirmed access to exquisite horses and allow her to escape the scrutiny of her stepmother, but was it worth it?

Lord Stildon had been all anyone could talk about at the assembly and before and after church, especially within Bianca's hearing. Her well-known connection to Hawksworth and the fact that she'd stood up with him first had somehow made her the primary target for all the newsmongers.

Obviously she'd kept her early-morning blunder to herself and insisted that it was merely chance that he'd noticed her first when looking for a dance partner. Her lack of knowledge wasn't shared by everyone, and by the time the sun set yesterday, details others couldn't possibly know about the man had been flying about in conversations.

Despite the suppositions about his past and his character, one thing was certain: Lord Stildon was the current target for every marriage-aged female in the area. If Bianca wanted Hawksworth, or rather the viscount, for herself, she needed to press her one advantage quickly.

The thought could far too easily be uttered in her stepmother's voice. Somehow that woman had gotten into Bianca's head and convinced her that manipulation was the only way to get what she wanted.

Yes, she wanted to marry the viscount, but she refused to connive her way into a match.

With angry swipes, Bianca jerked the pins from her hat and dropped it onto the dressing table before attacking the curls. With a swipe of her brush, a twist, and a few hairpins, she tucked all her hair away like it was most mornings. With a yank, the lace fichu drifted to the dressing table, and then she positioned her hat in its normal position, making the woman in the mirror far more recognizable than she'd been moments before.

At the assembly she'd displayed her social skills. Now she would woo him with her practicality.

Maybe.

What if he wasn't even a morning rider? What if he kept Town hours and hadn't even risen yet? Not every aristocrat took advantage of the hours in which they were allowed to ride the Heath at will before it was closed for races, challenges, and training.

All the questions threatened to have her second-guess her decision to wreck the elegant hair dressing, so she pushed away from the dressing table and left the room before she could give in to the urge to tuck the lace back into position.

Her father's study door was open as she passed, and she stuck her head in to greet him.

His white hair was long and pulled back in a queue, though the style was far from fashionable anymore. Bianca's knock drew a welcoming smile to his face, and he beckoned her in. "Off to Hawksworth already?"

"Yes. My mount came up lame the other day, so I didn't get much of a ride in."

"You could have ridden one of our horses, you know," he said with a frown.

Was it possible her father didn't realize the difference between the grandeur of Hawksworth and the meager stable of Kendal Hall? Bianca gave a small hum of acknowledgment, unsure what to say. Father kept two aged carriage horses and an even older riding horse. She could walk faster than any of those animals plodded along.

"I've heard the new viscount moved in," Father continued.

"Yes. He attended the assembly on Saturday." Bianca moved farther into the room and sank into one of the chairs across from her father's desk. It wasn't often that the man was in the mood to chat, and Bianca wasn't going to pass up the opportunity, even if it delayed her ride. "We danced."

"Good, good. Mrs. Snowley tells me he'd be a fine son-in-law."

"I'm sure she did," Bianca murmured, trying not to wince at the idea of Marianne as the mistress of Hawksworth.

"She meant he'd be a good match for you, I'm sure."

She gave a noncommittal murmur. If her father wanted to think his second wife thought of Bianca as a daughter, was there any point in correcting him? What good would it do?

Father frowned. "She and I have discussed that you need to marry before Marianne, being the elder and all."

Bianca shifted in her seat. Would her father's encouraging of Mrs. Snowley's involvement help Bianca's intentions or hinder them? "I have every intention of marrying, Papa. I'll find the right man."

"I want both of my daughters well settled. My wife has asked me to mention Marianne to a few men at the club. You'll let me know if I need to do the same for you."

Bianca had never thought to involve her father in the procuring of a husband, but it sounded as if he was paying far more attention to it than she'd thought. If tensions rose between Mrs. Snowley and Father because Marianne was set to marry before Bianca, what would that mean?

The truth was, marriage had only recently become an active goal for Bianca, while Marianne had been planning her marital approach for years. If the viscount didn't offer for Bianca, or if he took a long time to do so, Marianne could very well reach the altar first, and then Bianca would be a pitied spinster with an uncomfortable home life.

Perhaps she could temper her father's expectations.

"I would like a partner. I'm trying to be like you and select someone who will bring what I need to the partnership."

Father had rushed into his second marriage, somewhat desperate to provide a mother for his infant daughter. There were times

Bianca got the feeling he wished he hadn't been quite as hasty in his decision, so she was determined to take her time to learn the measure of the man in question before committing to him, even though the idea of staying in the house with Mrs. Snowley after Marianne married was terrifying enough to send her running off with the traveling horse circus troupes.

Father shuffled a few papers about on his desk. "Yes, well, there's no need to decide today. Everyone isn't back in town yet, so the pickings at assemblies will be light."

All the more reason for Bianca to establish her place in the viscount's mind early. Soon the area would be flooded with eligible ladies.

"Speaking of being back in town," Father said, reaching for a box on the corner of his desk, "I brought you something from my recent trip. Oh, and your brother sends his greetings."

Bianca eased forward on the chair and stretched her neck to get a look as he opened the box. "How does Giles like being a sixth-year student?"

Sparkles of jewels greeted her gaze, and her excitement fell a bit. She adored a good bauble as much as any other young lady, but the ostentatious jewelry her stepmother and sister preferred had always felt cold and heavy. She much preferred the small collection of pendants and chains her mother had fancied.

"Good, good," her father said. "Same as always. He likes his language studies, hates maths." Her father's thick fingers reached into the box, pushed aside a bracelet covered in emeralds, and then emerged with a brooch. The smooth, delicate curves of the golden edges could be seen, along with the clasp at the back, but the front was entirely hidden. He looked down at the jewelry with a small smile before laying it faceup in his palm and extending it toward her.

Bianca gasped. The brooch nestled in his palm was a cameo, intricately carved to show a woman standing beside a horse. The horse's neck was curved around the woman so the head pressed against her chest. It was a charming and intimate look at a woman and her equine best friend.

Her hand trembled a bit as she reached for it. "It's lovely, Father."

"There was a larger one," he said with a shrug, "but I thought it would be cumbersome to wear while you were riding. This one seemed . . . well, it made me think of you."

Bianca curled her fingers around it. He hadn't lost sight of the fact that she was different from his other daughter or his wife. She circled the desk and placed a kiss on his head before straightening and affixing the brooch to her riding jacket. "It's perfect."

"As are you," he said with a gentle smile. "Now, go on with you before the sun gets too high and you miss your ride. I'll say an extra prayer for you this morning that your horse doesn't come up lame again."

Bianca laughed as she moved to the door. "I appreciate it greatly, Father. Perhaps your petitions along with mine will convince God to ease my way."

"Bah." The man waved his hand through the air. "He's already planned it out. Our prayers are to help us remember that."

Her mind stayed on the conversation as she took the well-worn path between the estates. She couldn't help but tack one additional request onto her prayer. If God's plan included Bianca's having a stable of her own one day, she would dearly love it to be Hawksworth.

Eight

Arriving at the stable during the early morning hustle was far different from slipping in while the horses were off being exercised. The busyness distracted him from wondering when Miss Snowley normally made her appearance.

Several grooms bustled about the wide stone central corridor, leading horses and seeing to their care. In the middle of it all stood Mr. Whitworth, occasionally making a notation in a notebook. Hudson waited for a pause in the flow of grooms and made his way over to the manager.

"There's a race in a few weeks," Mr. Whitworth said by way of a greeting. "I'd been planning on entering Apollo in it."

Hudson nodded, hoping he looked as if he knew enough about the lay of the land to have an opinion. He wasn't even certain which horse was Apollo. "You can move forward with those plans. I'd like to know about the horse's training later."

"Of course." Mr. Whitworth made a note in his notebook. "I've made a few changes to his training this year that should improve his performance. He's going to have a good year."

That was as good an opening as Hudson was going to get. "What do you know about the horse Hezekiah?"

All of Mr. Whitworth's attention hit Hudson as the man lowered his notebook to his side and cocked his head to study his employer. Action ceased in the two nearest stalls as well. A gruff man with deep wrinkles worn into his tanned face stepped out of a stall and approached.

"This is Mr. Knight," Mr. Whitworth said with a nod. "He's your head groom. When did you hear about Hezekiah?"

"At the assembly."

One side of Mr. Whitworth's mouth kicked up. "How did that outing go?"

"As well as could be expected." Assuming a man wasn't riding the unrealistic childhood expectation that life was going to go easily at some point.

Mr. Knight grunted. "What was said about the horse?"

Hudson crossed his arms over his chest and considered the two men. How interesting that these men were far different from the ones collected around the card table two evenings ago, and yet the conversation was so very similar. "Apparently Hezekiah is going to be available this year. Is that uncommon?"

Mr. Knight snorted while Mr. Whitworth nodded. "Lord Gliddon doesn't truly need the money, but he enjoys the exclusivity and how everyone fawns about trying to get him to select their request. Of course, the fact that every horse sired by Hezekiah has done well means whomever he honors with his blessing pays an exorbitant sum. He never chooses more than two per year."

Mr. Knight looked over to Hestia's stall. "Hezekiah and Hestia. Just imagine the fine specimen they could produce. That horse would be the envy of the country."

Hudson had been intrigued by the idea before, but the awe on the head groom's face all but solidified it for him. If he could make this happen, he would gain the respect of everyone far sooner than he would if he had to wait years to see if he'd made a breeding misstep. Hudson glanced at Mr. Whitworth. "You agree?"

"That Hezekiah and Hestia would make a fine foal? They certainly have the potential, and their foal would be one everyone would watch." Mr. Whitworth clearly held a bit more caution than Mr. Knight, but his gaze was somewhat unfocused as he looked toward Hestia's stall.

He blinked a few times and then turned back to Hudson. "I've heard a few rumors about Hezekiah myself. More than the horse is on the market this year."

"I heard similar rumors at the assembly." Would Mr. Whitworth volunteer other information? Was Lady Rebecca a complete harridan? If so, he'd have to find another way to succeed. But if she wasn't? If she was sweet, biddable, and everything his father had told him Englishwomen were? He didn't see why he shouldn't attempt to court her.

Mr. Whitworth narrowed his gaze. "You'd make a lifetime commitment for a chance at a champion horse?"

Mr. Knight stepped back before looking from one man to the other. After a moment, he returned to the stall he'd been working in.

Hudson met Mr. Whitworth's steady regard. "You don't believe in subtlety, do you?"

"Not really. I've better things to do with my time than try to decipher a man's meaning as we pretend to talk about another subject entirely."

"Which explains why you went into horses instead of politics."

"Politics tends to require legitimacy. Horses don't care which side of the blanket you're born on as long as you strap theirs on right."

Hudson wasn't going to maneuver this man by making him uncomfortable, as it seemed that was the manager's preferred form of manipulation. If they both tried to use it on each other, the conversation could move from awkward to embarrassing rather quickly.

He could use a bit of candidness right now, though. "Is Lady Rebecca a shrew?"

"Hardly." The manager sighed and rubbed one hand against his temple. "She's an English rose of the highest order. Her father is an earl, her mother the granddaughter of a duke. She's beautiful, admired, and accomplished, according to all accounts."

"Which means I won't be the only man with this idea."

"No, you won't. You aren't." He sighed and shook his head. "You have Hestia. That might be enough of an inducement on its own. You should simply make the request. Lord Gliddon is a horse man after all."

Hudson might know pitifully little about English etiquette, but he did know that a man only had one chance to approach a prospective partnership. If he asked about the horse and was turned down, his asking for the lady's hand would not be well received.

Besides, just yesterday he'd determined that a well-positioned wife would solve other problems as well.

Still, a champion mare wasn't enough to overcome his shortcomings. He couldn't afford to look like a fumbling colt who didn't know his own legs in each new social situation.

"I'm afraid India is far more different from England than I anticipated." Given the reaction to Mr. Whitworth's presence at the training grounds, it was unlikely the man would be able to help, but Hudson didn't have anyone else to ask. "I don't suppose you know the particulars of moving about the local society, do you?"

A splutter of a snicker sounded from the taller man, who quickly pressed his lips together until his face began to turn red. Then he released a loud laugh that startled more than one nearby horse and caused a roaring echo of thuds and jangles to fill the stable.

"I say, whatever could make you laugh with such boisterousness, Mr. Whitworth?" A gentle, somewhat familiar female voice cut through the cacophony. "I'm not sure I've seen you do more than crack a smile in all the time I've known you."

Mr. Whitworth turned toward the newcomer, and his smile shifted into one of indulgent exasperation. "What's there to laugh about when I'm dealing with your pestering presence?"

"I'm a delight and you know it." Miss Snowley grinned at the manager before sneaking a hesitant look Hudson's way. Her smile drooped and then propped back up, somewhat stiffer than it had been before. "Besides, if I didn't exercise some of these horses, you'd have to hire another groom."

Mr. Whitworth shook his head but said, "I have to admit that I would—or rather, Lord Stildon would."

"Of course." She swallowed hard and looked at Hudson. "Good morning, my lord."

Hudson met her look with an assessing stare. This woman had more than saved his reputation Saturday evening, but he still wasn't sure what to make of her. A slash of red crossed her cheeks, and she turned her attention back to Mr. Whitworth. "Whatever the reason, I'm glad to see you happy."

"It isn't often I'm asked to manage a man's entry into society."

So much for the man being trustworthy. Hudson glared at the manager, refusing to meet Miss Snowley's gaze, which would likely have shifted from hesitant to mocking. What sort of viscount asked his stable manager for social assistance?

Hudson's glare didn't make Mr. Whitworth squirm. Instead he shrugged and nodded in Miss Snowley's direction. "You need help, and she's the best option you've got."

"I'm flattered," Miss Snowley said, her mock surprise tempered by the wide smile on her face.

Mr. Whitworth glanced around the stable. "Well, you didn't have much competition for the title of most helpful. Everyone else here is about as socially useful as a saddle without a girth."

Hudson wanted to argue, but the idea wasn't a horrible one.

Wouldn't one woman be the best person to teach him how to manage another? It was like learning to ride. One might start on a cart horse before riding a thoroughbred. He turned to fully face Miss Snowley. "I believe we worked well enough at the assembly."

"We did indeed." Her impish grin remained as she nudged Mr. Whitworth. "I'm surprised you would admit to Mr. Whitworth here that you don't even know how to dance, though."

Another chuckle erupted from the manager, and it was echoed by several of the stable hands who were now standing in the entrances to their respective stalls, not even bothering to pretend that they weren't listening.

"What exactly is it that you need assistance with?" she continued, ignoring the mild uproar she'd just created.

"He wants to join the hoard of gentlemen stuffing flowers into Lord Gliddon's drawing room."

Hudson was fast coming to realize the downside of Mr. Whitworth's candidness.

"Oh," Miss Snowley said quietly. Her head dropped until all he could see was the top of her hat. After a few moments, her face reappeared, the smile still in place, though somewhat smaller. "As it happens, I'm the perfect person to help you. I'm not an intimate of Lady Rebecca, so I can't personally recommend you, but I am excellent at maneuvering through Newmarket without stepping on any toes."

"What about the dance floor, though, Miss Snowley?" called a voice from down the stable.

Hudson spun around, trying to guess which groom had spouted such irreverence, but it was impossible to tell.

Miss Snowley seemed to know, however, and she didn't look the least offended. "I've never stepped on any toes there either. I'll need some help teaching Lord Stildon the same skill. I assume you'll be my first volunteer, Miles?"

A groom stepped out with a wide smile splitting his dark face. "Of course, Miss Snowley, whatever you need."

Mr. Knight shook his head and pointed at Miss Snowley.

"You're not stealing away my grooms, now. I've horses that need tending."

"And apparently an employer as well," Miss Snowley returned. "I can hardly teach him to dance without assistance."

More chuckles scattered through the stable, and the man named Miles simply grinned larger.

"Horses, Miss Snowley. Horses." Mr. Knight crossed his arms over his chest, but he looked more like an indulgent father telling his child she could only have two biscuits instead of an irritated head groom.

"I'll need Arthur and Ernest too. You'll have them back within the hour."

Mr. Knight shook his head but waved in her direction as he turned his attention back to the horses.

"I'll even take two horses for a ride when I return as a thank-you."

"How nice of you to offer such a sacrifice. I suppose next you'll volunteer to ride Hestia for me?"

Miss Snowley gave a sigh. "If I must."

Hudson blinked. Didn't Mr. Whitworth say that she wasn't allowed to ride one of the thoroughbreds?

Mr. Knight shook his head. "You can have my grooms but not my sanity. You can ride Odysseus later and that will do fine."

"Very well, then." Miss Snowley moved back toward the door she'd recently entered. "Come along, Lord Stildon. You too, Mr. Whitworth. Since Mr. Knight won't let me take more grooms, you'll have to help, too."

Mr. Whitworth grunted. With a grin, Hudson nudged the man forward. "At least she won't be running amok in the stable."

"No," Mr. Whitworth returned, "she's going to make a mull of your life instead."

Nine

When she'd dressed this morning, the seams of her tailored riding jacket had lain in smooth, perfectly fitting lines. As Bianca led her coerced group of men away from the stable toward the decorative gardens on the other side of the house, the seams constricted until she could scarce take a full breath.

She circled a hedge and moved toward a semi-secluded section of lawn where they could have their lesson in some form of privacy. Somehow she had to get control of herself.

Yes, his plans contrasted hers, but that didn't explain the keen sense of disappointment now stabbing through her. It wasn't as if she was in love with the man, and in truth he held a higher status than she'd ever aspired to. Still, she'd thought that maybe her connection to his stable and ability to enter his space gave her an advantage.

It would seem that was not the case. Like so many other men, he was besotted with the idea of Lady Rebecca.

Bianca wished she could dislike the woman, but the truth was that Lady Rebecca was everything rumor made her out to be. She possessed beauty and connections enough to entice many a man, but she was also sweet and intelligent. Honestly, her greatest flaw was being so perfect as to be boring.

Lord Stildon would be one of many suitors. Would he be as appealing to Lady Rebecca as he was to Bianca? There were loftier titles, men with greater social presence.

All Bianca could do was establish herself as a helpful and appealing part of Lord Stildon's life and hope that either Lady Rebecca chose someone else or the competition was so tedious that Lord Stildon preferred the ease with which he could court Bianca.

And if he still married Lady Rebecca? Bianca shuddered at the thought of living with Mrs. Snowley's undivided attention without having Hawksworth as a retreat.

She stopped in a circle of grass ringed on two sides with elaborate flower beds and the other with rows of tall trees. "This should do nicely."

Her strange little crew stumbled into a cluster around her, varying levels of bemusement on their faces. Grooms were hardly the ideal choice of dancing tutors, but she couldn't trot out here with her sister and the ladies who came around to tea every now and then.

"Why do I have to be here?" Mr. Whitworth asked, arms crossed, head cocked to the side. "Not that I don't think it will be entertaining."

"Because it is in your best interest for your employer to be well connected." Bianca met Mr. Whitworth's gaze and then dropped it, realizing suddenly that it was possible Lord Stildon would one day soon elect to manage the stable himself and put the other man out of work.

Of course, it was also possible he wouldn't.

Bianca was working on optimism today.

She liked Mr. Whitworth, with his bold frankness and lack of charm, and they'd formed an odd sort of camaraderie over the past year and a half. It would be a sad thing if he were no longer in her life because Lord Stildon did away with his job.

This moment was about Lord Stildon, though, not for her to

try to name why Mr. Whitworth felt like more of a brother than her own did.

"Before we begin," she said to Lord Stildon, "I have to ask how it is possible that you have reached the age of . . . I say, how old are you?"

Bianca frowned and considered the viscount. It was so difficult to determine a man's age once he'd passed two and twenty. That is, until he approached something closer to forty. That left a rather large range of possibility.

"Eight and twenty." He narrowed his eyes at her and took a deep breath through his nose.

Only four years older than she was, then. She pressed on. "How is it that you reached the age of eight and twenty without learning to dance?"

"By not dancing." The flat voice implied the answer should have been obvious and that her questions were useless and unwelcome. New to England, he was now in a corner of his own grounds surrounded by employees and taking orders from a woman who'd tried to beat him with a boot. It was understandable that he found the situation somewhat uncomfortable.

"They don't dance in India?"

"Not like they do here." He glanced around the small group of people. "Some of the areas of the country with a higher concentration of English families might have had some dances, but there weren't any where I was."

"Well." Bianca turned her gaze to the people she'd coerced into helping her lesson. "This will be simple enough to solve. Mr. Whitworth, will you please—"

"I don't know how to dance either."

"Nonsense." Bianca frowned. "You stood up with Helen after that beastly Lord Davers implied that she shouldn't have even been allowed to attend Mrs. Wainbright's party last year."

"The lady was not very appreciative of my gesture."

No, she hadn't been. While Helen might have only been a lady's maid, she was a respectable one. Dancing with a man who worked for a living would have been difficult but acceptable, as she, too, had been forced into service. It was the fact that the man was illegitimate that had made Helen feel her partner was too far beneath her.

No one ever said whom he was the son of, though Bianca had heard enough innuendo to assume his father was aristocratic. But everyone knew the status of his birth, and Helen wasn't going to lower herself to associate with him.

"The point is," Bianca rushed on, "that you danced. Now, please take Andrew and stand at the top of the formation."

The wiry young groom with a wide toothy grin that took up a large portion of his face loped to the place Bianca pointed. "I say, does this make me the woman?"

"Yes," Mr. Whitworth said quickly.

She could have told Andrew he was standing in for the family dog and he still would have smiled at her. Nothing kept the man from being happy, except a problem with one of the horses.

What would it be like to love life that much?

Ernest, the third groom she'd called into service, was too shy to tell her no, while Miles wouldn't have stayed away even if she'd asked. He was drawn to anything that could be considered bizarre. She waved those two grooms into position beside Mr. Whitworth and Andrew.

"Don't worry," Miles said. "I'll be the lady in our pairing."

"Yes. Well. Now." Bianca turned to Lord Stildon. How was she going to do this? "With only three couples, this won't be much like a full dance, but it should suffice for explanation of basic formations."

Her half-formed idea soon devolved into utter disaster. While Mr. Whitworth gave a valiant effort to go where he was supposed to, he'd been honest in saying that his skill was lacking. It didn't help that his companion hadn't a clue as to what he was doing.

The second pair had even less of an idea. Ernest made matters worse by refusing to look anywhere but at his own feet, so he never managed to move before Andrew would collide with him.

The entire business was such a mess that she couldn't even spare a moment to consider her actual pupil, beyond making sure he was physically where he was supposed to be.

"I think it is safe to say," Bianca said, clasping her hands together in front of her after her attempts to demonstrate one of the popular country dances had failed even more spectacularly than the last, "that at the very least, the next time you dance you will wear a genuine smile while remembering this moment."

Lord Stildon chuckled, the first noise he'd made since the lesson started. "Perhaps I can dance with a woman who has a keen interest in her shoes. I'll spend the entire set rescuing her and come off as gallant instead of inept. It's possible I could get out of the dance entirely by escorting her to a corner to recuperate."

Bianca couldn't restrain her own laugh. "To think all along we women have been doing it wrong. We've been striving for accomplishment when we should strive to need rescue instead."

"Any woman who scares off a horse thief with her riding boot isn't going to want a man to rescue her from the dance floor."

"No, I suppose not," Bianca said, refusing to drop her gaze to her own toes but having no qualms about a sudden interest in Ernest's. Surely the man had found something interesting to look at for the past twenty minutes.

"You've no need to be rescued when you are fully capable of doing the rescuing without even leaving the dance floor." He swept into the edge of her vision with a bow worthy of a royal courtier. "I merely seek my own level of ability because I cannot aspire to yours."

"Well," Bianca said, trying to will away the heat making its way from the tips of her ears to her neck, "they may not dance in India, but flattery seems to be alive and well."

"Admiration is a universal occurrence."

If Lord Stildon possessed this much charm when he wasn't try-ing to be appealing, her chances of becoming mistress of Hawks-worth were slim indeed. How could Lady Rebecca not find him engaging?

"Yes. Well." She lifted her face while avoiding meeting anyone's gaze—particularly Mr. Whitworth's. "We've not enough people to do a quadrille, but we'll try to make do."

The next half hour felt approximately like four hours as she attempted to instruct Lord Stildon, and, by extension, the three grooms. Mr. Whitworth was somewhat better at the quadrilles and offered a few helpful suggestions, as he had performed the dance as a man maneuvering around ladies' trains and, well, she'd always been the one in the skirt.

When she attempted to show Lord Stildon a reel, it was such an utter failure that she abandoned all hope. Likely this entire morning had caused more detriment than Lord Stildon's simple admission of inability would have done.

"I think," she said through heaving breaths that proved dancing one part of a reel was nowhere near as difficult as attempting to dance six parts, "that we've done quite enough for today."

Ernest and Andrew all but fled from the clearing, the ordeal proving too much for even Andrew's indomitable spirit.

"Will it be enough?" Lord Stildon asked.

"You won't be proficient." Bianca paused to catch her breath. "But you won't be entirely clueless."

"You can blame any other fumbling on it not being a popular dance in India. None of them will know any different." Miles gave a shrug before ambling off in the same direction as the other two grooms. "The others are going to love hearing about this," he called over his shoulder. "Don't worry, my lord, I'll keep it in the stable."

Bianca winced. Why hadn't she considered that this foray would cost Lord Stildon some of the respect due an employer? Mr. Knight was not going to thank her for that or the work he'd have to do to set it all to rights.

Mr. Whitworth crossed his arms over his chest and looked from Bianca to Lord Stildon and back again. "You aren't going to teach him how to waltz?"

"I don't really think—"

"I saw the announcement for next Saturday's assembly. Every third dance will be a waltz."

Bianca frowned. There was nothing wrong with the waltz, and she never gave a second thought to dancing it at assemblies, but here, in the privacy of Hawksworth's garden, she understood why some thought the dance scandalous. Without the benefit of other couples, it seemed far more intimate, especially given her intentions toward the man. As her goals were now in jeopardy, she wasn't sure she wanted to participate in an activity that might encourage more emotional attachment.

Disappointment she could handle. She wasn't so sure about heartbreak.

Mr. Whitworth smiled, but it didn't hold the same quality his rare smiles normally did. His gaze was narrowed instead of glinting. "A woman being courted will expect Lord Stildon to waltz."

"Yes," Bianca murmured. This awkward situation was of no one's making but her own, and now she had to see it through to completion.

"Very well," she said with an outward smile and an inward wince. "I'll teach him to waltz."

And she dearly hoped she wouldn't regret it later.

Ten

In the amount of time it took for a horse to make a chunk of sugar disappear, Hudson's dancing lesson shifted from an indulgent amusement to a treacherous threat. Until that moment, it had been rather like putting a horse in a race with a pack of goats—amusing, but not noteworthy and certainly not productive.

In the face of Mr. Whitworth's suggestion, Miss Snowley's confidence disappeared, even as she agreed to its necessity. Was a waltz some sort of painful or traumatic ritual that he would be expected to perform in order to court a lady? Perhaps England was not as civilized as he'd been raised to expect.

He cleared his throat. "What is a waltz?"

"A dance." Mr. Whitworth looked from Hudson to Miss Snowley and back again, his face devoid of expression and his arms crossed tightly over his chest.

"A scandalous one." Miss Snowley lifted her nose in a gesture that should have appeared haughty but only made her look more nervous. "We don't even know if Lady Rebecca has permission to dance it."

Hudson's brows flew upward. A few moments ago, Miss Snowley had taught him—or rather attempted to describe—how to do a dance in which he spent as much time, if not more, dancing with the other ladies in the set than with his chosen partner. To Hudson, that seemed rather scandalous, not to mention ridiculous. This waltz was supposedly more so, though, enough that special permission was required. Did he have to attain that as well? Where would he get it?

"She's had permission, almost from the first of the Season," Mr. Whitworth said as he relaxed and clasped his arms behind his back. The tight smile he'd been wearing earlier changed to a grin. "Even if she didn't, Lady Jersey is hardly going to appear and harp on what happens in Newmarket's assembly hall."

Miss Snowley's eyes narrowed at Mr. Whitworth's grin. Some sort of unspoken conversation was transpiring between the two of them, and Hudson didn't have nearly enough information to try to interpret it. Where was his manager's frank way of speaking now?

"How do you know she has permission? I thought you didn't dance," Miss Snowley said with a smug smirk.

"I don't. But I can assure you that gentlemen enjoy gossip as much as ladies do." He darted a quick look in Hudson's direction before returning his attention to Miss Snowley. "I have friends in London. I hear things."

With a decisive nod, Mr. Whitworth turned in the same direction the other men had recently run. "Now, as the waltz requires only two people, I do believe I'll leave you to it."

"But—but, you can't!" Miss Snowley took a step toward a retreating Mr. Whitworth. She then turned back to Hudson before seeming to think it better to go after the manager again. Back and forth she went, making her heavy riding habit swirl about until she appeared to be doing some strange dance of her own.

Hudson waited. He didn't know dancing and he didn't know about the habits of English women, but he knew how to wait out a businessman who was warring through his options in his own head. This seemed a rather similar moment.

Finally, she turned back to him, her smile brittle, her every mannerism telling him she was as likely to bolt as she was to stay.

At that moment, his need to prove himself, his dislike of nearly everything about his new homeland, and his confusion over the new society fell away and left behind a burning need to know what this woman was thinking. Why, when she'd simply barreled through with her plans to teach him to dance everything else, did this one cause her trepidation?

She was acting like a skittish horse, and those he knew how to handle.

The tension he'd been holding in his body as he feared making a misstep even among a group of horrible non-dancers disappeared, and he eased forward, arms wide, palms facing outward. He dropped his gaze to her shoulder, trying to gauge her reactions in his periphery vision. He didn't have any food with him, and he rather thought beckoning her with a morsel of chocolate or a tea biscuit would be more insulting than helpful, so he began to talk in the same low voice he used with his horses.

"If learning this waltz is essential to my making a bid for Lady Rebecca's affections, I would be most appreciative of any help you can provide. I realize it is asking a lot of you, though, and you've already done quite a bit."

"That's what friends do," she said in a thin, high-pitched voice. He fought a grin at her failed attempt to sound unaffected and calm.

Were they friends? The concept was foreign to him. Not the idea of friends in general, but the idea of female ones. The women he'd encountered until now were to be revered and respected but kept at a distance. Still, he had to admit that since leaving India his best conversations had been with this unpredictable woman and an unconventional employee who both was and wasn't of his social class.

"This waltz, then, is a dance?" The foolish question would hopefully prompt her to start explaining. Maybe once she was instructing him again, she would forget whatever was causing these nerves.

"Yes, though it's fairly new to England, or at least in London and here. It is nice for courting couples, though, as the pair stays together for the entire dance."

"I can see how that would be advantageous." A step forward brought him within touching distance of her if he stretched his arm fully forward, so he came to a stop. The next move would have to be hers. "What do we do first?"

"Well." She looked up at him. "The waltz is a series of movements performed in a circle. It won't be easy to hide that you've never properly learned."

"Isn't that a problem you are correcting?" He gave her a grin that he hoped conveyed jovial humility.

A small answering smile curved her lips. "I can hardly make you an expert in a matter of minutes."

"Very well." He drew himself up tall. "At least save me from total ignorance."

She laughed and dropped her gaze, and an uneasy feeling curled through Hudson's middle now that he was no longer having to focus on keeping her from bolting. This was sounding an awful lot like a flirtation. As he had his intentions set on another woman, that wasn't a proper thing to indulge in.

"Where do we start?" He dropped his smile and his eye contact and looked at his feet, as if waiting for her to command him as she'd done earlier.

"With the arms." She pulled the pins from her hat and placed it near a tree. "That would be constantly bumping you in the nose if I left it on."

Hudson blinked. They were going to be that close to each other?

With brisk movements, she shifted his arms until one curved in front of him and the other reached above his head.

Then she stepped into the space created.

Her back settled against one hand while she reached up and took hold of his other. Her second hand came to rest on his shoulder. Her upturned face was only inches from his own.

No wonder the waltz was considered scandalous.

"Then what?"

"We go about in a circle. Sometimes we walk hand-in-hand, other times we'll pirouette about, but for the most part, we slowly spin."

She hummed a tune as she directed him through their first pass around the small section of lawn. Once he got past the idea of this being a dance, he realized how similar this felt to riding and guiding a horse. By the second pass around, he felt quite confident in the basic movements.

"How does one keep this from being an awkward interlude?" he asked. "The other night you said I am not allowed to dance multiple times with a single lady. That means I am sure to find myself in this position with a woman I am not courting."

"Such as now?" She peeked up at him with a mischievous grin.

Hudson coughed. "Yes. Such as now."

She tilted her head, considering him as he continued to guide her about the grass. "You talk."

"About what?"

"Anything. I think that's part of the scandal, you know. A couple can hold a personal conversation that only they can hear while still maintaining propriety. It's as close to alone as some couples can get, at least in the city."

Hudson chuckled and experimented with their pirouette in a way that drew a small laugh from Miss Snowley. "Does that mean I shall get to hold a conversation that is not about the weather or the antics of a drunken idiot? The only other conversation I had at the assembly speculated upon Lady Rebecca's arrival, and I hardly think the lady would like to discuss that."

"No, I would think not." Miss Snowley grinned up at him, and he felt a bit of tension leave her as her back settled more solidly against his hand. "You could talk about your own arrival. That was what everyone else discussed on Saturday."

Hudson winced. "I supposed as much. Please tell me that will eventually become an uninteresting topic."

She smirked. "How long have you been in England?"

Hudson counted back the days, surprised to discover his feet had been on solid ground for only a mere week. "Not long. I'm afraid I still have quite a few adjustments to make."

She pinched the lightweight fabric of his jacket. "Such as clothing?"

He nodded. "I've pressed one of the footmen into service as a valet. I heard him grumbling about my clothing as he unpacked. Said the fabrics were fit for a women's shop."

"We do tend to wear far thinner fabrics than the men."

He shuddered. "How do you keep from freezing?"

"Capes?"

"Hardly practical."

"When practical clothing is called for, we wear heavier fabrics. See my riding clothes? Your coat should be made of wool such as this." She rolled her shoulders. "Admittedly, it is making this dance far more difficult than normal, but I rather think your coats will be cut a bit differently from mine. Eventually you'll become accustomed to it."

"I fear there are many things to which I need to become accustomed." He slid his hand a bit lower on her back to guide her around a plant he'd accidentally brought them too close to. "Is all English food dreadful?"

"I, er, well. . . . Admittedly, Mr. Pierre isn't known for arranging particularly delectable refreshments, but there are other foods."

Hudson grunted. He wished he was only referring to the paltry offerings at the assembly, but indeed he'd now suffered through several meals within his own home that had been sufficiently filling but hardly enjoyable. "I wonder if my cook is of the same mind as Mr. Pierre."

"I doubt it. While Newmarket has more than its share of aristocracy thanks to the horses, working at Hawksworth isn't a position a servant wants to risk losing. You can't think the servants aren't trying to impress you."

"You mean to tell me that all English food is that bland?"

She laughed. "We make up for it with saucy women who attack men in their own stables."

"Ah yes," he said with a laugh, pulling her a bit closer before he thought to stop himself. Yes, this was a scandalous dance indeed, but he didn't cease their endless circle. "I think, given the choice, I'd rather have bland food than boring company."

"It's a rather good thing you met me then, isn't it?" she asked quietly.

"Yes, I think it is," he answered in a whisper, all too aware of the fact that there wasn't any part of her that was more than six inches away from him.

It was close enough to distinguish the warmth that came from being in the proximity of another living body. The sensation was quite different from being in the vicinity of a horse, though. While the animals could envelop a man in heat, this was a more delicate sensation, almost more of an impression than a feeling he could truly identify.

He wasn't sure which of them stopped the dance as they stumbled to a halt, but both of them jerked away from each other and looked anywhere but at the other person.

"There's—" She paused to clear her throat again. "There's more than dancing that you'll need to know. I'm assuming you've learned proper table habits in India?"

He pulled his gaze from a large pink flower to consider her. Was she being serious? "Yes. I've even been using a fork for a full year now."

A slash of pink started at her ears and slid across her cheek-bones even as she lifted a hand to hide her small smile. "Of course you have. I'm positive it's been at least two since you stopped slurping from your spoon?"

"Oh, nearly three." He looked her way and, thankfully, the strange sensations of moments ago were nowhere to be found. All he felt was the camaraderie they'd known earlier. "I'm afraid, though, that this is a case of not knowing what I don't know."

"If you want more help dancing before the next assembly, let me know," she said quietly. "I'm here most mornings anyway." She clasped her hands in front of her and lifted her chin. "To ride."

He bit his cheek to keep from smiling. "I do believe you are simply angling for access to my horses, Miss Snowley."

"Well," she said with a grin, "I have known the horses longer than I've known you."

"Speaking of riding—"

"Yes. Odysseus. Mr. Knight said he would have him saddled for me." She twisted her hands in front of her. Obviously she found this moment as difficult as he did. That was good. It would mean they would both avoid repeating it.

"I'll just . . . go for that ride now." She stepped backward a few paces and then gave a small smile before turning and walking away.

Hudson didn't move until her figure disappeared from view.

Eleven

Never again would Bianca think those Minerva Press novels that she openly teased Marianne about reading but sneaked into her own room in the evenings were nothing but silly nonsense. At this moment, flopped across her bed in her riding habit, she was as floaty and nonsensical as any heroine jumping at shadows.

She even felt that edge of fear along with her hesitant happiness. Lord Stildon was everything in a man that Bianca hadn't even admitted she was looking for.

Well, except for the fact that he was looking for Lady Rebecca.

Bianca was pretty enough, especially if she sat still while Dorothy properly attended to her hair and clothing, and she would be welcome in nearly every fine drawing room in Newmarket, assuming she could stomach making visits with her stepmother. But there were two things she didn't have and never would.

A title and a champion horse.

She pushed up into a sitting position with a sigh and set about removing her hat and her habit before she ruined both by wallowing on the bed.

Was she wishing Lady Rebecca ill to hope the woman chose a different man? Just because Bianca had never met anyone more appealing didn't mean Lord Stildon was perfect for everyone. Lady Rebecca would have every suitor imaginable making visits to Newmarket. She would have her choice of titled men. Why would she choose Lord Stildon?

"Why indeed?" Bianca muttered as she took the pins from her hair. If one meeting with the man had her feeling giddy, what would happen to Lady Rebecca when she encountered him while he was actually trying to be charming?

A knock at her door provided a welcome distraction from the mind-numbing swirl her thoughts were descending into. "Enter."

The last person Bianca expected to open the door was her stepmother, but there she was, fading blond hair piled up into fashionable curls and a curve to her lips that should have been a smile but somehow looked sour.

Bianca was fairly certain that Mrs. Snowley hadn't visited her in her rooms since she moved down from the nursery six years ago. She blinked at the woman but wasn't at all sure what to say.

Mrs. Snowley didn't have that problem. Her farce of a smile turned into a sneer as she took in the disheveled riding clothes. "You haven't changed yet?"

"I only just returned home."

"And you're going out again. Dorothy will be in as soon as she has finished with Marianne. I expect you downstairs in half an hour." Mrs. Snowley sniffed and turned back toward the door.

Bianca took several paces across the room, ready to snatch her stepmother by the arm if the woman tried to leave without explaining herself. "Where am I to be going?"

Mrs. Snowley heaved a sigh so strong that it caused her curls to tremble. "Marianne and I make calls on Mondays."

"Yes, I know. What has that to do with me?" Bianca didn't want to participate in those calls any more than Mrs. Snowley wanted to take her, so why the sudden insistence?

"Your father thinks I'm not giving you the same social advantages as Marianne. Half an hour." The older woman left before Bianca could decide on the appropriate additional question.

Dorothy appeared, a dress draped over her arm. Bianca's confusion and suspicion kept her still enough for Dorothy to make the necessary alterations to her appearance in the allotted time.

For as long as Bianca could remember, Mrs. Snowley had been the mother figure in her life, and she'd seen enough to guess what awaited her over the next few hours. She braced for censure, prepared for snide remarks, and shored up the defenses on her confidence against any and all attacks on her appearance.

Mrs. Snowley and Marianne were waiting in the front hall when Bianca came down the stairs, and soon they were bundled into the carriage and on their way. Bianca tucked the latest gossip sheet into her reticule so she could surreptitiously study it and be able to identify any sly remarks or comparisons made at her expense.

Receiving compliments from her stepmother was never even a consideration, so the visits that followed had Bianca wishing she carried a vial of hartshorn, because surely someone was going to faint in shock.

Possibly even her.

"She's so accomplished," Mrs. Snowley told Mrs. Fernstone at their first stop. "You've seen her at the assemblies. Everyone likes her, and she's as light and graceful as a feather."

Bianca narrowed her gaze at her stepmother. The nicest thing Mrs. Snowley had ever said about Bianca was that she evened up the numbers at a dinner party well. What was she doing listing Bianca's abilities? How did she even *know* Bianca's abilities?

Know them she did, because everywhere they went, she extolled Bianca's slightest virtues.

"Her pianoforte is exemplary when one considers how little she gets to practice because of the time she spends riding. That might not be an asset everywhere, but this is Newmarket," she said to another matron whose name Bianca couldn't remember. The woman had a horrific dog that huddled underneath a chair and stared at Bianca throughout the visit.

By the third visit, Bianca was positive something nefarious was underfoot. It sounded as if Mrs. Snowley thought Bianca was a horse going off to auction. Was this what the woman normally did on her Monday visits? Did she go about telling everyone how amazing Marianne was? Surely not. They'd never be invited anywhere.

Speaking of Marianne, the girl had been oddly silent all day.

Bianca turned in her sister's direction. Did she know what was going on? Her eyes met Bianca's before quickly looking away, but that was not enough to declare the younger girl's guilt. If she were truly hiding anything she'd shift her hips and—there! Bianca barely resisted the urge to point at her sister and cry out "Aha!" as Marianne pushed against the edge of her chair to turn her hips slightly away from Bianca.

A sisterly chat was obviously in order when they returned home. It might involve pinning the younger girl down and threatening to pummel her with a pillow, but Bianca would learn what she needed to know.

Marianne's easy capitulation was the only way Bianca managed to stay a step ahead of her stepmother. When Mrs. Snowley had gotten an irrational and sudden desire to clean out the attic before Bianca's first Season, a bit of sisterly coercion had learned the reason. Bianca had barely had time to move the two trunks of her mother's mementos and belongings before the dastardly woman could find them herself and subject them to whatever form of damage she thought she could get away with and have it look natural. Likely water and some form of mouse infestation.

"Perennial, dear," Mrs. Wainbright said, leaning slowly toward Mrs. Snowley, "Marianne has far better chances this Season. Don't you think Bianca is a bit long in the tooth?"

Bianca clenched her jaw to keep from gaping. Was the woman implying Bianca was too old to marry?

"Not yet," Mrs. Snowley said firmly before giving a dramatic, overdone sigh. "That's why we've decided we finally have to let her go. It's been selfish of us to discourage her leaving until now. She brightens up the house so much. But parents must put their child's welfare over their own." She gave a sniff and a nod. "It's time."

Bianca was going to be ill. Or faint. Or run screaming into town as the woman before her revealed herself to be possessed by some mind-altering spirit. Mrs. Snowley had never encouraged Bianca to do anything except be silent or, on occasion, to be gone.

One thing was now clear, though, and that was that Mrs. Snowley had decided, with some urgency, that it was time for Bianca to marry. The only question that remained was, did she have a particular target in mind?

If BIANCA THOUGHT she would be able to corner Marianne as soon as they arrived home from the plethora of exhausting visits, she was sadly mistaken. Upon their return, they walked into a house in hectic preparation.

Bianca recognized the bustle of midday cleaning and the various aromas competing for the identifying dish of the evening meal.

She'd forgotten Mrs. Snowley was having a dinner party. With the Meads.

If there had been any doubt that Bianca was being served up on the night's menu, the day's conversations with mothers, aunts, sisters, and even sisters-in-law of every eligible man under the age of fifty would have confirmed it.

"Do you have an even number for dinner? I understand if you need me to eat in my room." The ploy wasn't likely to work, but Bianca felt she had to try.

Mrs. Snowley frowned. "Successful pairings don't simply happen, you know. One must constantly work to position herself to her best advantage if she wants to make a good match, and receiving invitations requires one also issue them."

"Strange how my lack of participation in these invitations wasn't a problem until recently."

Mrs. Snowley ignored Bianca's snide comment and shooed the girls toward the stairs. "Your gowns should be laid out and ready. I'm afraid we haven't much time."

Bianca dressed as hurriedly as possible, barely managing to hold still long enough to avoid being burned by Dorothy's curling tongs. She wanted to be downstairs when the guests started arriving. The last thing she wanted was Mr. Theophilus Mead thinking she'd timed her entrance in order to impress him.

As she started down the stairs, familiar voices drifted up from the front hall, and she paused with her foot in midair and her hand on the banister. Hoping she was mistaken in the speaker's identity, she squatted down and tilted her head to see the hall without descending into it.

Cold ran through her body, raising the hairs on her arms and making her fingers curl into her palms as the first man stepped into view. Mr. Octavius Mead, one of her father's dearest friends.

She was too late.

The elder Mr. Mead was innocuous enough, though somewhat strange. He was married, but as far as anyone knew, his wife preferred to stay in Bath these days. No, the problem with Mr. Mead was that he rarely went anywhere without his odious son.

His odious, unmarried son who was likely in the hall now, positioned to admire her as she came down the stairs.

Was it too late to plead a headache or some form of digestive ailment?

"What are you doing?" Marianne asked, plopping down to sit next to Bianca on the step.

"Er," Bianca said. She could hardly tell her sister that she was contemplating creating an excuse to avoid the gathering. Nor could she now feign illness since Marianne had seen her dressed and hale on the stairs.

"I caught my slipper on my hem and had to fix it so I didn't tumble down the stairs." She straightened to a stand and adjusted her skirts, wincing at the lie, hearing the vicar extolling on the evils of dissembling in the back of her mind.

"Oh. I'm glad you didn't fall." Marianne stood as well and gave Bianca one of those smiles that was impossible to interpret.

Did Marianne dislike Bianca as much as her mother did? Did she dislike her for other reasons? Did she perhaps not dislike Bianca at all but just smiled strangely? Was she thinking about something else entirely?

It was simply another unsettling thought to plague Bianca's mind as the sisters continued down the stairs. At least the strange conversation had delayed them enough that the men had retreated to the drawing room.

Mr. Theophilus Mead was the first to see them enter the room, and his lips twisted into a curve that said he assumed they would be honored to be in his presence. Even his hair, with its thick swoop to the side and carefully pomaded disarray, looked smug and condescending. If the man spent half as much energy on his horses as he spent on his hair, she'd find him far more appealing. No, that was too far. She'd find him far more respectable.

Bianca took a deep breath and set her jaw. She could and would make it through this evening without embarrassing her father. Even if she had to make idle talk with a man who ran his horse ragged despite the pebble in its shoe and then sold it away when it turned up lame like a pouty little boy who'd broken his own toy and didn't want to admit it.

Maybe she wouldn't be sitting near him?

Unlikely, given the day's revelations.

The Wainbrights arrived, along with another of her father's good friends, which created an even number for dinner but an imbalance between the men and the women.

Mrs. Snowley could only have been more obvious if she'd tied

Bianca up in a carriage and had her delivered to Mr. Mead's door-step.

By embedding herself in a stunningly boring conversation about Mrs. Wainbright's roses, Bianca managed to avoid the younger Mr. Mead until it was time to progress into dinner.

There, the loathsome man had been seated to Bianca's right while his father was on her left. The elder would prove no help whatsoever, as he'd been seated to her father's right and would spend the entire night conversing with Mr. Snowley.

No matter. She would simply employ the same philosophy she used when forced to sit for tea with Mrs. Snowley. She would focus on taking the smallest bites of food possible. Even the most meticulous governess had never imagined someone giving as much attention to the cutting of meat as Bianca was about to do. And not even Mrs. Snowley could find fault with Bianca's not talking with food in her mouth, no matter how tiny the morsel.

"May I say you're looking particularly fetching tonight."

No, you may not. Bianca ground her teeth together. "You flatter me, sir. Thank you." She shoved a bowl in his direction. "Potatoes?"

He took the bowl, but his gaze never left her. "Are you attending the assembly this Saturday?"

Not if you are going to be there. "I imagine so. We usually do." She served herself a bit of beef and then passed the dish on before Mr. Mead had managed to move along the potatoes. Bianca didn't care. The sooner her plate was full, the sooner she could begin eating, and the sooner she could blame her lack of conversation on good table manners.

"I bought a new horse last week." He juggled the meat platter in one hand while waiting for Mrs. Wainbright to take the pota-toes. "A beautiful chestnut stallion. I believe he'll do well in the races next month."

Provided you don't run him lame before then. "How exciting. Do you intend to ride him yourself?"

"Of course not. I wouldn't want to miss the fun of watching the race from the sides." He leaned toward Bianca and lowered his voice. "I may even garner an invitation to the duke's stand. I've been working on that for a year now."

"Turnips?" She slid the bowl between them to force him to sit upright once more, and he was required to drop his gaze and attend to his plate if he didn't want to risk dropping one of the dishes Bianca was pushing his way.

Finally there was enough food before her that she could begin eating. Unwilling to be completely rude, she tried to make appropriate nods and murmurs as the man went on about all the ways he'd tried to maneuver himself socially in order to gain the coveted invitation to the duke's stand.

What she wanted to do was roll her eyes to the ceiling. She understood how much of a game Newmarket's society was and how it connected to the actions of the Jockey Club, and therefore the races. After all, hadn't she agreed to help Lord Stildon navigate the confusing business?

The difference with Lord Stildon was . . . well, it was . . . She frowned at her pudding. There was a difference, wasn't there? Was Lord Stildon's goal of a marriage and a stallion any more honorable than Mr. Mead's desire to stand atop the duke's stand and attain a better view of the races?

She poked at the dessert with her spoon. When looked at objectively, Lord Stildon's goal was less honorable, as it affected poor Lady Rebecca. Or could possibly affect her. The lady was likely to be inundated with similar attempts to gain her hand, if not her affection, so it wasn't as if Lord Stildon would be trying to trick her.

Her dislike wasn't based on the action, then, but the man himself. Even more reason to avoid her stepmother's machinations. Listening to the man speak made her hope he somehow stabbed himself in the lip with his fork.

Why had her stepmother orchestrated such an obvious matchmaking attempt? Never had Bianca indicated any sort of interest in the man.

She glanced up from her pudding, but before she could spear her stepmother with a glare, she saw Marianne and Miss Wainbright with their heads angled together and wide smiles as they darted looks toward Bianca over their nearly untouched desserts.

Bianca stabbed at her pudding with such vigor that a portion of it slid over the back rim of the bowl to plop onto the table. Once this torturous evening was over, Bianca was going to find out exactly what Mrs. Snowley was up to.

Twelve

Being cold was bad.

Being cold with the knowledge that the weather was only going to get colder was worse.

Being cold while knowing that everyone else thought the temperature was perfectly pleasant was downright miserable.

Hudson wrapped his hands around his cup and glared at the low-burning fire in the grate. After several moments, he gave his attention back to the book he'd propped against another book in order to be able to read it without having to hold it. Eventually he would become accustomed to the weather—hopefully—but the dreary, misty almost-rain that had moved in as the sun lowered in the sky had sunk a chill under his skin that refused to be chased away.

After drinking as much tea as his stomach could bear, he'd taken to having the servants send up pot after pot of hot water so he could pour a cup and hold it as it cooled. When combined with the strange look they'd briefly given him when he requested a fire, Hudson could only assume they thought him some sort of delicate flower.

This was yet one more botheration he could lay at the feet of his dead paternal figures. He hadn't been prepared for the dismal weather, the horrid food, or the different social manners. Yes, he was alive, which he supposed he should thank them for, but his father and grandfather had left him in a rather embarrassing quandary. Had his grandfather foreseen these issues and given them as an argument for Hudson's return? Had he put off Hudson's requests to come because he knew his father's denial would raise a son that might embarrass the title?

Chills apparently induced self-denigration.

He reached the end of the page and turned to the next one quickly so he could return his fingers to the warmth of his mug. A slight knock broke the quiet of the room, and he answered without looking up. "Enter."

"What is that?"

After several hours of the timid kowtowing of the servants desperate to keep their positions, the bold question of his stable manager was rather welcome. Hudson glanced down at the cup in his hand before looking up at Mr. Whitworth standing two steps inside the library door. "Hot water."

"Hot—" The man broke off his sentence with a chuckle. "I had been asking about the, well, I'm not quite sure what to call it. Robe? Jacket? But now I'm rather curious about the teapot as well."

Hudson looked down at the brightly colored sleeve of his banyan. He was so accustomed to using it as a dressing gown that he'd forgotten he was wearing it. Unlike he'd done in India, though, he'd left his normal clothing on before donning the vibrant garment tonight. He'd even left his jacket on when cramming his arm into the wide sleeve and hooking the clasps until it covered him up to his chin.

Hudson rolled his shoulders and settled deeper into the warmth it provided. "It's a banyan. A, er, dressing gown of sorts, I suppose. Don't you have those here?"

Mr. Whitworth shook his head with another short chuckle. "Not like that." He gestured to the teapot. "Feeling chilled, I take it?"

"Hmmm." Hudson turned the page he hadn't read and lowered his eyes to the book. He had only been at Hawksworth three days, and he was well and truly tired of feeling out of place. "I assume you have a reason for coming here this evening?"

Mr. Whitworth held up a pamphlet. "The racing calendar. The major races won't be until October, but there are others worth considering. I thought you might like to discuss a plan without your well-meaning stable staff overhearing. Now I think you need a fencing partner instead."

"Are you volunteering?" The skepticism he was feeling likely laced the statement, but he wasn't in a mood to bank it down. The way he understood it, fencing was a sport of the elite in England.

One of Mr. Whitworth's brows lifted in a gesture that reminded Hudson that a nameless arrogant aristocrat's blood ran in the other man's veins. "If you need it, I'd be happy to disarm you."

"What a shame I haven't any foils available, then," Hudson murmured, quite glad for the fact that his mediocre fencing skills wouldn't be challenged this evening. It didn't sound as if Mr. Whitworth was at all unsure of his own ability.

"Yes, a pity." Mr. Whitworth dropped the pamphlet on the desk beside a stack of mail Hudson had been ignoring.

He'd opened several of the letters, but each one had left Hudson feeling more overwhelmed than the one before it, so he'd chosen to ignore them instead.

Mr. Whitworth poked a finger through the pile, nudged one particular invitation away from the others, and stared at it for several moments, still as a statue. Finally, he looked back up at Hudson and sighed. "Have you cards?"

Hudson glanced around the room. Did he have any cards? There were still vast corners of the house, even of the main rooms, he'd yet to explore. "Probably. Why?"

"Because while Lady Rebecca will be on the dance floor, Lord Gliddon will be at the card tables."

"You wish to subject yourself to more of my lack of English awareness?"

Mr. Whitworth huffed. "No, I wish to keep your insipid self-pity from ruining one of the best stables in Newmarket."

Hudson was torn on whether or not to feel offense at the man's statement but decided instead to be glad for his continued honesty. He stood and dropped his lap blanket onto the chair before stalking through the room, opening doors and cabinets.

"Haven't had time to settle into your new home yet?" Mr. Whitworth chuckled as he positioned a chair on the other side of Hudson's table, as far away from the pitiful fire as one could get while still being able to reach the flat surface.

Hudson grunted in response, unwilling to admit that he'd counted his ability to get to the library from his room without getting lost as a significant accomplishment. The fact that he'd had to go to the breakfast room first because that was the only place he knew how to get anywhere from was entirely beside the point.

"Did my grandfather have this place built?" Infernal cornerless house.

"I believe he added the east wing and the corridor connecting the stable to the main house. His father built the central section, though."

Three decks of playing cards jostled against each other as Hudson jerked open another drawer in one of the built-in wall cabinets. He pulled one out and then ran his finger along the top of the curved drawer front. "Why round?"

"Why not?"

"Why not?" Hudson shut the drawer with more force than was required for the ten-foot-tall solid wood door in the front hall. Obviously hiding his displeasure was no longer on tonight's agenda, assuming it ever had been. "Perhaps because a round house has no corners. There are no corridors. Just room after room circling about that winding staircase that somehow, despite it being in the very center of the building, never seems to be where I think it should be. I can't remember how to get anywhere because there is no such thing as 'turn left' or 'turn right.' There's merely 'wander around until you see the red carpet and then use that door to reach the library.'"

He threw the cards onto the table, jerked the lap blanket from his chair, and dropped back into his seat. "That"—he snapped the blanket in the air before draping it over his legs—"is why not."

Mr. Whitworth smirked but said nothing as he removed some of the cards from the deck. After a moment, he began to shuffle the remaining ones. "I am assuming you know whist."

"Of course." Hudson wasn't a complete lackwit. He was simply cold and wanted food that didn't taste like his lap blanket. He nodded to the lightened deck. "One uses all the cards for that."

"So they do. For piquet, however, we only use thirty-two."

As Mr. Whitworth dealt the cards three at a time, Hudson was loath to admit he hadn't any idea what the other man was doing or why. Pride wasn't going to help him if he found himself at a table with Lord Gliddon or any of the other men he'd met who were simply waiting for him to show himself a fool.

Hudson looked at the series of piles in front of him. "Am I to assume this is a two-player game?"

Mr. Whitworth nodded. "And a complicated one to learn. Playing it is simple, though, so if two gentlemen want to make a deal without meeting in private, this is as good as it gets."

"It sounds like a useful game to know, then." Hudson adjusted his seat to more fully face the table.

Twenty minutes later, when Hudson's grasp of the game shifted from nonexistent to adequate, Mr. Whitworth rose and crossed to the desk. "I believe you're ready to keep score now. Have you paper and pencil, Lord Stildon? Or have you not had time to find that yet either?"

Hudson winced at the name and at the friendly jab. Stildon

was his title—his name now, really—and had been for a year, and thus far it hadn't brought him anything particularly good. But since Mr. Whitworth had arrived, he'd forgotten, at least a little, that he was miserable. "Call me Hudson. If you're going to be party to my most embarrassing moments, you might as well have the liberty." He glanced over to the tall man, who stood frozen, partially bent over the writing table. "Oh, and paper and pencil are in the left-hand drawer. I saw them when I was looking for the cards."

Mr. Whitworth didn't move.

Hudson resettled his lap blanket and looked up to see the only movement the other man had made was to turn his head and stare at Hudson.

The unblinking consideration was somewhat unnerving.

"You know which side is left, don't you?" Hudson asked. "It's the one you mount a horse from."

The stable manager blinked and looked down at the table he'd braced his hands on. Finally, he opened the drawer and extracted the writing implements. His return to the game table was equally slow and pondering.

Hudson thought back through the past five minutes, at a loss as to why the man was suddenly different. Nothing stood out, so he studied Mr. Whitworth, seeking a clue from the other man.

After Mr. Whitworth had taken his time easing back into his chair and set the paper and pencil on the table, his pale eyes stared hard at Hudson. "You wish me to use your Christian name?"

A suspicious heat crawled through Hudson, making him unsure whether he still needed the lap blanket. Adjusting it gave him a reason to drop his own gaze and shift his position in his chair. Hopefully the heat wasn't showing on his face, thanks to his now lack of any sort of tan.

"You don't have to, of course. I've no wish to make you uncomfortable." Even though Hudson was far from any sort of ease at the moment. "I only assumed that calling each other by name was a custom in England."

Mr. Whitworth set about shuffling the cards and dealing them out once more. "The only men of rank who have asked me to use their name are the ones with whom I went to school. We started as boys and never saw need to change it."

Hudson scooped up his cards and began to sort them. "You consider these men friends?"

"Of the highest order."

Hudson moved a king to the end of his hand and then a jack to the beginning, with no rhyme or reason to the movement. Too many ideas were shuffling through his mind.

The men Hudson had encountered at the training grounds had been clear that associating with Mr. Whitworth was not in Hudson's best social interest. However, the man had willingly danced with a groom for Hudson's benefit.

What was Hudson to do? He could take the offer back, reset the ordinary order of things. But that would only leave Hudson to spend the rest of his evening brooding about how low the fire was.

Or he could try something unexpected.

Instead of taking anything back, Hudson chose to be deliberately obtuse. If nothing else, it would make Mr. Whitworth the uncomfortable party for once.

Hudson stacked his cards together and tapped them on the table, even though they still resembled utter chaos. "It is quite understandable that you would hold those men in higher esteem than you hold me. For now, we can simply settle for Stildon. Perhaps one day you'll feel I've earned being addressed as Hudson."

A sense of satisfaction melded with Hudson's considerations as Mr. Whitworth's face went slack and his cheeks flushed. Hudson had to lift his cards and fan them out in front of his face to hide his small smirk at finally flustering the unflappable stable manager.

There was a surprising truth in what he had said, though.

He certainly counted Mr. Whitworth among the men whom he wanted to earn respect from and knew the stable manager's frank attitude would make that regard mean all the more when he finally earned it.

"I'm not . . . that is . . . I don't think . . ." Mr. Whitworth cleared his throat and quickly regained his confident equilibrium, at least in appearance. "I believe this might be another area in which you are unaware of the customary English traditions."

Hudson tilted his head and pretended to think. "I don't believe so. Father tended to be rather formal at times in India, particularly among the local aristocratic class." He exaggerated his thoughtful expression, in part to keep the smile from his face. "He was always very passionate about teaching me about the title that would one day be mine. Of course, I think he intended to have it himself first, but life rarely goes as we expect. Still, he taught me that the use of a man's name is a particular honor that shouldn't be granted to simply anyone. I understand your withholding that honor."

Mr. Whitworth shuffled his cards about in his hand, and two of them fell to the floor. He took far longer than necessary to retrieve them. When he rose, he sat back in his chair with a smile that Hudson didn't quite know how to read. In the brief moment the man had been beneath the table, though, he'd come to some form of decision, because he suddenly looked far more comfortable than he ever had before.

"Are you going to exchange any cards?" Mr. Whitworth nodded to the small stack still sitting in the middle of the table.

"Oh, er, um, yes." Hudson fanned his cards once more and actually looked at them before pulling out three and replacing them with cards from the center.

Mr. Whitworth exchanged two. "You would get on well with Graham and Oliver, I think. 'Tis a shame neither are in the district right now, though one never knows when they'll make an appearance."

"I would be honored to make their acquaintance." Hudson frowned at his cards, hoping Mr. Whitworth thought it was because he was thinking and not out of frustration that the conversation wasn't going the way he'd hoped. He gave his concentration to his cards for a moment, trying to remember in what order he made his declarations. "Point of five."

"Equal." Mr. Whitworth shifted in his seat before mumbling under his breath, "In the cards, anyway."

That was better. The man wasn't as comfortable as he was attempting to appear. "I believe I've"—Hudson paused—"forty-six points."

A slight smile formed on Mr. Whitworth's face. "No good."

They finished the opening declarations and point adjustments without interruption, and Mr. Whitworth noted them on his paper. Hudson led the first trick with his ace of diamonds and waited.

When another card didn't hit the center of the table, he looked up at his opponent.

"My name is Aaron. It's probably best if we use *Stildon* and *Whitworth* in public, though." Then he tossed down a five.

Hudson scooped up the trick with a great deal of satisfaction. "I'd hoped you'd come around. Now, let us also hope Lord Gliddon is as easily won over."

"And his daughter as well?" Aaron lifted a brow in inquiry.

"Yes." Hudson laid down the queen of diamonds. "And his daughter as well."

Thirteen

There had never been any question as to whether Mrs. Snowley was smart. Her manners, integrity, and overall morality could certainly be questioned, but not her brain, which was why it didn't surprise Bianca that she was nowhere to be found the moment the door shut behind last evening's dinner guests.

More surprising was that Marianne also wasn't available. She either managed to slip away soon after the meal was finished or went to bed in her dinner gown, but she was fast asleep when Bianca stopped by her room.

Which meant Bianca had spent the night staring at the ceiling, pondering options and considering possibilities, and now she wanted answers. Neither woman usually emerged from her room until midmorning, and Bianca wasn't about to miss her morning ride over this, so she was delighted to see Dorothy moving toward Marianne's room after finishing with Bianca. Her younger sister's early evening must have caused her to rise earlier than normal.

Bianca slid into the room behind Dorothy. "You're awake early."

A wide smile split Marianne's face. It was difficult to tell if her extra blinks were due to having just awoken or if she was trying to avoid Bianca's gaze. "I think I wore myself out with excitement last night. All I could think about was the coming week."

Bianca moved to perch on the side of the bed, leaning back

against one of the tall, carved corner posts. "You've plans for the week, then?"

More hazy blinks. "Don't you? Mother said it's time I marry because I'll never have as much opportunity as I'll have with all the men following Lady Rebecca here."

From coloring to temperament, there weren't many similarities between the sisters, but did Mrs. Snowley truly intend for them to compete for the same men? "Are you ready to marry?"

A small shrug shifted the end of Marianne's tight, neat braid. "It does seem the next thing, doesn't it? I had last year to become acclimated to being out of the schoolroom. What else is there but for me to marry?"

What indeed? There were women who didn't have to rely on others to support themselves. Bianca wasn't so fortunate. While she knew her father and half brother would never leave her to starve, she didn't particularly want to be the crazy spinster aunt living in the attic.

Nor could she see Marianne embracing such a fate. Bianca smiled and patted her sister's hand. "I wish you great success, then."

Marianne's pale blue eyes widened. "Thank you. My success isn't as assured as yours, of course, but I hope to soon follow in your footsteps."

Bianca choked on air. "My footsteps?"

"Of course." Marianne picked at the bedcover. "When Father asked Mother what her plans were for us, she had much more detailed ones for you than for me."

Confusion left Bianca speechless. There were many times she didn't understand what Marianne said, but this might be the most boggling. Mrs. Snowley would care much more about whom Marianne married than whom Bianca settled down with. "Did she share those plans?"

"Oh yes. She said it would look bad if I made an excellent match before you, so she was going to give you her best efforts first. She even selected candidates with good horses, since she knew that mattered to you."

Bianca almost laughed at the idea of Mrs. Snowley knowing anything about what Bianca would want in a husband, but Marianne wasn't finished relating her mother's thoughts. "She's given it a great deal of thought because she doesn't want you to discover that no man truly wants a wife with callused fingers or a strong seat. That was why she invited Mr. Mead to dinner last evening. She said the family connection would increase your appeal."

Increase her appeal indeed. Bianca was absolutely certain that Mrs. Snowley knew how little Bianca cared for Mr. Theophilus Mead. She was also aware of how often the elder Mr. Mead and Father had joked about marrying their children off to each other. It was the perfect revenge. Mrs. Snowley would make her husband happy and her stepdaughter miserable with one single act.

"Father refuses to take me for a Season in London because we have such likely society here, so Mother has made it her goal to get you engaged within the month so she can focus on me."

Marianne reached over to pat Bianca's hand. "I don't mind going second. I know if Lady Rebecca makes her choice quickly most of the quality men will be gone, but many will be back for the races." She smiled widely. "And there's always next year. I'm only twenty, whereas you, well . . . Mother worries."

Bianca's thoughts swirled until all she could hear was "within the month," and the phrase induced something akin to panic. How far was Mrs. Snowley willing to go to get Bianca out of the way in a manner Father found suitable? Would she damage Bianca's reputation and force her into a match? Would she lie to Father about how Bianca felt about Mr. Mead?

She nearly groaned at the thought of trying to explain to her father that she despised his closest friend's son. She adored her father, truly she did, but it wasn't as if she snuck into his study and confided in him. He was her *father*.

No, she had to find a way to solve this herself. The easiest way, of course, was to find a husband other than Mr. Mead. Mrs. Snowley wasn't foolish enough to ruin Bianca's chances with another man if that match still accomplished the main goal of removing Bianca from consideration.

It would appear waiting for Lord Stildon's courtship of Lady Rebecca to falter was not going to be an option after all. She needed a new plan, and the best place to think was on the back of a horse.

She managed a few more minutes of conversation with Marianne before she could excuse herself without raising suspicion, then hurried toward Hawksworth. It didn't matter if Mr. Knight put her on the back of a plow pony this morning. Bianca just wanted to ride.

The biggest problem, as she saw it, was that although she knew the ins and outs of society's rules enough to teach Lord Stildon how not to embarrass himself, she hadn't the first idea how to indicate to a man that she would like his attentions. She could hardly do the proposing herself. She couldn't even ask a man to dance with her.

Determination was all well and good, but it didn't take a girl very far if she didn't know where she was going.

Her conversation with Marianne had delayed her, and most of the riders had already departed from the stable. Owen was waiting for her, though, with Odysseus saddled and ready.

The black-and-white Spanish Jennet was the fastest of the horses she was allowed to ride, and Bianca sent a thankful glance heavenward that God had nudged the grooms toward readying this particular horse.

As she approached, Owen pushed away from the side of the stable where he'd been leaning and then helped her mount with a silent nod.

After thanking him, Bianca set off before Owen had a chance

to mount Hestia. He wouldn't have any problem catching up with her. The horse might not have won many races, but she could still best Odysseus any day of the week.

Once clear of the fenced areas, Bianca gave Odysseus plenty of rein and let him stretch out into a run. Wind pulled at her hair and tested the security of her hatpins, but it also seemed to clear her muddled thoughts. As the hoofbeats pounded beneath her, one thought slid through her head over and over.

She needed help.

But whom would she ask? Yes, she was friendly with many of the other women in Newmarket, but none of those friendships extended beyond social pleasantries. She couldn't remember the last time someone had come to visit her or she'd made the effort to visit someone else in particular. She saw people when she saw them, and their interactions were always enjoyable enough.

There was also the question of how they would respond when they learned Bianca was actively competing with them for the attentions of the eligible men.

Not to mention, if the conversations in the retiring rooms were anything to go by, none of the other girls knew how to get a man to offer for them either.

What Bianca needed was a man to tell her how to find a man. The irony was not lost on her.

She directed Odysseus to slow and the horse trotted along, his sides heaving from the run. A few feet to Bianca's right, the strong lines and smooth movements of Hestia's gait drew her attention.

"You took a mighty quick line on that ride, Miss Snowley." Owen gave her a respectful nod. The wind had mussed his long brown hair until his queue looked more like a fuzzy halo. His disheveled appearance didn't at all match the beauty of the horse he rode, but he handled the animal well. That skill was likely what kept him employed despite his less-than-professional attitude and appearance.

The horses slowed to a walk as they turned back toward Hawksworth. Other horses raced across the Heath, some draped in heavy blankets, others lining up for mock races, and some running a line like Bianca had just done.

The colorful chaos was a beautiful sight that normally calmed Bianca's nerves. Today, it was merely the background to her thoughts. Determining what she needed didn't mean she knew how to get it.

Owen was unaware of Bianca's wish for silent introspection. "Imagine if you were on Hestia here. You could show those riders a thing or two."

Bianca ducked her head a bit to hide her chuckle. Owen was sweet, if a bit clueless. She was positive he meant his statement as a compliment, even if, in reality, he was tempting her with a carrot she could never have. "Thank you, Owen. Have you had a good morning?"

Owen frowned. "Busier than normal. Mr. Whitworth's horse was still stabled there this morning, so Mr. Knight insisted we do some of our regular chores before we exercised the horses instead of after."

Mr. Whitworth's horse had been in Hawksworth stable and Bianca had missed it? Yes, she'd been preoccupied, but when had a male dilemma ever drawn her notice away from the horses?

Why Mr. Whitworth had stayed overnight at Hawksworth when he lived only a few miles away was also an intriguing question, though for Bianca's purposes, the more important one might be, would Mr. Whitworth still be there when she returned to the stable?

Granted, Mr. Whitworth wasn't a true gentleman like the ones she would be considering for marriage, but he was a man who, from all appearances, had been raised in a similar fashion. Would he have advice she could use? "Has Mr. Whitworth departed yet?"

"No, ma'am," Owen said with a shake of his head. "Haven't seen Lord Stildon yet this morning either."

Owen expertly guided Hestia up to a fence and leaned down to open the gate into Hawksworth's fields. "Mr. Knight says to act like he's always there, since he could come in at any moment."

He shrugged as he backed up his horse to allow Bianca and Odysseus through the gate first. "Doesn't make any matter to me, as I do my best by the horses anyhow."

Bianca smothered a grin. Owen might do his best by the horses, but his other work could certainly be questioned. He always seemed to do more lurking than working. "You do a fine job with the horses, Owen."

It was all she could do to keep her horse at a walk as they made their way back to the stable. Now that she had a glimmer of hope that there was a solution to her problem, she was anxious to get back to the stable and put her idea in motion.

Mr. Whitworth might not be willing to help her, but he was her best chance. She'd offered to help Lord Stildon accustom himself to English traditions, but that had been more to give her a reason to seek him out and spend time with him than any true intention to help him.

If Mr. Whitworth could tell her how to use that time more wisely, she might be able to still attain her original goal.

"What sent you tearing across the Heath this morning?" Owen leaned forward in the saddle to look beneath the brim of Bianca's hat. "I know the others think I don't understand people, but I know a ride of frustration when I see one." The man straightened, and deep grooves formed around his mouth as he pressed his lips into a grim line. "I don't like seeing you frustrated. I like you. You always treat the horses well, even when you're upset."

"Thank you," Bianca mumbled. She could hardly pour her heart out to Owen. Though he was male, he wasn't even on the fringes of propriety. At least Mr. Whitworth had attended schools and knew how to behave in polite society.

"Roger says when a man rides a horse hard, there's usually a woman behind the whip. Is it the same for women? Have you got a man causing you grief?"

Imagining the gruff, grumpy groom muttering such a quip

through his scruffy dark beard made Bianca smile. "No, Owen, there's not a man causing problems for me."

It was the lack of a man that was causing her issue.

"Oh." He looked at somewhat of a loss. "What is it for women, then?"

"I think," she said slowly, trying to give the man's question honest consideration, "that a woman would probably ride hard to get away from another woman as well. The problem is in a different capacity, of course, but that doesn't mean we don't know how to make trouble for each other."

Another woman was the crux of Bianca's issues anyway. Mrs. Snowley had the ability to make Bianca's life truly difficult. Until this morning, Bianca's life had been a well-ordered, easy existence. She avoided her stepmother as much as possible, which allowed her father to continue in the blissful belief that everything was as it should be, and Bianca herself then ordered her days in a most enjoyable manner. Even her decision to marry had been her own.

All of that was now threatened.

"Makes you women sound like a great deal of trouble," Owen said with a tone of bafflement as they arrived at the stable. He smoothly dismounted before tying Hestia to a post and then assisting Bianca down. Once her feet were on the ground, he gave her shoulder an awkward pat. "I think you're one of the good ones."

But was she good enough to get a husband quickly? She knew plenty of gentlemen, and none of them had ever offered for her. Still, she managed a smile for Owen's benefit. "Thank you."

He flushed red from his neck to his fuzzy, mussed hairline and then took Hestia into the stable for a rubdown. Bianca took Odysseus by the reins and followed with a slow shake of her head.

She tied Odysseus in his stall and rubbed behind his ear. He gave a brief *whuffle* and bumped his head into her shoulder. At least she knew what this male wanted from her.

"Good morning." Mr. Whitworth appeared in the stable, approached Odysseus's stall, and began unbuckling the saddle. "Did you have a good ride?"

"Hmmm." Bianca scratched behind the horse's ear once more. She should question the manager as to why he'd spent the night at Hawksworth, but she had something else to ask him before she lost her nerve. "Have you ever been courting, Mr. Whitworth?"

"I don't think we'd suit that well, Miss Snowley." Mr. Whitworth gave her a crooked grin, though the face around it looked somewhat hardened. "But I'm flattered you'd think about it."

"Not courting *me*." She shook her head, trying and failing to find a bit of indignation. Surely he'd thought to turn that charm on a young lady at some point, hadn't he? "I meant, have you ever considered courting in general?"

He shrugged and adjusted his hold on the saddle. "I suppose every man's thought of it in a general sense, but I've never met a young lady worth changing my life over."

Bianca frowned. "Is that how you view it? Is that how all men see it?"

For her whole life, marriage and family had simply been an extension of the life she was already living. If men saw it differently, though, she had more of a challenge before her than she'd thought.

"I can't speak for men of your ilk, Miss Snowley."

Bianca snapped her gaze from where her finger was tracing one of Odysseus's spots to take in Mr. Whitworth's countenance. Had she inadvertently insulted him? Did she owe him an apology?

The man was grinning at her, though, and this time it looked far more natural than it had moments before. "There's a fair difference between me and, say, Lord Stildon. Why don't you ask him?"

Ask Lord Stildon when previously she'd been plotting how to become his choice of bride? She thought not. She shook her head and turned her focus back to Odysseus. "I don't think it's a good idea to ask Lord Stildon."

"Ask me what?"

Fourteen

Hudson glanced from Miss Snowley to Aaron and back to Miss Snowley again, a sense of unease crawling up his spine with each passing moment.

Aaron was looking at the ceiling, a saddle held to his chest and his lips pressed tightly together, while Miss Snowley's face grew ever pinker as she stared intently at the horse's black mane.

"Ask me what?" Hudson repeated.

Aaron's attention dropped from the ceiling to Hudson as he gave a small shrug. "Miss Snowley wants to know how men decide it's time to court a woman."

Her head snapped up, the flush on her cheeks growing to a bright red. Hudson was rather afraid his face might be heating to match.

"I did not say that," she muttered.

Aaron gave another shrug. "It's what you meant. I've never courted a woman, but that doesn't mean I haven't spent any time around them." He edged past Hudson and out of the stall. "I think I'll put this saddle away now."

Oh no he wasn't. The man was not going to drop this on Hudson and then slink away. He stepped sideways and blocked Aaron's exit. "I think one of the grooms could manage that, don't you?" He flagged down one of the men from the previous day's dancing

126

lesson and gestured to the saddle. Without a word, the young man nodded and relieved Aaron of the burden.

Aaron sighed but leaned against the stall dividing wall, one booted foot crossing over the other at the ankle, while his arms crossed over his chest.

"Now." Hudson cleared his throat and tried to look like he was in charge instead of utterly confused. "What is going on here?"

Aaron nodded toward Miss Snowley. "Your courting expert has questions."

"I taught him to dance. I never said anything about courting." Miss Snowley snatched up a currycomb and began working it along Odysseus's side.

"One's part of the other."

Hudson picked up another comb and slid into the stall opposite Miss Snowley to work on the horse's other side. Perhaps if he were busy this would be less awkward. "Why the sudden need to know about . . . courting?"

In his exceptionally limited experience, men decided to court a woman because it was advantageous to do so. Cold, perhaps, but true as far as he knew it.

She dropped backward to lean against the feeding trough. The horse nudged her shoulder before returning to the hay. "My stepmother has decided I need to marry. My father has noticed his daughters don't get the same treatment and admonished her for it. I fear she's afraid other people will think ill of her if my sister marries before I do. My stepmother can make my life difficult if I don't follow her wishes."

Aaron grunted. "I never thought having no one care about me could be a blessing. I do know something of being the unwanted older half-sibling, though."

"Oh my, I'm so sorry," Miss Snowley said, straightening away from the wall. "You're right, of course. My situation really isn't all that bad. I should be grateful."

"I think that's the opposite of what I said," Aaron murmured, taking the comb from her and working on the horse. He looked over the horse's back and met Hudson's gaze. "And women think men are confusing."

Hudson didn't know what to make of the entire conversation. Something about it bothered him on a very personal level. That he should feel even a mild anger on this woman's behalf confused him. Yes, Miss Snowley had been one of the first people he'd met in England, certainly one of the first who had been anything of a friend, but he didn't really know her well.

"Has she indicated that she has someone in mind for you?" Aaron asked.

"Mr. Theophilus Mead."

Aaron froze, the comb mid-circle on the horse's back. "You would die married to that man."

The low rumble of anger spiked within Hudson, and he leaned closer. He vaguely remembered meeting a man of that name but couldn't remember any sort of particular impression. "What's wrong with him?"

"Nothing," Miss Snowley said quickly, just as Aaron said, "Everything."

Aaron shook his head. "You're a top sawyer when it comes to riding, Miss Snowley. You respect the horses, so you could never respect Mr. Mead, and he would never forgive you for that."

"I'm well aware," Miss Snowley said, a smile pushing at the side of her lips and a brassy note to her voice that clashed in Hudson's ears. "That's why I've decided I need to find another man to marry." She gave a delicate shrug. "Problem solved. We can stop discussing it now."

Aaron smirked. "If that decision solved the problem, you wouldn't have asked about courtship in the first place."

"I could help you." No one looked more stunned by Hudson's statement than he himself. He was the last person who could help

128

Miss Snowley. Not only was he completely out of his element while navigating English society, he didn't even know anyone not currently standing in this stable.

Still, he couldn't allow her to be forced into a terrible match, could he? He rubbed harder at the horse. "I mean, it is only fair that I help you since you are helping me."

"I'm not *helping* you." She straightened, her thin nose pointing higher into the air. "I *helped* you. We have no ongoing agreement."

"Perhaps we should." The more he considered it, the more the idea had merit. "I'm sure to rub shoulders with some of the men you say are going to be coming to town to try to gain Lady Rebecca's attention. Perhaps I could steer a few your way. Once you find one you like, you can ask Whitworth if he's worthy of riding a carriage pony."

"How did I become part of this?" Aaron asked.

"I certainly don't know which men she should avoid."

"I'm beginning to think 'all of them' is the appropriate answer," Miss Snowley muttered.

Aaron looked hard at Hudson before turning his attention to the woman next to him, whose head was bent so that all Hudson could see was the plumes of feathers extending from her riding hat.

When Aaron's attention came back to Hudson, there was something in his expression that Hudson couldn't identify. "I'll do it."

"What, exactly, is it you are doing?" Miss Snowley asked, trying to cram her hands onto her hips in the tight confines of the stall but bumping an elbow into Odysseus instead. She patted the horse and murmured an apology.

"You keep me from making a social misstep and I drop your name in conversation." Hudson thought it a rather perfect plan.

"I'm not socially inept, you know." Miss Snowley's glare narrowed at Hudson, her brown eyes almost disappearing. "I rather think you need me more than I need you."

"That's true." Hudson shrugged.

Aaron chuckled.

Miss Snowley jerked back. "Have you no pride?"

Probably too much, which was why he wanted so badly to prove to everyone that he could and would make a success of this stable. It wasn't enough to know his own abilities. If everyone else knew them too, his life would be easier, and he would have far more respect in town.

And he would be able to go to sleep knowing he was living up to the legacy his father had raised him for.

Sometimes it was necessary to choose where one gave his pride away in order to salvage it elsewhere.

Still, he had enough pride not to want her to know that. "I believe I dropped it in the ocean on the way from India." There was some truth to that. He'd certainly been humbled while casting his accounts overboard. "I'll add to the purse. Not only will I help you find a respectable gentleman to marry so you can thwart your evil stepmother, but if you help me marry the woman I need, at the end of the racing season, I'll let you ride Hades."

"What?" she breathed.

"What?" Aaron nearly yelled.

The echo of the word through the stable was not simply the manager's yell bouncing off the stone walls. Hudson really needed to remember that no discussion in this stable was truly private.

Miss Snowley licked her lips and wrapped a hand in Odysseus's mane. "You're proposing that I spend time with you, teaching you about Newmarket society?"

Hudson nodded. That was a strange way to phrase it, but it was the same idea. "And I'll help you know what men are thinking."

She swallowed hard. "I'll do it."

"Excellent." Finally Hudson felt like he was taking control of his life here in England instead of simply floundering from one confusing encounter to the next. "We can begin tonight." He thought of the invitation Aaron had separated from the pile of mail. "Did you receive an invitation to the Wainbrights' card party?"

"Mrs. Snowley probably did."

Hudson glanced at Aaron.

"Don't look at me." He held both hands up. "I don't get invited to anything."

It briefly crossed Hudson's mind to wonder if the lack of invitations bothered the man, but he'd said he had friends, so perhaps he just led a different social life than Hudson's should be. Could be. Would be.

"You'll come riding with us tomorrow, then."

"I will?"

"He will?"

Honestly, why did these two question each of Hudson's statements? Didn't they see the obvious? Was he the smartest of the three of them?

"Yes. You mentioned that it's public knowledge that Miss Snowley rides here, so it will draw no concern if she's seen riding with us. I may not know everything about English society, but I do know three are more proper than two."

Aaron snorted. "And you think I make a proper chaperon?"

"I think I trust you." A truer statement might never have been uttered. Hudson was placing his trust in these two people for nearly everything. If they steered him wrong, it was possible Hudson's reputation would never recover and he'd spend the rest of his life on the outside looking in.

He prayed he wasn't being foolish.

BIANCA SPENT THE ENTIRE WALK home alternating between pondering the wisdom of this new agreement with Lord Stildon and contemplating how she was going to invite herself along to the card party without making Mrs. Snowley suspicious.

By the time she passed her father's small, mostly empty stable, neither subject had come to any sort of satisfactory conclusion. She was hardly the best person to guide Lord Stildon's social life, and now that she'd had some time to calm down and think, she didn't think her stepmother's threat to push her into marriage so quickly was all that dire. What could the woman really do?

"There you are." Mrs. Snowley looked her up and down as she entered the house, her lips curling into a sneer as if Bianca had dressed as a maid instead of in a perfectly fashionable riding habit.

Bianca said nothing, merely stood where she was, waiting for Mrs. Snowley to finish whatever she was determined to say.

"Marianne and I are going out tonight."

This was hardly anything new. The only difference on this day was Mrs. Snowley's feeling the need to inform Bianca.

"I've instructed the staff you are eating in the dining room tonight instead of having a tray sent up to your room," Mrs. Snowley continued.

Bianca's eyebrows lifted. "And if I don't?"

"The door to your room will be locked from seven this evening until ten, and no food is to go anywhere other than the dining room or your father's study. Anyone disobeying the order will immediately be dismissed without a reference."

A stunned chill lifted bumps along Bianca's arms, and her mouth dropped open slightly. "What?"

"Your father intends to meet with Mr. Mead tonight, and his son will likely come with him. If you are available, it improves the chances that he will make an offer." Mrs. Snowley cast her gaze down Bianca's wardrobe once more. "I've already selected the gown you will wear. I suggest you make the most of the opportunity."

The dilemmas Bianca had been pondering fell into sudden clarity. She needed to marry, she couldn't wait on Lord Stildon, and she needed all the help she could get, even if it was less than knowledgeable.

"Where are you and Marianne going tonight?"

Mrs. Snowley's eyes widened and her lips pursed. "A card party at the Wainbrights'."

Bianca swallowed hard and smiled. "That sounds fun."

Pale eyebrows arched upward. "I beg your pardon."

"I would like to go to a card party."

"You were not on the invitation."

It was entirely possible that was true, and there was little chance she'd be able to prove otherwise. But if her father's opinion was influencing Mrs. Snowley as much as Bianca thought it was, she could afford to push back a bit.

Bianca kept her smile in place. "I'm sure Father would appreciate your asking Mrs. Wainbright to extend her invitation further."

Mrs. Snowley's gaze narrowed more. "Yes. I'm sure he would."

"What time do we leave?"

After a tense moment during which the two women stared at each other in silence, Mrs. Snowley told Bianca when they would be departing. Bianca silently determined to be ready an hour before her stepmother had said in case she intended to use Bianca's tardiness as a reason to leave her behind.

Bianca nodded before ascending the stairs without looking back. She was near to shaking by the time she reached the safety of her room—the relative safety, anyway. Mrs. Snowley had just proven that even this sanctuary wasn't out of her reach. There wasn't a single servant who would come to Bianca's assistance when his or her livelihood was threatened.

She spent the afternoon going through her wardrobe, making lists of the men she knew, and trying to create a plan of some sort that would get her out of this house without landing her in an even worse position somewhere else.

It was frightening how little she had to work with. Somehow she'd always thought marriage would just happen one day. Waiting was no longer an option.

Dorothy wouldn't meet Bianca's eyes when she came to dress her for the party, not even in the mirror. In a matter of hours, Mrs. Snowley had removed Bianca's comfortable existence.

Bianca could probably speak to her father, but there was that small part of her that wasn't entirely positive her father would go against his wife. From childhood he'd said it was Mrs. Snowley's job to raise the girls. There was no question that he loved Bianca, but she couldn't remember the last time he had truly stepped into her life.

THE PARTY WASN'T overly large, but Mrs. Wainbright was bustling about as if she expected the entirety of Newmarket to descend upon her drawing room.

Miss Wainbright rushed to Marianne's side, her cheeks flushed in a way that might not be entirely natural. "He's accepted."

"Who?" Bianca asked before she could stop herself.

Marianne laughed and gave Bianca a scathing look that called into question every time Bianca had excused her actions because she'd thought the other girl simple. "Is there any other *he* right now?"

Bianca certainly hoped so. She'd never taken part in the competition, preferring to stay away from the men all the girls were giggling over, but now she needed a *he* of her own, and she hoped there were enough to go around.

"Lord Stildon, silly." Miss Wainbright smirked. "I would have thought you of all people would know what a catch he is."

Of course Bianca knew Lord Stildon was a catch. She also knew he intended to be here. Before she'd trudged home, she'd left him with instructions to accept the invitation as well as make another trip to the tailor.

She made a noncommittal noise that could have been agreement but was more along the lines of a strangled growl. "I believe I'll get some punch."

A murmur ran through the small group behind her as she retrieved her punch from the table. On principle she didn't look, but she had a feeling Lord Stildon had arrived.

She made herself take two sips before turning around and verifying her suspicion. Lord Stildon greeted Mr. Wainbright and was introduced to several people as Bianca worked her way through her cup sip by sip. She was halfway done before Lord Stildon excused himself for his own refreshment.

"I predict we have a matter of seconds before every young lady in this room becomes entirely parched."

"I feel like I'm being paraded about like Sir David Ochterlony's wives on their nightly elephant ride," he grumbled before taking a large gulp of punch. His face immediately scrunched up. "This may be worse than the drink on Saturday."

Bianca hid her grin by taking another sip. "What card games do you know? I didn't think to ask you earlier."

"I know how to play cards," he grumbled. "Shall we find a whist table?"

Was it wise to partner him in whist? She could see how he interacted with others and give him appropriate advice, but already people were associating her with him because of her time at Hawksworth. Would a potentially interested man assume her attentions were already engaged?

Then again, if people associated them together, perhaps he would as well.

She shook her head. Either she tried to capture Lord Stildon's attentions, or she looked for another potential husband. She couldn't continue doing both.

"I think you'd be better off asking someone else. Lady Rebecca may be your goal, but until she begins making appearances in Newmarket, you should make a point to mingle."

"So I don't look mercenary when she arrives?"

"You said it, not me."

"I'm not being mercenary, though I can see where others might call it so. Should the lady be completely unsuitable, I will form a new plan, but I must marry sometime, and it may as well be advantageous."

Bianca couldn't fault a single piece of his statement. More to the point, no one was going to find anything objectionable about Lady Rebecca unless they had something against perfection.

She took a breath to utter her agreement, but the first of the guests descended upon them.

As she settled down to games of cards, she did her best to split her attention between watching Lord Stildon's interactions, which were excellent, if somewhat stilted and awkward, and examining the men around her for their potential suitability.

Most of these men she'd known for years, and though she tried to smile more, simper more, bat her lashes more, and generally do everything she'd seen other women do, her interactions with them seemed the same as they'd always been—polite and meaningless, with a hint of utter boredom.

Those were still better qualities than a life with Mr. Mead would garner, but she'd always hoped for something more.

A peek in Lord Stildon's direction proved that boredom was not something he was currently risking. He played game after game and partnered many different women, but still managed not to anger the men who also sat at his card table, conversing with them as much, if not more than, the ladies.

If Lady Rebecca wasn't taken by his pleasant manners and mess of dark curls framing bright blue eyes, Bianca would volunteer to eat these cards. There wasn't a man in the room who could compare.

And he was the one man she couldn't even attempt to set her cap for.

Fifteen

've another stable to manage, you know, and preparing two slates of horses for the next racing season is somewhat time consuming. My answer is no. It's bad enough that you're taking up my morning with this ride when I could be looking in on the training."

Hudson didn't bother restraining his chuckle as he pulled Hades to a halt and turned his mount so the view of Aaron and Miss Snowley facing off was unobstructed. She was on Midas this morning, while Aaron rode Poseidon. The grey thoroughbred was at least two hands taller than the chestnut horse, putting Aaron's head well over a foot above Miss Snowley's.

That didn't prevent her from glaring up at him from beneath the brim of her riding hat.

While he certainly understood Miss Snowley's suggestion that Aaron attend the next assembly with them so he could point out which men he thought she would find suitable, he could also comprehend the man's stern rejection.

Miss Snowley turned her glare on Hudson, her mouth pressed into a thin line, and he tried, or at least tried to appear like he was trying, to stem his mirth.

With a huff, she turned back to Aaron. "Don't be a child, Mr. Whitworth. I'm not asking you to attend a private dinner party or even a ball. These are public assemblies. I'll even front you the money for the subscription."

Hudson couldn't stop his laugh from sputtering out, and he tried to mask it by coughing into his hand. He knew how much Aaron was getting paid to hire trainers, schedule races, care for the horses, and research prospective breeding opportunities. A subscription fee for the season of public assemblies was not the issue.

"I don't need your money," Aaron growled through gritted teeth before prodding his grey stallion back into a walk.

Miss Snowley nudged her chestnut into motion alongside him, while Hudson regained his composure enough to steer his horse into the group so that Miss Snowley was positioned between the two men.

He grinned at Aaron over Miss Snowley's head. The other man scowled at him, but that only made Hudson grin wider. Had he ever had this much fun before? He couldn't remember anyone back in India with whom he'd been comfortable enough to tease, but perhaps the upheaval of his life had allowed him to open himself up to relationships he'd have overlooked before.

Or perhaps he simply recognized the camaraderie of a man who knew as much as he did about horses—possibly even more. Whatever it was, Hudson was enjoying it immensely, and he couldn't resist teasing the man an iota more. "Not to worry, Aaron, I'll give you the coin if you don't wish to take it from a female."

Miss Snowley's mount was suddenly pulled to a halt, and she fell behind the men for a few paces before trotting back up into position. She looked from one man to the other and back again, eyes wide.

A tinge of exasperation joined the irritation in Aaron's frown. Hudson had agreed to call him Whitworth around other people, but it just didn't seem like Miss Snowley really counted. She was a co-conspirator.

Aaron shook his head. "It's not the money that bothers me, *Hudson*, it's the wolves this termagant wants to throw me to."

"I say, are men always so quick to become such intimate friends?" Miss Snowley asked, still looking back and forth between Hudson and Aaron. "Miss Wainbright is my sister's dearest friend, and I'm not even certain I know what her Christian name is. Is it different for men? It's a wonder the assemblies aren't littered with *Johns* and *Williams* instead of *Lords* and *Misters*."

"Speed is contingent upon extenuating circumstances," Aaron said with the briefest of glances in Miss Snowley's direction. "I spent more than a few hours sweating in his library, teaching him card games."

"That's how he knew all the games at the party last night." She bit her lip as she stared at Aaron, the reins limp in her hands as she depended upon Midas's contentment to keep her plodding along with them. "Why were you sweating? Wait, no. That doesn't matter, although I suppose I can see how that would make you friends rather quickly. I feel rather on the outside of our little team now, but no, that doesn't signify at the moment either. I suppose I should thank you. While I can attend a card party, the cardroom at assemblies is somewhere I can't go. I don't even know if they play the same games in there. All the more reason you should attend on Saturday."

"I'm not an imbecile," Hudson grumbled, finding a little less humor in the discussion. "I've been carrying conversations with men for years." He frowned down at Miss Snowley. "It's the addition of women that seems to be giving me trouble."

"Don't they always?" Aaron smirked in her direction.

Miss Snowley did not find them amusing. "Perhaps I should simply leave you two to muddle through without me, then."

Hudson leaned down to better see Miss Snowley's face, as if her countenance would help him assess the sudden tension that seemed to fill the situation. She was blinking a great deal, far more than he would have thought necessary. They hadn't even made it to the Heath yet, so the wind couldn't be irritating her eyes. Had she picked up a piece of dust somewhere?

Aaron did not appear to share Hudson's concern. He sighed. "Save me from such easily miffed women. If it will ease your feathers, you can call me Aaron in private."

Miss Snowley blinked several more times while considering the offer. He didn't blame her for hesitating. There had been a certain grudging tone to the offer, but Hudson already knew—as the earlier conversation about assemblies could attest—that Aaron didn't do anything he didn't want to do.

"Does that mean you would call me Bianca?"

"I suppose I might."

Hudson didn't think he'd ever met a Bianca before. It suited her, the individuality and uniqueness. He wanted to test it out for himself, but his father hadn't been entirely remiss in Hudson's societal education. While he and Aaron could claim some sort of extenuating circumstances, it was a far different situation with a lady.

He liked thinking of her as Bianca, though. It gave him a connection in his mind that made her helping him more palatable. "Bianca is a pretty name."

She snapped her head in his direction, staring at him with wide, unblinking eyes for several moments before smiling and saying in a voice far tighter and higher pitched than it had been a moment before, "Thank you, Lord Stildon."

Hudson gave her a nod and a smile. "I'm still not accustomed to hearing the title said aloud. Lord Stildon doesn't feel natural yet."

It also looked strange when he signed it to paper. He'd seen the title in his grandfather's handwriting for so many years that it looked strange when written by his own hand. Hearing it was even stranger. Hudson's father had never referred to the old man by his title, simply calling him *Father* or *your grandfather*.

The discussion of names dropped a heavy weight onto the conversation that had been teasing and open only moments before. They fell silent, apart from the clop of horses' hooves and the creak of leather saddles.

Hudson spotted the final hedge of his property with great relief. Beyond that hedge lay the open expanse of the Heath and freedom from whatever had just entered his life. England might be bland and boring when it came to the weather, clothes, and certainly the food, but he was finding the interactions with the people to be more uncertain than anything he'd encountered in India.

Aaron seemed to be as uncomfortable as Hudson because he heaved a sigh as they passed the boundary. "Wonderful. Now, can we run? If you want me to look into some of those other breeding options, I'm going to have to leave for London tomorrow. It would be nice to go somewhat faster than I can in Hyde Park."

Hudson scrunched up his brows in momentary confusion before his thoughts cleared and he looked over the Heath. Aaron's departure would mean he and Bianca were on their own, a prospect that seemed daunting enough for him to choose to ignore it for the time being. "A race, then. Would you care to name the marker?"

Bianca pouted as Aaron described the markers and paths to Hudson. "Don't mind me," she sighed. "I'm sure I'll catch up eventually."

"Good." Hudson grinned. "We'll run it again when you've earned the right to ride on Hades here."

The grooms and Aaron might have been horrified by Hudson's deal, but she was a good rider. He didn't have the qualms the others seemed to have, especially if it maintained her assistance with Lady Rebecca.

"Very well," she said, running a knowledgeable eye over the sleek black coat of Hudson's horse and then setting her mouth into a determined line. "As I will have no reason to cry foul, I'll indicate the start."

To Hudson's surprise, when he and Aaron lined up at their determined starting point, Bianca put Midas right in line with them. Despite the fact that they all knew what her place in the race was going to be, she refused to be left behind. She was certainly a stubborn one.

He shook his head and shifted his grip on Hades's reins, more than ready for the thrill of a race to pound away the tension.

BIANCA WANTED TO BASH THEM both as she started the race and gave Midas a hearty kick. She wasn't going to beat them on her horse, but she would gladly beat them both with her boot.

She closed her eyes and gave Midas his head for the first few paces, as the brief flurry of dust kicked up by the thoroughbreds filled the air. Soon their pounding hooves were enough in front of her that she felt safe enough to open her eyes.

There was no way she could keep them from pulling farther and farther away from her, but she couldn't be mad about it. Watching two glorious animals, one just out of his prime and the other a few years past it, power over the grassy expanse was worth being left behind. Hades's sleek black mane and tail streamed behind him as he took the lead, and Bianca gave Midas another kick. She'd never catch the men, but she could enjoy feeling the wind in her face and the steady rhythm of her horse's gait.

Both men had pulled their horses to a stop beside each other when Bianca finally passed the marker, but they and the animals were still catching their breath, so she'd count that as a win, even if they did laugh at her determination to cross the set finish line.

"Whitworth!"

Bianca looked over her shoulder as she slowed her horse to a walk. Another horse had ridden over to Lord Stildon and Aaron. The deep brown former racehorse had a white stocking on each leg and a scattering of lather that indicated he'd already had at least one good ride on the Heath this morning. The horse pranced in a circle until the rider could face Aaron and Lord Stildon.

A sudden tightness looped around Bianca's throat as she turned Midas to walk back toward the group. It was Lord Brimsbane. She'd never interacted with him much, but she knew who he was. If he was back in town, it meant Lady Rebecca likely was too.

Given that he was her brother and all.

Lord Brimsbane nodded to Aaron. "Testing the stock yourself these days? Bit tall for a jockey, aren't you?"

"Simply showing Lord Stildon what his stable contains." Aaron gave a polite nod toward both men, the smiles and easiness of moments before nowhere in sight. "My lord, may I present Lord Brimsbane, heir to the Earl of Gliddon."

"Ah, the new viscount. I'd heard you'd finally made it home from India. Is it as rustic as they say?"

"I've never found it lacking, but I suppose it would depend upon where one lived."

Lord Brimsbane nodded. "Capital. I'd love to hear about it. I always wanted to travel, though perhaps not quite so far afield. Maybe through Europe, now that peace has settled."

Midas walked close enough to the group to catch Aaron's attention. The other men soon followed his glance and noticed her presence. Bianca tried to smile as she would if encountering Lord Brimsbane in a ballroom, but it felt strangely formal from the back of a horse.

"Ah, Miss Snowley. Always a pleasure to see a woman who knows how to ride. Can't get my sister out here in the mornings, you know."

Bianca allowed Midas to take a few more steps in until the four horses were nearly standing nose to nose. The agreement she'd made was suddenly all too real. If she were going to actively assist Lord Stildon's pursuit of Lady Rebecca, it started now. Her brother's opinion would surely weigh into her final decision.

She nodded her head to Lord Brimsbane. "I'm sure Lady Rebecca's time is being taken up by other equally important endeavors."

Lord Brimsbane shook his head. "Only if one considers flowers essential to life. We're hosting a ball soon, and she and Mother are acting as if the Prince Regent intends to come."

"Are you sure that he won't?"

"Come now, Miss Snowley, we both know our esteemed Regent won't show his face in Newmarket anymore. He didn't take kindly to those cheating accusations."

Right. She glanced at Lord Stildon but quickly reverted her attention back to Lord Brimsbane. Local gossip was something Lord Stildon wasn't going to be familiar with, especially gossip that was years old.

Lord Brimsbane looked at Lord Stildon as well and was a bit slower in returning his gaze to Bianca. "Still riding the Hawksworth horses, I see."

"They are convenient." She nearly winced at the statement, as it implied she couldn't care less about who owned the horses. If word got around, though, that she and Lord Stildon had formed some form of *tendre*, as the hesitance on Lord Brimsbane's face seemed to speculate, neither of them would achieve their goals. Well, *she* might, but she'd determined at the outset not to win a husband by manipulation.

"I see." He glanced between the two of them once more. "You would not be opposed to riding another stable's horses, then?"

"No," Bianca said, dragging the word out as she contemplated what the man might mean with his question. Midas shifted beneath her and bumped his nose into Poseidon's neck. Aaron took the opportunity to back his way out of their small circle. She hated that he felt the need to do so and that she felt grateful for his discretion.

She pushed her smile wider as she gave her attention back to Lord Brimsbane. Now was not the time to speculate upon the unfairness of the world, especially when there was nothing she could do about it. "Even if the Prince Regent doesn't come to your mother's ball, I'm sure it will be a well-attended gathering."

"Don't remind me. We're doomed to be overrun." He turned his horse in the direction Bianca had recently raced from. "May I join you as you ride back to Hawksworth? I confess I'll take any excuse to prolong my morning ride. The back of a horse is the only place I'm likely to find sanity until my sister marries."

"Do you truly expect it to be as bad as all that?" Lord Stildon asked as he too turned his horse toward home.

"I suppose not," Lord Brimsbane mused, "since Meadowland Park is far larger than our London residence and therefore easier to hide in. Still, I'd rather escape the whole business entirely."

Should Bianca ride Midas between the men? Should she go next to Lord Stildon or over to Lord Brimsbane's side? Etiquette books were sadly lacking in horse-riding protocol. Should dinner escort rules apply here? What about orders of precedence? Not that either of those helped her any, as she was the only woman among three gentlemen.

Oh bother, she would let the men sort out where to situate themselves. She gave Midas a kick and let him burst into a brief trot that pulled her ahead of the men and then slowed him to a walk.

A horse came up on each side of her. It was similar to the position she'd been riding in with Aaron and Lord Stildon as they left the stable, but it didn't feel as easy now.

She smiled up at Lord Brimsbane. "At least you've a fine animal to escape on, if you must ride away. You could always join us on our morning rides."

In the immediate silence that followed, she questioned her own boldness, but truly it was time to commit to helping Lord Stildon, and she needed to push past the uncomfortableness of playing matchmaker. Lord Stildon was going to need some form of advantage, besides Hestia, and a friendship with Lord Brimsbane could be it.

Had she pushed too hard, though?

She held her breath until Lord Brimsbane replied in a quiet voice, "I might take you up on that."

They walked along in silence for a few minutes, then Lord Brimsbane spoke again. "Will you be at the assembly Saturday? Rebecca insists on attending. She was rather miffed that our return was delayed and she missed the first ones."

"I'll be there." Bianca swallowed. "I believe you were saying something about attending as well, weren't you, Lord Stildon?"

"Yes."

Bianca nearly rolled her eyes. Hadn't the man claimed to know how to converse with other men? If this was what he considered successful conversation, it was a wonder he'd accomplished anything in India.

At the hedge border of Hawksworth, Lord Brimsbane said his good-byes and trotted off. Bianca looked around to see that Aaron and Poseidon had fallen quite far back, though he moved the horse a bit faster as Lord Brimsbane rode away.

As she turned back to Lord Stildon, she was surprised to see him frowning. "What?"

"How are we supposed to make plans on our morning rides if he is riding with us?"

"Lord Brimsbane *is* a plan. If you become friends with him, your access to Lady Rebecca increases dramatically."

"So you don't have designs on him yourself?"

Bianca blinked. Designs? On Lord Brimsbane? "I am a gentleman's daughter. Perfectly respectable, I assure you, but I'm hardly going to marry an earl."

Aaron, who was now riding beside them once more, cleared his throat. "If one wants to be particular, he's actually a viscount at the moment." His gaze fixed hard on Bianca's face. "Same rank as our friend Hudson here."

"If we're being *particular*, our friend currently outranks Lord

Brimsbane, as a viscount outranks the eldest son of earls, but I'd be a fool to set my cap for a man who will one day *be* an earl."

"Does that mean you wouldn't be a fool to set your cap for a viscount, then?" Aaron widened his eyes in feigned innocence.

Bianca glared at the manager. She did not need him doing . . . whatever he was doing. She was Lord Stildon's friend. Nothing more. And as soon as she found herself a man she could reasonably see herself marrying, she would have no problem remembering that.

Sixteen

Lady Rebecca's arrival sent ripples throughout Newmarket, but the men who followed her caused waves of gossip to crash through the drawing rooms and shops. At the modiste, the latest pattern book was surrounded by young ladies and mothers, all debating the merits of the current fashions.

Bianca wasn't immune to the excitement, and she ran her hand along a selection of fabrics she never would have considered before. She also wouldn't normally come here with her stepmother, but here she was.

"Did you see the new sleeves?"

"I think the waistlines are even higher on this one."

"How do you think this one would look in blue?"

"I would have it done in green."

Bianca glanced at the group that included Marianne and Mrs. Snowley. Would that be her if her mother had survived? Or even if Mrs. Snowley had claimed Bianca as her own? It wasn't a thought she often considered, but as she entertained this new philosophy of life, she was realizing just how lonely her existence was. She didn't have anyone she could giggle with like Marianne did, didn't have anyone offering her advice on colors and cut like Miss Turner did, and didn't know where she would begin to look for someone to do either.

Her two closest friends were a stable manager who eschewed most of society and a viscount who was everything she'd ever wanted in a husband but had his eyes on someone else—or rather had his mind on someone else, because his eyes hadn't yet seen Lady Rebecca.

Bianca moved toward another of the pattern books, one that had arrived a few months ago, and flipped through the pages without really seeing them.

"Did you hear who arrived in town this morning?"

Bianca angled her head to better hear the conversation. The last attention-getting arrival had been Lord Stildon, and he was proving rather life changing for her.

"Lord Rigsby."

Three feminine gasps met the news. Bianca frowned. She'd never heard of Lord Rigsby.

"Mrs. Vernon said he took rooms on the south side of town," Miss Wainbright said. How did she always know the latest *on dit*? Did the woman simply wander from drawing room to drawing room all day?

Miss Turner sighed. "Of course he did. That's near Meadowland Park."

Several women murmured their own disappointed agreement.

"Don't forget, ladies," Mrs. Snowley said, "Lady Rebecca can only marry one man. All you have to do is catch the eye of the others."

The murmurs turned a bit more excited.

"We should stand near each other Saturday at the assembly," Miss Turner said. "That way, when the men escort us to the side after dancing we can meet all of them."

Given the amount of effort she'd had to put in last Saturday to position herself for Lord Stildon, who had been a co-conspirator in the meeting, she couldn't imagine how difficult arranging introductions could be.

"We should meet for tea to discuss the best topics of conversation. We can't mention the same ones everyone else is or we won't stand out," Miss Wainbright added.

Bianca blinked. She'd never considered putting so much thought into a conversation she wasn't even sure she'd be having. On this, at least, she knew she had an advantage. The men coming to town would mostly be horsemen, and there wasn't a girl on the current marriage market who knew horses better than she did.

"Whatever you do," Mrs. Wainbright told the girls, "don't bring up racing or horses. You don't want them to start thinking about Hezekiah while dancing with you."

Bianca sighed quietly. Why was this so complicated? Life had been so much simpler when she had just done whatever she pleased and enjoyed it for the moment it was. Not only had it never drawn an ache into her head like the one forming after hearing this conversation, but she'd never been faced with how few people she truly knew. It didn't escape her notice that no one was inviting *her* over for tea to contrive introductions or plot conversations.

"I think we should see if Madame Bridget can make this one for you in a pale pink," Mrs. Snowley said to Marianne, pointing at the book. "It will look quite fine with your complexion, and I'm sure Lady Gliddon will be holding a ball at some point."

Mrs. Snowley and Marianne moved away from the book, passed by where Bianca was standing, and started perusing the available fabrics.

Neither of them even glanced her way.

Bianca looked back down at the book in front of her and the ball gown that had been the height of fashion four months ago. What was the point? Could she alone, save two men who hadn't mentioned anything like the strategies these women were discussing, hope to compete for the attention of the eligible men in town?

The idea of a new dress, which had been somewhat exciting

moments before, now seemed like a desperate effort to cling to the mane as one fell off a horse.

"I'm just going to step outside for a bit," she said in the direction of her stepmother.

To her surprise, the woman heard her and glanced over. "Take Dorothy with you. We can't have you marring your reputation right now."

Bianca opened her mouth to ask when would be an acceptable time to mar her reputation but snapped it shut again as Mrs. Snowley turned back to inspecting the fabrics.

After collecting Dorothy from the cluster of other waiting maids, Bianca stepped out of the shop and leaned against the wall outside, watching the people go by. There were indeed a great many more young men on the street than there normally would be. It wasn't unusual for Newmarket's population of rank to swell during the racing season, but these men were a good month earlier than normal. The July races were long past, and the next large meetings weren't until October.

The prize at stake in this race wasn't a purse, though. It was a woman.

Or, more specifically, it was the horse that came with the woman as an unofficial part of her dowry.

Perhaps Lady Rebecca was in an even worse position this year than Bianca was. Bianca knew what it was like not to be wanted— her stepmother had made quite sure of that—but she didn't know what it was like to be wanted for all the wrong reasons. She rather thought she'd prefer the honesty of the former.

HUDSON DEPARTED FROM THE TAILOR'S SHOP, where he'd promised a large sum of money to have some of his new clothing delivered by tomorrow. People streamed down the pavements on either side of the town's main street, while horses and carriages clogged the actual road. There were no street stalls, no tents, and the people were all entrenched in their cloaks and hats.

All in all, the town felt very . . . closed.

He glanced back at the store he'd just departed. The large windows displayed finely tailored goods, but the door dumped one right out onto the pavement. There was no overhang, no open-air portion.

The closeness of it all made him long to return the few short miles to the openness of his estate, but if he wanted to find his place among the turf set, he had to make forays into town, particularly to the taverns and coffeehouses around the Jockey Club in the afternoons and to the gallops, where the horses trained in the mornings.

He'd also have to wade through the astonishing number of invitations that had landed on his desk. He couldn't see Aaron nudging the appropriate ones his way on a regular basis, but perhaps he'd haul the whole lot to the stable and get Bianca to go through them after their ride tomorrow. In India, the group with which he had to socialize was small and, for the most part, lived close together. He'd never had to choose between four different events for a single evening before.

His stomach grumbled as he entered a tavern and the smell of food filled his senses. He couldn't tell what it was—wasn't even sure if it smelled good or bad—but at this point he would welcome anything as long as it simply had a distinct taste to it.

First, he had to decide where to sit. A long table to his left was empty at one end, so he took it and placed his order, hoping he'd managed to request whatever it was he was smelling.

At the other end of the table sat three men. One of them he recognized from the training stable, and another from last week's assembly. They were leaning in to listen to a young lad talk about a horse. His words were somewhat slurred, and the empty tankard in front of him as well as the half-empty one in his hand attested as to why. His other hand rested over a small stack of coins.

"He's off his feed, that's for sure. Been running poorly in his morning gallops. If you wanted to challenge, now's the time."

"Is Crawford aware of this, or will the stakes still hold high in the betting?" one man asked.

"Ain't nobody paid me enough for this but yous." The lad shifted to the side, his shirt stretching across muscles formed by the hard labor of a stable, and he gathered the coins into one of his pockets. "Shubert ain't telling either. Refuses to admit that his horses might not win anything this year."

The serving lass set Hudson's meal in front of him. The aroma wasn't quite appealing, but it was at least something.

"Would he accept a challenge?"

The lad shrugged and belched before taking another gulp of drink. "Not if he thinks he'll lose."

"I've an unknown," the man with curly hair said. "If no one else knows Gypsy isn't running well, my win will look impressive."

Hudson frowned. That didn't make any sense. He turned his head to look at the group at the other end of the table. "Won't it look worse when your next win isn't as impressive, though? Your horse will gain a reputation that he can't uphold."

Three dark looks told Hudson that just because the men had been having this conversation in an easily accessible location did not mean they welcomed someone else approaching them.

"Stildon, isn't it?"

"Yes." Hudson narrowed his gaze, trying to make out the details of the man in the dimly lit room.

Ah. It was Lord Davers. If Hudson had noticed that earlier, he'd have kept his mouth shut. The other man had taken a dislike to Hudson from the beginning, though he wasn't entirely sure why.

"As you put no coin into this particular endeavor, I suggest you have the decency to stay out of it," Lord Davers sneered. "Or didn't they teach you common courtesy in India—if that's even where you are truly from."

The stable lad drained the rest of his drink and rose from the table, less than steady on his feet but not dangerously so. As long as he could find his way home, he should be fine. "Pleasure doing business with you, my lord."

Lord Davers slid another coin into the boy's hand. "See that no one else learns of this."

With a shaky nod, the boy swaggered off while the three men shifted to Hudson's end of the table.

Hudson took a bite of the meat pie that had been delivered to him. It was hot and filling, and while the flavor wasn't anything dramatic, it had been seasoned with something. In all honesty, it might be the best thing he'd eaten since leaving India.

The company, however, was proving less desirable. Were these really the men he was supposed to be like? Were these the men his father had spent years teaching Hudson to fit in with? He'd heard over and over that he couldn't become too comfortable with the Indian way of doing things, because where he truly belonged was with his peers in England.

Well, he was in England, and by all accounts these were his peers, but he must have picked up too many bad habits somewhere along the way, because he didn't think he wanted to have very much to do with them.

He shoved another bite in his mouth.

"It's a shame that a jewel like Hawksworth would fall into the hands of someone without a notion of what he is doing." Lord Davers shook his head. "I suppose time will tell if you can manage it. In the meantime, I'll help you out."

Hudson had a feeling that any help Lord Davers dished out would go down worse than his cook's morning mush. He took another bite of pie.

"A challenge."

The other man shifted restlessly and leaned in a bit closer. Would it be too obvious if Hudson slipped and dropped his tankard of ale, dousing the lot of them? The fact that there wasn't an angle that would sufficiently do the job convinced him that he was better off merely taking a sip for himself. After setting the tankard back down, he looked at Davers. "What sort of challenge?"

"One that will let us see what you're made of. An informal race. Four-mile run. Your best against my best. One hundred pounds to the winner."

Everything about this seemed like a bad idea. Aaron had left for London, and Hudson's knowledge of his racing stock was limited. He knew he had three horses in training but had no knowledge of his jockeys or the protocol for gentlemen's challenges in England. Was it the same as it was in India?

What was worse? Muddling through and making a mistake or backing down from a bully?

"I'm still settling in, but perhaps two weeks from tomorrow?" he offered. That gave him time to sort things out and, hopefully, keep this little race from drawing too much attention. He did know enough about England's racing rules to know that if it didn't happen during a meeting it didn't count, so win or lose it wouldn't officially hurt his stable. His reputation, on the other hand, was another matter.

He had to use this week to establish a connection with Lady Rebecca, then, one that could sustain a small blow if he made a minor mistake with this challenge. Winning her hand was more important than ever. If he managed to win against the other men in that course, they'd have to respect him on the turf as well.

Now he just had to learn which of his horses was the best, where his jockey was, and if a four-mile run was a particular course or a type of race. Those were all questions he would normally have asked Aaron, since that was, after all, the man's job. Would Bianca know any of the answers?

"Lord Stildon?"

Hudson looked up to find another man standing next to his table. He nodded at the man, who then sat at the table and proceeded to introduce himself. Subtly, Hudson glanced around the room and noticed quite a few men looking in his direction.

It appeared this was going to be a very long meal.

Seventeen

Bianca had given up expecting her arrival at Hawksworth stables to follow any sort of predictable routine, but her wildest imaginations couldn't have created the scene that awaited her the next morning.

A small table and two chairs had been set up in the middle of the aisle. Horses were being led alongside it, and grooms rushed by, going about their morning duties as if the furniture were a normal fixture.

Lord Stildon sat in one of the chairs, staring at a stack of letters piled in the middle of the table.

"Is your study too comfortable these days?" she asked.

"Which of these is Lady Rebecca likely to attend?" Lord Stildon picked up one of the papers and tapped it against the edge of the table. "This is absolute madness. I had a large enough stack of correspondence yesterday morning, but then another wave arrived in the afternoon after I met a few men at the tavern in town."

Bianca nodded, trying not to smile. The man truly looked put out by his instant popularity. "Many apologies, my lord. It must be awful to have everyone want to be in your presence."

Lord Stildon grunted. "I think they just all want a firsthand account of my moment of failure."

Unfortunately, Bianca couldn't deny the sentiment. There were certainly people who would want to see that. "We'll simply have to make sure that doesn't happen, then." She sat in the chair opposite him and began to pick through the pile. "When did you go to the tavern?"

"Yesterday. I was passing by after visiting the tailor again and the smell drew me in."

Bianca looked up at him in surprise. She couldn't remember ever passing by the local taverns and being enticed by the smell.

He sat back and rubbed a hand across his face. "I simply cannot stomach the bland food my cook keeps trying to give me anymore. The meal didn't quite live up to its aroma, but it at least had flavor."

"Sounds like you should hire a new cook," Bianca mumbled, most of her attention going to sorting through the many invitations he had received. She tried not to think about how many of these hadn't come to her house—or if they had, she hadn't seen or heard of them. Despite the fact that she'd grown up here, most of her social life had consisted of enjoying the company of whoever happened to be in the vicinity. She hadn't sought them out, and it would seem they had reciprocated the lack of gestures.

Given her lack of effort, one would think she wouldn't mind the lack of invitations, but a few were from people she considered friends. One was from a lady she'd seen in town the day before and chatted with at length. Never had she mentioned a gathering of any sort.

No matter. Bianca straightened her spine and her shoulders. She was changing everything now. It just might take a bit of time.

Time she didn't have.

"I would accept these." She handed three invitations to him. "Lady Rebecca is likely to have her mornings filled with callers, so I don't know how much of her evening calendar she intends to fill. There's also the chance that Lady Gliddon will be holding her own dinners. That could explain the influx of invitations. Everyone is trying to get your commitment before she requests your attendance."

Stuck between two of the invitations was a folded letter. She picked it up and handed it across the table. "This looks like it might be more personal." She smirked. "Have you a friend in India who would have mailed you a letter already?"

Lord Stildon gave another grunt and set the invitations aside. "It would have had to be on the same boat I was on to get here so soon." He broke the wax seal and unfolded the letter. "I hardly think any of them were missing me before I even departed the coast. It will likely be a year before I receive any correspondence from them. I know I have no intention of writing until I have something noteworthy to share. Since many of them grew up in England and then moved to India, all of my experiences thus far would only make them laugh at me."

Yet another reason for the man to have his eyes on Lady Rebecca. While her name wouldn't mean much to anyone, the Earl of Gliddon's would—as would Hezekiah's, if his friends had followed racing before going to India.

The sadness that curled through Bianca surprised her. Was she still somehow hoping Lord Stildon would swoop in and save her from the maudlin situation she found herself in? That he would forget about Lady Rebecca and allow Bianca to be the lady of Hawksworth's house and stables?

She picked at a flake of paint on the edge of the table. Maybe, if she put forth the effort, she would find another gentleman in Newmarket with whom she could converse as easily as she did Lord Stildon.

"Well."

Bianca looked up from her musings. Lord Stildon was leaning back in his chair, eyes flicking over the letter again and again.

"Who is it from?"

"My uncle."

Bianca blinked. "You've an uncle? I thought you were the last of your family."

"He hasn't been in Newmarket in . . . thirteen years? Maybe fourteen? The solicitor said he moved to Ireland in 1804 and lived in London before that, so you've likely never met him."

"Well, that's simply lovely that you still have family, then. Is he coming to visit?"

"I certainly hope not."

"Oh?"

"My father claimed his younger brother wanted the title badly enough that he feared for the lives of any future children, particularly since he and my mother weren't having a great deal of luck having any. They moved to India to see if the climate would help her health. When I was finally born, he kept us in India to keep me out of my uncle's reach."

Lord Stildon looked up at Bianca, and for the first time she saw something of the lost little boy in his eyes. No matter how unstable or unsure he'd been, there'd always been a solidity to him, but now his hand shook a bit as he set the letter down. His gaze was softer, and he looked more than a little vulnerable.

She wanted to reach out, to comfort him, but what could she do? "Wait, he wasn't the man who tried to claim the horses after the death of your grandfather, was he?"

Lord Stildon's eyebrows lifted. "I beg your pardon?"

"You'll have to ask Aaron for the particulars, as I wasn't here at the time, but a man showed up and claimed he'd inherited all the horses and was going to start a stable in Ireland with them. The grooms set up a constant watch for three weeks. Was that your uncle?"

"Very likely. He would have assumed he was the heir." Lord Stildon jabbed a finger at the letter. "I didn't find out until I arrived here that my father hadn't merely kept me in India, but he'd also kept any knowledge of my existence in India. There's no indication that my grandfather told anyone except the proper authorities. The solicitor said my uncle was furious when he came to the London office, but mentioned nothing about him coming here."

A dry, scratchy tightness crawled up Bianca's throat. There'd never been much love lost between her and her stepmother, but she'd never feared for her life. Her sanity, possibly, but never her existence. "Is he . . . that is, do you think he . . ." She couldn't bring herself to finish the sentence.

"Still wants to kill me?" Lord Stildon shrugged. "I don't know. I would think it'd be far harder now than it would have been when I was a child. People would be far more suspicious at least."

"Does the letter say anything?"

Lord Stildon picked up the paper and refolded it, pinching the edges into sharp lines. "It says a lot of things. I think most of them are the blatherings of a hurt, angry man."

Bianca shook her head slowly. So far, Lord Stildon hadn't shown a great deal of ability to read between the lines of an Englishman's meaning. She'd seen what men were capable of doing to each other to get a better position in a horse race. How much more would they be willing to cheat to gain a title? "You should still take precautions. Be careful if you see him in town."

Lord Stildon gave a short laugh. "I don't even know what the man looks like."

"I do." Mr. Knight's voice came from a stall a few feet behind Lord Stildon. The head groom stepped out into the aisle. "I'd be surprised if Mr. Albany showed his face here after we ran him off last time, but if he does I'll be sure to let you know." He shook his head, the deep grooves of his face making his frown look even grimmer. "I was only a stable lad the last time he visited his father, but I remember all the other grooms telling me to stay away from him. If he was going for a ride, they made sure his horse was ready and tied to the post outside before he ever came down to the stable. The slightest interaction could make him angry enough to get a boy fired."

"That doesn't sound pleasant," Bianca whispered.

Lord Stildon said nothing, simply stared down at his folded letter. Finally, he tossed it into the pile of rejected invitations and picked up the three Bianca had told him to accept. "These are the ones, then?"

She nodded, trying to swallow in an attempt to ease the dryness of her mouth and throat. "Yes. And the assembly on Saturday, of course."

"Of course." He stood abruptly. "Shall we go for a ride?"

Bianca scrambled to her feet. "What? Oh. Yes. Of course."

Mr. Knight gave a nod. "I'll get Odysseus and Hades saddled for you." He cast a look between Lord Stildon and Bianca. "And I'll send Owen, seeing as Mr. Whitworth isn't here to accompany you."

"Neither man is exactly a proper chaperon," Bianca said with a shake of her head.

"Around here, they're proper enough to keep the tongues from wagging. They're accustomed to seeing you on Hawksworth horses. They ain't accustomed to seeing you alone with Lord Stildon."

Nor should they become so, not if Bianca wanted to gain the attention of another man. She sighed. Life was so much simpler when she hadn't cared.

NEARLY TWICE AS MANY CANDLES as normal had been placed about the assembly room, making Bianca's usual hiding spot available to prying eyes. Still, she hovered near the edge of the room, astounded at the number of people in attendance. Mr. Pierre was probably beside himself with glee over the swell in subscriptions.

Bianca was beside herself with fear.

It was strange, the number of these she'd attended without a single concern, but now, when she was forced to consider the ramifications of every action, every accepted invitation, every non-forthcoming invitation, she understood why so many girls ended up in the retiring room in need of remedies to calm their insides.

The entire prospect of the evening became nerve-racking when one considered the fact that for the next few hours she was going to have access to men she normally wouldn't be able to see without some sort of favor or social manipulation.

Her father skirted the crowd, his arm tucked low and close to his body. There was something in his hand that he seemed to be hiding, but she couldn't tell what it was.

As he came closer to her, she could make out what looked like a small plate. When he got to her side, he extended his prize.

She gasped at the round crisp circle on the plate, the artful pattern of piercings making the small treat as pretty as it was appetizing. "Is that a Shrewsbury cake?"

"Indeed it is." He turned his back to the room and shielded the plate from view as he held it out to her. "Compliments of the spread in the cardroom."

Though she had yet to take a bite, Bianca somehow swallowed wrong and started to choke. Perhaps surprise could solidify in midair? "Mr. Pierre put food in the cardroom? He barely includes refreshments with that awful punch."

Her father chuckled. "I'd wager you'll still find the offerings at the main table lacking. He's put his efforts where the influx of young gentlemen will notice it."

Of course he had. "I thank you for seeing to my needs, then." Bianca reached for the sweet treat and broke off a bite before popping it into her mouth and chewing slowly. "That is spectacular."

Father chuckled. "I have a feeling the young dandies who've come here for a wife won't see a single pastry, though. The fathers are snatching them up." He turned toward the mass of bodies floating about the room. Small clusters of conversations mixed with parading young ladies and speculative matrons.

"Have you got your eyes set on one yet?" Father asked.

Bianca shook her head. "They aren't here for me, Father."

None of them were. She'd tried hard to shake the loneliness that had crept over her as she looked at Lord Stildon's piles of invitations, but even Odysseus's hard run hadn't blown them out of her mind.

"Bah," her father scoffed. "Might as well be here for you. It's not as if Lady Rebecca can court them all, or even dance with them all. She certainly can't marry them all." He shook his head. "Gliddon would be better off selecting someone to receive Hezekiah's attentions before it comes to bear on the actual marriage. Seems a shame to subject his daughter to a union like that."

Bianca tilted her head to consider her father. "Do you truly think so? That marriage shouldn't be a business arrangement?"

"'Course I do." He pressed his lips together in a firm line. "Marriage is a choice that impacts the rest of your life. If done right, it can be the best thing to ever happen to you." He puffed out his chest in a show of pride. "That's why I told your stepmother I didn't intend to approve a match for your sister unless she was putting as much effort into helping you find a suitable match too."

She reached out and took the last portion of cake and shoved it into her mouth to keep from chiding him. She knew he was trying to help, that he wanted her settled and cared for and happy. If only the pursuit of such could be done without the oversight of her stepmother.

"I'm off to the cardroom before the dancing begins," Father said, tucking the empty plate to his side. "I want to get a good seat at a table with the other fathers who simply want to pass the time. I've no interest in sharing a table with men who want to play for large amounts."

She watched him walk away, an indulgent smile tugging at the edge of her lips. It was little wonder where she'd learned to live life in its current moment. Unfortunately, she hadn't the same freedom to indulge such an easygoing nature.

"Any words of advice tonight, O wise one?"

Bianca startled at Lord Stildon's low voice as he came to stand by her shoulder. She covered her jumpy movement by brushing nonexistent crumbs from her fingers. "Advice on what?"

"Dancing, of course. That is the main amusement, is it not? Or did I suffer your tutelage for nothing?"

She tried to look stern even as she battled the urge to laugh. "Do try to remember what I taught you tonight. Your poor performance will reflect on me, should anyone learn of the source of your knowledge."

"I believe my attempts at avoiding folly will be more motivated by a desire not to embarrass myself, but if it makes you feel better to think they are in honor of you, I don't mind."

Bianca smiled. Bantering with Lord Stildon was enjoyable, but she'd already committed to helping him with his plan, and she would see it through. Clenching her jaw for a brief moment, she nodded toward the side of the room where Lady Rebecca was holding court. "Your chosen conquest is over there. Dark hair, yellow dress. Lord Gliddon is the man standing a few feet to her right in a green waistcoat."

He took a moment to survey the room. She should be as calculated as he was, but it still didn't sit well with her to identify each man in the room by how well he could save her from her current predicament. Lord Stildon's suit of Lady Rebecca certainly wasn't going to be an easy endeavor, but then again, how else would he ensure that the first horse he bred as Hawksworth's owner was a champion? Matching Hezekiah and Hestia was as close to a sure thing as horse breeding came.

"Is there any man in particular you'd wish me to send your way? I confess I've never done any sort of matchmaking before, so my attempts might not start off well, but I'm sure I'll learn."

"I can't think of anyone." If she could, then maybe this entire business wouldn't feel so cold.

"Will you wish me luck," Lord Stildon said, breaking into Bianca's confused musings, "or is something else done in England?"

"Good luck."

He nodded and walked into the fray. As she watched the crowd, she noticed Mr. Mead standing near the refreshment table, searching the room intently. Was he looking for her? If so, she needed to risk her stepmother's attention and find herself a dancing partner soon.

With a deep breath, she traced the same path Lord Stildon had just taken, hoping a little of that luck she'd wished him was still available for herself.

Eighteen

Over the course of the night, Hudson learned three things. First, everyone had not been overestimating the appeal of Lady Rebecca and Hezekiah on a subset of England's elite population. He was fairly certain he was in the midst of every influential stable owner in the southern half of England who had a single son of marriageable age or was of marriageable age themselves.

Second, there were plenty of women who didn't have a single qualm about feeding off Lady Rebecca's discards, as he was also certain that he was in the midst of every eligible female of good family from at least three counties.

Third, and possibly most important, he learned that the men were trying to impress each other as much as, if not more than, Lady Rebecca. As the cluster around the serene young woman grew, the men looked at each other in overt assessment, as if Lady Rebecca's hand was going to be awarded by the vote of some sort of committee.

Hudson glanced at Lord Gliddon, holding court with a puffed-out chest to the lady's right, and Lord Brimsbane, just beyond him. It was possible that Lady Rebecca's future husband would be a committee decision, but none of these men would be on it.

He blew out a frustrated breath and glanced around. If he

patiently waited his turn to approach the lady, he'd get to greet her just before her new husband's horse beat Hudson's in a race.

A string of women stood behind him, hoping to gain attention and a dancing partner. It wouldn't be much interaction, but perhaps he could position himself to talk to Lady Rebecca as they passed in formation during one of the dances.

A young woman with blond hair and large, guileless blue eyes in a wide, round face stood on the edge of the group. Unfortunately, he didn't know her. Bianca had informed him that he was not to greet a lady in public if he hadn't been properly introduced to her, but wasn't the entire point of an assembly to meet other people?

He glanced around, but there was no way for him to know if the men and women talking to each other had prior acquaintance.

Lord Davers approached, a gleeful sneer on his face that told Hudson he might have made a mistake in making any sort of indication of interest in this particular girl. He couldn't take it back now, though, as the man drew near.

The girl beamed up at the other man, and Hudson half hoped that Davers intended to ask the young lady to dance, even though that would still leave Hudson without a dance partner.

"Miss Marianne, have you had the pleasure of meeting Lord Stildon? He's still new in town and, I believe, lacking a partner for this next set."

There was nothing untrue about what Lord Davers had just said, but it left Hudson feeling as if he should defend himself. The momentary dimming of the girl's smile didn't help his confidence any. Perhaps she held an affinity for Lord Davers. He'd introduced her as Miss Marianne, indicating she was a younger sister. Hudson bowed his head in greeting, and she curtsied.

"I'm pleased to make your acquaintance, my lord."

"The pleasure is mine." The lie tasted bitter. Meeting her wasn't a pleasure. In fact, he'd derived little pleasure from the evening at all. In racing, one trained, prepared, and then gave the race everything he had, hoping that skill would mix with a smidge of luck and produce a victory. So far this matrimony competition seemed to rely entirely on luck. Perhaps it was time to apply a little strategy.

He smiled at the lady. "Would you care to dance?"

She placed her hand in his, and he led her to the floor, making sure he joined the same configuration in which Lady Rebecca lined up.

"The weather was fine today," Miss Marianne said as they took their places.

Considering that the morning sun had only managed to create a slight glow among the grey clouds of the sky that had given way to rain somewhere around noon, *fine* was not the word he would use. The best he could manage as a response was "I managed to avoid getting caught out on the Heath in the rain."

This was his seventh discussion of the weather, and all of them had led him to believe the English natives were accustomed to incredibly dreary conditions. Only two of them had agreed that the day had been somewhat dismal, but he had a feeling that was because they'd asked to hear his thoughts first and were ready to agree with whatever he said.

If this dance followed the path his other ones had taken, Miss Marianne's next words would be about the mighty crush the assembly room had—

"It's quite a crush tonight, isn't it?" she chirped as she laid her hand on his elbow and they began their first sequence of steps.

"Hmm," he responded as they parted. How he'd love to take them to an Indian market so they could know what a crush truly was.

"I, for one, am quite thankful for the crush," the woman in the pair beside them said. "It's been a spell since I danced this much."

The gentleman across from her smiled back. "There are so

many people that you can dance with the same lady twice without anyone noticing."

A giggle came from the lady, whom Hudson assumed was the two-time dance partner in question.

"Have you a lady you wish to dance twice with, my lord?" Miss Marianne asked, looking up at him through her lashes.

It was a strange habit he'd noticed of Englishwomen, turning their face down but then looking up. Didn't it hurt? "I've only been in town for a week." He cleared his throat, glad the movement of the dance gave him an excuse to look away. "There are still people I've yet to meet."

"Such as me?"

Hudson curved his lips into a polite smile. "Yes, but now that has been rectified."

He stumbled as he turned the wrong way in the dance. There'd been so many dances tonight that all the sequences were starting to blur together in his mind. For the most part he'd been holding his own, but unless he was dancing a waltz—which had been deuced uncomfortable the two times he'd done so tonight—he still occasionally forgot which way he was supposed to go.

Two more sets of steps brought them side by side with Lady Rebecca and her partner.

She was beautiful. Dark ringlets framed her pale, thin face and sweet smile. Her countenance and manner had remained delicate and peaceful despite the chaos her presence created. A man couldn't ask for more poise in a wife.

He'd crossed paths with her in other dances, of course, but then he'd had some sense of fairness in not wanting to draw her attention away from her partner or ignore his own.

His sense of propriety was quickly eroding.

"I hear you are planning a ball," Hudson said as he met Lady Rebecca in the middle and took a turn about her dancing partner.

Her eyes widened. "Where did you hear that?"

Was he not supposed to know? Suddenly the cravat, which already felt overly starched, tight, and thick, threatened to choke him outright. "Er, well, I met your brother out riding."

"And he told you? How odd."

"Well, I suppose he was telling Miss Snowley, but I was there." Could he sound any more inane? He'd made himself sound like a puppy tagging along behind his mistress instead of the titled owner of a prestigious racing stable.

She smiled as he walked her back to her place. "Oh, you must be Lord Stildon. Arthur mentioned you." She dropped her face and did that strange looking-up thing. "He said that I should accept, should you ask me to waltz."

"Perhaps the next one, then?" Hudson slowed his steps back to his own side of the line, forcing Miss Marianne and Lady Rebecca's partner to dodge around him.

"That one's taken, but I can reserve the one after that for you."

Hudson swallowed, trepidation and the thrill of success swirling in his gut and making him glad he'd avoided the refreshment table. "I would like that."

Miss Marianne glared at him as she took her own circle on the arm of Lady Rebecca's partner. Hudson was man enough to admit the stare induced a bit of guilt. It wasn't Miss Marianne's fault that her father didn't own a champion racehorse. She deserved his undivided attention for the rest of the dance, though if they didn't come up with something more to talk about, that attention was going to look a lot like silent staring.

As they continued up the line and Miss Marianne began to speak, Hudson found himself craving awkward silence. "My hair was positively dreadful earlier, and my maid had to redo it twice."

Why couldn't the dance be more intricate and fast so she wouldn't have the breath to talk?

"It made my sister perturbed, of course, since we share a maid, but I simply couldn't arrive without an appropriate coiffure."

What sort of coiffure had her sister arrived with, since Miss Marianne had taken all the maid's time? Not that he would ask. His only goal was to remain polite and attentive for the remainder of the dance.

"Your hair is lovely," he replied.

She preened. "Thank you. Bianca said it looked exactly the same as the second time, but she's wrong. These ringlets are a full inch shorter."

Hudson swallowed and looked closer at the lady in front of him. How many women here tonight were named Bianca? He didn't see any resemblance between Miss Marianne and Bianca, but that didn't really mean anything, did it? Especially given Bianca had mentioned a stepmother.

He shook his head. Not knowing the local connections was threatening to give him a headache. He had to tread carefully around everyone because he never knew when someone would turn out to be the sibling or cousin of someone else.

Finally, the dance ended, and he was able to escort her back to the side of the floor. "Thank you for the dance."

"It was lovely." Miss Marianne smiled at him. "If you wanted to stand up with me again sometime, I wouldn't say no."

Hudson blinked and nearly stumbled to a halt. That was rather forward, wasn't it? Then again, Lady Rebecca had just done something similar, so maybe it wasn't? All he knew was that the two interactions felt incredibly different.

"I, er, uh, thank you for accompanying me." He bowed his head as an older, though still beautiful, woman who definitely bore a resemblance to his recent dance partner stepped up. She examined him as if he were a specimen in a gallery.

Everything was suddenly too much. The crowd, the heat, everything. Hudson made his way through the crowd and stepped out onto the balcony, not caring if it rained on him.

Another man had already escaped to the calm of the outdoors

and was leaning against the balustrade, watching the dancers through the windows. Beside him, being quite obviously ignored, stood another man. The tension on the balcony was almost as thick as that in the ballroom, but at least out here Hudson could breathe while he suffered the awkwardness.

The area wasn't significantly large, so Hudson was only feet away from the other two men when he approached the railing in order to look out into the night. It wasn't entirely dark, as lanterns and glowing windows from the town spotted the view, but it was calm.

He couldn't prevent his curiosity and took another peek at the gentlemen to see if he knew them. One of them he assuredly didn't know, but the disgruntled, ignored one was Mr. Theophilus Mead.

Hudson's single encounter with the man the week prior hadn't been anything exemplary, and the poor opinions of Bianca and Aaron were enough to solidify an inclination to dislike him. The sneer on his face as he looked from the silent gentleman to Hudson only verified the notion that the man was very capable of shedding his gentlemanly demeanor when it suited him.

Mr. Mead's gaze connected with Hudson's, and the man's countenance shifted immediately into a mask of civility. "Stildon."

Hudson's eyebrows rose. Even in India a man didn't drop the honorific unless some semblance of relationship had been established. "*Mister* Mead." He gave the other man a nod of greeting because Hudson was going to be a gentleman no matter what, and then turned to the silent man. "I don't believe we've met. I am Lord Stildon."

The man with a thick, dark shaggy cap of hair looked from Mr. Mead back to Hudson before nodding a greeting in return. "Lord Rigsby."

"As you're new to England," Mr. Mead said, his smile hardening until it gave the impression of being a sneer once more, "I'll save you a bit of confusion. Rigsby is a courtesy title. He's the heir to a marquis." He splayed out his hands in front of him. "We wouldn't want anyone not to know where they stood."

It wasn't Hudson's preconceived notions coloring his view. The man was definitely sneering.

"It isn't your lack of title I object to," Lord Rigsby said calmly and without expression, "but rather your lack of decorum."

What on earth had transpired before Hudson came out to the balcony?

Mr. Mead straightened his shoulders. "If you'll pardon me, I believe I shall see which ladies are pining for the loss of men within their reach. I should have my pick at the moment, though I've my eye on a particular one."

As glad as Hudson was to see the man go, he was praying fervently that Bianca was already engaged for the next several dances. She absolutely needed a different husband than that man.

Should he follow Mr. Mead back into the room to ensure Bianca's safety? He was poised to do just that when he saw Mr. Mead engage another woman in conversation.

Thankful he didn't yet have to venture back into the fray, Hudson relaxed against the stone behind him and turned to Lord Rigsby. "Friend of yours?"

The man gave a short laugh. "Hardly. I met him about ten minutes before you came out." He sent an assessing look Hudson's way. "Yours?"

Hudson shook his head. "Met him in the cardroom last Saturday."

Lord Rigsby nodded before turning around to look out at the view. "What brings you out into the night, Lord Stildon? Escaping the madness or strategizing how to be a part of it?"

"Both, I suppose. I would certainly like to talk to Lord Gliddon about Hezekiah, and Lady Rebecca is a very appealing woman. I've reserved a waltz with her later." He wished he was looking forward to it, but the waltzes he'd participated in thus far were nothing like his whirl about the garden with Bianca.

Lord Rigsby nodded. "That she is." He glanced over his shoulder. "Not worth that price, I'm afraid—at least not to me. I'm in the area to look it over before racing my horses here in October."

"I'm of little assistance to you there. I've yet to experience a Newmarket race myself."

The two men continued to talk as the music drifted out of the room behind them. It was the most enjoyable conversation Hudson had held outside his own stables since arriving. These assemblies weren't what he'd expected when he came to England. He'd thought the entire experience would be much closer to this balcony encounter—a mutual meeting of similar minds and a sense of camaraderie.

As the music shifted from one dance to another, Lord Rigsby nodded to the room. "Shouldn't you be getting back in there?"

Yes. Though he certainly didn't want to. "Do you intend to rejoin the dancing?"

Lord Rigsby sighed. "I suppose. My father is pressuring me to marry. He wants assurance that his line will continue." He shook his head. "I don't know that I want to join that frenzy, though. Other than appearance, how is one to know if they are committing themselves to spending twenty minutes with someone interesting? Just because a girl lives in Newmarket doesn't mean she enjoys riding, or even living in the country."

This man could be perfect for Bianca's needs. So why was Hudson having such trouble getting the suggestion out of his throat? "I may know someone."

Lord Rigsby laughed. "You've got a sister?"

"No. My neighbor. A friend. Of sorts."

"With a beautiful personality?" He shook his head again. "Obviously you think well of her but not enough to court her yourself. What's wrong with her?"

"She doesn't have access to any champion bloodlines."

"A shortfall she has no hope of overcoming." The man looked

175

past Hudson to the couples visible through the open doors of the gathering room.

"If you need some extra incentive," Hudson said, truly wanting to feel like he was helping Bianca avoid the clutches of her stepmother's marital choices, "she is the young lady Mr. Mead has his eye set on."

Rigsby's eyebrows flew up and a small smile curved his lips. "Intriguing. Tell me, if you were free of this horse obligation, would you be considering her yourself?"

"One year ago I was living in India in blissful ignorance of the fact that my grandfather was dying. If I didn't have a horse obligation hanging over me, I'm not positive I'd even have left the house tonight."

Lord Rigsby's question gave Hudson something to consider. He only got to marry once. He only got to make one first move as a stable owner. He only got one chance to start this new life. Lady Rebecca seemed the perfect way to properly make all those firsts in the right way, but was that what he would choose if he didn't feel any pressure?

"Is she here tonight?" Lord Rigsby's question broke into Hudson's musings.

"Yes." He looked to the dancers. "Do you want to meet her?"

"Just point her out to me. I can facilitate my own introduction. Don't want the lady to feel like you're trying to shuffle her off somewhere."

The two men stepped closer to the window, and Hudson directed Lord Rigsby's attention to Bianca as she pranced by, her pale green dress swirling about her and her brown curls bouncing in time with the music.

Lord Rigsby nodded. "And where is your lady?"

Where was Lady Rebecca? It took him far longer to find her in the configuration, but he finally located her on the arm of Lord Davers, circling another couple.

"Best of luck to you." Lord Rigsby clapped Hudson on the shoulder and then moved to the door. "And next time we meet, feel free to call me Rigsby."

Hudson returned the offer and then followed the other man back into the assembly room, his shoulders feeling somewhat less weighed down than they had earlier. Perhaps God hadn't dragged him to England to lead a life of constant tension. Aaron, Bianca, and now Rigsby had entered his life by unexpected chance. Perhaps he just needed to be a bit more patient with God's plans.

With a decisive nod that committed to doing just that, he went in search of Lady Rebecca to claim his waltz.

Nineteen

If asked a month ago, even a single week ago, if she thought she was an overly particular person, Bianca would have said no. She felt that, generally speaking, she was easy to please.

She never complained when her least favorite foods appeared on the table. Whenever her stepmother summoned her—which hadn't been often until the past week—she'd gone along without a murmur, at least not one anyone else could hear. If the weather was poor, she didn't mind donning an oilcloth cape for her walk to Hawksworth.

In fact, the only time she could remember feeling truly put out was when the weather was so bad or her schedule so confining that she didn't get to go for a ride.

All her experience told her she was an easily pleased woman.

Such was not the case at tonight's assembly.

She rarely sat out a dance and she enjoyed the activity, so it wasn't the abundance of dances or even the longer formations necessitated by the crowd that was upsetting her.

No, it was her partners. Even though many were men she'd stood up with countless times before, tonight she found them vexing.

They were too talkative or too quiet, too tall or too short, too plain or too handsome—well, none of them fell into that category, as all the exceptionally handsome men were surrounding Lady Rebecca.

Poor girl. Perhaps she should have just sent Hezekiah in her stead. Wouldn't that be something? A horse trying to dance the waltz?

She smiled at the thought.

Her smile faded as she saw Mr. Mead moving toward her. The next dance was a waltz. She didn't want to dance with Mr. Mead, and particularly didn't want to waltz with him.

Perhaps she should develop a sudden need to visit the retiring room.

Another gentleman appeared at her side before Mr. Mead could reach her. She turned with grateful expectancy, which plummeted as she realized she didn't know the man.

"Please forgive me if this is an etiquette blunder, but I do believe as it is a public assembly that I may introduce myself?"

Could he? She couldn't remember ever having been told one way or the other. Then again, she'd grown up in Newmarket and normally knew everyone at these dances already. There was something charming about his demeanor, and he wasn't Mr. Mead, so she smiled up at him.

"I don't know, but I promise not to tell anyone if you don't."

"It shall be our secret, then. I am Lord Rigsby."

Other than the mention of this man in the dress shop, she'd never heard of him before. It was likely his title was a courtesy one, but she didn't want to admit that she was so removed from social gossip that she hadn't a clue whom he was the heir of. "Miss Snowley."

He gave her a small bow. "May I have the honor of this dance, Miss Snowley?"

A burst of pleasure warmed her cheeks. This man had sought her out specifically to ask her to dance. That had to mean something, didn't it? Perhaps she could actually find another man to marry.

If she weren't making her way onto the dance floor, Bianca

would have kicked herself. Why was she contemplating marriage with every man she met? Wasn't this the very thing she scorned other women for?

Yes, Lord Rigsby was attractive, and he delivered four sentences with adequate personality, but she required more than that in a marriage.

She'd once thought she needed nothing but horses and civility, but that was before.

Before Lord Stildon.

Oh, drat the man. He surely wasn't comparing Lady Rebecca to her, so Bianca wasn't going to compare Lord Rigsby to him.

"Are you new in town?" she asked as he guided her into the dance.

"Merely visiting. I intend to bring my horses here to race in October." He looked around the room. "I didn't realize the town would be so busy already."

"It normally isn't. Have you never raced your horses here before?"

"My father has always refused to bring our horses to New-market. I've bought two of my own, though, so he can't dictate where they race."

There had to be an interesting story behind his father's aversion to Newmarket, but Bianca couldn't think of a polite way to ask about it.

They fell into silence for a full round of the dance floor, but it didn't have that heaviness that silence often had. Lord Rigsby was an excellent dancer, and Bianca was able to enjoy the movement as they whirled among the other couples.

She needed to come up with something to talk about, though, as this was the first man who had piqued her interest. Then again, she'd only been looking for a week. Still, she knew a lot of people, and she'd given many of them consideration tonight.

None of them had drawn her regard.

"Did you ride the Heath for yourself this morning? The weather was a bit of a deterrent, but the ride is still nice."

Gracious, had she just mentioned the weather? It wasn't that she hadn't had many a conversation about the weather, but she always tried never to be the one who brought it up.

"I confess I have not had that pleasure yet. Hopefully Monday."

She nodded as they fell silent again. This time, it was somewhat less comfortable.

"In your opinion, what should I be sure to see of Newmarket while I'm here? Apart from the Heath, that is." He guided her gently around another couple who had turned the wrong way.

"Well." Nothing came to mind. It was silly given how much she loved her town, but she was completely blank as to what someone should see when they visited. "You'll want to see the training stables, of course. Since you intend to bring your horses here."

He nodded. "Does your family race horses?"

She gave a short laugh. "My family has a pair of carriage horses that couldn't even outpace a man at a brisk walk. I visit my neighbor's stable frequently though."

"Ah yes. Lord Stildon. I met him earlier."

Bianca maintained her smile, but inside her enjoyment of the dance faded a bit more. The viscount was keeping his promise to send eligible men her way. He truly wanted her to marry another man.

It wasn't a surprise, wasn't even a new idea, but for some reason it was suddenly real.

They passed her stepmother, who was chatting with Mr. Mead and sending occasional glares in Bianca's direction. Did Mrs. Snowley know Lord Rigsby? Did she not approve of him? Did she approve of him too much and want him for Marianne?

Not that Bianca cared one way or another. The only thing her stepmother represented was Bianca's need to get busy starting her own life, and as Lord Rigsby was the best candidate she'd seen, he deserved every bit of her attention.

She pushed her smile wider and looked up at him. She didn't care one iota about it, but Newmarket did have one other claim of import that many people enjoyed discussing. "Have you had a chance to see the remains of the palace?"

IT WAS HARD to say what was more disconcerting—the stares of the other bachelors or the assessing gaze of Lord Gliddon as Hudson waited for Lady Rebecca to return to her father's side so that he could claim her for the waltz.

"Lord Stildon," Lord Brimsbane said, stepping into the space between Hudson and Lord Gliddon. "Good evening."

"Lord Brimsbane." Hudson swallowed and kept his gaze on Lady Rebecca as her previous partner escorted her back.

"So, you truly are interested in marrying my sister?"

What was the correct answer here? He'd never had a sister, never really had a woman in his life at all other than his mother and Bianca. Just minutes ago, he'd sent Lord Rigsby to find Bianca because the man had been interested in meeting the woman, not simply finding a suitable bride.

How much more would such a distinction matter to a brother? "I'm interested in getting to know her."

"Hmmm."

The other man's expression remained impassive, but Hudson could feel the scrutiny. When they'd met on the Heath, there'd been a sort of curiosity, but this felt harder. Was it Hudson's own discomfort causing that sensation, or was it something unspoken that the other man was somehow indicating? Hadn't Lady Rebecca said her brother recommended him?

Society was confusing.

Lady Rebecca caught her brother's gaze before smiling at Hudson. "I believe this is your dance, my lord."

Hudson bowed and took her hand. "I believe it is."

He led her onto the floor and guided her into the waltz. Up close, her smiling face didn't look as delighted as it had from a distance, though her curls were just as perfect and her manner as graceful.

He should say something. "I recently arrived from India."

The corners of her eyes crinkled a bit. "I recently arrived from London."

"I mean that I grew up in India and recently arrived in England from there."

"Did you like India?"

Did he like it? It was all he'd known. He'd heard tales of other places, but India was his entire existence. There were things he liked and things he didn't, but he really didn't have anything else to compare it with, other than a week in Newmarket and six months on a ship.

"It was a fine place to grow up," he finally settled on.

She nodded and continued to smile gently as they danced. Didn't her cheeks hurt?

Over her head, he spied the refreshment table as they twirled by. "Have you tried the punch tonight?"

She nodded. "It parched my thirst."

Indeed.

There had to be something they could talk about that would drive this conversation for more than two sentences. "Do you ride?"

She laughed, the sound as gentle and soft as her appearance. "With my father? Of course I do." She lifted one shoulder. "I have a mare. Her name is Daffodil."

Ah, horses. Yes, this was a topic that should last them a while. "What kind of horse is she?"

Her nose scrunched up, though she somehow managed to keep a slight curve to her lips. Perhaps her mouth was simply made that way? "I forget the exact name Father called it." Her face smoothed out once more. "I confess that I enjoy attending the races and don't mind riding, but the little details quite escape me."

Another topic trampled beneath the feet of the many waltzers.

This time he would wait until she came up with something.

"Have *you* tried the punch?"

Or she could repeat something.

Had he tried the punch? Yes. And then promptly poured the rest of the glass into a potted plant and gone to the cardroom in search of something—anything—else. That was hardly polite conversation, though.

Perhaps that was his problem. He had no issue talking with Bianca because he was boldly blunt. Would Lady Rebecca appreciate the same thing?

He nodded once. "I did try it earlier. It was rather awful." He took a deep breath and plunged ahead. "I poured it into a potted plant."

She blinked up at him and then turned her head this way and that, looking about the room. "Oh? Which one?"

"That one." Hudson nodded his head toward a plant in the vicinity of the refreshment table. He couldn't remember which plant had assisted him with emptying his glass, but he didn't think it much mattered.

With her head tilted to the side, she considered the plant a moment. "Do you think the punch will do it ill?"

"The plant?" Hudson blinked. It was a plant. Didn't they thrive on far worse things than horrible-tasting punch?

She nodded. "It's barely fit for human consumption, so one can only wonder what it will do to a plant. We shall have to check on it at next week's assembly."

"Yes. Yes, we should do that."

On the one hand, Hudson was happy. She wanted him to seek her out next week, and perhaps even before then. On the other hand, while the topic had gone further than two sentences, the conversation was now dead once more.

They danced along. Twice, he caught sight of Bianca and Lord Rigsby. They seemed to be getting along well enough.

What did he and Lady Rebecca look like? Would her brother and father think everything was going well between them? The best he could say for this current activity was that it didn't feel awkward. Painfully exhausting, perhaps, but not awkward.

The relief he felt when the dance came to an end didn't bode well for his future. As he walked Lady Rebecca back to her father, he again saw Bianca and Lord Rigsby. She was smiling up at him as if the dance had been the best of her life.

At least the evening had gone well for one of them.

Hudson just wished he was happy about it.

Twenty

Bianca stood in the middle of her room, dressed in a riding habit with her hair slicked back into a bun and her hat pinned securely in place. She held her leather riding gloves in her hand and her toes wiggled within her boots.

Yet she didn't move.

Her normal routine would have had her quickly finishing the food that had been brought up on a tray and then making her way to Hawksworth.

So why wasn't she leaving? Why wasn't her scrambled mind fleeing to the peace that riding a good horse would bring?

Because Lord Stildon came along with the horse, and he wanted her to marry someone else.

They'd both said that before Saturday's assembly, but seeing him dance with Lady Rebecca while Bianca danced with the man he'd sent her way had made their bargain real. Up to that point, she'd seen it more as a game.

She wasn't sure she wanted to play anymore. What choice did she have, though? Walking away decreased her chances of finding an acceptable husband. Finding more to like about Lord Stildon's humor and personality every time they met was simply a pain she was going to have to handle.

Unless she could get there and mounted before he came down to the stables. Then it was a pain she could delay.

The longer she stood there staring at the loose thread on her bedcovering, the lower her chances of being able to leave the stable before he arrived and the greater her chances of encountering her stepmother on her way out.

Both were very good reasons to get her feet moving.

Unless she didn't go riding this morning. She *could* change into a morning dress and join her stepmother and sister in whatever they were doing, but life was certainly not that bad yet.

That left her two options.

One, she could go to Hawksworth as normal and hope Hudson wasn't up and about yet and simply deal with the consequences if he was. Two, she could ride one of her father's horses. It wouldn't be the same, certainly, but it would get her out into the fresh air.

A soft knock preceded Dorothy's entrance into the room. "If you please, miss, you've a visitor."

"A visitor?"

"Yes, miss."

"It's"—she glanced at the clock—"not even seven."

"I know, miss, but he's out on the drive, and he's asking for you."

Curiosity freed her feet from the carpets, and Bianca all but flew down the stairs and through the front hall. She stumbled to a halt as she crossed the threshold because, sure enough, there was a man waiting for her on the drive.

Lord Brimsbane held the reins of a cream-colored horse in one hand and his hat in the other. Behind him, a groom held the reins of Lord Brimsbane's glorious chestnut and another mount.

"Miss Snowley. I wondered if you would do me the great honor of going for a ride with me."

Well. This was an option she hadn't considered.

A firm nudge between her shoulder blades sent her tripping two steps forward. "Of course she would."

Bianca turned to see her stepmother keeping to the shadows

187

of the doorway but definitely making sure she was involved in whatever was happening in front of her home. How quickly had she thrown on those clothes in order to be downstairs already? Normally she wasn't even awake yet.

Bianca whirled back to Lord Brimsbane and smiled. "Of course I would."

"Don't mess this up," Mrs. Snowley whispered. "Connections to an earl would do a great deal of good for our family."

As annoying as that thought might be, it wasn't a reason to turn down Lord Brimsbane's invitation, especially as it aided two of Bianca's growing problems—how to get in her ride this morning and how to find someone who piqued her interest as much as, or hopefully more than, Lord Stildon did.

The original plan might have been for Lord Brimsbane to meet her and Lord Stildon at Hawksworth, but she wasn't going to quibble over the change when it suited her so well.

She stepped forward and rubbed her hand down the pale horse's neck, appreciating the strength and warmth of the animal before tugging on her riding gloves. "I would be happy to accompany you, Lord Brimsbane."

"Excellent."

Moments later, everyone was mounted, and they were riding toward the Heath, the groom staying a steady three lengths behind like a well-trained maid.

"What is her name?" Bianca shifted in the saddle to settle more firmly on the unfamiliar horse.

"Daffodil. She's Rebecca's horse."

Bianca turned to look at Lord Brimsbane, unable to hide her surprise. "Oh."

"She insisted."

"Please express my appreciation to her."

He nodded. "I will." As the rolling green lengths of the Heath came into view, already dotted with an abundance of horses, he guided them away from the area where she normally rode. "Do you mind if we take this side of the Heath?"

"No, of course not." Obviously Lord Brimsbane relished the idea of encountering Lord Stildon as much as she did. The two seemed to have gotten on well enough in their previous encounter, so the decision must have been because of her.

The idea inspired pleasure, but there was also a brick of dread in the bottom of her stomach.

They rode along, switching at times from a brisk walk to a trot, and then slowing back down again. Conversation consisted mostly of the horses they passed, which ones would do well in the races, which riders were having a good day.

"Are any of your horses out here training this morning?"

"Of course." He looked around and then gave her a sheepish grin. "I'm afraid I'm not sure where, though."

"No matter," she laughed. "Probably wouldn't be very ladylike of me to speculate on the quality of your horses in front of you anyway."

He feigned being stabbed in the chest. "You wound me. Are you so loyal to Hawksworth that you doubt my father's stable's superior reputation?"

Loyal to Hawksworth? Perhaps only in sentiment. Loyal to Aaron's insistence on following different training methods than most of the other owners? Definitely.

Speaking of such would be going too far in her knowledge of horses, though. She wanted to be a match for a good horseman, not try to be his better. Although she wouldn't want to hold back too much, since she wouldn't be able to hold her tongue for long.

They rounded one of the low hills on the edge of the Heath, and a long, flat expanse spread before them.

"Shall we run?"

He laughed. "If you wish. Though I must tell you Daffodil is no match for Uzziah."

Of course she wasn't. Bianca never got to ride the truly fast animals. "To that far hill?"

He shook his head and laughed. "Would you like an advantage?"

Did she? Normally she would turn one down on principle, but that meant she never won, so how good a principle was that? "That would be lovely, thank you."

He nodded, his grin wide. "I'll count to ten, shall I?"

She nodded.

"One."

She nudged her horse and shifted her weight so that she didn't slide off as the horse ran. Daffodil was a glorious animal. If Bianca were being honest, this was a finer horse than the ones she rode at Hawksworth. Of course, this was also the personal horse of an earl's daughter.

Wind whipped across her face, and she couldn't help but laugh aloud at the wonder of being in a race without watching the backside of her opponent's horse the entire time.

Hoofbeats thundered up behind her, and she urged Daffodil to go faster, though the finish line was far enough away that she had no hope of reaching it before Lord Brimsbane's thoroughbred caught up with her.

Still, when his mount flew past hers, she could see the finish marker, and she passed by it only a few moments after he did.

She slowed the horse, still laughing. "I almost had you."

He shrugged. "I counted to fifteen."

"That was an interesting race."

Bianca and Lord Brimsbane turned their horses toward the new voice.

Lord Rigsby sat atop the most gorgeous bay thoroughbred Bianca had ever seen. He had a sleek coat that shone with dark red undertones, legs that faded evenly down to black right at the knees and hocks, and the clearest white star on his forehead. In appearance, at least, this animal could rival Hezekiah for beauty in proportion and power.

"Do I know you?" Lord Brimsbane steered his horse in between Bianca's and Lord Rigsby's.

She should appreciate the gesture—she *did* appreciate the sentiment behind it—but they were surrounded by hundreds of people. What did Lord Brimsbane think was going to happen if they conversed with a stranger?

With a shake of her head, she steered her own mount from behind Lord Brimsbane. "Allow me to make the introductions. Lord Brimsbane, this is Lord Rigsby."

The men nodded at each other but continued to stare. Bianca looked from one to the other. What was she missing? If the two men weren't on horseback, she'd think they were considering coming to blows.

"Are you new in town?"

"Visiting for a few weeks. I'll be bringing my horses here in October, and I wanted to learn my way around the place."

Lord Brimsbane relaxed and Lord Rigsby smirked.

Bianca grew more confused.

Obviously there was some conversation going on that she didn't understand. She tried to take in every single detail so she could relate the encounter to Lord Stildon later. Perhaps he could explain it to her.

Just thinking of Lord Stildon sent a wave of goose bumps to ride across the skin of her arms and a swirl of intensity to hit her in the middle. Not once in her interactions with Lord Brimsbane had such a thing occurred, nor had she felt this way upon seeing Lord Rigsby.

She sighed. The heart was certainly inconvenient.

THE STABLE AT MEADOWLAND PARK WAS FULL. Every stall held a horse, and three more were tied to a post.

Apparently Hudson hadn't been the only one to have the idea

of visiting Lady Rebecca this morning. In all honesty, he wouldn't have had the idea if he hadn't heard someone else talking about morning visits after church yesterday.

He'd been slow to leave the church because he'd still been pondering the sermon. It had taken him a while to give it his full attention because he'd felt conspicuous sitting alone in an enclosed pew. The St. Mary's he had attended in India was filled with rows of cane benches.

At the St. Mary's in Newmarket, he had a pew in a box that his grandfather had paid for several years in advance. The entire business felt strange, but eventually he'd managed to focus on what was being said.

The passage had been out of Romans, so even his full focus didn't keep it from being at least a little bit confusing. He had caught the phrase, "For I know that in me (that is, in my flesh,) dwelleth no good thing." Then there'd been something about not doing the good that one wants to do, but instead doing evil. It had raised a great deal of questions, but it hadn't provided any answers.

Then he'd heard two women talking about which men they thought might come to pay them a call the next morning.

Luck? Coincidence? An answer from the Lord? Who knew. What he did know was that he refused to sit around considering the meaning of the pastor's sermon when he could be doing something that might show him the right direction.

So, with questions still racing through his head, he dismounted and handed Hades over to one of the stable boys. There was nothing for it but to wade into the fray.

The butler took his card—thank goodness the tailor had mentioned how conveniently sized the coat pocket was for holding a card case, and Hudson therefore procured one along with the necessary cards—and showed him into a large drawing room.

Ten other men milled about the room. Three of them stared out the room's windows, ignoring all the others, as if that would make them disappear. Four sat on the chairs and sofas, occasionally chatting, and one appeared like he was considering taking a nap. One man paced the room, while two more played a game of piquet at a corner table.

It looked more like a strange men's club than a formal drawing room.

No one greeted Hudson upon his entry, though a few of them looked over in acknowledgment of his presence. He now understood the position of the three men at the windows. Had there been an empty set of panes, Hudson would have taken up a position in front of them just to pretend this whole business wasn't happening.

A newspaper lay folded on a table, so he sat in a chair close by and opened it. If he had ten visits to wait through before getting his turn, he might as well settle in.

The butler appeared in the doorway, and everyone came to attention. Three men on the sofas sat upright, the card players set down their hands, and the men at the window turned toward the room. Only the fellow who'd fallen to the lure of slumber didn't move.

"Mr. Wansford."

Eight men groaned and huffed as one of the men stood from his seat on the sofa and moved to the door. The butler escorted him out of the room. After a few moments, everyone returned to what they'd been doing before.

Another gentleman came in, looked about the room, shook his head, and left. Hudson couldn't blame him. It was a rather daunting prospect. Only the idea that Hudson held an advantage in Hestia gave him enough confidence to remain.

He supposed his title shored up his suit some as well, but as he was lower ranking than the woman's father, he rather thought being a viscount wouldn't matter much.

To Hudson's surprise, he only had to wait through three more visits before his name was called. Obviously this was a merit selection, not a timing one.

That meant he was a better choice than the sleeping man but not the card players. Considering the one who won this particular contest was the man on top, it didn't bode well for Hudson's chances.

Twenty-One

The butler escorted Hudson to a smaller parlor just across the front hall from the drawing room where the men were waiting.

Lady Rebecca and a woman he assumed was her mother sat side by side on a settee, while Lord Gliddon occupied a large chair in the corner to the left of the settee, reading a newspaper.

When Hudson entered, Lord Gliddon folded one side of the paper down and glared at him. Hudson met his stare for as long as he felt able, but eventually the need to blink forced him to break contact first.

Lord Gliddon gave a slight nod and lifted his paper back upright.

Hudson moved across the room to where Lady Rebecca sat, wearing that same small, serene smile she'd worn at the assembly. He glanced at Lord Gliddon's looming presence once more before sitting in the chair across from Lady Rebecca.

This couldn't be normal, could it? If it was, it was a wonder anyone in the aristocracy got married. Hudson was losing an entire day at his own estate to make this one short visit. If a man had to do this three, four, or more times, he'd have nothing to support his wife with by the time he finished courting her.

"Lord Stildon, have you met my mother?" Lady Rebecca looked at the woman beside her.

"No, I have not had the pleasure." He nodded and smiled as Lady Rebecca handled the introductions.

After that, he didn't know what to do. Was he meant to converse with Lady Rebecca as if her parents weren't there? Should he give them extra consideration? Did they want him to tell them about himself or simply see if he could manage polite discourse?

Why hadn't the two women outside the church included that information in their conversation?

"It is a pleasant day," Lady Rebecca said. "Did you ride from Hawksworth or walk?"

"Er, ride. I came over on my horse Hades."

"Is that the one you've decided on for your personal mount, then?" a gruff voice came from the corner.

Hudson snapped his gaze back and forth from Lady Rebecca to Lord Gliddon. He couldn't be rude and ignore the man, but it was more than a little awkward trying to angle in his seat in a way that would include everyone in the conversation. "Er, yes. His temperament suits me well."

"Fine stepper, that one. Told Stildon that myself. The old one, obviously."

Hudson swallowed. "Obviously."

"You've still got his dam in your stable, haven't you? Hestia?"

"Yes." Hudson swallowed the burst of anticipation. Was Hestia the advantage that had gotten him brought in ahead of some of the others?

A grunt was Lord Gliddon's only response, so Hudson shifted his focus back to Lady Rebecca. "You said you've a horse?"

She nodded. "Daffodil."

"I grew up with your father, you know." Lord Gliddon turned his paper down once more and caught Hudson's eye.

"Actually, I didn't know that, but it does make sense." Hudson looked back at the ladies, who seemed to see nothing unusual in the happenings. Whether or not this was the way they normally did things, Hudson had come today to visit Lady Rebecca, not her father. Though he wanted to impress the man, she was the one he'd be marrying. "Lady Rebecca, did you spend most of your childhood in this area?"

"We split our time between here and Yorkshire." She tilted her head. "You grew up in India?"

"Yes. My whole life until recently."

"Smartest thing your father ever did," Lord Gliddon said as he turned the page in his paper. "Your uncle always struck me as an odd sort of fellow. Went to school, you know."

"I had always assumed he had, yes sir. Did you attend a school somewhere, Lady Rebecca?"

She shook her head. "Governesses and tutors."

"He claimed he was going to become a lawyer," Lord Gliddon continued as if no one had spoken. "He did study law, but only for a year or so. Rumor was he only ever wanted to know about the trying of aristocrats and the legalities of title inheritance."

That description certainly fit with what little Hudson knew of his uncle. Still, what was Hudson to say in response? He could hardly agree with the man, given that Hudson's only interaction with his uncle was an angry, disgruntled letter that he hadn't even answered yet.

He looked over at Lady Rebecca, who sat still with her hands folded in her lap. He could only hope the smile he gave her looked more natural than it felt.

"What are you . . ." His sentence faded away as he realized he hadn't the faintest idea what to ask her. The unfinished sentence dangled in the air, taunting him.

It was ridiculous, really. Hudson was a man of many talents and accomplishments. He could shoot, ride, and manage property— everything a gentleman was supposed to be able to do, or so he had thought. His entire life had been dictated in such a way as to make him a proficient Englishman.

Yet here he was, without a single notion of what he was to do. Never had his father indicated how much of a viscount's life was spent socializing.

He cleared his throat and tried again. "That is to say"—*Think, think, think! What would you ask Bianca if she were the one sitting there?*—"are you looking forward to the cooler weather?"

That was most definitely not what he would say to Bianca, but at least it was a full question.

A few wrinkles appeared between Lady Rebecca's eyes, but the tiny frown soon smoothed away. Lady Gliddon's gaze narrowed on him and then looked over at her husband.

"I've never cared much for the cold," Lady Rebecca said.

Finally! Something they had in common. "I'm not anticipating it greatly either. I find that even now the air is far more chilled than I experienced in India."

"Oh? Was it very warm there?"

"Yes. Less rain as well."

"Oh." She paused and then sat a little straighter. "There's not many clouds in the sky today, so it probably won't rain."

"No, probably not."

Silence descended again.

Lord Gliddon's paper rattled once more, and Hudson held his breath, hoping that he would interrupt the conversation again, if only to give them something to say in return.

After a few tense moments, it was Lady Rebecca who came to his rescue. "Did you spend any time in London before coming to Newmarket?"

Not any more than he'd had to. "Only long enough to meet with the solicitor and make arrangements to travel here."

"You should have been here earlier," Lord Gliddon grumbled.

While Hudson agreed, he didn't much care for this stranger's opinion. Prospective father-in-law or not, Hudson wasn't about to discuss such personal details as how Hudson felt about his grandfather's constant encouragement to stay in India. "The ship that brought me here was the same ship that carried the news of his passing. I could not have arrived any earlier."

"We didn't even know you existed until Mr. Albany started shouting about collecting his horses in the pub one day. Said he'd come all the way from Ireland to collect his claim only to be told there was another heir. Thought he was going to bust the place up."

That this man knew more about Hudson's family than he did was disconcerting enough that Hudson wished desperately for something to do with his hands. Reins, a paper, a teacup, even a glass that he could swirl a swallow of brandy around in.

This must be why men had clubs. Ladies might be able to sit through tense moments such as these, but Hudson was agitated. Lord Gliddon must feel the same way. Hudson had a feeling the man had been reading the same paper throughout all the social visits this morning.

The butler arrived in the doorway. "It has been a quarter hour, my lady."

It had only been a quarter of an hour? It had felt like at least double that. And what was he supposed to do now? Depart, obviously, but it seemed like there should be some sort of notion whether or not he'd advanced his chances in the past few moments.

Lady Gliddon smiled at Hudson. "Thank you for coming."

He said his farewells and stood. Two steps from the door, Lady Rebecca stopped him.

"Lord Stildon?"

Hudson turned to look at her. "Yes, my lady?"

"I've nothing scheduled Thursday morning. If you wished to go for a walk, that is."

That was an indicator of success, wasn't it? "I would be honored to escort you on a walk."

There was a lightness in his step as he returned to the stable to collect his horse. Hades had been moved to one of the stalls, and Hudson stood to the side while the horse was collected and saddled.

Lord Brimsbane rode up, holding the reins of a riderless cream-colored horse in one hand.

"Lord Stildon." He dismounted and handed both of the horses over to stable boys. "Did you have a pleasant visit?"

"Quite." Hudson gestured to the pale horse. "Did you have to chase down a runaway?"

Lord Brimsbane laughed. "Hardly. I took a lady riding this morning. Rebecca graciously offered me the use of Daffodil so I could impress her."

Some of the happiness he'd been feeling moments earlier curdled and landed heavy in Hudson's gut. "And was she?"

"I believe so." Another laugh as the man tugged off his riding gloves. "Of course, Miss Snowley wouldn't tell me if she was better than the stock at Hawksworth, but she didn't seem to have any complaints."

"I see no reason why she should." Nor was there any reason why he shouldn't be happy with the news.

Yet, as he rode away, he had to resist the urge to send Hades galloping across the countryside.

BIANCA WAS RATHER NUMB when she returned to the house. She walked inside and paused in the middle of the front hall, mesmerized by the swirling pattern in the floor tile.

What had just happened?

Very well, she knew *what* had happened, but she didn't know why, and she didn't know how she felt about it. Or what she thought about it. Or even if she wanted it.

No, that wasn't right. She knew she wanted to be courted and get married. She just wasn't sure she wanted that with Lord Brimsbane.

She'd known him for years, or at least known who he was. It wasn't as if they'd been childhood friends or anything, but they'd been passing acquaintances.

What had changed to make him now willing to rise at an unheard-of hour in order to catch her at home before she went to Hawksworth for her morning ride?

That made about as much sense as she and her stepmother suddenly becoming—

"Oh good. You've returned."

Bianca looked up from the floor to see her stepmother in the drawing room doorway. "Did you need something?"

Mrs. Snowley gave Bianca a smile that looked more genuine than any she'd ever seen before. "I thought you might want to join me for tea."

"Tea."

"Yes."

Had she woken up in someone else's life this morning? Bianca gave a longing look to the stairs she should have escaped up immediately, but then moved toward the drawing room. She couldn't really say no, could she?

Considering the fact that Bianca was willing to actively pursue marriage in order to prevent the older woman from being detrimentally manipulative, she should at least sit down to tea with the woman and try to guess what was on her mind now.

A tea service was already set up in the little seating area in the far corner of the drawing room. It was a more intimate arrangement than the one Mrs. Snowley sat in to receive guests, and the drive, along with the lane beyond, could be seen through the window.

Beside the teapot sat two fine china cups.

Bianca stumbled to a halt. "Where's Marianne?"

"She's gone to town with Miss Wainsbright."

"Oh." Bianca sat gingerly on the edge of the chair, acutely aware that she was still in her riding habit, which bore the dust of a long ride and carried the aroma of horse and leather. The smell didn't bother her at all when in a stable or among the animals, but in a drawing room it made her feel at a distinct disadvantage.

Bianca accepted a cup of tea and bit her lip in order to keep from wincing. Mrs. Snowley never fixed Bianca's tea correctly. While the other woman preferred her tea with only the barest hint of sugar, Bianca liked it quite creamy.

In fact, she preferred it the exact color of the brew in her cup.

She had most definitely awoken in someone else's life.

After peering about the room to see if someone was lying in wait—to do what she didn't know, but it did feel as if she were being placed in a position to be caught off guard—she took a hesitant sip of the tea. It could have done with a bit more sweetness, but it was far better than what she normally received from her stepmother.

"I thought we could talk about what you were going to wear to the assembly Saturday." Mrs. Snowley set her cup down. "There's still time for us to make alterations or even buy you a new gown."

Bianca set her own cup down, ready to flee the room at a moment's need. "I believe the evening dresses I have are sufficient."

Mrs. Snowley continued as if Bianca hadn't spoken a word. "We could have Dorothy take in Marianne's pink dress for you. The one with the embroidered lace. What do you think?"

She'd rather try to dance in her most cumbersome riding habit.

"I've the perfect necklace and bracelet set to go with it," Mrs. Snowley continued. "The center stone is a ruby, but then the gems grow paler as they get farther from the middle."

Jewels as well? Absolutely not. "I would prefer to wear my own dresses and jewels. There is a reason I chose them, after all."

"Yes, yes." Mrs. Snowley waved one hand through the air. "But now you've attracted the attention of a future earl. I had no idea you had such potential. We must support it so you can make the most of this opportunity."

Bianca's shoulders straightened as she sat a bit taller. "If he's already seen me in my normal clothes and chosen to come for a visit anyway, I don't think I need to change my closet."

"You need to show him how much more you can be to secure him. Surprises keep a man interested." Mrs. Snowley took a sip of her tea. "Not to mention that everyone else will be wondering how you caught the attention of someone such as him."

Never, not once in all of Bianca's life, had she and her step-mother had a conversation like this one. While the words suggested that Mrs. Snowley was trying to be helpful and caring, it didn't feel like it.

"Why do you care? I thought you wanted me to marry Mr. Mead."

Another dismissive wave of her hand. Another stalling sip of tea. "That was before."

Bianca's gaze narrowed. "Before what?"

"Before I realized you could do better. One can't begin to fathom why Lord Brimsbane came to call on you. If it had been at any sort of normal time, I would have thought it possible he was trying to see Marianne, but no civilized lady is up and dressed at that hour."

Bianca's mouth gaped open a bit, but she didn't respond. How was someone supposed to answer anyone who made such a state-ment, much less someone who was supposed to be a sort of pa-rental figure?

"A woman isn't meant to understand the minds of men, though. They are such illogical creatures. It would make far more sense for him to be enraptured by Marianne, but since there's something about you, I'm committed to helping you expand upon it."

"By changing me," Bianca said flatly.

"Of course. Everything can be improved upon, don't you think? I've decided Mr. Mead isn't enough for you. Even if Lord Brims-bane comes to his senses, you've proven you can land a much bigger catch than Mr. Mead."

Mrs. Snowley sighed. "It will sadden your father, of course, but don't worry about that. I'll brave it in order to see you set up. We'll have to see to it quickly, of course, since Marianne is sure to marry this Season and we wouldn't want you to appear less desirable. I can make it happen, though. You've nothing to worry about."

Oh no, Bianca had everything to worry about. Mrs. Snowley wasn't doing this out of the kindness of her heart or some sudden arising of maternal instinct.

It was far too late for the other woman to be a mother to Bianca, and certainly not if she simply wanted to turn Bianca into the spitting image of Marianne. If this was what passed as affection and attention from Mrs. Snowley, it was potentially worse than being pushed aside.

"I believe"—Bianca rubbed her hands along her skirt and stood—"that I'll go get cleaned up."

While she was at it, she would contemplate her own plan for securing Lord Brimsbane. Preferably one that didn't leave her feeling like she'd sold her soul.

Twenty-Two

The next morning Bianca had no trouble getting out the door early. She wanted to avoid her stepmother, her father, Marianne, everyone. If she could have gotten dressed without Dorothy's assistance, she would have avoided her too.

She'd gotten little sleep, spending most of the quiet hours staring at the ceiling before falling into a fitful bout of slumber, then waking to stare at the ceiling once more.

Not a single conclusion had come her way.

One thing she did know was that she couldn't go back to the way it had been, even if that became a viable option. She understood now, as she hadn't then, that she'd been living a lonely existence. When she'd craved company before, she'd simply gone out. Everyone she encountered seemed happy enough to see her, and that had appeased her.

The arrival of Lord Stildon had thrown everything off course, and now she was too aware of what she lacked to return to idyllic naïveté.

Unfortunately, she also didn't know how to move forward. The only people she wanted to seek out were at Hawksworth. Lord Stildon, Aaron, the grooms. Spending time with them didn't move her toward her ultimate goal. If anything, it made finding a solution more difficult because it made the awkwardness of other interactions starkly obvious.

Would she be happier if she had no easy friendships, nothing to compare her other interactions to?

It was enough to make a girl feel very, very isolated. Even in church on Sunday, instead of feeling cozy and secure, the walls of her family's box pew had seemed like divisions between her and everyone else.

Even God.

Why would He allow her to get to a place where her only actual friends were a handful of grooms and a cantankerous stable manager? Oh, and an ignorant but confident viscount who made her notice everything she was missing but had no interest in filling those gaps himself?

Ah, but she needed a ride. A good, long ride with just her and a horse.

The answers that had eluded her all night would come on the back of the horse.

They had to.

Because if not, she didn't know what she would do. Continuing on in this disconcerted state of mind wasn't an option.

Apparently, she wasn't the only one with such a plan this morning.

Hades was tied to a post outside the stable as she approached, Lord Stildon standing at his side, ready to mount.

The horse greeted Bianca with a neigh and a slight bounce of his dark head, and then Lord Stildon turned, looking like he'd been caught doing something he shouldn't.

Bianca sighed. "Good morning."

"You needed to think too?"

"Yes. I can return home, though. Ride one of my father's horses." It was what she should have done to begin with. Even though the old carriage horses wouldn't bring the same pleasure, she would have been assured a private ride.

And she wouldn't have been faced with a reminder of what she couldn't have.

"There's no need." He gestured to the open door of the stable. "I've plenty of horses and can only ride one at a time."

He paused and looked down at his hands, taking a few moments to straighten gloves that already looked perfectly positioned. "Would you like to mount up with me or take a groom?"

Just moments ago she'd been hoping to avoid him, but somehow the fact that he offered just such a scenario gave her a peace about riding with him.

It would seem men were not the only illogical creatures.

"Why don't we go for a walk first?"

It was difficult to say who was more surprised by her statement, but once it was out, Bianca liked the idea immensely. Perhaps it wasn't the right time to outrun her thoughts. It wasn't as if pondering her problems on her own had kept her from thinking about him. Maybe thinking about them in his presence would present a solution.

And maybe she was a glutton for punishment.

"A walk first sounds lovely."

They strolled along the drive, even though her hem was already soaked through with morning dew from crossing the fields. Golds and yellows streaked the ground as the sun finished its climb above the horizon.

"What are you needing to contemplate?" Bianca asked. She rather thought he'd had everything planned out. What was he reconsidering? The spark of hope that surged through her was almost enough to make her turn around and run home.

"I visited Lady Rebecca yesterday."

"Oh?" The spark fizzled and crashed low in her gut.

"It didn't go as I had hoped it would."

"Oh?" Once more the flame sputtered to life.

"I was given permission to take her on a walk Thursday, so

I suppose it wasn't a complete lack of success, but it was all so very strange."

"Oh." Doused. Again. Apparently Lady Rebecca was indeed everything Lord Stildon wanted in a wife, and meeting her hadn't made him rethink his plans. It would also seem that Lady Rebecca—or Lord and Lady Gliddon—saw something promising in him.

"Are all courtships like this? Is there something else I should be doing?"

"I'm afraid I don't know. I've never been courted."

"You danced with Lord Rigsby," he said. "And went riding with Lord Brimsbane."

"How did you know about that?" Bianca turned her head sharply to study his face.

He gave a shrug. "I was leaving the stable as Brimsbane returned. He told me he'd been riding with you."

And the news had meant nothing at all to Lord Stildon. If she needed any more proof that he wasn't suffering from the same overwhelming attraction she was—and really, any sane person would have had more than enough—there it was.

"Did you enjoy your ride?"

"Yes." Bianca looked down at her toes, watching the boots appear and disappear as she walked. "He brought me a fine horse."

She pushed a smile onto her face and looked up at him. She'd still committed to being his friend, and given her recent realization of how few of those she had, she couldn't afford to lose even an unconventional one.

"What makes you think it was strange?" she asked. "Perhaps that's simply the way courtships are done in England, Lord Stildon."

He chuckled. "If we're going to continue to have discussions such as this, I do believe a less formal address would be appropriate." He took her elbow and guided them into a slow arc so that they were strolling back in the direction of the stable. "Perhaps meeting you and Aaron before anyone else ruined me. I don't really find the discussions of clouds interesting when I know conversations can be so much more."

She nodded along with everything he said, but part of her was stuck back at his casual offer of the use of his name. It was an intimacy she shouldn't allow since they weren't courting. Then again, they *were* friends.

How convenient an excuse that was for her to continue torturing herself.

Mentally accepting it, though, didn't mean she was ready to utter the man's name. "I think clouds can still be interesting." She pointed into the sky. "That one rather looks like a horse."

He laughed and came to a stop as he tilted his head up. "So it does." He pointed to another cloud farther to the right. "I believe that one is a teacup."

They pointed out clouds and shapes for several minutes until their interpretations became rather ridiculous. When she declared a long, thin wisp of a cloud looked like a riding crop, he declared they should return to the stable and go on their ride.

He offered her his arm and she took it without thought, then immediately wished she hadn't. Especially when he said, "Would it be presumptuous for me to ask permission to use your given name? Only in private, of course. Miss Snowley feels so . . . formal. Of course, you may use Hudson."

That seemed like a very bad idea. The granting of that leniency would make her an utter fool. "You may call me Bianca."

She must have enjoyed her sleepless night more than she realized.

"Bianca." He gave her a warm smile. "I like it."

The sound of her given name in his voice rolled through her ears, down her arms, raising the hairs as it went until it settled into a low thrum at the point where her arm connected with his.

"Bianca," he mused again, and she couldn't decide if he should stop saying her name or continue saying it over and over. "You still haven't told me what you think I should do."

He didn't want her to answer that question. Not really. At least, not truthfully. It would rob them both of this strange camaraderie.

She took a deep breath. Perhaps, if she treaded lightly into dangerous territory, he would join her there. "I think that going after what you truly want with honesty might be simpler than all this planning."

He pursed his lips and nodded thoughtfully. "I agree."

Perhaps she'd treaded a little too lightly. "I think . . ." She drew out the word to buy herself and her gathering courage more time. "Such honesty requires boldness. You have to look at what you really want and articulate it." Another deep breath, and she plunged on before she could stop herself. "Sometimes in doing that we learn what we actually want isn't what we initially thought."

"I think I know what you're saying." The look he gave her was soft and thoughtful.

Bianca's heart pounded so hard she could feel the vibration of her chest. "You do?"

He nodded. "I should be honest with Lady Rebecca. I should tell her that though my initial interest was inspired by something else, there are many traits about her that I admire and I am fully committed to getting to know her better."

He was choosing another woman.

And she couldn't even be mad about that, because it was the woman he'd chosen from the very beginning.

He escorted her back to the stable. "Shall we go for that ride now?"

Odysseus had been saddled while they were walking, and Bianca all but flew to the horse's side. Now she definitely needed the mind-clearing wind of a good, long ride.

Unfortunately, all she felt as the morning breeze bit through her jacket was cold.

HUDSON SPENT THE rest of that day and the next in and around town. He needed to know people, to know the area, to see and to be seen before he took Lady Rebecca for a walk.

It was also time to really take control of his horses. The lands had already been planted for the year, and there wasn't much he could do to manage this year's harvest.

Races, however, were just around the corner. Aaron had already lined up the entries for the October meeting, and Hudson was interested in seeing some of the different training regimens the stable manager had instituted.

Aaron had ordered the trainer not to sweat the horses, so they did their morning gallops without heavy blankets wrapped about their bodies. Combined with the abundance of box stalls he had created, the man was a visionary. Everything he had done so far seemed to result in high-quality horses, so Hudson decided to reserve judgment until he saw the effects.

While hanging about the training gallops, he'd encountered Brimsbane multiple times. After several conversations, Hudson came to a simple conclusion.

His potential future brother-in-law was as dull as a horseshoe.

He was loyal, noble, and honorable—everything Hudson had been told a lord should be, and perhaps that was the problem. His travel had been decent, his school exemplary, his childhood antics nonexistent or easily pushed away from memory. Even his preference of horse and clothing was predictable.

He was a textbook gentlemanly aristocrat.

Which meant he was exactly what Bianca was looking for. After all, Lady Rebecca was a portrait of ladylike sensibilities, which made her ideal for Hudson. Why should her brother be any different?

Hudson adjusted his coat and wiggled his toes in his new boots as he walked down the street. He'd taken to having at least one meal in town most days, though whether it was to be in the midst of a crowd like he'd had in India, to see more of the town, or simply to eat something other than his cook's fare, he didn't know.

What he did know was that he was tired of eating alone. Everywhere he went he either sat by himself in silence, endured numerous introductions, or received endless speculation on whether or not Hawksworth could survive with Hudson at the reins.

Those last conversations made Hudson want to punch something, preferably the one speaking, but he also understood. He had to prove himself to these people, and he would. As soon as possible.

Still, he'd like to eat a meal without having to defend himself.

Lord Rigsby was exiting the Jockey Club as Hudson walked by.

"Lord Rigsby." Hudson nodded at the building behind the man. "Are you a member?"

"No, but I'd like to be. I was delivering a message for my father." The man shrugged. "It could have easily been sent by messenger or even the post, but delivering it myself gave me an excuse to talk with the members."

It sounded as if Lord Rigsby had something to prove as well. "I was heading to eat. Would you care to join me?"

"I've heard the food at Rutland's is commendable."

Hudson looked around the immediate area. "Do you know where that is?"

Lord Rigsby looked around. "There aren't that many roads in Newmarket. We should be able to find it."

It took them two wrong turns and one case of retracing their steps, but they located the restaurant.

The food was almost as bland as what Hudson got at home, but the company was the most interesting he'd had outside his own stable.

If only the man hadn't asked so many questions about Bianca.

Twenty-Three

On Wednesday night, Hudson attended a musicale at an estate north of town. The room felt nearly as crowded as the public assemblies, and the conversation was equally as inane, though here it seemed more peppered with empty flatteries.

They should simply parade everyone around in a circle like a horse auction. It would be more honest.

Lady Rebecca stood next to her brother near the center of the room, a cluster of people around her, both men and women. Other groupings of people radiated out like flower petals.

Hudson was pleased to realize that he recognized many of the people in the room, even if he didn't feel particularly inclined to talk to them. That, at least, was a familiar feeling. In India, he lived near Fort St. George and frequently found himself in a room with the officers stationed there.

Perhaps his discomfort with those men who were born in England and saw India as a land to be conquered instead of embraced should have told him that he wouldn't be quite normal when he transplanted himself.

None of that mattered now. Hudson knew what he could do with his horses, was confident he knew enough to manage the rest of the estate, though the manager his grandfather had put in place seemed more than competent, and thought that a fresh look on the world might be just what the peerage of this country needed.

All he had to do now was convince everyone else.

He rolled his shoulders to adjust the fit of his jacket collar and started working his way across the room to Lady Rebecca's large circle.

It had been a while since he'd ridden in a proper race, since he'd outgrown the size for a jockey, but he still knew how to take advantage of small gaps when people shifted, and he soon found himself in the center of the group.

"We meet again, Lord Stildon." Lady Rebecca smiled at him.

It was the same smile she gave everyone, the same one that seemed a permanent fixture on her face. How was he to know if she was happy to see him or not?

"Yes, we do," he replied. "Have you heard tonight's singer before?"

She nodded. "In London. She's very good. She's Mrs. Englebert's cousin."

The way she said the sentence seemed like it was supposed to have some sort of significance to him, but he hadn't a clue why it should matter. Still, he nodded and gave a murmur of understanding because he didn't see how what he was missing could matter overmuch.

They discussed all the normal subjects, including many of the other nearby people in their conversation. Hudson knew some of the names that were mentioned in the gossip portion of the conversation, which came after the weather and comments on the number of people in attendance, but he didn't know why anyone cared about these details of their lives.

Very well, he could see why someone might be interested in knowing that Mr. Mead's horse had thrown him into a bush this morning. The man had probably deserved it, though the horse was likely to pay the penalty.

Finally, it was time to sit for the musicale, but Hudson hadn't positioned himself in such a way as to be able to claim a seat beside Lady Rebecca or even one in the area immediately in front of or behind her. He glanced around and noticed Bianca and Lord Rigsby sitting three rows back.

Bianca might not appreciate Hudson interrupting her conversation, but she would understand his desire to sit beside someone he knew for the next hour, so he moved to join her.

"Good evening," he said as he sat on her other side.

Lord Rigsby arched an eyebrow, reminding Hudson of the way Aaron looked just before he told Hudson he was wrong about something. All the man said, though, was "Good evening."

Bianca nodded at him, her smile wide and welcoming. "Are you anxious to have a taste of English music?"

Hudson glanced down at the card he'd been handed with the evening's list of songs on it. "It appears to be rather French in nature."

Lord Rigsby chuckled. "Don't let anyone else hear you say that. Just because the words are in French, it doesn't mean the performance is French. It means it's fancy."

A suppressed laugh escaped Bianca for a moment. "And expensive."

"That too," Lord Rigsby said with a nod.

For the first time, Hudson felt like he was intruding when in Bianca's company.

He didn't care for the feeling.

"You need a new ball gown."

Bianca looked up from the book she was reading in the upstairs parlor. It was in an area of the house that was only used by guests, so her stepmother never ventured up here, yet there she stood in the doorway, Marianne trailing behind her, looking around as if she hadn't lived in this house all her life.

After sticking a finger in her book to hold her place, Bianca gave Mrs. Snowley her attention. "Why do I need a new ball gown? I've only worn the one I ordered in the spring twice, and Dorothy changed the trim on last year's so that it practically looks like a new dress."

Bianca's evening dress collection was quite extensive and replenished regularly, but ball gowns? There weren't that many events that called for them, since the aristocracy came to Newmarket for races and more casual interactions before or after the extravagance of their London springs.

Mrs. Snowley pressed her lips together in the disappointed expression Bianca was accustomed to. At least that false attempt at strangling motherly guidance wasn't making a reappearance.

"You cannot wear a dress you've worn before to the Gliddon ball," she gritted out. "This is going to be the event of the year, I'm absolutely certain. Any number of matches will be decided that night."

"As I'm fairly certain Lord Gliddon hopes to announce Lady Rebecca's choice there, I do hope no one intends to claim the gathering for their own."

"Of course not," Mrs. Snowley said, an unspoken derogatory name dripping from the end of her sentence. "Pairings will be decided there, though, I'm certain of it."

"Miss Wainbright intends to see if Lord Davers can be lured out into the garden," Marianne said idly, as if she hadn't announced that her dearest friend was plotting to trap one of the town's confirmed bachelors into marriage. "She said the Gliddons' garden is perfect for getting caught in."

Instead of looking appalled, Mrs. Snowley's face grew thoughtful as she turned toward her daughter. "Did she say how she intends to do this?"

"By risking her reputation, obviously," Bianca murmured.

Mrs. Snowley jerked her head to face forward. "Yes. Well.

You still need a new dress. I'm taking you to the modiste this morning."

If Mrs. Snowley took Bianca to the modiste, she'd end up with a dress of flounces and ribbon, with uncomfortable embroidery irritating her skin all evening.

"I will agree to a new dress," Bianca said slowly, "but I'm going to the shop on my own." She resisted the urge to add that she'd been doing so for the past six years. "I'll take Dorothy."

"Dorothy is mending Marianne's dress for this evening. You can take Helen."

Mrs. Snowley's lady's maid would report back to her mistress everything Bianca chose, right down to the thread color, but it was a sort of compromise, so Bianca agreed. Besides, she was more interested in knowing where Marianne was headed this evening.

"I thought there was nothing on tonight's calendar. Where is Marianne going?"

"Dinner at Lady Kelbrooke's." She waved a hand through the air. "I didn't think you would be interested, so I declined on your behalf. It'll leave you plenty of time to finish your book."

How many other invitations had been turned down on Bianca's behalf before? She would love to attend dinner at Lady Kelbrooke's. It was said they had some of the finest horse-related art in the world hanging in their house. They even owned a Gainsborough painting.

Lord and Lady Kelbrooke also had an unmarried son who didn't tend to socialize much. A dinner party at their house would definitely attract the attention of any marriage-minded girl and her mother. And, apparently, inspire that marriage-minded mother to leave her stepdaughter out of the running.

Bianca snapped her book shut and set it aside. "Since I've so much time later, I suppose there's no reason I shouldn't go to the modiste now."

If nothing else, it would get her out of her stepmother's presence.

DESPITE KNOWING THAT Helen was trying to subtly take notes in a little notebook about everything Bianca chose, she enjoyed her time at the dressmaker.

The pattern she selected had a great deal of decorative flounces, but since they circled the skirt from the hem to the knee, she wouldn't have any of them rubbing against her arms or getting in the way while she danced.

The short bodice was a silk so thin it was nearly sheer, layered over a dark green, with only the underlying coloring and the neckline as decoration.

Bianca was absolutely in love with the dress. She couldn't wait for it to be ready for a fitting.

Her buoyancy lasted until she stepped out of the shop and into the path of a promenading couple. She'd known, of course, that today was the day Hudson was taking Lady Rebecca for a walk.

She hadn't thought she would have to see it firsthand.

Yet, there they were, arm in arm, being watched over by Lord Brimsbane instead of a maid. Hudson was correct that this courtship didn't seem to be going as normal. Bianca wasn't sure if she should confirm that for him, though.

She intended to smile and nod her greetings, but none of the party seemed interested in letting her escape so easily. After exchanging pleasantries, she moved to go on her way when Lord Brimsbane stepped up. "Would you care to walk with us?"

"Please do," Lady Rebecca said. "It will make Arthur stop looking like an overbearing brother."

"I am an overbearing brother."

She shook her head and gave a light laugh. "Be that as it may, there's no reason to tell the world. Two couples on a stroll will garner far less attention."

Lord Brimsbane offered Bianca his arm, and there was nothing she could do but accept it, especially since Helen was already scribbling away in her notebook.

She took his arm and smiled brightly. "Where are we walking to?"

"I haven't the slightest," Lord Brimsbane said with a shrug. "Rebecca chose the way."

Lady Rebecca looked back at her. "Why don't you lead for a while? I was simply showing Lord Stildon the town, since he is new here."

Bianca gladly accepted the role of guide, partly because it gave her something to focus on, but also because it meant Hudson and Lady Rebecca were now behind her and well out of her line of vision.

She'd tried to settle herself on the idea that Lord Brimsbane would make a suitable husband. He was everything a girl could ask for. It wasn't as if many husbands and wives spent a great deal of time in each other's company. At least she knew he would be kind to her.

But if her future meant a lifetime of watching Hudson with Lady Rebecca, she would have to reconsider.

Or get over this crazy infatuation with Hudson.

Perhaps both were in order.

She directed them toward the center of town and the one Newmarket site Hudson probably hadn't even known existed.

They walked along in companionable silence, Lord Brimsbane occasionally remarking on a store window as they passed it, until they reached the stone pillar at the center of town.

Bianca threw her arm out with a great flourish. "And this is where it all began."

Hudson looked from her to the pillar to the building just behind it. "The Crown? I wouldn't have thought the pub your normal establishment. Is this a frequent haunt of yours?"

Bianca tried not to smile, truly she did, but she couldn't help laughing as she said, "No. This is where the races began. We've other courses now, obviously, but this is the starting marker. Racing from here to the center of Cambridge is thirteen miles."

Hudson looked down the path, and Lord Brimsbane shared the history of the straight path that once lay between the towns and how the courses and landscape had changed over time.

Bianca was impressed with his knowledge, but not with the man's delivery or his timing. The longer they stood here discussing racecourses, the longer she had to watch Hudson and Lady Rebecca arm in arm.

A man exited The Crown and grumbled about them blocking the road, which gave Bianca the perfect excuse to suggest they continue walking.

She also took the opportunity to disconnect herself from Lord Brimsbane's arm. As perfect as the man seemed, walking so close to his side had made her feel awkward and crowded.

Pointing at a brick building, she said, "The palace was there." She frowned. "Or is still there? The Duke of Rutland turned that part into an inn not two years ago, but the rest still belongs to the king, I think. There are rumors that they intend to sell off the other sections of the palace. It's just as well because—"

"Watch out there." An arm snagged around Bianca's waist and swung her clear of a large puddle.

Instinctively, Bianca threw an arm around her rescuer's neck as he lowered her to the ground. She was plastered to his side, and it didn't feel at all uncomfortable the way walking had a moment ago.

Then she looked down and saw that the arm around her waist wasn't encased in grey wool. It was wrapped in the brown that Hudson was wearing.

Twenty-Four

In one hand, he held the elbow of the woman he hoped to marry, while his other arm was wrapped around the middle of the woman who had vowed to help him accomplish that.

His mind should have been awash with the awkwardness of such a situation, but all he could think about was that here, away from the horses and leather, she smelled like sunshine. There wasn't a perfumer in the world who could accomplish such a feat, but there she was.

And here he was, still holding her pressed to his side.

He jerked his arm away and stepped back, securing Lady Rebecca's arm more solidly against his own and pulling her side into contact with his upper arm. Though he tried to ignore it, there was no denying the difference between the two women. It had been impossible to miss the strength Bianca had acquired as an avid horsewoman, just as he couldn't help but notice the softness of his walking partner.

Lord Brimsbane rushed to Bianca's side and placed a steadying hand on her back, even though she'd already righted her own balance. "Are you all right?"

She laughed and nodded. "Of course I am." She stuck a foot out and shook it. "As are my slippers." She turned her smile in

Hudson's direction, but she didn't meet his gaze. "You may consider your rescue successful, my lord."

"Yes. Good." He looked down at Lady Rebecca. "Shall we continue our walk?"

"Around the puddle or over it?"

Hudson blinked down at her. Had Lady Rebecca just made a joke? Her expression was the same as it always was, leaving him confused and off balance.

He guided her around the puddle, looking anywhere for something to talk about, but there was nothing but people he barely knew and the building they'd just been looking at. That was better than nothing, he supposed. "So, this was the palace?"

"Yes." Lady Rebecca nodded. "Built by Charles the Second."

"Of course."

They lapsed once more into silence as they strolled farther down the street. Hudson shouldn't have been aware of the couple now walking behind them, but the echo of each soft step on the pavement refused to be ignored.

"Mr. Whitworth manages your stable, does he not?" Lady Rebecca asked.

Hudson almost missed a step and had to shift his feet quickly to maintain their rhythm. It was the first time she'd given any indication of interest in his horses, his stable, or even his estate. "Er, yes. My grandfather hired him when he took ill."

She nodded and then gestured down a side street that rolled through the south end of town. "The other stable he manages is about two miles down that road."

"Oh?" He didn't know much about the other stable Aaron managed, only that Aaron avoided running them against each other for anything except the largest and most important of purses.

The question was, why would Lady Rebecca know? Or care?

"It's owned by the Earl of Trenting," she said. "He doesn't come to town much, but we saw him in London. I thought he and his son were going to have a fight in the middle of the ballroom because they didn't realize their tailor had made them the exact same jacket until they arrived there."

He relaxed with a slight shake of his head. For a moment he'd thought they were going to talk about horses. He had to admire that Lady Rebecca had found some way to connect the information to him, but it also baffled him that the most she'd ever said to him was a story about a party in London. Did she miss the city? Was she hoping to spend more time there?

He had to admit that life in the countryside was the only thing he'd adjusted to quickly in England. He very much enjoyed the space in Newmarket, as opposed to the tight streets of India. "Do you plan to return to London soon?"

Her gaze dropped to the pavement. "Probably not. Father goes for the Parliament, of course, but he prefers it here in the country."

That answer didn't settle Hudson's budding concern.

"I see our carriage up ahead," Lord Brimsbane said. "Father must have known you would walk too far and planned accordingly."

Had Hudson taken her too far? The Gliddon residence was on the edge of town, and Lady Rebecca had suggested that they make their way down High Street, but perhaps Hudson should have insisted upon a shorter route?

"It is more likely that Mother was concerned about the possibility of rain and didn't want to be unable to dress my hair for tonight." Lady Rebecca placed one hand on her bonnet and angled her face toward the sky. "Does it look like it might rain?"

Hudson glanced up. "Not particularly, though there are clouds." He pointed at one. "Look. That one looks like a rabbit."

Lady Rebecca tilted her head. "I suppose," she said slowly.

"The one beside it could be a carrot," Bianca said from behind him.

Lord Brimsbane stepped forward. "There's no sense not using

the carriage since it is here. May we offer you and your maid a lift home?" He looked toward the woman who'd been trailing several feet behind the group. "I'm afraid she'd have to ride up with the driver, but we should be able to manage."

Hudson held his breath while he waited for Bianca to answer. As successful as he felt this walk had been, it was still only with her and Aaron that he didn't feel like he was riding the wrong way on a racecourse.

Not that he needed her presence. He'd been getting along well enough with Lady Rebecca before they bumped into Bianca. It was just that he would welcome someone else coming along to help carry the conversation.

"I, well, yes, thank you. That would be lovely." She slid her hand free of Lord Brimsbane's arm in order to prepare to climb into the carriage, but she remained looking up at him, a smile on her face.

Had Bianca decided upon Lord Brimsbane, then? Did she have designs for the other viscount? Even though she'd been sitting beside Lord Rigsby at the musicale, it might have simply been because she couldn't get to Brimsbane.

Then again, weren't women known for changing their minds or hiding their true intentions? That was certainly the prevailing sentiment in the assembly cardroom and at the training stables. Bianca had always seemed different to him, but she was still a woman.

If he needed confirmation of that, he had only to remember what it felt like when he'd swung her away from that puddle.

Bianca's choices weren't what was important right now, though. He slid his hand into Lady Rebecca's. "May I assist you into the carriage, my lady?"

"Yes, thank you."

Brimsbane followed his sister into the carriage after helping the maid up onto the driver's bench. His expression was unreadable as he gave Hudson a good, long look before climbing into the conveyance.

Hudson could only try to guess if that meant the man was contemplating throwing him out of the moving carriage.

The ladies were chatting about a gathering scheduled for tonight. It didn't sound as if Bianca was attending, but it was one of the ones she'd told Hudson to attend.

Hudson sighed. Another basketful of invitations had arrived since he'd gone through the pile with Bianca. He needed to hire someone to handle his affairs. It was as good a conversation to have with a man as any.

"I haven't had a chance to hire personal servants," he said to Brimsbane. "Have you suggestions on where to hire a secretary?"

As with his discourse on the original race path, Brimsbane had a great deal of information to deliver with very little inflection. Was it because the man was boring, or had he decided he didn't like Hudson after all? The conversation wasn't brusque, but it wasn't friendly either.

The carriage rolled to a stop a few moments later, and Hudson didn't recognize the house they pulled up to. Its blocklike structure was far more conventional than his round house, though he still marveled at the plainness of it. No one of any wealth lived in something this simple in India.

The front door of the house opened, and two women spilled out. Bianca sighed as she saw her stepmother and sister but managed to smile and thank Lord Brimsbane and Lady Rebecca for the ride.

Hudson moved toward the door. "I'll assist the maid down, shall I?"

He climbed out, and Mrs. Snowley's eyes widened a bit. "My lord." Her gaze flicked sideways to see Bianca emerging from the cab. "Thank you for seeing her home."

Hudson nodded and went to assist the maid.

Brimsbane followed Bianca out of the carriage. "It was our pleasure."

Hudson turned from the maid in time to see Mrs. Snowley eying the brother and sister the way a horse watched a lump of sugar. She stepped closer to the carriage, where Lady Rebecca was framed by a square of light created by the open door.

"We were pleased to receive an invitation to your upcoming ball, Lady Rebecca. So kind of you to remember us."

"Of course," the young woman said, her voice carrying a pleasant iciness that hadn't been present in any other conversation Hudson could recall. It would seem there *were* people Lady Rebecca didn't care for. "Bianca tells me you intend to be at Lady Kelbrooke's gathering tonight."

Hudson frowned. Hadn't Bianca said she wasn't attending anything tonight?

"Yes," Mrs. Snowley said, glancing at her daughter and then back to the carriage. "We wouldn't miss it."

"We shall see you there."

That was the handiest, most polite dismissal Hudson had ever witnessed. Such polite rudeness wasn't a prevarication he'd had much practice with, but he could certainly see its occasional advantages.

It was obvious that Mrs. Snowley knew exactly how to take Lady Rebecca's comment, as her smile tightened and she stepped away from the carriage to allow Hudson to climb back in. Once he was situated inside, the door shut and the carriage rolled into motion.

For the first time he could remember, Lady Rebecca wasn't smiling. The expression on her face was very clearly a frown. He hadn't even been positive her face could contort into such a shape. Then she seemed to remember she wasn't alone, and she sat back, clearing her face of all expression.

Brimsbane laughed. "You can likely speak freely, sister. If Lord

Stildon counts Miss Snowley among his companions"—that un-
interpretable hard look came Hudson's way once more—"and I
believe we can assume he does, he wouldn't hold Mrs. Snowley
in high esteem."

"I don't make a practice of speaking ill of others in company,
Arthur. Even if we are all in agreement."

Brimsbane laughed again. "You never speak ill of anyone. You
simply make it quietly clear they are beneath your touch."

"It is the ladylike thing to do." She glanced at Hudson once
more before lowering her head to stare at her hands.

He could hardly say it, but the truth was, her ability to behave
in such a way only convinced him all the more that Lady Rebecca
was the right wife for him. Given how little he knew about navigating English society, having a wife with honed skills in doing so
would be nothing but an advantage. Yes, every moment he spent
with Lady Rebecca proved she was ideal for his needs.

So why did the idea of spending life with her at his side fill him
with dread?

Twenty-Five

Bianca had been out in society at functions both large and small for six years. Never, in all that time, had she felt the need to hide in the retiring room.

Until now.

The maid assigned to oversee the room was beginning to look at Bianca with a pitying expression, and Bianca couldn't even blame her. There had to be something wrong when a girl fixed the same curl fifteen times in a row. At this point, she was pretty much flicking it and watching it bounce.

On Friday morning, it had been raining too much for even Bianca to brave the elements, and she'd been stuck inside the house. In a moment of weakness, she had accepted her sister and stepmother's invitation to paint screens with them.

In addition to the creative pursuit, she received a very long diatribe on the goings-on of the party she'd been spared from attending. Marianne would have done a gossip paper proud with all the details she remembered.

Particularly around every woman Lord Brimsbane deigned to pour attention onto.

"Truly, it's better you hear it from us," Mrs. Snowley said as she tilted her head to study her flower. "Even I was caught up in the idea that he might fancy you for a moment, but water does always seek its own level eventually."

Marianne sighed. "At least Lady Rebecca is showing a marked preference now, which means some of the men are more seriously available." She dabbed at her screen. "Of course, some of them are convinced that Lord Stildon could still falter, but she spent nearly half the night talking to him and danced with him twice."

"He's a mystery that holds a certain amount of appeal." Mrs. Snowley smiled at her daughter. "You've still got a bit of that, as this is only your second Season. Everyone already knows Bianca and look where that's gotten her."

Nowhere. It had gotten her precisely nowhere.

Bianca's landscape had started to look a great deal like the stormy one beyond the window.

And then her life followed suit.

With Lord Brimsbane seemingly seeking other company, Mrs. Snowley had once again set her sights on Mr. Mead for Bianca. It was enough to make Bianca consider running off with the chimney sweep.

If she knew who the chimney sweep was. Surely it couldn't be that difficult to find him.

Bianca twirled her curl one more time. She really should go back out there, but everywhere she went, she encountered Mr. Mead. He'd been waiting near the entrance when she arrived at tonight's assembly and immediately offered to escort her to the refreshment table—as if anyone wanted to visit that particular area of the room before they were desperate. But her father had beamed at the idea of his dearest friend's son escorting his elder daughter, so Bianca had agreed. It was a cup of punch. How bad could it be?

As it turned out, very bad. Punch turned into the first set of dances. In the second set he managed to get himself lined up directly next to her, so he might as well have been her partner again.

And through it all, he complimented her.

Loudly.

And with great insult.

"That coiffure is lovely. I can hardly tell that your forehead is as wide as a horse's hoof."

"Have you started taking care to remove yourself from the sun more often? No? Perhaps that gown simply makes you look paler."

"I meant to tell you at the Wainbrights' card party last week that you play very well for one who never gave proper care to her education."

Did he think Bianca was going to be flattered by his statements, or had he decided she needed to be publicly brought down?

Whatever it was, Bianca had had more than enough. As she'd told Hudson before, though, leaving before midnight wasn't really an option. Hiding out in the retiring room, however, was. She'd now been in there long enough to make anyone who'd noticed her departure very concerned.

The retiring room door opened, and Lady Rebecca poked her head in. "There you are."

Bianca's eyes widened, and her gaze met Lady Rebecca's in the mirror. Aside from that very strange stroll through town the other day, they'd never had cause to spend much time in each other's company. "You were looking for me?"

"Yes. I was hoping you would agree to partner Arthur for the next waltz."

"I . . . well . . ." Everything her mother had said the day before about Lord Brimsbane's behavior flooded her mind. She rather doubted the man was in need of partners. There wasn't a girl around who would turn him down. "Does he *want* to partner with me?"

Lady Rebecca winced and came farther into the room so she could perch on a chair next to Bianca's. She bit her lip and sighed.

Never before had Bianca seen Lady Rebecca look unsure. Meek, yes, but not unsure. "He hasn't confided in me, of course, but I do think he's finding this whole evening quite wearisome. I was . . . well, may I be frank?"

"Do you think you can?" Bianca almost bit her tongue at the uncouth question. "I'm sorry, that was rude."

"It's understandable," she said, nearly making Bianca sigh and wish the other woman would stand up for herself for once. "Arthur has been by my side all evening. He's stood up with me, stood next to me, and stood in the way so that only one gentleman at a time could approach me. He's been trying to give me all his attention, and it's making some of the women rather angry and desperate. They've been quite insulted when he's paid more attention to my conversation than to his partner. I don't blame them for getting upset about it, but Arthur is simply worried that I'll end up with someone horrible because Father will declare I have to. You've never shown much inclination to marriage, and you and Arthur have seemed to get on well together of late, so I think you'll either finally allow him to focus on something else or forgive him if he's a bit distracted."

Bianca blinked, opened her mouth to speak, and blinked again. Was that how people saw her? Did everyone in Newmarket think she had no interest in marrying? Was that why Lord Brimsbane had been giving her attention? Did he think her safe?

She swallowed and tried to smile. It wasn't Lady Rebecca's fault. In fact, Bianca should be thankful for the woman's uncommon candor. "I don't think I've ever heard you put that many words together at a time."

Lady Rebecca frowned. "I usually don't need to. Or don't get a chance to." She sighed. "I normally don't have that much to say at one time."

Bianca couldn't stay in this room forever, and if anyone out there was going to be significant enough to keep Mr. Mead away, it would be Lord Brimsbane. Even if Bianca was unsure of a future with him if it included Lady Rebecca as Lady Stildon—or if he thought her a dedicated spinster—she didn't mind spending time with the man.

It didn't excite her overmuch, but she didn't mind.

And if it made Mrs. Snowley wonder once more if Bianca was going to marry in a way that let her outrank her sister, that was an added benefit.

"It would be my honor to, well, save your brother from himself, I suppose."

The smile she got in return was sweet and perfectly proportioned.

The chambermaid opened the door for the two ladies and gave Bianca a pitying smile that did nothing to boost her confidence.

She stuck close to Lady Rebecca's side, knowing that she would be as good a deterrent as any to whomever else her stepmother thought to send.

"I found you a partner for the waltz, brother."

Bianca winced. Her only saving grace was that Lady Rebecca had said the words softly enough that no one heard them besides Bianca and Lord Brimsbane.

Her brother turned with a sigh. "I don't need you to—oh." His forbearing expression slid into a smile. "Miss Snowley."

Bianca gave a small curtsy. "My lord."

"I hope my sister didn't put too much pressure on you to accept her invitation on my behalf."

"No." Bianca glanced at Lady Rebecca before pressing on. If these social gatherings were going to be a disaster anyway, she might as well be herself while being miserable. "It is a favor among ladies, you know, to distract the older brothers long enough for a woman to enjoy a waltz."

Lord Brimsbane had no reaction, but Lady Rebecca suddenly found the floor immensely interesting as her shoulders gave a slight shake.

"And here I thought I was being of assistance by managing the hordes."

"You are," Lady Rebecca said, "but my next waltz is with Lord Stildon, so I think you can relax for a while."

"Hmmm."

Bianca was thankful neither of them seemed to expect her to say more as the music started and the couples formed. Lord Stildon collected Lady Rebecca and sent a strange look in Bianca's direction before leading his future wife away.

Even the prospect of riding Hades didn't lessen the impact of that view.

Lord Brimsbane offered his arm, and she took it. Soon they had joined the crush of couples whirling about the room.

"Have you been riding lately?"

He nodded. "I ride every morning."

"Even yesterday? Did you get caught in the rain?"

He nodded again. "My horse, Uzziah, doesn't care for storms, so it took me a while to get back, but I dried out well enough. Were you out in it?"

"No, it was raining before I could leave the house."

"What about this morning?"

Something was off about Lord Brimsbane's tone. Had Bianca become suspected of some crime she didn't know about? If Lord Brimsbane were the local magistrate, she'd wonder if Mrs. Snowley hadn't decided to try to get Bianca out of her life another way.

"Er, I rode one of my father's horses this morning."

He tilted his head and watched Bianca as he guided her around. "You didn't go riding with Lord Stildon?"

"No." She swallowed. She'd thought that her known presence at Hawksworth would temper the gossip about her and Lord Stildon. Was she wrong? Had Lady Rebecca arranged this dance because she was worried about the relationship between her and Hudson?

Bianca swallowed, wondering how she could defend herself while still maintaining her dignity. "Hawksworth has always generously allowed me the use of their horses, as my father's stock is somewhat lacking."

"Hmmm."

They danced in silence, but the tension seemed somewhat less. Had she convinced him that she wasn't a threat? Because she wasn't. Hudson had made that abundantly clear.

Eventually, his gaze wandered the floor until he located his sister. It was quite masterful that he was able to guide Bianca while watching Lady Rebecca, but she had promised to do the girl a favor, so she attempted another distraction. "Have you decided which horses to enter into the races this year?"

His attention dropped back to her. "I believe Ahab has another year in him, though Father disagrees. We might be running Jehu. And Solomon, of course."

"Perhaps you could alternate the two, enter multiple races in a day."

He nodded and snuck another quick glance in Lady Rebecca's direction before answering. "If we do, it's likely I will sponsor one and Father will sponsor the other. The idea of family rivalry will likely draw people to enter so the purse will be larger."

"That's rather brilliant." People would want to be part of a friendly feud between father and son, even if the reality was that they both hailed from the same stable and the same money. It was well known that the earl was proud of his son, who'd taken two firsts at Cambridge and was never mentioned in the scandal sheets, except in a most exemplary manner.

"Do you attend the races?" he asked.

"Of course. Every one, if I can manage it. I love watching them."

"You should join us. The duke won't make many of them this year, and he gave Father free usage of his stand."

Air backed up in Bianca's lungs at the invitation. She wanted to ask if he meant it, but that would be insulting. The stand was big, but not so big that he could hand out invitations to it without care. This was truly a privilege that he was seeming to bestow with nonchalance. "I would be honored to join you in the stands."

Unless Hudson and the new Lady Stildon were there. And they

likely would be. Perhaps they wouldn't marry until after the October meeting and she could enjoy at least one set of races before voluntarily extracting herself.

Another smile came her way. "Excellent."

They spoke of nothing of consequence for the remainder of the dance, but he managed to focus on her for the most part. At the end of the waltz, he seemed genuine as he thanked her for the dance.

Bianca was confused all over again. Was that manners or interest?

She couldn't return to the retiring room, but she wasn't sure she wanted to participate in the next dance either, so she moved straight to the refreshment table, eyes glued to the punch bowl to deter anyone from interrupting her.

"Is there a prize if I get there first?"

Bianca turned her head to identify the speaker and nearly stumbled. "Lord Rigsby! I didn't know you were here."

"I'm not surprised, giving how much time you spent . . . indisposed."

There was no denying the heat in Bianca's cheeks—no, her face, perhaps her entire body. Pleasure warred with embarrassment over the fact that Lord Rigsby had noticed her enough to pay attention to her whereabouts. "I was . . . fixing my hair."

"Oh?" His eyebrows rose. "Not avoiding people?"

"Perhaps that too."

"As you didn't know I was here, I am going to assume I was not one of the people you were avoiding." He gave her an exaggerated frown. "Don't correct me if I'm wrong."

She laughed. She couldn't help it. "Obviously I was not avoiding you."

"I'm also going to assume you won't start avoiding me now that you know I'm here. May I escort you the remainder of the way to the refreshments, or shall we choose a different marker and race there?"

She took his offered arm, knowing that once more her stepmother would be stewing. Bianca hadn't worked up the nerve yet to admit she didn't know who Lord Rigsby was, but she'd heard enough snippets of gossip to know that he was well sought after. A grin spread across her face.

"That looks like quite the smile. I don't think the mushrooms inspired it."

The last thing she could do was tell him what she'd been thinking, so she fell back on her normal favorite topic of conversation. "Will you tell me more about your horses, Lord Rigsby?"

"If that's your required topic of conversation, I shall tell you anything you wish to know."

Bianca's cheeks heated again, but she also couldn't prevent a smile. Lord Rigsby didn't make her feel fuzzy, she didn't think about him when he wasn't there, but the man was entertaining, even if she was forever feeling embarrassed around him. "It is not a requirement, but it is a favorite topic of mine."

"You've seen one of them. I've others, though. I hope to set up a base here in October. From what I've seen of Newmarket thus far, I can't imagine why my father never chose to bring his horses here." He handed her a cup of punch. "I saw you riding several days ago. Do you ride often?"

"Whenever I can. Lord Stildon generously allows me to exercise some of his horses."

"Have you a favorite area of the Heath to ride?"

"Oh yes." Bianca smiled just thinking about her favorite path to run.

"Shall we find a corner so you can tell me about it?"

Bianca looked at him, steadily meeting his gaze. She didn't know much about this man, where he came from, who his family was, or if he even had horses beyond that truly exemplary specimen she'd seen him riding last week.

She enjoyed his company, though, and the more knowledgeable ladies wouldn't be trying to catch his eye if he wasn't respectable. Was that enough?

As the conversation continued, part of her mind wandered. Lord Rigsby? Lord Brimsbane? Did either of them want to marry her? Did she want to marry one of them? Did what she wanted even matter? She wasn't in a position to turn down an offer from a man whom she could tolerate or even like.

She'd once thought she wanted nothing in life but peace and access to horses. Now it would seem that she was discovering, possibly too late, that there might be something in her life more important than riding.

And that something just might be herself.

Twenty-Six

Hudson considered staying home on Sunday instead of going to church and sitting alone in his grandfather's pew, but he went, dragging himself through the door at the last possible moment to still be considered polite.

Lady Rebecca's family sat across the aisle and one box forward. She didn't turn around, but he stared at the back of her head the whole time.

Would she soon be sitting next to him?

The thought didn't excite him very much, so instead he pictured Hestia carrying a colt that was the envy of everyone in Newmarket.

Even that thought didn't excite him like it once did.

What was wrong with him?

As soon as the service was over, Hudson slunk out and made his way home. He wrapped himself up in his study with a book, but the novel lay forgotten in his lap as he stared at the fire he'd had the staff stoke to a normal level.

It was time to admit the truth to himself.

He didn't like England.

The problem was he couldn't go back, even if he wanted to. Yes, he could physically return to India. He could get on a ship and suffer six months of torment and be back in the town where he'd grown up before the next monsoon season.

But he wouldn't belong there. He would know all of this was here. Aaron, Hades, Odysseus, even the tenants. No matter what sort of care he left them all in, he would know he'd left them.

Knowing that would make him not like India either.

So where did that leave him?

No home. No father. No grandfather. Only an uncle who hadn't been happy to learn about his existence, and even now might decide to cause trouble. And a house that had been designed by a madman.

And he was all alone in it.

Or was he?

He looked down at the novel in his hand, tossed it on his desk, and went to the corner where he'd set the trunk containing his pitifully small collection of books. He'd yet to find the time to add to the shelves, but it shouldn't take long to find what he was looking for.

He moved his books aside to reveal the contents on the bottom of the chest. Most of it had been there since he'd cleaned out his father's room after he died. Three tied bundles of letters sat neatly next to a large Bible.

He untied one of the strings and found letters from his grandfather, the counterparts to the ones he'd found in his grandfather's personal study. There were sure to be answers to his curiosity in there, but at the moment he was interested in resolution for his future more than his past.

Setting the letters aside, he took the heavy Bible back to the desk. Hudson flipped it open for the first time in eight years. They'd gone to church every week when he'd been growing up, and his father had always admonished him to listen to the sermon with open ears. He'd heard the man pray and heard him mention doing things the Christian way, and Hudson had thought that was all there was to it.

Yet there'd been this Bible beneath his father's pillow.

It hadn't been there when Hudson had been a child. He knew because he'd frequently hide in his father's bed to get away from his ayah since it was the one room in the house she refused to enter.

When had he put it there, and why hadn't Hudson ever wondered that before now?

Some of the pages were more wrinkled than others, and a few were even slightly torn at the corners. A single red ribbon marked one of the pages.

Hudson turned to it and found the ribbon was attached to a thin medallion of woven hair. The rich blond hair of his mother. He had no idea his father had kept any of her hair, much less had mourning jewelry made from it. A folded paper sat between the marked pages. Hudson set it aside to look over the pages.

One verse had been underlined. *If God be for us, who can be against us?*

Hudson ran a thumb over the ribbon and read the underlined words over and over, then started at the top of the page and read all the way down.

Was this why his father had always lived the way he had? With boldness and determination and more confidence than one would have thought he should have?

He picked up the folded paper. The creases were worn from so much folding and unfolding that he had to handle it carefully or risk tearing it as he flattened it onto the desk. He wasn't sure what he'd expected to find, but a letter to himself wasn't it.

Hudson,

As I write this, you are sleeping on the sofa in my office. You fall asleep there most nights since your mother died. Though you are too big now for me to carry upstairs, I won't stop you from staying in here. I understand the need to know you're safe.

I like knowing you are safe too.

He remembered falling asleep in his father's study. Most evenings he would arrive with a book in hand and then inevitably nod off, only to be led up the stairs when his father decided to retire.

What he didn't remember was the habit being tied to the death of his mother. Nor could he remember when he'd stopped doing it, but it had been sometime after the death of his father.

You'll be fifteen this year. I should take you to England, but I can't. Perhaps it is cowardice that keeps me here, but I couldn't bear walking this earth without you, particularly if your demise came at the hand of my own blood.

Hudson shook his head, smiling at his father's direct words, even as a fresh sense of loss filled him.

I didn't want to come to India. It was your mother who insisted all those years ago, but I've learned to love God here, and I've been able to see His hand in my life so clearly. I can scarcely remember what it was to live anywhere else now.

Would Hudson one day feel like that in England? Had his parents felt utterly alone those first weeks in India? It was little wonder that his father had entrusted his wife's hair to the Lord after her death. She'd likely been the one thing to keep him from complete despondency when he'd moved to a new land.

What I remember of England probably isn't enough to ease your way. I think my father knows this. I received a letter from him today, angry that once again I've delayed your voyage to England, this time until you turn eighteen. He and I disagree about how to raise you, and he has threatened to disown the product of my decisions.

Since his other potential heir is truly insane, I think you've nothing to worry about on that front.

Hudson ran a hand over his face. That had been his greatest fear, the one that had him obeying his grandfather's request that he stay in India. He'd been terrified that his grandfather would meet him and be disappointed.

It didn't feel uplifting to know his fear was justified.

What I have learned here is how important it is to be a better man of God than I am an Englishman. To seek God's approval instead of man's. Goodness knows we're a fickle lot anyway.

This letter is for me, son. Not you. It is a promise that I am making to raise you to understand what I have learned. I don't always find the right words, but I pray I can at least live my life as an example.

This world is not our home, but while we are in it we prepare ourselves to one day arrive there.

Your mother is home now. I miss her everyday, but one day I'll join her. Before I do, I need to prepare you for what is to come. I need to face my own fears of returning to England.

God is with us. May I remember that. My promise to you, son, is that I will keep searching God for the courage to leave what has become familiar and to face what must be.

There was another note at the bottom of the paper, still in his father's scrawl, but obviously added at a later date.

You barely fit on the sofa anymore. You will be eighteen in two months. Will you hate me for not taking you to England? Will you be angry at how much you don't know?

I read this promise every night. I haven't found the courage yet. God willing, I'm one step closer.

Maybe one more year.

Hudson set the letter aside and braced his elbows on the desk before laying his head in his hands. So many things his father had said over the years, particularly in those last years, suddenly made sense.

Was it possible Hudson had been relying on the wrong interpretations of his father's teaching? Had he missed the point?

He looked back to the open Bible on the desk.

If God be for us, who can be against us?

Who indeed?

A small voice in Hudson's heart whispered that it just might be himself.

HUDSON WAS ROLLING his shoulders in an attempt to work out the discomfort than had arisen from sleeping in a chair in his study for half the night when he walked into the stable the next morning.

"I leave you for a mere week and a half and you fall apart." Aaron greeted him from his position near Athena's stall. He nodded to the mare. "I've got it all lined up for Athena here. We'll send Miles and one of the occasional stable lads with her, and when she returns, you'll have yourself the beginnings of a new racehorse."

"Hmmm," Hudson murmured. "It's a good pairing?"

Aaron nodded. "It has the potential, anyway. Breeding horses is always a gamble."

"Good."

"Any developments while I was gone?"

Had it truly been less than two weeks since Aaron had gone to London? It seemed like months. Would his life always move at this pace? Was there a way to slow it down?

He scrubbed his hand over his face and rolled his head around on his neck to relieve more tension.

"That bad? Did you run off and get married while I was gone? If you did, I'd love to know what horses you used to get to Scotland

and back so quickly." Aaron opened his notebook and moved on to the next stall.

"I did pay Lady Rebecca a visit."

Aaron's brow rose, and for a moment it looked like he wanted to say something, but then he simply nodded and murmured, "How did it go?"

"Well. We've been for a walk. Her father knew my father and uncle, of course."

Aaron nodded and moved on to the next horse. "Have you checked in on the training?"

"Of course. I, er, might have been challenged to a race."

"Did you accept?"

"Yes."

"Idiot."

Hudson had rather felt like that as well, but it sounded far worse hearing it from Aaron. "Well, it's on Thursday, and I intend to see it through."

"Of course you do. You aren't that much of an idiot." Aaron sighed. "Is it you or your horse?"

"Horse. Apollo."

"At least you chose the right animal. I'll arrange your jockey and have the horse there that morning."

A loud rap against the stable door announced a visitor before a man with blond hair and an engaging smile stuck his head inside. "Good morning."

Hudson looked at Aaron, but he'd stepped back the way he did at the training stables. Whoever the man was, he must be of some importance. "Good morning."

"Can I bring my horse in, or shall I leave him tied up out here?"

Without Hudson having to say anything or even look around, Andrew came scampering out of the tack room and headed for the man's horse.

The newcomer's head disappeared for a moment, but then the

entire man came strolling into the stable, arms clasped loosely behind his back.

Andrew led the man's horse, a fine dappled grey that was certainly not a racehorse, former or otherwise, to an empty stall at the far end of the aisle.

"If you'd allow me, I'd like to introduce myself."

Hudson couldn't stop himself from emitting a sound of surprise. "That would be preferable, yes."

"Lord Trent Hawthorne." He offered his hand.

"Lord Stildon." Hudson shook the man's hand.

Lord Trent looked beyond Hudson to where Aaron was standing. "I assume you are Mr. Whitworth, are you not? I've heard about you, of course, but never had the chance to make your acquaintance."

Aaron nodded, set his shoulders, and came to join the two men. "I am Mr. Whitworth."

"Excellent." Lord Trent rocked back on his heels and looked from Aaron to Hudson and then around the stable. "I like what you've done with the place. I haven't been here since I made arrangements with the previous Lord Stildon, but I can see the improvements."

"Arrangements?" Hudson asked.

Aaron jabbed his thumb in Lord Trent's direction. "Lord Trent buys horse byproduct from a couple of the stables in the area."

"Horse by—" Hudson lowered his voice to a whisper. "Aaron, there's no such thing as horse byproduct. Horses don't produce anything. They aren't cows."

Aaron just looked at Hudson with that irritating expression that said he was simply waiting for Hudson to catch up with him.

Lord Trent was laughing. It was a quiet laugh, more of a silent shoulder shake, but a laugh nonetheless.

"The only thing horses produce comes out the back end," Hudson continued.

"Apparently that's a required element for growing pineapples," Aaron said dryly.

"Pineapples?" Hudson asked. "Horse manure helps pineapples grow?"

"That it does," Lord Trent said, still grinning. "I buy the other stuff too."

"For pineapples?" Hudson simply couldn't wrap his mind around this idea, but Lord Trent didn't seem to realize how strange his words were.

He nodded. "For pineapples."

Hudson had eaten pineapple several times in India, but he'd never seen it grown. Now he didn't want to. "I'm never eating pineapple again."

Lord Trent laughed and gave a shrug. "You can just set it on the table and let it look pretty until it rots, then. I've sold plenty of them for just such purposes."

Hudson wasn't sure what to say. He was even more flummoxed when Lord Trent clapped Aaron on the shoulder and asked, "Is he treating you right?"

It wasn't often Aaron looked out of his element. Out of sight, yes, but not out of his element. Right then, with Lord Trent's hand on his shoulder, Aaron looked at a complete loss.

When he didn't answer, the blond man's grin faded a bit. "Surprise or concern got your tongue?"

"Why do you care?" Aaron finally asked.

"We're practically family," Lord Trent said. "We need to watch out for each other."

Family? Aaron was illegitimate, and Lord Trent certainly wasn't. They didn't share a father, did they? If they did, Hudson was going to have to find the contract he had with this fellow and see how to break it. He wasn't going to have his stable be one of the areas Aaron felt unwelcome.

Aaron wasn't looking angered by the claim, though. Instead, it seemed to relax him as he said in his normal voice, "We're hardly family."

"Depends on your definition."

"By *anyone's* definition."

Lord Trent pretended to look thoughtful and then he turned to Hudson. "I am a person, correct?"

Aaron groaned. Hudson agreed, because there was no way he couldn't.

"Very well. We'll say by my definition, then." Lord Trent nodded. "Family."

Hudson was tired of not knowing what was happening. Everything in his life felt questionable. On this, at least, he would have answers. "How are you two connected?"

"We aren't," Aaron said.

"Of course we are. Through Graham."

"You don't even know Graham."

"We've met."

"When?"

Lord Trent waved a hand in the air. "I don't remember when, but I know we have."

Hudson cleared his throat. "It doesn't sound like a very close connection."

"Between Graham and me?" Lord Trent asked. "Of course not. The connection is through Graham's wife."

"Whom you have also never met."

"Yes I did. At Jess and Derek's wedding."

Aaron shoved his notebook into his pocket and placed his hands on his hips. "You went to the wedding?"

"We all did. Sat on the bride's side."

"You don't know the bride."

"Of course I do. She was Ryland's parlormaid. And just to save time, since we both know the next point in the connection, don't even think of saying I don't know my brother-in-law." Lord

Trent crossed his arms over his chest and looked very satisfied with himself.

"*I* have never met your brother-in-law," Aaron said, "and I pray I never do."

Hudson winced at the insult and waited for Lord Trent to bluster and stomp away.

Instead, the man laughed. "Terrified of him, are you? Smart man."

Aaron simply grunted.

Hudson hated to ask, really he did, but he hadn't followed any of that. "Would someone please explain this connection again?"

Aaron sighed. "My friend Graham—I've mentioned him? Lord Wharton? He's married to a woman who is friends with a friend of Lord Trent's brother-in-law."

Hudson tilted his head. "That seems rather . . . distant."

"Not when you consider the people involved." Lord Trent shrugged. "They gossip like old women." He turned his grin on Aaron. "They're worried about you."

What in the world could anyone say to such a statement? Fortunately, Lord Trent didn't seem to need an answer, as he turned his attention to Hudson. "I came by to meet you. Lady Adelaide and I would like to extend an invitation to dine with us. You are invited as well, Mr. Whitworth."

Aaron narrowed his gaze. "Did you specifically wait until I was back in Newmarket to come for your visit?"

Lord Trent grinned and rocked back on his heels again, but he remained silent.

It was so silent, in fact, that Hudson knew every single groom was listening to the exchange. He really should stop having private conversations in the middle of the stable.

The silence was broken not by the sound of men working or the continued conversation, but by Bianca.

"Oh good, I haven't missed the ride yet."

Hudson turned toward her entrance, unable to prevent a smile of greeting. Not that he would want to. There wasn't a reason in the world why he couldn't smile at the arrival of a friend.

She came to a stop two steps into the stable. "Oh. Lord Trent."

Lord Trent bowed his head in greeting. "Miss Snowley, isn't it?"

"Yes, er, I can . . . come back later."

"No, no, don't leave on my account. Are you here for Lord Stildon or Mr. Whitworth?"

The fact that the man even offered Aaron as an option made Hudson inclined to forgive some of his eccentricities. What else could be expected of someone who chose to be in a business that required the purchase of horse waste?

"I . . . I . . . that is—"

"She's actually here for the horses," Hudson said, stepping up to draw Lord Trent's attention. "Mr. Whitworth believes in daily exercise for all the animals, so she assists by taking one for a ride." He turned to Bianca. "I haven't seen you in a while—that is, you haven't been by to ride in several days."

Her throat worked as she swallowed hard and kept a steady connection with his gaze. "Rain," she choked out, "and, um, my stepmother."

What had Mrs. Snowley been making Bianca do? He'd thought the fact that she was talking so often with Lord Rigsby and Lord Brimsbane would have settled the older woman's concerns.

Neither man was ideal for her in Hudson's opinion, but he rather thought her stepmother wouldn't look further than their titles.

A movement in the corner of his eye caught his attention, and he glanced sideways to see Lord Trent leaning against the stable wall, looking from Hudson to Bianca with a grin on his face.

Heat slashed across Hudson's cheekbones. He hadn't realized how close he was standing to Bianca or how long they'd been silent. Dropping his gaze to the floor, he took a step back. "Is she still causing you problems?"

She cast her eyes to the ceiling. "I think she will always be a problem, but yes. She's still . . . overly concerned. Though what she is concerned about seems to change with regularity."

He wanted to ask how but was very conscious of the stable's abnormal occupant. An occupant who was still grinning as he looked from Hudson to Bianca and back again.

"Do you intend to come to any of the assemblies this year, my lord?" Bianca asked.

"Gracious no," Lord Trent said with a laugh. "Certainly not until all the craziness subsides. It makes my wife nervous." He looked over at Aaron. "Lady Rebecca had almost as grand a time in London."

Aaron yanked his notebook from his pocket. "Is this a business discussion you need me for, or a social call that doesn't require my presence?"

A momentary frown crossed Lord Trent's face, but it was gone just as quickly. "Well, it isn't business. My deliveries have been arriving on schedule, so I've nothing to complain about."

Aaron nodded and stalked away, shoulders hunched, to the stall at the farthest end of the stable.

Lord Trent appeared unbothered by the abrupt departure, instead engaging Bianca and Hudson in a discussion about how full the social events had gotten in the past two weeks.

He abruptly ended the conversation with a nod. "Well. I won't keep you from your ride. Be looking for my invitation. We'll have you come early so we can play a game of cricket."

Had the man said *cricket*? Hudson could have hugged him in happiness. He'd been asked once or twice to join a man in a game of billiards, and while Hudson's skills with a billiard mace were mediocre at best, he was adept with a cricket bat.

"I will accept with gladness when the invitation arrives."

Lord Trent looked at Bianca once more before grinning at Hudson. "See that you do."

Then he nodded farewell to both of them, collected his horse, and rode away.

"Many apologies for interrupting," Bianca said.

"You didn't interrupt anything," Hudson assured her. "It was barely a conversation." Yet somehow, as Lord Trent had departed, the significance had seemed far greater.

Twenty-Seven

"What are you doing?"

Bianca paused in the act of lifting a mug of tea to her mouth. Because she'd refused to spend another morning staring at her own room in indecision, she'd moved her pondering to the breakfast room, never imagining that her stepmother would appear.

Yet there she was.

"Breakfast?" There was a plate of toast in front of her and a mug of tea in her hand. She knew that most people waited until later in the morning to eat, but she'd long ago discovered that riding on an empty stomach made her feel ill.

Her stepmother knew this, didn't she? Bianca had been having early toast and tea for nearly ten years.

"I can see that," the woman spit out. "I meant, what are you doing with your life?"

Now there was a weighted question if ever there was one. Though she was sorely tempted to say *wasting it*, she didn't. It was likely her stepmother would agree and would use Bianca's sardonic statement to get her to do something she didn't want to do.

Instead, she stayed silent. Mrs. Snowley was sure to expound soon if she didn't get the answer she wanted.

"Do you truly think Lord Brimsbane is going to offer for you,

or"—she fanned herself as if the concept was too much to utter—
"Lord Rigsby? You think you could become a countess or a marchioness?"

Bianca blinked. Lord Rigsby would be a marquis one day? No
wonder all the girls wanted his attention.

Mrs. Snowley continued, "Your gallivanting about on horses
all the time is all good and well in Newmarket, but those men are
going to be peers. True ladies—London ladies—don't do such
things."

Bianca was fairly certain a countess or marchioness could do
just about anything she pleased, particularly if it was to ride horses
about Newmarket, but that wasn't the true point here.

Mrs. Snowley's question was whether Bianca expected an offer
of marriage from either of those men.

Bianca's question was whether or not she wanted one.

"I thought you would be pleased with my association with the
most eligible men in town," Bianca said slowly.

Mrs. Snowley huffed and crossed her arms. "Seen with them
once, perhaps twice, yes. It makes the other men take notice and
puts the rest of the family in greater social standing. You don't
want truly appropriate matches to get the idea that you aren't
available, though."

Bianca broke off a corner of toast and watched the crumbs dance
around on her plate. "Appropriate matches? How could either of
those men ever be inappropriate?"

"Inappropriate for *you*." Mrs. Snowley shook her head. "Women
who reach above their station end up miserable."

"Did you give this same advice to Marianne?"

"Of course not. A man of rank would make an excellent match
for her. I raised her to be a lady."

"But you didn't raise me to be one?" Bianca's grip on her toast
tightened until it mushed together into a crumbly mass.

Mrs. Snowley sighed. "I did the best I could, but blood will tell."

The desire to chuck her plate at her stepmother raged through Bianca, but contrary to what the other woman seemed to think, she was too much of a lady to follow through on the act.

This time.

Next time? Who was to say?

The statement required an answer, though, and one that was firm enough to keep her stepmother from ever saying something like that again. "My, my. What would Father say if he heard that?"

"Your father is well aware of his first wife's shortcomings."

Bianca wanted to refute that statement, needed to refute it. Her father had loved her mother dearly. She knew this. He'd sat with her when she was a child, before Giles was born, and told her story after story about her mother.

Just because he'd loved her, though, didn't mean she was perfect.

Just because he loved Bianca didn't mean he didn't see her as flawed.

She used to take problems to him, but he always said that it wasn't his place to take over his wife's job of raising their daughters. Was that because he thought she truly needed such correction? Did he agree with Mrs. Snowley's assessment of Bianca's character and capabilities?

Every governess had been diligent in making sure that Marianne appeared the more dutiful child.

Every misdeed, every delay in lessons, every poorly trimmed candle had been blamed on Bianca.

He might have been persuaded to believe her less than capable or refined.

"I see you understand," Mrs. Snowley said, obviously misinterpreting Bianca's silent trip down memory lane.

What Bianca understood was that she hadn't a single ally in this house.

She had to marry, but what if Mrs. Snowley was right and neither Lord Brimsbane nor Lord Rigsby intended to offer for her?

She couldn't stay in a house with only her father and stepmother as the other residents. Where did that leave her? Traveling about, claiming a closer friendship with her many acquaintances than she truly had? Depending upon the kindness of others to house and feed her until her brother was home to act as some form of buffer?

She had to marry the first man who asked.

"Now"—Mrs. Snowley clasped her hands together—"I've arranged for your father to invite Mr. Mead and his son over this morning. I suggest you be at your prettiest because I've talked to Mr. Theophilus Mead, and the man might very well offer for you. Possibly even today."

Perhaps not the first man who asked, then. How long could she manage to avoid Mr. Mead? Was marrying him better than living with the growing barbs of her stepmother? Was it better than watching the man she prayed and wished would notice her married to her sister-in-law? Was it better than entering into marriage with a man whose company she enjoyed but whose situation was a complete mystery?

When she looked at it that way, there wasn't an appealing option in her life right now.

Mrs. Snowley curved her lips. It was a smile by definition, but there was no kindness to it. Perhaps some happiness, as she seemed to get a great deal of glee out of making Bianca miserable.

"Now. I've told Dorothy to ready your best morning dress. She'll be upstairs to get you ready. You should probably remain in your room until Mr. Mead arrives. It will be quite dramatic if he sees you coming down the stairs." She clapped her hands together. "It will also prevent you from being a distraction when Sir Joseph comes to collect Marianne. She and the baronet are going for a ride in his phaeton."

A baronet. Marianne was trying to land a baronet, which was more than respectable for the daughter of a gentleman. It also explained why she was no longer hoping for a continued connection between Bianca and one of the viscounts.

To buy herself time, Bianca took a large gulp of tea. "You wish me to skip riding this morning?"

Mrs. Snowley waved a hand through the air. "You've plenty of time to ride once you get married. I chose Mr. Mead for that exact reason. You want horses, I'm giving you horses. Don't think for one moment that once Lord Stildon marries his new wife they will take kindly to the amount of time you spend over there."

Her stepmother raised her hands and pressed lightly at the edges of her eyes. "Rising at such an hour to talk to you privately is simply exhausting. Oh, the things a mother does."

Bianca bit her lips to keep from laughing out loud.

"But you've thwarted me at every turn. Still, I'm watching over you. This offer from Mr. Mead will set you up in the life you want, or at least the one you've always said you wanted. There's nothing I can do if you've spent all these years lying to me."

Then she left the room.

Bianca pushed her plate away and stared at the mangled piece of toast. Her future was certainly looking bleak. One thing was certain, though—Bianca was about to thwart her stepmother once again.

She was going for a ride, and she'd be taking her father's horse.

Whether her stepmother had meant to or not, she'd helped Bianca this morning. When faced with the possibility of gaining what she'd always said she wanted, everything in her said no. So, what did she actually want?

It was time to truly look at her life in a way she never had before.

She pushed back from the table and headed to the stables, hoping the horses were feeling sprightly because it was going to be a good, long time before she chose to come back.

THE BLUE SKY mocked her as she allowed the horse to plod along at a walk. Given that she intended to roam the Newmarket countryside until she knew what she wanted to do, she didn't want to tire the horse out.

Still, the weather could have cooperated by being grey and dismal to match her mood. Instead, it was the sort of day that Hudson would have loved. Even now he was probably racing Hades along the Heath, glorying in the happy weather.

Did he wish she was with him?

She certainly wished she was.

But was that stopping her from seeing her true opportunities?

She dropped her head back and looked up at the sky, feeling entirely alone. She'd avoided the Heath and cut across the fields in order to have isolation, and the groom respectfully was staying several feet behind her.

It wasn't helping.

"Lord," she whispered, "I know it isn't Sunday, but I hope you're listening anyway. Have I gone too far down the wrong road? Is there no hope left for a happy life for me? Should I accept Mr. Mead?"

Nausea crawled up the back of her throat at the very idea of accepting that man, but wasn't the Bible full of people who'd suffered because it was the choice God wanted them to make? Had He given her a lifetime of learning how to be alone because she was destined to be lonely for the rest of her life?

It didn't seem right, but then again, what did she know? Should she ride over to the rectory? Would the priest laugh at her for such a question? Would he tell Mrs. Snowley, or worse, her father?

"Do you still deal in signs, God? Because I could use one now," she grumbled.

"Good morning, Miss Snowley."

The deep voice caused Bianca to jump until she'd nearly unseated herself. She had to grip the reins, mane, and even the front of the saddle to keep herself from spilling to the ground. She turned to look at the speaker.

Lord Rigsby was riding toward her atop the glorious animal she'd seen him on before. She had adored many a horse in her time, but never had she seen an animal like this. His powerful legs and intelligent eyes were the marks of a champion. It was obvious why Lord Rigsby hadn't braved the crowd to meet Lady Rebecca.

Bianca fixed her seat and straightened her riding jacket. "Lord Rigsby. I see you are out enjoying the first truly fine day we've had in a while."

"Yes." He glanced up at the sky and then took in the area around her. "This isn't where you told me you like to ride."

He'd remembered their conversation from the assembly? That was a good sign, wasn't it? Bianca might not wake up thinking about seeing Lord Rigsby, but he was a good man. She could learn to be happy with him.

She could.

She smiled. "I was thinking I'd try something different today."

"Perhaps I could accompany you for a ways?" He turned his horse until he was facing the same way she was.

"That would be nice." And it would be. Perhaps that was what Bianca needed. A ride without agonizing over her future, so that when she returned, everything would once more be in perspective.

They rode a path through a grove of trees, and the scattered shadows played across the horses' manes and the man next to her. The groom continued to plod along behind them, his expression conveying that he wasn't entirely sure what he was supposed to do in this situation.

Bianca wasn't either.

"Your horse is lovely," she said.

Lord Rigsby chuckled. "My father hates that I've chosen Sunset's Pride as my mount. Said he should be protected at an estate somewhere in the country."

"A beautiful stepper like that shouldn't be ignored."

He gave her a searching look. "I agree. I never saw the point of confining a horse to lack of exercise simply because he was good blood."

The conversation fell into an easy discussion of their favorite horses, their difficulties, and how he was starting his own stock so his father couldn't tell him how to run it.

Bianca bit her lip. "Do you think you'll choose Newmarket?"

"I might." He shifted in his seat. "I do like it, but I haven't decided yet if the society is the right fit. Since I intend to be involved with my horses, I want to choose somewhere I want to live."

Bianca chuckled. "And you haven't found everyone here to be to your liking?"

"I haven't met everyone here."

"How true. Have you ranged beyond the assembly-going set?"

"As social gatherings are where new people in town tend to meet others, no, I haven't," he said in a dry voice, accompanied by a tiny crooked smile that seemed somehow familiar. Perhaps it was simply the friendliness such an expression evoked.

"Well," Bianca said, "there are wonderful people who don't attend assemblies and card parties."

"Friends of yours?"

Bianca thought of the fun she'd had with Hudson and Mr. Whitworth and even the grooms of Hawksworth. "Yes."

"I would love to meet them, then."

Bianca blinked at the warmness of his tone. "You would?"

He nodded. "If they are friends of yours, I would be interested in meeting them very much."

As they approached the lane where Bianca needed to turn off and head home to give her poor horse a rest, Lord Rigsby nudged his horse closer. "We should do this again sometime—on purpose, instead of just by chance."

She had asked God for a sign. Was this it?

"Yes, we absolutely should."

They smiled at each other until the groom's plodding horse

came alongside them, then Bianca said her good-byes and turned her mount toward home.

The death of a dream she hadn't even known she had cried through her as she rode the short distance back to the stable.

Respect was more than some marriages had, so she really shouldn't be saddened over the prospect. When she considered her situation objectively, Lord Rigsby was a truly ideal choice. After all, she'd be a marchioness with horses and a kind man for a husband. What more could a girl ask for?

In time, she could possibly even learn to love him. It wasn't as if she was in love with Hudson—she was simply attracted to him, drawn to his personality, and admired the way he'd handled the challenge of moving to a new land. Very well, she also considered him a superb horseman and liked the way he'd accepted Aaron as an equal in the stable and how he'd believed her about her stepmother. She found his humor appealing and liked how he could laugh at himself.

But how was she to know that Lord Rigsby might not have some of those qualities? How was she to know if he did?

For the first time ever, she wished that she'd listened a bit more to Marianne as she went on and on about how women handled men. Bianca could steer a horse anywhere she wished him to go, but Lord Rigsby would likely resent having a bit put in his mouth.

Whatever it was she needed to do, she needed to do it soon, because he just might be her best chance for happiness in a marriage.

An hour ago she'd been crying to God to give her a solution. Now that she had one, she wanted to cry all the more.

Twenty-Eight

To say that Mrs. Snowley was perturbed by Bianca's missing the Meads' visit was putting it mildly.

The fact that she once more sent regrets on Bianca's behalf to a social gathering, took herself and Marianne off to it, and thought that was a punishment only emphasized how little she knew Bianca.

It also emphasized how little Bianca knew herself.

Not too long ago, she would have been devastated at being so intentionally left out of important events, but when the house settled quietly around her, she discovered it was somewhat easier to breathe.

Learning all these truths about herself was leaving her dizzy and insecure. How had she reached the age of four and twenty without having asked herself any of these questions before? She'd never asked herself if she enjoyed parties. She'd simply gone because it was what people did.

She read for a while and then wandered toward her father's study. Was he in, or had he gone out for the night too?

A lamp sent flickering light across the area in front of the fireplace where he sat reading. He nearly jumped when she knocked on the door. "Oh, Bianca. You didn't want to go to the party?"

Did he truly not know what Mrs. Snowley was doing? "I'm enjoying a quiet evening."

He nodded. "I enjoy the evenings too. Everything gets still. It's like you can hear God breathing."

Bianca sat in the other chair. "What do you mean?"

"Morning air is always bustling about with the birds and the new day and everything, but now, I suppose it's the peace of it. Like God's laying everything in place for it to whirl up again tomorrow."

"I've never looked at it that way." She tilted her head. "When did you become a philosopher?"

He laughed. "When life needed meaning, I suppose. It was either find the purpose or allow pain and regret to bury me. The second one wasn't an option. I had children depending on me."

Bianca sighed as she looked at her father. He cared. He showed it in his own way, but she'd never had reason to doubt that he cared about her. How many other men would even be willing to have their daughters intrude on their quiet solitude?

She rose and kissed him on the head. "I love you, Papa. I'll leave you to listen to God breathing."

His chuckle followed her out of the room, and she paused in the corridor to listen to it fade into a happy sigh.

As she trudged to her room, her mind was awash with thoughts. She'd been allowing fear, desperation, and who-even-knew-what-else to push her around. Perhaps it was time she sought out their purpose instead.

THE NEXT MORNING her riding habits were missing. Every. Single. One. Dorothy hadn't come to her room yet, and the sun was peering over the horizon.

All her steady resolve from the night before was set aside and replaced with utter confusion.

She opened her door and saw Dorothy slowly making her way up the stairs, holding a tray with Bianca's tea and toast. All the way across the landing and down the short corridor and even into the room, the maid kept her face averted, refusing to meet Bianca's inquisitive gaze.

Bianca waited until Dorothy set the tray down to speak, so that the fragile-looking maid didn't drop the entire contents on the floor.

"Do you know where my habits are?"

"Yes, miss."

Bianca waited. No more answer. Still no eye contact.

"Where are they?"

"In Mrs. Snowley's dressing room, miss."

"In Mrs. Snowley's . . . why on earth are they there?"

Dorothy clasped her hands in front of her and lifted her face, but she still looked somewhere past Bianca's left shoulder. "She said"—the maid paused to clear her throat—"she said that you needed to be available for visits today, but she refused to get up early in the morning for you again, since you'd been so ungrateful last time."

Bianca dropped her head back on her shoulders and groaned. When she looked forward again, Dorothy was biting her lip and sneaking longing glances at the door.

"I am well aware that was a quote. I'm not mad at you, Dorothy." At the end of the day, both of them were at the mercy of the older woman's whims. "Did she also give instructions as to what I was to wear?"

Dorothy visibly relaxed and rushed to the dressing room. "Yes, miss. The yellow muslin with the green flowers."

"Let's put me in it, then."

An hour later, still well before Mrs. Snowley ever graced the world with her presence, Bianca was settled in the drawing room, poking a needle into a piece of embroidery. She didn't embroider often—in fact, this piece had been in her work basket for nearly two years now—but it gave her something to do, and she could pretend every stitch was her poking her stepmother with the needle.

After the visits commenced, she was far more occupied imagining ways in which the woman could be rendered mute.

Not anything truly harmful, of course, but something that would cause the temporary cessation of the ability to talk. A scratched throat, a cold, perhaps even a minor injury, so long as it didn't cause any real damage. Really, anything that forced the woman to stop making sly stabs at Bianca's already-weakened confidence would be wonderful.

"It really is a relief that only one of my girls is so particular about her clothing. Bianca's practicality makes trips to the modiste so much easier." Mrs. Snowley gave out a tinkling laugh, as if she'd just given Bianca a compliment and not veiled criticism of the boring simplicity of her wardrobe.

Neither Lord Rigsby nor Lord Brimsbane ever seemed to find her clothing lacking. Of course, they'd never been overly complimentary about her appearance either.

Really, though, how did excellent fashion sense make a woman a better wife? Her clothing was sturdy and constructed in a way that it could be cleaned after a day in the stable. No matter how particular Mr. Knight was about the condition of the stable, horses were dirty. They walked about in the dirt and mud, got it caked in their coats and hooves, and occasionally—well, almost daily— some of that dirt got transferred to her. Silks and satins would be ruined in moments, whereas her wool habits had been in circulation through her wardrobe now for months.

Maybe wives weren't meant to be practical.

Mrs. Addington laughed along with Mrs. Snowley and Marianne.

Marianne always joined in the laughter. When they'd been younger, Bianca had assumed the other girl didn't truly understand what her mother was laughing at. As a woman full grown, Bianca could no longer grant her such an excuse.

One more relationship that should have—could have—been so much more than it was.

Bianca sighed and slumped into her chair. It wasn't as if she had any hope of impressing her stepmother and Mrs. Addington. Why did people have to be so exhausting?

In truth, it wasn't people so much who were exhausting. Most of the time, Bianca liked people in general. It was trying to navigate a relationship that went beyond occasional greetings that drained her.

"Madam," the butler said, coming in with a card on a silver tray. "There is a lady requesting your permission to call."

With lifted eyebrows and pursed lips, Mrs. Snowley lifted the card from the tray, holding it with two fingers, as if she thought it would cut her.

Maybe it would. On the throat. Just a little tiny paper cut that made it uncomfortable to speak.

A moment later, her mouth dropped open before curving into a wide smile. Both hands gripped the edges of the card, and she nodded to the butler. "Of course. She's most welcome here."

Marianne's blue eyes were round as she watched her mother. Mrs. Addington shifted in her seat, trying to subtly crane her neck to view the card.

Bianca didn't even try. With her luck it was Lady Gliddon, or perhaps even Lady Rebecca. Either of them would throw an extra scoop of torture into the mix.

The woman who appeared in the doorway was not Lady Gliddon or Lady Rebecca or indeed anyone Bianca knew by more than sight.

Bianca glanced to her stepmother and sister. Both of them sat on the edge of their seat, eyes wide and smiles even wider.

What was Lord Trent's wife doing here?

"Lady Adelaide Hawthorne," the butler announced.

Mrs. Snowley sprang from her seat and crossed the room to greet the newcomer. Lady Adelaide's serene smile reminded Bianca of Lady Rebecca, but there the similarities ended. She had dark hair, though a swath of it had been cut short to fall across her forehead, and black wire spectacles. Her dress was simple but unquestionably elegant. Everything about her, even the way she moved to the seat Mrs. Snowley offered, exuded sweetness and peace.

Which did beg the question of why she was in the Snowleys' drawing room.

Mrs. Snowley immediately called for tea to be sent. Bianca snuck a look at their other guest. Did Mrs. Addington realize the same courtesy hadn't been offered to her? It didn't appear so. She was too agog to notice.

Within a few moments, everyone was resituated. Once more Bianca had been given a cup of tea that was nearly black. She quietly set it aside.

"To what do we owe the pleasure of your visit, Lady Adelaide?" Mrs. Snowley tilted her head and gave what was likely meant to be a welcoming smile.

Anyone else probably thought it looked welcoming. Bianca thought her stepmother looked like a viper.

"My husband." The woman's voice was as sweet as her appearance. In a different setting, Bianca thought she would really enjoy the prospect of getting to know this woman. "We spend so much of our time in the area, and he wishes to expand our social circle."

The spectacles made the woman's eyes enormous, and there was no missing the way her gaze cut over to Bianca as she finished her statement. Did that have some meaning, or was she simply being polite?

"We're honored that you chose to bestow one of your first visits upon us."

"First visits?"

Mrs. Snowley laughed, an edge of discomfort creeping into the tone. "Well, yes. Everyone knows you don't pay calls."

"Oh, but I do. Just to a very small set of women."

The discomfort disappeared, as Mrs. Snowley all but preened

under the implication. "We'll have to have you and Lord Trent over for supper and cards. It will take a few days to arrange, as Newmarket is ever so much busier than normal just now. Why, Marianne and I are scheduled to be out every night this week."

Bianca blinked. They were? Had her stepmother kept Bianca away from every single invitation? She knew of nothing besides Saturday's assembly and Mrs. Wilson's monthly garden party, which was nothing more than a viewing of the orange plants in her conservatory.

"Oh?" Lady Adelaide looked about the room, her gaze clearly stopping on every lady, including Bianca.

With an expression that managed to look somehow abashed and yet arrogant, Mrs. Snowley lowered her voice, as if sharing a confidence with the woman she'd known less than five minutes. "Not all the invites included Bianca, though I assure you she doesn't mind. Evening clothes and droll social events don't appeal to her as much as her precious horses. There are times when a hostess must simply make decisions because of the numbers."

How could Mrs. Snowley, so concerned with her reputation, not know how that sounded? The implication that cutting out the elder daughter of a family was simply a sacrifice that must be made for social propriety?

That was an insult that no one could miss.

Lady Adelaide didn't seem the least disturbed by it, though. In fact, she leaned in a little herself. "That happened every day this week? Even tonight?"

"Yes," Mrs. Snowley said with a sad shake of her head. "Marianne and I are due to attend the Wainbrights' dinner and musicale."

Bianca almost laughed. That was probably the only invitation that actually hadn't included Bianca.

"My mother encountered many of the same dilemmas when my sister and I were out at the same time." Lady Adelaide gave Mrs. Snowley a sympathetic smile. "I completely understand."

Perhaps Bianca didn't like this woman very much after all.

Then Lady Adelaide turned to Bianca. "I know it is terribly last-minute, but since you are not otherwise engaged tonight, would you care to come to dinner? I had been afraid I wouldn't be able to invite you because it would require my being so rude as to not invite your entire family, but fortunately Mrs. Snowley is very understanding about numbers."

She placed a hand against her heart and turned to Mrs. Snowley. "Thank you ever so much for understanding. It has eased my mind greatly."

Bianca couldn't keep from smiling—indeed, could barely keep from laughing—as she accepted the lady's invitation.

"Excellent." She took a sip of tea. "I'll send the carriage for you, shall I? I assume your own family conveyance will be used to deliver the others to their gathering."

"I would appreciate it."

Lady Adelaide nodded and looked about the room. "This is a finely furnished room. Did you purchase the furniture locally?"

Silence ruled the room for several moments before Mrs. Snowley gave a stilted answer. Through it all, Lady Adelaide sweetly sipped her tea.

Then she asked about the tea service, the curtains, and even Mrs. Snowley's hair feathers.

When there was nothing else in the room Lady Adelaide could comment upon, she set her cup aside. "I must be off. Miss Snowley, would you be a dear and walk me out? I always feel so strange leaving a room by myself."

Bianca nearly sprang from her chair, desperate to have a private moment with this woman to learn what in the world had just happened.

In the hall, Bianca took a breath but held it when Lady Adelaide broke into a near trot on her way to the door. Bianca stayed right with her, unwilling to wait until tonight to gain answers.

Once they were out the door and on the front drive, Lady Adelaide stopped and pressed a hand to her middle. "Did I manage that well?" She took a deep breath in and blew it out through pursed lips. "Three years married to that man and you'd think his schemes wouldn't send my heart into flurries anymore, but I thought surely every one of you would be able to hear my heart in there."

Bianca opened her mouth but didn't know what to say. "I couldn't hear it at all."

She gave a sharp nod. "Good. I'll send the carriage for you at six."

"So there really is a dinner party?"

"Of course." Lady Adelaide waved a hand in the air. "And the numbers aren't even." She frowned. "At least I don't think they are. It depends on how many Trent decided to invite. This was all his idea, you know."

"To invite me?"

"Yes." Lady Adelaide pulled on her gloves and walked toward her waiting carriage. "He had some very detailed reason for putting together the gathering, but I'm afraid I missed most of it. Caroline—she's my daughter—started crying and I got distracted."

"Yet you came anyway?"

"Of course. He asked me to. He also told me he got the impression your stepmother liked to play favorites. Any lady trapped in such a situation has my complete sympathy." She glanced back at the house. "I'm not sure even my mother was ever that obvious about it, though." She gave another smile and climbed into the carriage. "I'll see you tonight."

Bianca dredged up a smile of her own. She had so many questions but could hardly detain the other woman to gain the answers. Instead, she had to survive approximately six hours without expiring of curiosity. That was, of course, assuming her stepmother didn't maim her first.

Twenty-Nine

For the second time this week, Lord Trent Hawthorne was at Hawksworth's stable. This time he was leaning against the wall, obviously waiting on Hudson and Aaron to return from their ride.

That morning they'd specifically ridden out to see the training of Hudson's horses. He wanted—no, needed—to win this first challenge race, even if accepting it had been foolish.

What he'd seen that morning gave him great confidence.

Seeing Lord Trent outside his stable gave him a vague sense of foreboding.

"Lord Trent," he asked as he dismounted, "you do remember coming to introduce yourself already."

The other man laughed. "Yes, yes. I also remember saying we should meet for cricket and dinner."

"So you did."

"Have you plans this afternoon?"

Even Miles, who had come out to collect Hades from Hudson, stumbled at the late invitation before hustling the horse into the stable under Aaron's glaring gaze. Andrew, who had come to retrieve Shadow from Aaron, ducked his head down and followed, leaving the three men alone on the drive.

Lord Trent nodded at Aaron. "You're invited as well."

"You meant that?" Aaron asked.

Hudson couldn't help but laugh over the shock on Aaron's face. "It takes quite a lot to surprise him. I'll accept for that gift alone."

"And here I thought my illustrious company was all the incentive one needed. Certainly seems to be when I go in the shops." The man lifted his hand to cup one side of his mouth as if he were going to share a secret. "Don't tell them that I don't do anything for this honorific. I rather enjoy my preferential treatment."

Perhaps there was hope for England yet if there were men like this for Hudson still to meet.

He looked to Aaron. "Will you be joining us?"

Aaron looked at his toes and then the stable before looking back at the men. "I'm afraid not. A friend of mine traveled with me from London."

"Bring him along. I'm guessing it's Lord Farnsworth, since you don't mention a wife." Lord Trent clapped his hands. "That was easily settled."

Aaron frowned. "How do you know it's Oliver?"

"Because you only have two friends. Possibly three now." Lord Trent gestured to Hudson. "You and this fellow seem chummy enough. That small a pool doesn't require a great deal of deductive skills."

"Is there anything about my life you don't know?" Aaron grumbled.

"Probably. Though if any of the women know it, chances are it's gotten around to me."

"Gossiping busybodies."

Lord Trent grinned widely. Was the man ever not happy? "Absolutely. This afternoon, then? Cricket, followed by dinner. You know where my house is, don't you?"

Without waiting for an answer, he poked his head into the stable and called for his horse.

Before he mounted up, he clapped Aaron on the shoulder. "Don't worry. We're going to get everything set straight."

Aaron's eyes widened, but he didn't say anything.

Hudson waited until Lord Trent had ridden away before asking Aaron, "What did he mean, get everything set straight?"

"I haven't the slightest idea," Aaron said, but he wouldn't look at Hudson while he said it.

THE CRICKET BAT felt almost as good in Hudson's hands as a horse's reins. It had been months since he had played, and even though the landscape, the environment, and the people were different, there was something so very comforting about playing the familiar game.

He idly swung the bat back and forth as Aaron, who'd arrived uncharacteristically late and with his dark hair still damp, introduced his friend Lord Farnsworth.

If Hudson had been dropped into a room full of men and told to find the one Aaron counted as a friend, Lord Farnsworth would have been the last man Hudson pulled. The man was perfectly polished, perfectly creased, and, when he spoke, perfectly cultured.

"School rules, I'm assuming?" he asked.

"With cricket?" Was there something Hudson didn't know? Was England even going to steal cricket from him?

"No, no. For names. As much as I would love to force Aaron into an uncomfortable night of trying to remember to call everyone aside from himself *lord*, I'm afraid I've grown too accustomed to answering to Oliver when he's around. It started in school, us dropping all the *lords* to keep Aaron from feeling left out."

"Let it be known that was Oliver's declaration, not mine."

"You didn't argue. Would you prefer Stildon or . . . well." Lord Farnsworth—or, apparently, Oliver—waved his hand about in the air. "Whatever your given name is."

"Hudson will do," he said, trying not to grin and then realizing there was no reason not to. Who cared if his mirth annoyed Aaron? That only made it more humorous.

"This is why more friends are just a bother," Aaron grumbled.

Lord Trent strolled toward the patch of lawn with the wickets already set. "Trent is my only option since all the titles went to my brother and brother-in-law."

"Why is your hair wet?" Hudson asked Aaron as they moved into position.

Oliver laughed. "Because one of my horses got into a mud puddle and then decided Aaron made for a good tree to rub it off with."

"It's not your horse," Aaron said. "It's your father's horse."

"Semantics."

"Tell that to the court."

Hudson laughed and moved into batting position. For the first time since he'd left India, and possibly for the first time ever, it looked like maybe—just maybe—he had found a group where he belonged.

"Why do you keep rooms in London?" Hudson asked Aaron as they stood to the side, watching Oliver wade into a clump of bushes to collect the cricket ball, while Trent shouted occasionally contradictory directions on how to get to the ball's location.

Aaron's eyebrows rose. "What?"

"Just a minute ago Oliver mentioned going by your rooms in London. Why do you keep rooms there? Is there much racing in London?"

Aaron adjusted his coat sleeves. "Not beyond Tattersall's, no. And since you and Oliver's dad are more breeders than collectors, I rarely have reason to go there."

"Why London, then?" Hudson hadn't seen much of the dirty,

crowded city, but he couldn't imagine a horseman wanting to spend any more time there than he had to.

"London is . . ." He trailed off, and Hudson had a feeling that whatever he had been about to say about London, he'd changed his mind. "London is central. From there I can take a stage to any of the racecourses or other stables. It's convenient."

"Convenient."

"Yes."

"Liar.

"That is left, not right. Didn't you have any tutors growing up?" Oliver grumbled as he lifted a ball high in the air and shook it at Trent.

"Yes. Even went to school. Where do you think I learned to enjoy making someone do something foolish?" Trent pulled the ball from Oliver's hand and moved back toward the pitch.

Aaron picked up his bat but didn't move into place. Instead, he stared Hudson down. "I'll make you a deal. You tell me why you want to marry Lady Rebecca, and I'll tell you why I have rooms in London."

Hudson's eyebrows drew together. "I thought it was obvious."

Aaron shook his head. "It's obvious why you'd want the horse. But you haven't even asked Lord Gliddon about it."

Hudson opened his mouth to argue, but he realized the other man was right. Was he always right? It was a rather annoying trait.

The fact was, Hudson had never tried to see if there was another path to Hezekiah. He'd never even questioned the gossip.

As if Aaron could read his mind, he shook his head and clicked his tongue against his teeth. "Aristocrats. All of you simply assuming a man would barter his only daughter for a horse."

"Or he's using the horse as bait to allow that daughter her choice of suitors," Hudson said to defend himself. The reasoning sounded flat, though, even as he said it. "She's going to make a fine wife."

Aaron shook his head. "Doesn't bring out the suitors, not the real ones, and a crowd like that, well. Just imagine the perfect match for Lady Rebecca and see if you can picture him pushing through that crowd."

As Aaron walked away, ready to take his turn at bat, Hudson stayed rooted to the spot. He'd thought Aaron supported Hudson's courtship of Lady Rebecca. And while he didn't need his friend's approval to make decisions, not having it certainly increased the questions that had already been forming in his mind.

Perhaps it was simply something that Hudson, who had been raised by an aristocratic father, might understand more about than his stable manager. Most aristocratic marriages were built on practicalities, such as business and connections. If they weren't, more dukes would be marrying commoners.

Of course, practicality didn't have a man storing his wife's hair in a Bible after her death.

BIANCA HAD NEVER RIDDEN in a carriage all by herself, and every time the carriage paused, she switched seats simply because she could.

It was a childish act, but she was desperate to distract herself from what awaited her at the end of the ride. Why had Lady Adelaide—or really, Lord Trent—invited her to dinner?

The carriage pulled up to the house, and Bianca gripped the seat with both hands as the door was opened.

A stool was placed on the ground outside.

Still, she didn't move.

The footman cleared his throat once, but otherwise everything seemed frozen in time, waiting for her to take the next step.

With a prayer for courage, she poked her head out and accepted the footman's assistance with exiting the carriage. The door to the house flew open, but it wasn't a butler who greeted her. It was Lady Adelaide herself.

"Come, come, there's someone I want you to meet."

There was? Curiosity doused enough of Bianca's trepidation that she was able to get her feet moving. Up the stairs and through the door she went, and then followed her hostess to the drawing room, where another woman was sipping tea and examining two paintings that were leaned up against one of the walls.

"Miss Hancock?"

"Oh good," Lady Adelaide said with a sigh. "You've met. That makes this ever so much easier."

"Of course we've met," Miss Hancock said. "I occasionally associate with the other people in town. It is you who is the hermit."

Lady Adelaide sighed. "I enjoy my quiet life."

"And so you should." Miss Hancock pointed to one of the paintings. "I like that one better, but no matter which one you hang, you'll have to redecorate the whole room."

"Hmmm. Miss Snowley, do come give me your opinion. Which of these should I hang in here?"

Bianca walked forward slowly. Given her current predicaments, she rather envied Miss Hancock. The woman had traveled extensively throughout her formative years, and then, when she was Bianca's age, she'd moved into her own small cottage on the north side of Newmarket. She'd been living on her own now for nearly three years. She even had her own horse that stayed in a small barn behind her cottage.

Bianca looked at the paintings because the other two women wanted her to, but she didn't see much difference. One was more of a water scene, while the other was a mountain. Both paintings used a good deal of blue.

She nodded her head toward the middle where the two frames bumped against each other. "That one."

Both women looked at her and then laughed. Lady Adelaide's was a gentle giggle, while Miss Hancock's echoed about the room in mirthful glee.

"You can say you've no opinion," Lady Adelaide assured her.

"I've no opinion."

"Hmmm. You know, I'm not sure that either painting is right for this room." She tapped a finger against her lips. "Perhaps that's why it is so very difficult to choose between them. Neither is the right one."

Miss Hancock pressed her lips together until her face turned an eerie shade of pink, and then she burst into laughter again. "If that subtlety works, I'll plan a trip to the altar myself. You don't jar a woman loose from erroneous thinking with a metaphor about paintings. If her ideas were that delicate, she'd have dropped them already."

Bianca took a step back. Were they talking about her?

Lady Adelaide frowned. "You're going to scare her."

"I think she's made of sterner stuff than that." She crossed the room and dropped onto a sofa. "I was beginning to question your decorating taste, though."

Lady Adelaide hooked an arm through Bianca's and all but dragged her over to the seating area, where she positioned her in front of a chair and stood there until Bianca decided to sit. Then she seated herself on the settee.

"Trent spent hours visiting the club and chatting to people in taverns so that he would know what was going on. This was all his idea."

"Somehow I don't think he imagined it going like that."

Lady Adelaide frowned. "Well, no. I changed it somewhat. I thought it was a clever idea."

"Perhaps. I just have a feeling it's too subtle."

Bianca clasped her hands together. "I'm sorry. What are you talking about?"

"You know?" Miss Hancock said with a tilt of her head. "I have no idea. Do you play cards?"

Lady Adelaide sprang up and moved to a decorative wooden box to extract a deck of cards. "That's a splendid idea."

"When is dinner?" Bianca asked. She wanted to pursue the

earlier line of questioning, but Miss Hancock intimidated her too much for her to press the point.

"When the men finish their cricket match. I saw two of them digging through the bushes for a lost ball, so it might be a while yet."

Bianca moved over to the card table, glancing toward the back of the house as if she could see through walls. Which men were back there?

Half an hour later, Bianca was hoping the men's cricket game would last for hours. Miss Hancock was still exceedingly intimidating, perhaps even more so as she shared some of her travel stories, but she was also captivating and undeniably likable.

"I know I've seen you at other gatherings before," Bianca said, "but I've never heard any of these stories."

"I can't share stories like these at assemblies. People would be far too scandalized. These are reserved for friends."

Friends. Was that what these women wanted to be? The bold and brassy Miss Hancock and the sweet Lady Adelaide? Had they particularly claimed her to pull her into this circle? "Why me?"

"Because Trent said he thought we would get along well. He can converse with anyone, but I've never been that comfortable with new people. He also knew I would want to rescue any woman living on the short end of the attention scale."

Bianca shifted her cards. "You mentioned your mother favored your sister."

"Hmm. Yes. I didn't know what love really was until I married Trent. We discovered it together, and now I'm afraid he's rather obsessed with spreading the knowledge."

Bianca frowned. What did that have to do with her? She felt like she'd sat down to watch a play but missed the first act.

Lady Adelaide sighed and dropped her hands to the table. "I'm making a right mess of this explanation. What's important is that Trent thought, after seeing you at Hawksworth, that the two of us would be friends, and he's rarely wrong about people."

"I'm out." Miss Hancock tossed her cards into the middle of the table with a sigh.

"Why?" Lady Adelaide asked.

"Because," Bianca said with a wide grin of her own, "you just showed us that you have the ace, king, and queen. We'll never beat you."

She frowned down at her cards. "So I did."

A maid came in and curtsied. "If you please, Lady Adelaide. The gentlemen are going to be joining you soon, and Lord Trent asked that you bring Miss Caroline down."

Lady Adelaide's entire expression changed. Her smile shifted sideways, her eyes softened, and even her posture pulled in. Never had Bianca seen a woman more obviously in love.

"That man," she said with a sigh. "He does enjoy showing off his daughter."

As Lady Adelaide left the room to collect the little girl, Bianca and Miss Hancock moved back to the seating area. Even as her new friend regaled her with the story of another adventure, Bianca couldn't stop watching the door.

Who was going to come through next?

Thirty

Hudson had always thought that the features of children in paintings were somewhat exaggerated, but the small child on Lady Adelaide's hip had a shock of dark hair over the largest green eyes he'd ever seen on an actual human.

Lady Adelaide was coming down the stairs as the men entered the front hall, and she immediately crossed to her husband. "She's here, though I can't imagine why you wanted me to bring her down now."

Trent grinned as he took the child easily into his own arms. Did all English fathers behave that way? Hudson didn't think he'd ever seen it before. Certainly not a father with his daughter.

The child giggled as her father tickled her foot. "I did it so the numbers would be even." Trent grinned at his wife. "You know I always try to keep you from lying when I can."

Lady Adelaide pinked and then whirled away toward the drawing room. Trent followed with a chuckle. "This way, gentlemen. I'm sure dinner is ready, but we should meet up with the ladies before going in."

The ladies? Which ladies? Hudson's heart pounded up into his throat, threatening his ability to both talk and breathe.

"The truth is," Trent continued as he entered the drawing room, "that I simply wanted to show off my little pineapple."

Lady Adelaide sighed and gave Trent an indulgent look before moving to a small sitting area on one side of the room. "So you know, her name is not Pineapple, no matter what Trent tells you. It's Caroline. Considering that she was named after his mother, you'd think he would be more proud of that, but no, he'd rather refer to her as a crop."

"'Napple!" The young girl clapped her hands together.

The child was adorable, but Hudson wasn't looking at her. All he could see was Bianca, whose head was bent to hear what another woman was saying. Everything about her was lit up, from her smile to her eyes. There was something about her that was more captivating in that moment than he'd ever seen before.

He was not supposed to be captivated by Bianca. She was his friend. Nothing more.

Lady Adelaide reached to take the child back. "You've had your fun."

Trent danced a step away. "No, no, not yet. First I want to show them her new trick."

An immediate flush washed over the lady's cheeks, and she pressed her hands to her face. "Trent. No."

"Adelaide. Yes." He looked around. "This isn't a formal gathering."

"Nor is it family."

"Of course not. My brother isn't nearly impressed enough by little Pineapple's tricks, and Ryland turns it into a competition even though Henrietta is considerably older. It's hardly fair."

"Neither is you putting me through this."

Trent shrugged. "If you're jealous, you can hold her while she does it. I assumed you would rather have me do it so the attention wasn't on you."

She shook her head and moved to the side table to get a cup of claret. "Miss Snowley, as you are the only one in this room whose opinion I am concerned about, please do not lay what is about to happen at my feet."

Bianca nodded solemnly, but her lips were pursed so hard that her cheeks were sucked in against her teeth.

She was utterly adorable. Even more so than the child.

Trent gave a dramatic gasp. "Do be careful, wife, you'll insult our gentlemen callers."

"Somehow," Lady Adelaide murmured, "becoming a responsible adult has only made you more senseless."

"It's my love for you that does it, darling."

Lady Adelaide pinked again.

Was this what marriage was like when it wasn't built on practicality? Hudson had to admit it looked far more enjoyable than he'd ever thought marriage could look. Could he and Lady Rebecca ever be like this? It was difficult to picture.

Hudson looked back to Trent, who was trying to get Caroline to cover her eyes and then scream in surprise when she uncovered them and saw her father.

Was this a common thing for children to do? He glanced at Aaron and Oliver, who seemed as confused as Hudson was. That made him feel a bit better.

Trent looked over with a wide smile that fell into a dramatic, despondent sigh. "Apparently none of you appreciate it either. Very well. I'll take her back to the nursery. If dinner is ready, feel free to go on in without me."

Only the low murmur of the women talking in the corner could be heard in the wake of Trent's departure.

Finally, Oliver spoke. "Fathers are strange."

Aaron scoffed. "As you are the only man in this conversation who has one, we'll take your word for it."

"You have a father," Oliver said, "he's simply . . . distant."

"If Trent is considered a father, then mine doesn't deserve the appellation. I'm going to start calling him my life sponsor."

Hudson choked on a sudden laugh.

"I didn't realize you ever referred to him as anything," Oliver said.

Aaron continued, seemingly oblivious to the other two men.

"Like an aunt sponsors her niece for a Season. She doesn't want to. She's got her own daughters to put into society, but familial obligations mean she has to. So she steps in, does a little hand-shaking so that the girl is accepted in the right places, lends her name to give the girl some credibility, maybe throws a bit of money into the mix, and then goes back to her own children. A sponsor."

"That's . . ." Oliver coughed. "That's a rather apt comparison. Especially if the aunt brings out the real daughters to show them their responsibility toward their poorer relations."

"My crazy uncle living in Ireland doesn't seem like such a bad lot anymore."

"I don't know," Aaron mused. "At least my life sponsor never tried to bring an end to my existence."

"To my knowledge, the man never actually tried to kill me. He merely implied he would consider doing so."

"Given the way he reacted when he learned he couldn't take those horses away from Hawksworth, I'd believe him capable of doing it." Aaron gestured to the other side of the room. "Introductions are in order. Let's prove we've some gentlemanly qualities between us."

They joined the ladies, and introductions were made. Soon they were headed in to dinner, and Hudson found himself seated beside Bianca and across from Aaron. Oliver sat across from Bianca and Miss Hancock sat on Aaron's other side. With Trent and Lady Adelaide at the head and foot, it left Bianca and Hudson separated off in a way that felt significant, even though it shouldn't.

The dinner was both enjoyable and painful. Every resolve he'd had, every conclusion he'd come to, everything had been called into question in the last few hours.

Yesterday he'd known his course. Now? Now he wondered how well he even knew himself.

THE WAY BIANCA'S breath refused to fully inflate her lungs, one would think it was she who was competing in the challenge this morning instead of Hudson.

She crept quietly out of her house, taking care to avoid her stepmother and whatever diabolical plan she'd decided Bianca needed to implement today, and walked toward the Heath. Would it be a good thing or a bad thing if many people turned out to witness this race?

While winning would give Hudson something to stand on in front of his fellow stable owners, the gain would be minimal. After all, he hadn't bred this horse or overseen its training. Losing, however, would cause him great detriment.

It wasn't a fair outcome, but it was true.

The crowd milling about was sizable, increased by the number of well-to-do men in town on the lookout for anything remotely interesting to do. Most were gathered near where the race would finish. In the distance, she saw them setting up for the start.

"There are a great many people out today," Hudson murmured as he came to stand beside her.

"Yes." She pointed to the group in the distance. "Shouldn't you be over there?"

He shook his head. "Aaron said he'd see to the start. He shouldn't have any trouble making it to the finish line before the end, but he didn't want me to miss it. He'll come the short way, while the racers take the longer route."

Bianca nodded. "We should find you a good position to watch from, then."

A few people had driven their carriages up to the hill so they could watch the race in comfort, but with the fine day and only one challenge to watch, most of the people walked around, chatting with friends.

If it weren't for the horses, it would look like a garden party.

Many people walked by Hudson, some with congratulatory

remarks, others with speculative stares. No one stopped for long until Lord Rigsby came to join them.

"I laid my money on you, Stildon."

Hudson blew out a breath. "So did I."

"I've seen both of these horses race," Bianca said, hoping she could encourage Hudson to stop fidgeting enough to at least appear calm and confident. "If you don't win, there will be great speculation as to how Lord Davers could have interfered."

"Or they'll simply say I've run my grandfather's stable into the ground in a matter of days."

Lord Rigsby laughed. "That would take some considerable talent."

"I've learned that not everyone in England is logical."

Bianca placed a hand over her mouth to muffle her sudden burst of laughter while Rigsby let his out freely. "Was it any different in India?"

Hudson gave a shrug. "Not really. I'd heard tales of England all my life, though."

"Probably as true as the tales I've heard of India."

"Hmmm."

The three fell into silence as they watched the starting point. The jockeys were mounted now, and the red silks of Lord Davers and Hudson's blue silks stood out against the green landscape.

"Bold choice, to answer a challenge when the October meeting is only a few weeks away."

Bianca turned to see Lord Brimsbane and Lady Rebecca joining their little cluster.

Heat flushed through her face all the way down to her toes. She was, quite literally, standing between Lord Brimsbane and Lord Rigsby. What should she say? What should she do? Were either of them expecting to see some marked preferentiality from her? She prayed neither of them offered her his arm.

It wasn't the first time she'd been in the same space with the two men, but given that Hudson was there and everyone else was too far away to be considered any sort of distraction, it was enough to make Bianca's chest tighten even more, until it felt like only a sliver of air was making it through.

If one of the men was intending to indicate a formal intention to court her, she would prefer it be Lord Rigsby, but her preference felt weak when standing in close proximity to Hudson.

Her friendship with the man had done nothing to quell the infatuation she'd formed when she first met him.

"They're lined up now." Lady Rebecca jabbed her brother in the arm. "I do wish you'd let me bring my opera glasses."

"No one else has opera glasses."

"That only means that no one else can see either."

Bianca shook her head. "You wouldn't be able to follow them anyway. Much easier to simply watch for the colors and see the details as they come to the finish."

"Oh."

A stillness fell over the entire Heath, and then, in a flurry of movement and a chunk of thrown grass, the two horses were off.

The men who'd been on foot near the start ran for their own mounts to be able to cut the corner and see the finish for themselves.

The crowd noise rose as everyone cheered and yelled and speculated over the dots in the distance. The blue one was significantly ahead of the red as they went into the portion of the course that wasn't visible from the finish.

"I've never watched the race from down here." Lady Rebecca leaned across her brother to speak to Bianca. "It's quite excit— Oh!"

Lady Rebecca was not smiling as she looked over Bianca's shoulder with wide, almost panicked eyes.

Bianca spun around to see Aaron rushing toward them. She smiled in his direction. This was good. She had been wanting to see how Lord Rigsby reacted to her rather ostracized friend. If he treated Aaron well, it would be one more indication of the type of potential husband he would be. If she was going to be forced to choose practically, she was going to ensure he was the best he could be.

Lady Rebecca pushed past her brother and hissed directly into Bianca's ear. "Did you know he was going to be here?"

Bianca pressed her ear to her shoulder to relieve the strange tingle the close whisper had caused. "Of course. He's the stable manager."

Lady Rebecca's eyes darted about wildly. "Then why would you let—oh dear, he's here."

"They're running well," Bianca said as Aaron approached, "should be coming around the bend any moment."

He nodded as he came to stand behind Hudson and Lord Rigsby, watching over Bianca's head. "Apollo was looking frisky. It should be a good run."

Lord Rigsby jerked around so quickly that he nearly knocked Hudson over.

"Oh my, oh my, oh my," Lady Rebecca murmured under her breath, shifting her weight from foot to foot.

Bianca looked back and forth from Aaron to Lord Rigsby. Both men were staring at each other, expressionless. She looked at Hudson, who was taking in the exchange with a look that showed as much confusion as Bianca felt. A glance over her shoulder, however, showed not everyone was clueless. Several people, mostly the visitors, were watching the men instead of the race.

Most were whispering. Two men exchanged money. Lord Brimsbane pushed his sister behind him.

Bianca cleared her throat. "Lord Rigsby, may I present—"

"He knows who I am," Aaron bit out.

"Oh. He does?" She looked at Lord Rigsby. "You do?"

"I do."

Bianca looked at Aaron. "And you know who he is?"

"I do."

Hudson stepped closer, standing shoulder to shoulder with Bianca. "Well, I thought I knew both of you, but I've no idea what's going on here."

The glare Aaron turned onto Bianca and Hudson had her taking a step back and partially shielding herself behind the viscount.

"Do you know who his father is?" Aaron asked tightly.

The noise about them lifted to a roar as the men continued to stare at each other.

The horses flew by, but Bianca didn't even glance their way. Suddenly, people were moving everywhere, pulling Hudson away and shoving Bianca into the small space between Lord Rigsby and Aaron.

No one said anything until the noise had shifted far enough away to make yelling not required.

"I don't understand," Bianca said, looking from the man who'd been practically a brother for the past year to the man she'd been giving serious consideration about marrying.

"Do you know who he is?" Aaron asked.

"Lord Rigsby."

"He means," Lord Rigsby said, "do you know who my father is."

"I, well, no." Bianca frowned. She thought back through their conversations, and while he'd talked about his father often, it was always as "my father."

Lord Rigsby sighed. "I am the eldest son of the Marquis of Lindbury."

"The eldest *legitimate* son," Aaron added roughly.

Bianca pressed her hands to her cheeks. No, it couldn't be. Of all the people in all of England, this couldn't possibly have happened. "Oh dear."

"I suppose I know why Father avoids Newmarket now," Lord Rigsby said. "He should have warned me."

Aaron turned away from his half brother and looked past him. "Apollo won. My work here is finished."

Then he left before anyone else could say a word.

Bianca watched him stalk back to his horse and collect the reins before leading the animal away. He didn't even bother mounting up and riding away. He just kept walking, shoulders stiff and straight, and a hitch to his gait, as if his knees weren't quite bending correctly.

Should she go after him? Give him time to think?

She turned back to Lord Rigsby, who was looking at the ground. It seemed hours passed before he looked up at Bianca. His smile was sad as he reached out and brushed aside one of her curls.

"It was a pleasure to meet you, Miss Snowley."

"That sounds a great deal like good-bye."

"Because it is." He stared into the distance, where Aaron was nothing more than a blur. "I've taken enough from him, simply by existing. I won't take his friends too."

"It isn't your fault." She knew more than anyone that a child couldn't be judged by the parent. Gracious. She couldn't imagine having someone decide who she was based on their interactions with Mrs. Snowley.

"No," he agreed, "but it is true nonetheless. I enjoyed our talks." He gripped the tip of his hat and nodded in her direction before slowly walking away.

Bianca whirled around, wondering where everyone else had gone and if anyone had witnessed what just happened.

Neither Lady Rebecca nor Lord Brimsbane was behind her anymore. Had they been swept in with the same crowd that had swirled about, congratulating Hudson?

Where was Hudson?

She scrambled up the side of the ridge where the carriages had parked and looked down over the crowd.

There. She found Hudson.

And by his side, smiling as the congratulations flowed, was Lady Rebecca.

Thirty-One

With the way everyone was huddled around Hudson, one would think his horse had just won the Derby instead of an unofficial local challenge race. From what he'd heard, it wasn't as if the victory was even all that surprising, so why did it seem like everyone wanted to be around him?

Probably because he suddenly wanted to be anywhere but around them.

Not anywhere, actually. He wanted to be wherever Aaron was to find out what had happened between him and Lord Rigsby.

Finally, Hudson was able to thank his jockey and work his way out of the main crowd of people. Lord Brimsbane and Lady Rebecca stood off to the side. The lady's customary smile was tight at the corners, and Lord Brimsbane wasn't leaving her side.

Hudson crossed to them. "Do either of you know what happened?"

Brimsbane's gaze narrowed. "You mean you don't?"

"If I did, I wouldn't ask."

"Rigsby is Mr. Whitworth's brother. His younger, legitimate brother."

All the air left Hudson, as if an elephant had just stepped on his chest. "Do you know where he is?"

"Rigsby?" Lord Brimsbane's lips flattened into a tight line.

"No, Whitworth."

Some of the tension left Lord Brimsbane's expression. "He's gone. Took his horse and left. My guess would be he went home."

And Hudson had only a vague idea where his home was. What kind of friend was he? The kind who had been obsessed with making a name for himself, which wasn't much of a friend at all.

Lord Davers came up beside Hudson. "Celebratory drinks?"

As if Hudson could go laugh in a tavern without knowing if Aaron was packing his bags and taking up permanent residence in those strange London rooms of his. "Perhaps later."

Lord Davers gave him a strange look but departed with another group of men.

"He lives near Lord Farnsworth," Lady Rebecca said. "We can take you. Our carriage is at the end of the row."

"I would appreciate it."

He checked that a stable lad was taking Apollo back to the training stable, then joined the brother and sister in the carriage, holding his breath with every congestion-induced delay as the other conveyances tried to leave the area.

Once they were free of the Heath, it took little time to reach the estate.

"Where is the cottage?" he asked as the carriage rolled down the drive.

Brimsbane shook his head. "I don't know. I just know it's somewhere on this property."

Hudson nodded. Aaron would be a private sort of fellow. Maybe it wasn't such a sign of bad friendship that he didn't know where the cottage was. "Lord Farnsworth will know."

"Lord Farnsworth is here?" Lady Rebecca asked and then gave a small cough. "I thought he lived in London."

"He traveled with Mr. Whitworth when he came back from London."

The carriage stopped, and Hudson didn't wait for a footman to open the door. He pushed it open himself and jumped to the ground.

The front door opened as he approached. "What's wrong?" Oliver asked as he stepped outside.

"Where does Aaron live?"

Oliver's eyebrows flew up. He looked over Hudson's shoulder to the carriage, swallowed hard, then directed his attention to Hudson again. "Why do you want to know?"

"Rigsby," Brimsbane said from a few feet behind him.

Oliver looked over at his other impromptu guests once more. This time the pause was longer before he looked away, shoving a hand through his hair and mussing the perfectly smooth configuration. "What did Rigsby do?"

"He walked away," Hudson said, "but I need to apologize for having him there in the first place."

"Why would you do that?" Oliver ran his hand through his hair again and then placed his hands on his hips.

"I didn't know."

"You didn't ask?"

Hudson scoffed. "Do you go around asking men you meet if they are somehow scandalously related to every other man you know? I wouldn't even know Aaron was illegitimate if he hadn't announced it to me at our first meeting."

"He does like to get that out of the way these days."

"Oliver." Hudson drew the name out in a tone he hoped was menacing enough to get the man to give up the information but not threatening enough to make him keep it to himself.

"Three-quarters of a mile that way. There's a path just beyond those trees."

"Thank you." Hudson took off at a jog, breathing hard by the time he reached the little cottage.

A small barn, nearly as big as the cottage itself, stood to the side. Shadow was poking his head out of a window in the barn, so Hudson knew he was in the right place.

He gave the door two sharp knocks, then stepped back, trying to catch his breath.

Aaron opened the door. His eyes widened when he saw Hudson. He leaned out the door and looked both ways, as if making sure he'd come alone. "What are you doing here?"

"Apologizing?"

Aaron frowned. "For what? It's not as if you knew who he was."

Hudson placed one hand on his hip and gestured back in the direction he'd come from. "That's what I said, but Oliver thought I should have asked."

"That would have made everything awkward." Aaron stepped inside and held the door wide. "You may as well come in."

Hudson entered the little cottage, which was really a single room, divided into sections with furniture. "I didn't get to see everything, but they said you left angry—"

"Of course I did. I wasn't expecting to see him. The marquis has always avoided Newmarket. It's been a sort-of unspoken agreement between us that this was my area. They got the rest of the world."

Hudson frowned. "Why is he here, then?"

Aaron shrugged. "Because the rest of the world is not enough? Because his father didn't see fit to tell him not to come? I don't know. I do well enough when I know I'm going to see him, which isn't often. When I'm taken by surprise"—he shrugged again—"I leave."

"I see."

Aaron put a pot of water onto a small cookstove. "Do you?"

Hudson sat at the wooden table near the kitchen area. "Do I what?"

"See?"

Did he? He'd thought so. He understood why Aaron would

want to avoid Rigsby and why the surprise had made him angry. He understood that it would be easier for Aaron if Hudson picked sides, and he was willing to do so.

Suddenly, none of that seemed to be what Aaron was talking about, though. "I don't know. . . . Do I?"

"No. You don't." Aaron moved about, efficiently pulling out mugs, tea, and sugar from various places.

"Do you cook down here?"

"Just tea and the occasional breakfast. A boy brings my other meals from the house."

"Oh."

Aaron grunted and checked the water.

Hudson fiddled with a mug. "What don't I see?"

Aaron gave a humorless laugh and shook his head. "Do you know why I'll never marry?"

That was not what Hudson was expecting. "Um . . ."

"Because I've nothing to offer her but myself."

Hudson sent the mug spinning on the table as he sat back and crossed his arms over his chest. While he understood that statement, Aaron's saying it so baldly made him uncomfortable.

Aaron took each mug and scooped water from the pot before dropping a clump of tea into each one.

Hudson's mouth tilted up. "I don't think that's how you make tea."

"It's how *I* make tea. Take it or leave it."

Hudson sat forward and wrapped his hands around the mug, more to give them something to do than a desire to drink what was sure to be awful tea. "Explain."

"What is there to explain?" Aaron looked around the cottage. "I can't bring a wife home to this."

"I know how much I pay you. You could afford more than this."

"A better house, yes, but not a better life. My father acknowledged me. He sent me to school, forced London society to allow me to dally on the fringes, and made sure I wouldn't become a wastrel. As soon as his back is turned, though, they shut me out again."

"Not everyone needs high society."

Aaron shook his head. "Said the man who's willing to ruin his life for a good reputation."

Hudson looked up from the swirl of murky tea. "What?"

"You heard me. My birth means my wife would be ostracized, my children shunned. The happiest marriages are the ones that are more about the couple than the business, but even the strongest love will crack under enough pressure."

Aaron took a swill of tea. "What you don't see is that you don't have to worry about any of that. You can give a wife every comfort, but it will mean nothing if you don't give her yourself."

"How do you know that? Have you seen so many marriages that you're an expert on them?"

"From afar. You've seen them too, if you think about it. Lord Trent and Lady Adelaide?" Aaron shook his head. "That entire family is obnoxiously happy because they married for love. I thought it had something to do with the comfort of it all until I watched Graham fall in love."

He shook his head again and downed the rest of his tea in two long swallows. "It isn't the comfort that makes the love good. It's the life that makes their love good."

"Then why won't you marry?" If Aaron truly believed that love was most important, then it could overcome those other issues.

Aaron stood and grabbed his mug from the table. "Maybe I've just never met the right woman. You, however, have, and you're so busy being stupid that you're going to lose her."

He leaned both hands onto the small worktable by the cookstove. "Do you know how many times I prayed for a life like yours?" His voice was so low, Hudson had to stand and step closer to hear it clearly. "Every night for years, I prayed that God would work a miracle and I would wake up legitimate and in my father's house.

The day I met Rigsby I stopped praying, because I knew the position I'd asked God for had already been given to someone else.

"At that point, I vowed to go it alone, but Graham wouldn't take no for an answer, and he hauled Oliver right along with him. So I tried to hide in the stables, but Bianca kept trouncing in, and then you showed up. All of these people in my life with so much going for them and all of you are so very stupid, and I have to just watch because there's nothing else I can do."

Hudson wanted to be offended that Aaron had just declared him stupid, but there'd been such anguish in his voice that he couldn't bring himself to care.

"Go home," Aaron said, pushing up off the worktable to a standing position. "Go home and think about this. At the end of the day, it's your life." He shrugged. "And I could be wrong. Maybe you'll be perfectly happy with your decisions."

Hudson wanted to pry, to get Aaron to say whatever he was saying more clearly, because it seemed like he was bothered by something far more than Hudson.

Asking for more would be selfish, though. After a day like today . . . It wasn't as if Aaron had approached Hudson about this. Hudson had forced his way into Aaron's home. The man deserved to be able to say as much or as little as he wanted in his own home.

"Will you be at the stable tomorrow?"

"Of course." Aaron crossed his arms. "Likely in the afternoon, though. I've some work to do here first."

Hudson nodded. "I'll see myself out."

One side of Aaron's mouth kicked up. "Think you can find the door?"

Hudson gave a small smile in return and then left, his mind already churning over the possibilities Aaron had implied.

Thirty-Two

Hudson rolled his neck and tried to ease the strain of his muscles. He'd fallen asleep in the chair in his study. Again. When he'd gotten back to Hawksworth, he pulled out his father's Bible and flipped through it, his thumb rolling back and forth on the edge of the medallion on the bookmark.

How was one supposed to go about finding the answers to his questions in a book that was so old? There were stories of people asking Jesus for help and advice, but the man Hudson had related to the most was the one who had ended up on his knees, asking Jesus to help his unbelief instead of what he'd come asking Jesus for in the first place.

Hudson believed. He'd believed for a long time. That wasn't his problem.

Was it?

Just because he wasn't sure God was going to make something better didn't mean he didn't believe in God.

Or did it?

If he truly believed God was loving and powerful, wouldn't that mean he could trust that God knew what He was doing? That there'd been a reason for Hudson to spend years in India?

The night in his chair hadn't brought him clarity. Neither had a cup of coffee, nor practically dunking his head in the washbasin.

Perhaps a good, long ride would put everything in perspective, though the idea of going back to the Heath right now made him want to turn around and go back to bed. Still, even if he didn't go to the Heath, the back of a horse was a good place to view life from.

A familiar green riding habit was already in the stable when he arrived. It was possibly the first thing that had gone right for him since yesterday's race.

"I'm glad to see you," he said. "I've missed our rides."

"As have I. My father's horses simply aren't the same."

Hudson winced at the idea of even comparing his horses to the ones her father had, but he kept that to himself.

"I believe they've got our mounts ready. Shall we?" She stepped away from the horse she'd been petting, and a beam of sunlight pierced through the large window and lit upon her face, making her smile glow that much more.

He knew he'd been about to say something, but now the words were stuck somewhere behind the realization that his friend was more than pretty. She was beautiful. She hadn't needed anyone's help to secure a husband. She'd only needed to make herself available.

Which meant that soon he'd lose her. Would there be a way to maintain a friendship after she married? After he married?

Was this what Aaron meant? Had he seen that Hudson's friendship with Bianca had a time limit? Was he encouraging him to cherish it while it lasted?

He cleared his throat when he noticed she was giving him a strange look. How long had he been standing there, staring at her? "Er, which horse are you riding?"

"Odysseus," she said with a sigh.

"I thought you liked Odysseus."

"I do. He's just so much shorter than Hades."

"Then I'll ride Athena." The words were out of his mouth

before he could stop them. "She's still taller, but at least I won't be towering over you."

"Thank you," she said softly.

For a few moments, they stood there, not moving, not speaking, and for Hudson at least, barely breathing.

"Okay, then." She pursed her lips and stepped aside while the grooms scrambled to get Athena saddled. "We'll have to ride the lands. We're later than normal, and the Heath will already be closed for the morning."

"I'm sure the rest of the countryside is picturesque."

"Oh yes. There's a spot just west of here."

Hudson bowed low and swept his arm out wide. "Lead on."

She smiled that brilliant smile at him again—was it truly just the way the sunlight caught it?—and, once mounted, set off across one of his paddocks. Hudson spurred his horse to join her, and Owen followed several lengths behind on Atalanta.

The area was largely flat, but as they went west and skirted a few areas of farmland, small rolling hills joined the terrain. *Hills* might even be a generous term, but the slight embankments served to create a block to prevent him from looking back at Newmarket. He truly felt like he'd been able to leave life behind for a while.

"I enjoyed the dinner party at Lord and Lady Hawthorne's." Bianca shook her head and gave a little laugh. "I'd never met Lady Adelaide until she came to invite me, but I think I like her."

"Lord Trent gave an interesting introduction as well. I confess, I was somewhat nervous about it."

"I imagine dinner parties in India were quite different."

"Yes. Eating food is about the only commonality."

"What if he'd had a boar?"

"Isn't that a pig?"

"Mm-hmmm," she said with a nod. "The eyeballs are a delicacy."

"Only to someone who has never eaten them."

She blinked. "You've had boar's head?"

He shrugged, enjoying that, in this at least, he knew more than she did. "Goat. But I would think they'd be quite similar. Eyeballs are rather chewy. Really, the only way to eat them is just to swallow them down."

"No wonder you find our cuisine boring."

He wanted to correct her, that it was more an issue of blandness, but the truth was his cook made boring food. If he offered her a bonus, would she learn to cook with spices like turmeric, cumin, and cardamom?

She cleared her throat. "Have you seen Aaron since yesterday?"

"Yes. I went to see him yesterday. He's . . ." What was he? Right? Wrong? Bitter? Realistic? "I think he was more surprised than angry to see Lord Rigsby."

"That's good." Her gaze dropped to her reins.

What was she thinking? Was she thinking about Lord Rigsby? How close had the two of them gotten? Was she going to turn away from Aaron? "Are you thinking about Lord Rigsby?"

"What?" Her head popped up. "No. Well, yes, but mostly in that I didn't realize how much I didn't know about him."

"Should you have known a lot about him?"

She didn't answer. He didn't really expect her to, but he truly wanted to know. He wanted to quiz her about Lord Rigsby and Lord Brimsbane, wanted to make her promise she'd still come riding at Hawksworth after she married.

It had been mere weeks since she came into his life, but he couldn't imagine living in England without her. Restlessness drove through his body, making him want to spur the horse beneath him into a hard run so he could leave the sensation behind.

"My lord!"

Hudson and Bianca pulled their horses to a stop and looked back several yards to where Owen was dismounting from Atalanta at the base of the small rise they'd just come down. Without word, they both directed their mounts to return to the groom.

"I think she's picked up something in her shoe," the groom said as he ran a hand down the horse's leg. "She started hobbling coming over the rise. Nothing feels wrong, and she seems alright standing here." Owen straightened and tucked a wisp of hair that had escaped his queue behind his ear.

"At least we haven't gone far," Bianca said. "It won't be too long for you to walk her back to the stable."

Owen said nothing, just made a pointed look from her to Hudson and back.

Bianca gestured a hand over the empty countryside. "Who's even going to see us?"

Hudson coughed. "I don't think our immense solitude is an argument in favor of his leaving."

"If it makes you feel better, walk Atalanta back and then return with another horse. It won't take you long."

With a sigh, Owen agreed, because the only other option was for Hudson to take the horse back and let Owen ride Athena. That was probably what he should have done, but the idea of being alone with Bianca, even if it was on horseback in the middle of a field, was rather appealing.

Perhaps it was what he needed to sort out this mess in his head. If he could talk to her about it without distractions or attentive ears, would he be able to determine what was bothering him?

Owen took the mare's reins and walked her back over the ride toward Hawksworth.

After a few moments, nothing could be heard but the light wind rustling the grass and a distant bird calling to its mate.

"Shall we continue?" Bianca asked. "At the rate we've plodded along Owen will be able to catch us easily."

"Why don't we wait here for a bit? Rest the horses." He kicked his feet free of the stirrups and swung his leg over before Bianca could agree.

"What?" she said through a laugh. "It's not as if we've been on a cross-country trek. There isn't even a stump out here for me to remount with." She pointed to a scraggly group of shrubs. "Those are hardly going to suffice."

He wrapped Athena's reins around one of the inconsequential plants and then reached up toward Bianca. "I'll help you up when it's time to return."

She stared at him, eyes narrowed.

He wiggled his fingers. "Come along. I feel like this is a part of England I haven't seen yet."

"And you can't see it from the back of your horse?" She shook her head but shifted her hold on the reins so he could grasp her waist and help her down from her side-seated position.

He'd noticed her strength when they'd danced, and he noticed it again in a way that made his heart work just a little bit harder.

Once she was on the ground, he took her horse and secured it to another shrub before taking a few moments to try to get himself under control. Whether it was Aaron's statements, the Bible searching, or a night of sleeping in a chair, something was shifting in Hudson's mind, and he wasn't sure what it was.

All he knew was he didn't recognize it. Riding a horse wasn't clearing his mind. Perhaps sitting with her would.

When he came back to Bianca, she was looking out at the view, no longer smiling like she had been. Was this sadness new, or had it been there earlier and he just hadn't seen it?

She waved a hand in front of her. "Does India look like this?"

"Parts of it. Yet, at the same time, no. It doesn't look the same or feel the same, but there's something familiar about it."

Her toe dislodged a tuft of grass and kicked it his way. "I would think grass pretty much looks like grass no matter where you go."

He kicked the tuft away and then sat down to run his hand through the blades. "You would think that, and yet it isn't true."

He lay on his back and pointed at the sky. "Even the sky looks different. Not right now—though the sun never seems to be where

I expect it to be—but at night, everything looks strange. I remember on the boat, the few nights I managed to be well enough to walk on the deck, the sky told me I was farther and farther from everything I knew."

She sat next to him but didn't seem to share his relaxation.

A few feet away, the horses happily munched on grass, while overhead birds circled and chirped. Every living thing in the vicinity looked happy except for her.

"What's wrong?"

She jumped and looked down at him, her lips curving as quickly as they normally did. The corners of her eyes didn't crinkle though. "Nothing's wrong. Why do you ask?"

"Because this moment is sheer perfection and you aren't enjoying it."

"I'm enjoying it." She tipped her head back and threw her arms out to the side. "See?"

He rolled onto his side and propped his head on his hand. "I see."

Perhaps he was truly seeing now. Was this what Aaron meant about marriage being about giving oneself? Hudson wanted to make her happy, wanted to know what she was thinking, what she was feeling. He never asked Lady Rebecca questions like that—never even thought to.

He pictured Lady Adelaide and Lord Trent and the way they teased and interacted but still sent each other little smiles when they thought no one was looking. He'd never seen a couple like that, certainly never seen a marriage like that, but it looked ever so much more appealing than the ones he had seen.

And he could not even begin to imagine having a life like that with Lady Rebecca.

But what would it mean if he didn't marry Lady Rebecca? What would become of all his plans? Lady Rebecca made sense. But so did Bianca, in an emotional, gut-wrenching sort of way.

So, which was right? How did he make the correct choice? It had always been obvious before what he should do. There'd been only one true step forward, but now, there were paths.

He had to believe he could make the right choice. "Lord, help my unbelief," he whispered.

"What?" Bianca asked, turning to him and pulling up a blade of grass to run through her fingers.

He shook his head and looked back up at the sky. *Lord, help my unbelief. Not my belief in my own capabilities but my belief that you've got a plan for me and I should follow it, even if it doesn't make sense.*

"Lady Adelaide and Miss Hancock seemed like great friends." Bianca's statement broke the silence and Hudson's impromptu prayer.

"I think so."

"I don't have many friends. Aaron. You. It has occurred to me lately that it's something I'm not very good at. People are friendly if they see me, but no one goes out of their way to make it happen."

What could Hudson say to that? The truth was, if Aaron hadn't forced him to go into town, he'd have never met anyone, except Lord Trent, who'd pushed his own way in.

"Don't feel bad for me, though," she said, giving him a crooked, sad smile. "I don't put in a great deal of effort either. It didn't matter until I realized it. Now I can't seem to see much else other than how lonely I am."

She pulled up another tuft of grass. When she spoke again, her voice was tight, perhaps even on the verge of tears. "Do you think marriage will change anything?"

"I think that depends on whom you marry."

What if he did that? What if he looked at marriage as a companionship, an exchange of selves, like Aaron had described? Whom would he choose?

A woman who liked horses and riding. He lived and breathed the animals, so if she was going to spend life with him, she needed to as well.

A woman comfortable with joking and teasing. If she were someone he was going to give to on a personal level, he would have to respect her, and he could never fully respect someone who never challenged him.

A woman who could help him professionally by moving in the right social circles. Companionship mattered, but he still had a life to build.

She would be beautiful and feel right in his arms.

She would be someone very much like Bianca.

Whom was he trying to fool? It would *be* Bianca.

A puff of air released from her lips and slid across his own. How had she gotten so close? Had she moved, or had he? Likely him, as her arms were still wrapped around her legs.

Hudson lifted one hand to cup her cheek, thumb running gently over the soft skin. So many thoughts went through his mind he couldn't begin to articulate them.

Some of the things he'd been up most of the night contemplating were suddenly clear, and other things didn't seem to matter anymore. The idea that she would find someone, that the other men in Newmarket would suddenly see what they'd been missing, squeezed his chest until he couldn't breathe.

What would happen when he didn't see her every day? When she wasn't waiting in his stables?

"Hudson," she whispered, her face so close to his that his own name caressed his lips.

He leaned closer, wanting more of her breath mingled with his.

"This is a bad idea," she said, each word making her lips brush against his own.

Was it? Everything he thought he knew was suddenly in question. "I want to kiss you."

Her throat shifted against his fingers as she swallowed. "I want to kiss you too."

Then they both leaned in to remove that last bit of distance, and their lips met, bonding together just as their words had moments before.

What Hudson had thought was a moment of sheer perfection five minutes ago was nothing compared to what he was experiencing now.

This was bliss.

This was joy.

He shifted his balance to free his other arm and wrapped it around her as he tilted his head to deepen the kiss. She leaned farther into him, accepting his embrace and offering her own, though the twist of her body from the way she'd been sitting kept him from being able to pull her fully into him.

It was that inability to bring her closer that prompted him to pull back from her sweet kiss and search her face.

Her eyes fluttered open slowly, a dazed expression in her brown eyes that made him want to kiss her again.

With one more blink of her eyes, his future went from planned to uncertain, but it also went from dull to colorful. He'd been complaining about the food all while being willing to settle for a bland life.

No more. His path might be uncertain, there might be questions, but he'd rather walk it with Bianca than anyone else.

He needed to do it right, though. He needed to end his attentions to Lady Rebecca, needed to ask Bianca's father, needed to . . .

Needed to calm Bianca down, because the dazed expression had left her face and been replaced by something that could only be described as terror.

Thirty-Three

He'd kissed her.

Bianca blinked her eyes open to see Hudson staring back at her, so close she could see the darker rim of navy around his blue eyes.

He had kissed her. Really kissed her.

His arm was still around her, and she pushed it away, but since it had been the only thing holding her up, she fell backward onto the grass.

She scrambled to her feet, tripped again because she was standing on the long drape of her riding skirt, then made another attempt to rise after kicking the fabric away.

By the time she was firm on her feet, her heart was thudding in her chest, her breathing was faster than a galloping horse, and a blade of grass had gotten stuck in her hair and was dangling in front of her face.

She snagged the grass and threw it aside before glaring at Hudson. He still sat on the ground, one hand outstretched, as if he had attempted to catch her when she tripped.

"What"—she heaved through two breaths—"was that?"

He grinned at her. The man who might be announcing his engagement at a ball in less than a week, but had kissed another woman just now, grinned.

She wanted to kick him.

"In India, we called that a kiss. I think that's an English word, so it shouldn't need translating."

No, she didn't want to kick him. She was going to bring one— no, both!—of the horses over here and let them do the kicking.

She didn't know what she felt, didn't even know what she thought. There was a question swirling about in her brain, and she couldn't hold on to it long enough to form it into words, so she simply spat out, "Lady Rebecca."

He winced.

Then he sighed.

Then he stood.

What he didn't do was tell her that he'd told Lady Rebecca he wasn't going to be seeking her out anymore.

"I would like to return to the stable now. Actually, no, I'd like to go home. You can send Owen to collect the horse." She shook her head. "The groom is smarter than I am. He knew I shouldn't stay out here alone with you."

She stomped toward the horses, a sudden burn in her eyes telling her that her departure wasn't going to happen quickly enough.

Especially since she couldn't mount up without his help.

"Bianca, I didn't plan this."

She coughed out a mirthless laugh. "No. I should think not."

"Bianca, please turn around."

"No." If she did, she'd cry. She was going to cry anyway, but if she was very, very lucky and got on this horse very, very soon, she might be able to do it in private.

Never in her entire life had she ever thought a kiss could be like that. That it could feel like riding a fabled winged horse through the clouds while the best musicians in the world played along.

And now she would have to live with never experiencing it again.

"Bianca, I'm going to talk to Lady Rebecca." He sighed. "I

didn't expect . . . I didn't realize . . . I did some thinking last night, and . . ."

No. He was not going to give her hope. She'd waited for someone like him for years without realizing she was waiting, and then he'd chosen another, so she'd resigned herself to someone else.

Only now she didn't even have that, did she? A life with Mr. Mead had looked bad enough before. How much more so now?

And Hudson had gone and ruined everything on a whim? A spur-of-the-moment thought? An unexpected indulgence?

"When you decide how to finish one of those sentences, let me know." She took a shaky breath and gritted her teeth. Finally, she was able to squeak out, "In the meantime, help me onto this horse."

Unfortunately, there was no way to get on the horse that didn't involve her facing him and him putting his hands on her.

The moment was as disastrous as she'd feared.

As soon as his hands touched her waist, her control slipped and the tears poured out.

He wrapped her in his arms. "I'll make everything right, I promise."

She shook her head, wiping her tears and who-only-knew-what-else on his jacket. "Do you even know what you want?"

"Do you?" he countered. "I'm not the only one who has been making different plans for their life in the last few weeks."

"I only made mine because you made yours," she yelled into his chest. She really hadn't meant to tell him that. She sniffled and pushed away from him. "Put me on the horse, Hudson. Now."

He lifted her up onto the saddle, but his hands remained in place. "Can I call on you tomorrow?"

Would she be ready to face him? Would she know how she felt? Shouldn't she decide what she wanted before listening to him?

"I'll let you know," she said. Then she gathered up the reins and rode away.

THE ONE BENEFIT to years of practice sneaking around the house and avoiding her stepmother was that she knew how to get to her room without anyone the wiser.

Once there, she flopped across the bed and piled her pillows, her blanket, and even her dressing gown on top of her head so that she could sob without anyone knowing. The last thing she needed at this moment was some form of motherly advice that wasn't the least bit maternal.

When there were no more tears, she crawled out from under the soft mountain and draped herself on top of it, staring at her ceiling as the shadows shifted through the day.

Had Hudson kissed her two weeks ago, she'd have been thrilled, but time and again she'd seen him in the company of Lady Rebecca, and they'd looked so perfect. It hadn't been a long time, but who needed time when the match made such sense?

Who needed time when it was right?

But was it right? Could Hudson kiss Bianca like that and still want to marry Lady Rebecca? If he did, then he wasn't the man she thought he was, and it was a good thing he was marrying someone else because she'd fallen in love with a man that didn't exist.

Love? Was she really in love with Hudson? It had been three weeks. Could someone fall in love in three weeks?

Maybe.

If they'd spent their whole life waiting, subconsciously looking for the other half of themselves and never, ever finding it, it wouldn't take much to recognize it when it appeared.

Or did she want love so badly that she'd made Hudson something he wasn't?

How in the world was she supposed to determine that?

There were no answers in the night, nothing but more questions. She was so very tired of questions. Why couldn't God just tell her what she was supposed to do?

The last time she'd asked for a sign, Lord Rigsby had come

riding by. Obviously, he was no longer an option, even if she was willing to balance him and Aaron—which, honestly, she wasn't. She'd never do that to her friend. It would have been nice to have been given the choice, though.

Instead, it had been Lord Rigsby who'd walked away.

Maybe Bianca wasn't very good at determining signs.

"God, is it too much just to not want to be alone anymore? I want somebody to talk to, to share stories with, to laugh and enjoy life with. Someone who will care if I don't show up to something."

The truth was, she wasn't the smart choice of wife for Hudson. Her dowry was decent, but he didn't need money, and if he did, what she brought wouldn't be enough.

Of course, when looked at that way, she wasn't a good choice for any of the men she'd been spending so much time thinking about. A practical marriage required she have something practical to offer.

Finally, mentally exhausted and unsure, she fell asleep.

Some time later, Dorothy was shaking her awake. "Miss Snowley, please wake up. You've got a visitor, and we need to make you presentable. I didn't even know you'd gotten home."

"What?"

Bianca sluggishly blinked awake as Dorothy tugged her from the bed.

"There's a man downstairs to see you, and Mrs. Snowley's about got the house in shambles over it. I need you to change clothes right now."

Dorothy was already tugging at Bianca's clothing, loosening tapes and ties and dragging her riding habit off.

The skirt was still dropping to the ground as the maid slipped another dress over Bianca's head. "Arms in sleeves, if you please, miss."

"Who's downstairs?"

"Now your hair."

"Ow!" Bianca jerked sideways as Dorothy jabbed a pin into Bianca's head.

"I don't have time to fix the curls. I'll just rearrange them."

Three jabs later, she was tugging Bianca toward the door and down the corridor.

Bianca nearly tripped down the steps as the maid gave her a little push. As much as she wanted to slow her descent to an elegant crawl, curiosity had her hastening her step.

Was it Hudson?

Did she want it to be?

It wasn't Hudson.

It was Lord Brimsbane.

"Have you decided to take up residence in the stables, then? The round house finally chased you out?"

Hudson didn't even flinch from his position near the end of the stable aisle, looking from box stall to box stall at his thoroughbreds. Contrary to what his staff likely thought, he wasn't in a total stupor. He still heard the grooms moving about, heard the horses, and, most of all, heard his own thoughts.

And those scared him.

"Wasn't the round house," he said before turning his head to look at Aaron. "Might have been you, though."

"Me? I haven't even been here." Aaron leaned against the stall wall and propped one booted foot against it while he crossed his arms. Athena nudged at his head through the stall bars.

"It took me an hour to break free of all the congratulations yesterday," Hudson said. "Davers even invited me to the pub, and I thought the man hated me."

Aaron shrugged one shoulder. "Doesn't mean he likes you. Things are different on the Heath. Lord Davers even talks to me on race days, though I often wish he wouldn't."

"Hmmm." Hearing that what went on in the assembly room didn't necessarily carry over to the turf gave Hudson a new perspective, one that gave him a little more peace about what he was trying to get up the courage to do.

He took a deep breath and said, "If I don't ask Lady Rebecca to marry me—"

"Praise God," Aaron murmured.

Hudson snapped his gaze from the horse to Aaron. "Really? You dislike the idea that strongly?"

"I've never thought it was your best plan, no."

"Why didn't you say something?"

Aaron shook his head, laughing silently. "Hudson, I just met you."

"I've just met all of these people, and it feels like the rest of them are running my life."

Aaron pushed off the wall and gestured toward one of the grooms. "And why do you care what they think of you? That's the most finicky beast you'll ever ride. Trust me."

"My whole life I've been waiting for this moment, when I would be here doing what I'd been born to do. I have to be successful at this."

"I don't see any reason why you won't be." He opened Hades's stall door and grabbed the saddle the groom brought up. "The thing is, whose definition of success are you going to use?"

Aaron placed the saddle over the back of the horse and efficiently set about securing it. "Why do you think the Jockey Club doesn't let just anyone in? Even as a small group they have difficulty deciding what time the races should be. If it were open to public debate, nothing would get done."

"Are you saying my life needs a committee to run it?" Hudson asked as he took the bridle and gave the horse a good scratch behind the ears before sliding it on.

"I'm saying everyone's life has a committee. You need to decide who's on yours." Aaron gave the cinch a final tug and then propped an arm across the horse's back to look directly at Hudson. "And who isn't."

Hudson took the reins and mounted the horse. He knew what he was going to do, could feel a peace about the decision, even through the fear that it wouldn't go well, that it would change the direction of his life.

But maybe that was a good thing?

Lord, help my unbelief. This was the right thing to do. Lady Rebecca would make a wonderful wife, of that there was no question, but he couldn't see them building a life together. They would each have good lives that simply existed next to each other.

It was what everyone expected him to do.

That didn't mean it was the best thing to do.

Aaron had asked him why he wanted to marry Lady Rebecca, and the truth was he didn't. He was simply scared not to, and that was a terrible reason to make such an important decision.

It was time to set both of them free to find something better.

Thirty-Four

Lady Rebecca took the news far better than her father.

It might have been the happiest Hudson had ever seen her.

"You won't find anyone better, boy," Lord Gliddon said, not even bothering to hide behind his paper or in the corner. In fact, the three of them were standing in the man's study. Hudson could only assume they'd thought he'd come for an entirely different reason, which was understandable, given the past few weeks.

"It's not about finding someone better than Lady Rebecca," Hudson said carefully, not wanting to insult the lady or her father.

He just didn't want to marry her.

"Don't tell me this is about love," the earl grumbled.

Was it? Hudson hadn't really considered that, since love had never been a part of his expectations for life. But was that what he was looking for?

"Don't you think there should be some love in a marriage?" Hudson asked, giving the man a pointed look. Was he really going to stand there in front of his daughter and say that love wasn't important? Was he going to say he didn't love his wife?

Perhaps he didn't.

But Hudson knew that life with Bianca would be far different from life with Lady Rebecca, and that extra connection that love brought just might be the difference.

It was a difference Hudson wanted, and he wanted it enough to put his definition of success on the auction block. It was time to change goals from those that had been set for him to those he truly wanted.

He took a deep breath. "Lady Rebecca, you are a lovely young lady and marrying you would be an honor, but I know both of us could have a better life than that."

"Thank you," she said softly and glanced at her father before dropping her eyes to the floor.

"Lord Gliddon, I won't put you on the spot by asking about Hezekiah right now, but perhaps a conversation could be had in the future?"

"Perhaps it could, boy. Perhaps it could." Lord Gliddon shook his head. "You remind me of your father right now."

There wasn't much Lord Gliddon could have said that would surprise Hudson more. "I do?"

"When he went off to India with that bride of his, he said as long as she was with him he could find people to fill the rest of his life with." Lord Gliddon nodded at Hudson. "You're standing here today a fine man, so I guess he did well enough, but I can't imagine starting over like he did."

Neither could Hudson, but he was ready to try.

Lord Gliddon sighed and gave his daughter a sad look. "It's a shame. It would have been nice to make two announcements that night."

"Two, my lord?"

Lady Rebecca's smile tightened. "Arthur isn't home right now. He's paying a very important call."

Where Hudson had felt strong and sure before, his world felt like it was caught in a sudden monsoon.

Was he going to be too late?

BIANCA HAD NEVER considered herself a coward, but she hid for the next three days. She didn't go to the assembly, didn't come down for callers, even thought of pretending to be sick and missing church.

She knew Hudson had tried to come by at least once, but Dorothy had obeyed Bianca's instructions instead of Mrs. Snowley's and said Bianca was indisposed.

But now it was Monday, and she couldn't hide anymore. Even if she'd wanted to, she couldn't miss the ball.

She had a decision to make, and she'd promised to make it by tonight. The truth was she made her decision three days ago. She just needed the courage to admit it.

Mrs. Snowley looked grim as the family gathered in the front hall to depart for the ball. "I suppose you're happy with yourself."

Was she? Yes, actually, she was.

"Don't get too settled. Things could still go differently than you expect tonight." Her grim frown eased into a wicked smile. "You never know what could happen at a ball."

Bianca looked from Mrs. Snowley to Marianne, who was also looking strangely determined, given that they were going to what was sure to be one of the finest, most exclusive gatherings of the year.

"What are you planning to do?"

"Me?" Mrs. Snowley asked. "What makes you think I'm planning anything? I'm simply anticipating having my daughter's future settled."

It looked like Bianca could add one more thing to her list of concerns for the night.

HUDSON STOOD to the side of the ballroom, watching the door, waiting for her arrival. It had been the longest three days of his life, and that was including the time he'd spent on the ship from India.

He glanced over the dance floor to make sure he hadn't missed her coming in. It was easy to pick out Lady Rebecca as she danced with Oliver. She looked relaxed as she talked through the dance. He thought she might have even laughed. That was good. She should be happy.

His happiness wasn't on the dance floor, though, at least not yet. Hopefully he could get her there during the next waltz.

When she finally arrived, he thought his breath might fall out of his body. The dress she wore displayed her beauty and personality in a way that jolted him to the core.

Her family disappeared behind a cluster of people. In moments, Mrs. Snowley and Miss Marianne emerged, but not Bianca. Where had she gone?

Hudson started moving toward where he'd last seen her. A door was behind the group she'd vanished into. Had she left the ball-room already? Why leave so soon after arriving?

A footman entered through the door with a note in his hand. As he crossed the floor and handed the note to Lord Brimsbane, a sinking feeling hit Hudson's middle.

He hoped it was simply a coincidence, but what if it wasn't?

Lord Brimsbane frowned at the paper and glanced at the windows that overlooked the large garden and then nodded at the footman before stuffing the note into his pocket. He hastily made his excuses and started moving toward the door.

What if the note was from her? What if she hadn't told Brimsbane no yet? What if she'd told him yes? What if she had waited until tonight to answer?

What if the note had absolutely nothing to do with her and following Brimsbane would make Hudson the rudest and nosiest of guests?

He was willing to take that chance.

BIANCA LEANED HER head against the wall in the shadowed alcove she'd sought out soon after their arrival. She'd never been so nervous. What if she was wrong? What if he'd changed his mind?

What if that kiss hadn't made him rethink everything in the entire world the way it had done for her?

One thing was certain, she wasn't going to find any of those answers while hiding outside the ballroom.

As she came around the corner to rejoin the ball, she saw Hudson making his way toward the gardens.

Why was he going out there?

Her stepmother's determined face flashed through her mind.

Oh no. What if she'd taken Miss Wainbright's idea seriously and intended to trap Hudson into some form of compromising situation?

The son of an earl had proved Mrs. Snowley wrong and extended an offer of marriage to the stepdaughter she'd discounted.

Despite her surprise, she'd been additionally offended when Bianca hadn't immediately accepted.

Was she angry enough to do something drastic?

Even if Hudson had returned to his original plan after kissing Bianca, he didn't deserve to be a victim of this cruel social game.

Her fingers curled into fists, and she set off down the corridor to follow him into the garden. If he wasn't alone, he couldn't get caught.

THE GARDEN WAS DARK, and Hudson immediately felt like a fool.

If Bianca had sent that note, she wouldn't have brought Lord Brimsbane out here. Something else had lured the viscount, and it wasn't Hudson's business.

Curiosity was strong, though, particularly when he heard a muffled crash to his right, followed by a string of grumbled curses. Had Brimsbane fallen?

He moved toward the sound and entered a small, ornate clearing.

Where a man with round spectacles and a round hat was pointing a pistol at Lord Brimsbane.

"Whoa, now," Hudson said, spreading his hands wide at his hips. He didn't know what he stumbled into, but he couldn't leave Brimsbane to face it alone.

The gunman gestured to Brimsbane. "You look too much like your father to be anyone but Brimsbane. I'm not here for you. Move along."

"I think not." Brimsbane's back stiffened, obviously offended at the idea that he'd simply let a madman get at his guests.

"All I want is what's mine. It was stolen, and I want it back."

"And you think it's here?"

"No, but he is, that thieving . . ." The man swallowed hard. "They let me think it was mine, and they took it away."

An uneasy feeling worked through Hudson. There were no paintings of his uncle, no descriptions other than that he was a madman who wanted what his father had created. That description could fit the man in front of him. Was it possible?

"Who are you here for?" Hudson asked, easing farther into the circle.

The gunman looked him up and down, and Hudson was thankful he'd gotten his mother's coloring. He wouldn't look like anyone from this area, not in this shadowed garden.

"Hudson, don't do it!"

A small but strong body slammed into Hudson's back, nearly sending him to the ground.

Both Brimsbane and the gunman scurried about during the slight commotion, but Hudson managed to right himself and the woman who'd knocked into him.

He looked down at the warm bundle in his arms. At least he'd found Bianca, though he would far rather she not be anywhere near this situation.

"Hudson?" the man said. "You're Stildon?"

Should he confirm it? That didn't seem the smartest plan. "I'm sure there are many men named Hudson."

"But only one of them stole my horses."

Horses. Wasn't the man after the title?

"Who are you?" Brimsbane asked.

"Mr. Albany. I want my horses."

Horses. Hudson had horses, and if it got a madman away from Bianca, he'd give them away. "I'm sure we can arrange some—"

"Bianca?" a voice hissed in the loudest whisper known to man. "Are you back here?"

This clearing did not need any more people in it.

"Of course she's back here. She'll do anything to ruin everything for us, including ruining herself."

Bianca groaned as her stepmother and sister joined the fracas.

"What is going on here?" Mrs. Snowley asked.

"There's a man with a gun," Bianca said.

"Not helpful," Hudson said, even though it did make him want to laugh.

Miss Marianne screamed.

Bianca murmured, "Now that was not helpful."

And it hadn't been. Mr. Albany was nearly vibrating with anger. He didn't look disheveled or wide-eyed or have any of the other traits Hudson normally thought insane people would have, but there was no question that the man had gone somewhat mad.

"Well, this is not what I expected to find when I heard a woman scream in the garden." Aaron stepped into the clearing.

"What are *you* doing here?" Hudson and Brimsbane asked at the same time.

"Moral support."

"At a ball?" Bianca asked. "You wouldn't even attend an assembly when I asked you."

Aaron shrugged. "I didn't think you needed me there."

"And now I do?" Hudson asked.

"I'm not here for you," Aaron said. Then he gestured to the gunman. "Well, I am now. But I wasn't earlier."

A loud crack filled the air as the gun went off.

With shrieks and yells, everyone dove for the ground. Hudson shoved Bianca into the edge of the clearing as he went down, trying to push her farther out of the way.

With the shot still ringing in his ears, he lifted his head to see his uncle exchanging his spent gun for another in his coat pocket.

Slowly, Hudson climbed to his feet. The man had a look of desperation about him that made Hudson more than a little concerned about what he was going to do.

"There are too many witnesses," he said. "If you leave now, you've done nothing that will prevent you from returning to Ireland. Plenty an angry man walks free."

He thought Aaron might have laughed at that, but he didn't turn to check.

Mr. Albany moved slowly toward the edge of the clearing. Was this going to work?

"I don't believe you." Mr. Albany crept closer to the dark edge of the woods. "And what do I have to go back to? I'm training other people's horses. I was going to breed the best champions they'd ever seen once I had possession of the Hawksworth horses."

"Perhaps we can work something out."

The man sneered. "I don't want your castoffs." He moved so suddenly that it took everyone by surprise, and it wasn't until Bianca yelped that Hudson realized his mistake.

He'd pushed her away from him to protect her, but now he wasn't close enough to keep her safe.

Mr. Albany grabbed her arm and dragged her to her feet, swinging the gun back and forth from the group to Bianca.

If it was possible for a man's stomach to melt into his shoes,

Hudson's had just done so. He couldn't lose her. Not when he'd just realized how important she was.

"You stay where you are, and nothing will happen to her. I'll let her go when I feel safe."

Hudson wasn't sure what it would take for this man to feel secure, but anywhere farther than the path leading from the clearing was too far for him to take Bianca. "No."

Mr. Albany held Bianca tighter. "In this, at least, you don't get a say. This gun means that right now I'm in charge, and I say I'm taking her with me."

He dragged her to the path that led from the clearing, and all three men started to move but froze when he jabbed the gun into Bianca's side so hard that she cried out.

Her gaze found his, eyes wide with fear. "Hudson."

"Bianca." He wanted to tell her he loved her, to make sure she knew she'd become his closest friend in an impossibly short amount of time, that she was the person he couldn't imagine spending one more day of his life without, but he couldn't say any of those things.

"I'm coming for you," he promised, though whether he was threatening his uncle or reassuring Bianca he wasn't sure. Perhaps a little of both.

Mr. Albany growled and then showed the strength of a man who worked with horses by snagging Bianca about her waist and hauling her off her feet. Then he was running into the dark night.

As soon as he cleared the edge, Brimsbane, Aaron, and Hudson were on the move, the sound of their movements covered by the screaming and babbling crying of Mrs. Snowley and Miss Marianne.

Another gunshot cracked the air, and the three men dove to the ground once more. When they scrambled back up, Bianca and her captor were nowhere to be seen.

Thirty-Five

Bianca had never experienced an abduction before, but she had to wonder if they were all this clumsy. Even though it seemed that Mr. Albany hadn't planned this entire thing, she still couldn't manage to get away.

And she'd tried.

She'd wriggled and kicked, but despite how strong she was, he was stronger. He tied his cravat around her mouth before flipping her back over his shoulder and running. There was nothing she could do except beat on his back with her fists.

Beneath her she could see the blur of a long expanse of grass and then the edge of a lane before he threw her into the bottom of a small cart. Her head collided with the wall, leaving her dazed for a few moments, just enough for him to bind her wrists and throw a blanket over her head.

Still, she kicked and grunted, until he kicked back. "Keep quiet." His foot jabbed her in the stomach once more, knocking the air from her body. "I've no reason to hurt you."

A whip cracked, and the cart began to move. Faster and faster it went, bumping about enough to make her question whether or not he was taking one of the roads that led from the east side of town. If he had two horses pulling the cart, they'd be able to cover a great deal of ground very quickly.

And if he was crossing the countryside instead of staying to the lanes, it was going to be even harder for Hudson to find her. She was going to have to get herself out of this. Her captor had to stop eventually. And when he did, she would need to have a plan.

HUDSON LOOKED AT Brimsbane. It was possible, even likely, that they had ideas of marrying the same woman, but right now that didn't matter. He'd rather see Bianca married to someone else than in the hands of his crazy uncle.

"How many men in that ballroom do you trust to help with this?"

Brimsbane looked up at his house and pressed his lips tightly together. "None."

"Lord Trent said he was coming," Aaron added. "And I arrived with Lord Farnsworth. Though, in all honesty, he's not the best in these types of situations."

"You've faced a lot of abductions, have you?" Hudson couldn't help asking.

Brimsbane shook his head. "Farnsworth's leaving will be too obvious. If he's not here for the announcement, everyone will notice."

"Announcement?" Hudson asked. "Lord Farnsworth and Lady Rebecca?"

"They met in London," Brimsbane said.

"I might have gone to Town to tell him to get his lovesick self to Newmarket and do something about it," Aaron said with a shrug.

"I have questions, but they can wait. I'm going to find Lord Trent."

"Meet us at the stables," Brimsbane said.

"What should I do?" Mrs. Snowley asked in a small voice.

"Go home," Hudson said. "If she gets free, she might go there. Besides, if you go in looking like that, everyone will know something is wrong."

"What will happen to Bianca?" she asked.

Hudson wanted to ask why she cared, but that wasn't fair. Just because she preferred her own daughter to the one she'd gotten through marriage didn't mean she wanted Bianca dead.

Nor was it a conversation he had time to deal with. "Go home."

Hudson took off through the garden and had to pause to compose himself before going into the ballroom. Sending Mrs. Snowley home would be for naught if he gave the situation away.

It didn't take long to find Lord Trent. For a man who had decided to live a fairly quiet life, he certainly knew how to be the center of attention.

How was Hudson supposed to get him out of it?

Lord Trent noticed Hudson and gave a small nod.

Within moments, the crowd had dispersed, and Lord Trent was leading Hudson over to the side of the room.

"How did you . . . never mind. Bianca's been taken."

Lord Trent gave a nod and started moving through the crowd efficiently but without giving the appearance of haste. "Just need to find my wife first."

Hudson couldn't stand the crush of the ballroom. "I'll be outside." He retreated to the back corridor he'd entered from and paced. He was on his second loop when Lord Trent joined him. "Let's go."

In the stable, Brimsbane handed Hudson a set of reins. Hudson gaped in appreciation of the animal. Strong forelegs, wide chest, narrow head. "Who is this?"

Both of Brimsbane's eyebrows went up, and he said in a dry voice, "Hezekiah."

Hudson shook his head. He'd been so focused on doing something that would impress other people, he hadn't even looked into whether or not they were right about the horse.

He mounted up and joined the others, along with a small handful of grooms outside the stable.

"There are three roads from this area," Brimsbane said. "Four, if we count the one going back through Newmarket, but I don't think he'd go that way."

"He could have also gone cross-country," Aaron said. "That's what I would do."

"In short, he could be anywhere," Hudson said. "But we've got to start searching somewhere."

They split up and determined routes.

"Ten miles," Aaron said with surprising authority, given how outranked he was in the group. "We could run these horses ragged in the wrong direction. Ten miles, then you come back to regroup."

Everyone agreed, and they moved out.

As Hudson rode, he appreciated the animal beneath him, but most of his thoughts were prayers. If he was going to believe that God had a plan and it was better than his, then he had to believe that God knew about this too.

"Okay, God. Whatever happens, I'm trusting you. But please, God, please keep her safe. I need to tell her what she means to me."

Then he and Hezekiah went galloping off into the night, unsure of what they were even looking for.

ONCE BIANCA STOPPED MOVING, her captor stopped kicking. He then must have decided to take a road, because the ride got smoother.

Still, he didn't stop.

To Bianca's amazement, with the rocking motion and her own stillness, she fell into a fitful sleep.

She blinked groggily awake as the cart came to a stop.

How long had it been? Hours? Minutes?

She kept herself still and tried to listen. The feet shifted and then were gone, but the dull point of the gun replaced them.

The feet were preferable.

She didn't move, barely breathed. What was he doing? She assumed he'd stopped to change horses, but did he intend to simply stand there, pointing a gun at her the whole time?

Anger swelled. What would happen if she screamed? If she threw this blanket off and tried to stand? Were there other people about? Would he risk shooting her?

She hoped not.

It was a bet she had to make.

She wiggled her head first, trying to shift the blanket enough to allow her to take a peek at the situation.

After one look, she jerked her head sideways so that it would be entirely free of the blanket, and then she felt like a veritable idiot.

The cart had been pushed into the corner of a stable, and there was no one around. The gun had been wedged against the seat in order to keep it pressed against her.

If she shifted until it fell, would it go off? Could it? It looked like the gun he'd fired as he ran from the clearing, but he'd had plenty of time to reload it.

Had he left her here, or was he coming back?

Where even was here?

She could determine that after she determined what this gun was going to do.

She shifted.

The gun shifted.

Perhaps, if she moved very slowly, she could ease the gun to the bottom of the cart and not risk setting it off.

She held her breath and moved. The gun scraped the side of the seat as it moved down.

Shift. Scrape. Tiniest of necessary breaths. Shift, scrape. Shift, scrape. Shift, clunk.

She dropped her head to the bottom of the cart and took a moment to just breathe, even though the cloth tied around her mouth smelled like a wet horse. That wretched smell meant she was still alive.

Getting out of the cart with her hands tied behind her was something of a struggle, and her skirt was hiked up around her waist by the time she eased herself over the raised side of the cart, but once her feet were on the ground, her confidence grew.

What was she going to do now? She had no money. Depending on how far they'd gone, her name might not even be recognized.

Before she started to panic, Bianca took a good look around. She was in a large stable, though it looked like it was part of a nicer inn and not a private establishment. That was good. People were good, right?

To her left, a black tail swished above perfect black stockings, flicking a fly from a rich, red-brown rump.

She knew that horse.

Either Lord Rigsby hadn't left the area, or he'd come back.

Or she'd traveled much, much farther than she imagined.

She didn't really care one way or the other. All that mattered was she knew someone at this inn.

Now she just had to find him.

After being curled up in the floor of the cart, not moving for so very long, every muscle protested as she moved through the stable.

She was going to have to go into the inn. The bound hands she might be able to hide, especially since the ball gown would be a significant distraction.

The gag, on the other hand, was all too noticeable.

She looked around again. There had to be something in here that would help her get the gag off. No matter the stable, there were certain necessities each one contained. A hoof-pick, a leather awl, or even a comb might be enough for her to hook the gag and pull it free.

Her eyes lit on the bridle hooks at the end of the stalls. That should work. At least she wouldn't risk stabbing herself with something sharp.

It took three tries to hook the gag but only a few moments of tugging to get the loop of cloth to hang loose around her neck. She sagged against the wall, working her jaw back and forth and sliding her dry tongue across cracked lips. One problem down, and she wasn't even going to consider how many left to go.

It was dark, and the innyard was, for the most part, quiet. A sign reading *The Green Bear* in faded red letters hung from the entry post. Beyond it, a somewhat familiar town street.

Giddiness swelled in her. She knew where she was. If she was on a horse, she could be back at Lady Rebecca's home in a matter of hours. If she was on foot, especially in evening slippers and unescorted, and with a madman potentially looking for her, it might take a little longer.

Much better to find Lord Rigsby first.

Of course, there was no guarantee her captor wasn't also in the inn.

A young boy was sitting in the doorway of the stable, presumably on watch for customers or other people approaching the stable. She propped her shoulder against the wall, trying to keep her face at least somewhat shadowed.

"You there. Boy."

The boy jerked around and fell off his stool. "Well, I'll be. Where'd you come from?"

"Hmmm." She wasn't answering that question. Instead, she stuck her foot out from beneath her gown. "See these shoe clips?"

The boy slid across the floor and looked at the shoe. "Are those real diamonds?"

"Yes. And they're all yours if you deliver a message to someone in that inn for me."

The boy looked from her to the shoe clip. "I'm not supposed to leave . . ."

She wiggled her foot.

The boy swallowed. "What's the message?"

"Find Lord Rigsby and tell him there's a problem with his horse."

The boy scrambled up, grabbed a lantern, and ran past her. "Is there really? There can't be. He let me sit atop the horse and see what it was like. He's a nice fellow."

"Sunset's Pride is fine. But I need Lord Rigsby to come out here without anyone else knowing I'm here."

The boy licked his lips. "And I get both shoe clips?"

Why not? It wasn't as if she ever understood their purpose. Mrs. Snowley simply insisted on them. "One shoe clip alone won't do me much good, so yes."

He looked back and forth at the stable one more time before giving a sharp nod and running to the inn.

Bianca sagged against the wall inside Sunset's Pride's stall and dropped her forehead to the horse's side. Everything was going to be all right. She would get home and then . . . and then . . . well, she'd be home. Everything else could be figured out later.

Footsteps hustling across the floor alerted her to an approaching presence. The boy had certainly been fast.

"What's wrong with—Miss Snowley?"

"She promised me shoe clips," the boy piped up.

"Oh yes." She stuck her foot out. With her hands bound behind her back she couldn't exactly remove them herself. "Go ahead."

The boy started to kneel, but Lord Rigsby grabbed his shoulder. "Wait." He reached into his pocket and pulled out a bank note. "Cash is always better."

The boy stared wide-eyed at the money and then stuffed it into his pocket.

"Make sure no one comes back here," Lord Rigsby added.

The boy nodded and ran back to the front of the stable.

Bianca tried to give him a carefree grin. "I don't suppose you've a knife on you?"

"Of course, but—"

"I'd be ever so grateful." She turned and presented her bound wrists to him.

He muttered something harsh but reached down to his boot.

The rustle of fabric. Cold metal against her arm. A few quick tugs. Finally, blessed, aching, painful freedom. Every inch of her arms protested as she tried to move them to a more natural position.

"What happened?"

How could she explain? She wasn't entirely sure what had happened, and she'd been there. "I somehow managed to get between Hudson and his uncle."

Lord Rigsby's eyebrows rose. "Hudson, is it?" He gave a nod. "I suspected as much."

Heat flooded Bianca. Welcome in the cool night air, but not by her pride. "It's not like that."

"Then you're both idiots."

She wasn't an idiot. *She* had been quite aware of her feelings and ready to admit them. Whether or not he was, she didn't know, because she'd been avoiding him.

Perhaps they were both idiots.

"Be that as it may, I was hoping you could assist me in getting home."

"Is your abductor in the inn?"

"Does it matter?"

"Yes. If someone is going to shoot when they see you with me, I'd rather smuggle you out in a burlap bag."

"I think he's gone. At least he said he intended only to keep me until he got far enough away."

He nodded. "I'm not taking you home. If someone sees us alone this late at night, it won't matter if you and Stildon are idiots or if you're friends with Mr. Whitworth."

"Lord Brimsbane saw the abduction. You can return me there."
Surely Lady Gliddon and Lady Rebecca would keep the whole
thing quiet. "Fresh horses will have us there in four hours."

He laid a hand on the back of his horse. "Sunset's Pride could
be there in less, but there's not a horse we could rent in this stable
that will keep up with him."

"I don't suppose you would let me borrow Sunset's Pride, would
you?"

"I'd rather buy you a nag."

Thirty-Six

Hudson left his assigned groom behind almost from the start. He abided by Aaron's ten-mile rule, but he searched a few side roads on his way. Hezekiah was walking slowly now, head drooping low. He'd never been trained for this sort of endurance.

Hudson slid from the horse's back and led him to a creek so small it barely needed an arch for the small bridge to cross it. It was enough for the horse to drink though.

He rested his head against the horse's sweaty haunches.

It was all he could do to hold on to his newly formed belief that God was in control of everything. It had seemed his father had believed it. The evidence was there that his father's faith continued even when his mother had fallen ill and died.

Hudson would hold on to his as well.

Once Hezekiah finished drinking, Hudson led the horse down the road by its reins. There was no sense in making the exhausted animal carry Hudson anymore. A mile south of Cheveley, he turned back onto the main road to Newmarket. Aaron was waiting there, arms resting gently on the saddle pommel.

"She's back at Gliddon's."

Everything in him dropped. His heart, his vision, even his knees gave way, and he crumpled to the ground, prayers of gratefulness on his lips. Bits and buckles jangled, and then Aaron was kneeling beside him.

"Take my horse. I'll walk Hezekiah back. Lady Rebecca has informed everyone that no one is seeing Bianca until she's rested, but everyone is welcome to fill her mother's private parlor."

Hudson looked up to see a smirk on Aaron's face. "Lady Rebecca said that?"

Aaron nodded. "I think there might be more to her than most people ever knew."

"But you did?"

He shook his head. "Not personally. Oliver might have mentioned it." He hauled Hudson to his feet. "Go on, get back. You'll hate it if you're not there when she emerges."

It took him three tries to mount the horse with his numb knees, but soon he was back trotting toward Newmarket.

She was safe. She was alive.

For now, that was enough.

BIANCA HAD NEVER wanted for anything in her life, aside from a glorious stable, but she could learn to be very jealous of Lady Rebecca's tub.

It had been a rough ride back to Meadowland Park. Lord Rigsby had pulled her up onto Sunset's Pride with him. Even carrying two people, the horse had been faster than anything she'd ridden before.

She didn't know where he'd gone after bringing her here, but she would have to find him later and thank him.

Her would-be rescuers had still been out searching when she arrived, but the ball had thankfully ended. To her surprise, it was Lady Rebecca who had pulled her in. She'd napped in Lady Rebecca's bed, eaten a light meal, and was now soaking in a marvelous tub. She felt so relaxed that it was as if the entire ordeal had been nothing but a nightmare.

Lady Rebecca hustled in, followed by two maids, one carrying a dress, and one armed with a comb and a cup of hairpins. "You can present yourself now. He's returned."

"Who?"

She shook her head and gave a quiet laugh. "Lord Stildon. I knew you would want to see him first, so I delayed everyone else."

"I . . . you . . . but . . ."

Lady Rebecca shook her head. "Lord Stildon is a nice man, and I'm sure we'd have rubbed along well enough. I picked him because he was the only one who asked about me, you know. Never once did he ask to go see the horse." She sighed. "Still, he wasn't . . . there'd been a man in London, but he let me leave, so I didn't think he loved me."

"But now he's here?"

Lady Rebecca smiled wider and brighter than the sun. "He is. Even if his friend had to drag him here, he was still the one who had to do the asking."

"So congratulations are in order?" Bianca was happy for her. Very much so. But she now had to wonder if Hudson had chosen Bianca, was settling for her, or had decided against her entirely.

After dressing and having her hair pinned up, Bianca went to join everyone in the family parlor. Hudson was braced against the window frame, head dropped and shoulders hunched.

"Darling, I'm so glad you're feeling better. We were all worried." Bianca hadn't even noticed her stepmother in the room, but now the woman was trying to wrap her arms about Bianca like she was some sort of puppy.

Bianca straightened her arms and pushed her way free. "I don't think that's necessary." She glanced around the room, noting who was in it. Though there were a few surprises, there was no one she didn't know. "No one here believes your sincerity, I assure you."

Muffled laughter came from her right, where Lord Trent and

Lady Adelaide were seated on a settee. Miss Hancock sat on Lady Adelaide's other side.

Lord Farnsworth sat in a corner, head lolling against the wall as he slept. Her father was rising awkwardly to his feet, holding his knees as if he wasn't sure they'd take his weight.

Once he was fully upright, he moved toward her. The smile he gave her held only a glimmer of his normal gaiety, a sheen of sadness disguising his spirit. "These old bones don't run around quite like they once did." He hugged her, and she reciprocated. "I've tried to protect you from so much, but I couldn't this time."

"You did?"

Father scoffed. "You don't think a gentleman lets his daughter tromp around in the woods and in a strange stable without ensuring her safety, do you?"

"He pays Owen's wages," Aaron said, not moving from his spot by the wall. "The man's job is to make your life safer and easier. Anything he does around the stable is simply to keep busy and avoid suspicion."

Bianca's eyes widened. She had always wondered why Aaron had never sent the man packing.

Father was frowning. "I didn't know you knew about that."

Aaron coughed. "I tried to have the man fired after two days of observing him in the stable, only to learn he didn't work for Lord Stildon."

"Why didn't I know about this?" Hudson stepped forward to join the gathering, entering Bianca's peripheral vision and reminding her that not quite everything had been set to rights.

"Because learning the particulars of your finances has not exactly been your goal these past three weeks." Aaron smirked.

Her father's expression hardened as he turned to Hudson. "If she tells you to go away, you will. But I expect you to continue to give her access to your stable."

Bianca closed her eyes and considered covering her ears like a child. She didn't want to hear this, didn't want to know, didn't want that final moment when Hudson told her he would never love her enough to make her his future. As much as she loved his horses, she wanted more. She wanted him to want more.

Several murmurs broke out around her, and then people were moving, feet were shuffling, and clothes and furniture were rustling. "Five minutes." Her father's voice finally broke through the chaos. "Not a minute more, and I'll be one room away."

"Thank you, sir," Hudson said.

If she got ill, could she still blame it on her ordeal?

"Give me one reason why I should leave." Bianca looked over to see Lord Brimsbane standing by the door. Was he challenging Hudson? For her?

"Lord Brimsbane, I told you—" Bianca began.

"Yes. I know what you told me, but that doesn't mean he doesn't have to treat you well. I'm happy my sister is getting to marry the man she loves, but I'm not sure I trust how quickly Lord Stildon's affections shift. We could make a good life, you and I."

"You don't love me."

His silence was confirmation, and she released the small breath she'd been holding while she waited.

"Her father gave me five minutes," Hudson said.

"I'm giving you four." Lord Brimsbane left the room.

Strong hands cupped her shoulders and slid down to grip her hands. "Bianca."

She couldn't resist his unspoken request. Her lashes fluttered upward, and his face filled her vision. Tears pooled along her lower lashes but didn't fall. His eyes searched her own. Whatever he was looking for, she hoped she was able to give it to him.

"Bianca," he whispered. "I miss you. I miss my best friend."

Bianca grimaced and dropped her gaze, but his hand was under her chin, nudging it back up before it had a chance to fall to her chest.

"I miss my best friend," he said again. "I want her back. I want her in my life, telling me what I don't know and sharing in my victories. I want her by my side when I watch my first races." He swallowed hard and shifted his weight. "I want her with me when I run my first horses, the ones I select and I breed."

"That takes years," she choked out.

He nodded. "I want you there."

Her heart thudded against her chest, even as part of her cautioned that he still hadn't said in what capacity she would be standing at his side.

He cupped her cheek. "I won't ask you to marry me yet. I want to do this right. Brimsbane is right when he says this has all been too fast. I want to make sure you know, without a doubt, how important you are to me. You come first. Before the horses, the stable, even my own reputation. Bianca Snowley, will you allow me to court you?"

Did life get any better than this moment? Could a woman expire from happiness? While Bianca hoped for many more wonderful moments, she was afraid the pounding of her heart would have her testing the limits of joy that her body could handle. "Yes." She nodded her head with enough energy that her vision blurred. "Yes."

His smile was wide, and he leaned in to press it against hers. The sensation was strange, but Bianca didn't care. She'd stay forever with her smile pressed against his if it meant they would always be this happy.

Eventually they both relaxed enough to deepen the kiss into something that made it a good thing her father was a mere wall away.

Moments later—seconds, minutes, hours, it didn't matter— their embrace shifted to one of comfort. Hudson's arms wrapped around her so tightly that those last vestiges of fear and insecurity didn't have room to remain. She tucked her head against his shoulder and breathed in the smells of horse and leather that still clung to him. With his heart beating steadily beneath her ear, she felt more at home than she could remember feeling in a very long time.

A delicate cough had her lifting her head as Hudson's grip loosened. With great reluctance, she pulled away from Hudson. Even though he'd all but promised his future to her, they needed to take time to do this right, with both of them focused on the same outcome. No distractions, no miscommunications, no ulterior motives.

"I hurried ahead, but they're right behind me," Lady Rebecca called from the door.

"I love you," Bianca whispered.

"I love you too," Hudson whispered back, "enough to make sure you know it."

Bianca stepped farther away. Hudson's hand trailed down her arm before snagging in her fingers and tightening around them, refusing to relinquish that final connection. Was she giving him a secret smile of happiness like he was giving her? They certainly weren't going to leave any question in anyone's mind as to whether they cared for each other.

Father and Lord Brimsbane reached the door at the same time, making no pretense of looking anywhere other than Bianca and Hudson and their joined hands.

Brimsbane shook his head and went to join his sister.

Father kept staring pointedly at their hands. "Have we an announcement to make?"

"Not yet," Hudson said, smiling down at Bianca and bringing his free hand up to brush a stray lock of hair from her cheek. "Soon. But not yet."

"Then I think a bit more distance would be appropriate, don't you?"

Bianca sighed. "Father."

"Daughter." He nodded at their hands. "You'll have plenty of time to enjoy those moments. I imagine you'll scandalize New-market with the number of waltzes you'll share. Take this time to know that you will also enjoy each other's company in the break-fast room." His gaze dropped to the floor and looked sad. "Trust me. It's too late to discover it's a problem after you're married."

Bianca dropped Hudson's hand and stepped toward the man who had watched out for her more than she'd ever realized. It didn't escape her notice that of all the people reentering the room, her stepmother wasn't among them. "Father?"

"Don't pity me, girl. I'm only now realizing that you suffered for that decision far more than I did. At least I got Marianne and Giles."

"I got them too, Father."

He lifted his eyebrows and gave a shake of his head. "I saw she ignored you, and I thought if I pressured her not to, you'd get a mother." He chuckled. "I think I could have done a better job."

"I think everything is turning out as it should," Bianca said with a smile.

"Be that as it may," he said sternly, giving Hudson a hard look, "I'll be paying more attention from now on."

Hudson grinned. "I wouldn't have it any other way, sir."

"Good." Father nodded. "Now. Ask her properly to go for a ride with you tomorrow. We all know she'll be at that stable when the sun rises, but I won't have you taking her presence for granted."

Thirty-Seven

Hudson's valet might be ready to quit after dealing with Hudson's maniacal attention to detail when dressing for his morning ride. Normally, he threw on a coat without thought, fidgeted while his cravat was tied, and gave no notice to the shine of his boots.

This morning he wanted to look perfect.

It didn't matter that Bianca frequently had seen him in his near-disheveled state. He wanted to show her that he was taking this time of courtship seriously.

Bianca and Aaron were already in the stable when he arrived, standing near Hestia's stall, feeding her a treat. Owen was grooming a horse nearby with tiny, minuscule strokes that the horse was certainly enjoying but was going to make the job take five times longer than normal. Of course, it also put him in a position to watch every move Bianca made.

What to do with Owen would be a decision for another day. He'd take over paying the man himself, but with Bianca's penchant for going riding, keeping a man employed to keep her safe wasn't a bad idea.

Especially since no one had been able to find where Hudson's uncle had run off to.

Hudson's grin widened. How nice it was to be thinking of the future in terms of Bianca, in terms of keeping her happy and safe.

That was so much more fulfilling than the solvency of his stable or the most impressive foal.

"Good morning," Bianca said with a smile.

"Good morning."

Aaron groaned. "All of you. Every single one of you. I've no friends left who aren't nauseatingly happy."

"Maybe you'll be next," Hudson said.

Aaron merely lifted a brow and shook his head.

Hudson nodded toward Hestia. "She's the only mare we haven't bred yet. Any ideas?"

"I have one," Bianca said quietly. "But I don't think you're going to like it."

"What is it?" Hudson was inclined to agree, even if she suggested her father's old carriage horse.

"Well," she said, primly folding her hands in front of her, "it seems silly to be thinking Hezekiah is the only one who could sire a winner."

"He's sired the last three winners of the Two Thousand Guineas Stakes and two of the last five Derby winners. He's as close to a sure thing as a horse gets." Aaron shook his head. "You can get a winner out of another horse, but you'll be holding your breath while you wait for it."

"Unless there's a better horse that no one knows about."

"I've only seen a better animal twice in my life. Both were in India." Hudson shook his head.

"I know of a magnificent animal named Sunset's Pride."

"There was a Sunset's Pride in India," Hudson mused. "He was perfection."

"I think it might be the same horse. The owner said he brought him over from India."

Hudson couldn't believe it—wouldn't believe it unless he saw the horse with his own eyes. "That's amazing. Why don't you think I'll like your suggestion?"

"Because . . . well . . . he belongs to Lord Rigsby."

Hudson stilled. Aaron stilled. The bustle of the stable around them stilled, proving once again that none of the conversation had been private.

Bianca rushed on. "He's not a bad man, you know. Well, you probably don't know, and that's understandable, but I think, maybe . . ." She sighed. "There's no reason Aaron has to have anything to do with it. Hudson and I—" Color sprang to her cheeks. "That is, Hudson can approach him and arrange everything."

"Are you trying to fade me out of a job already?" Aaron asked.

"Of course not, I—"

"I suppose," Aaron said slowly, "that there comes a time when the right thing to do is let go of the past. Even if it's difficult."

"Tell that to my uncle if you ever see him again," Hudson grumbled.

"I hope to never see your uncle again."

Bianca murmured agreement.

"I don't suppose the world will end if I go make a business proposition to the legitimate son of my wastrel father," Aaron mused.

"What happened to you isn't his fault," Bianca said. "I think he might be lonely." She reached out and clasped Hudson's hand. "I wouldn't wish spending life alone on anyone, even if they think they have all they need."

Aaron groaned. "I'll do it." He ran his hand over Hestia's nose. "I won't let you down, old girl. One more champion foal, coming up." He gave Bianca and Hudson a nod. "I'll get out of here now and let you two experience this lovely day." He glanced at the window. "I wouldn't stray too far, though. Looks like it might rain."

Hudson looked out at the now-familiar dismal grey. "It looks like a fabulous day for a ride."

Bianca laughed. "I agree."

He reached up to smooth an errant curl. "You are amazing."

Her returning smile lit up the dim stable like a sunny day in India.

"You are everything I didn't know I needed," Hudson said, "and everything I hadn't realized a man could hope for." He cupped her cheek. "I love you, Bianca."

"I love you too." She gave him a sweet smile, her eyes shimmering. "Now, I think the right thing for us to do is get out of this stable before we have to start over establishing our correct footing."

"I couldn't agree more." He offered her his arm and escorted her outside to where their saddled horses had been tied. He walked past Odysseus and over to Hades. "I do believe we made a bargain once. That if you helped me get the woman I needed, you would get to ride Hades, so"—he took her by the waist and, even as she shrieked and grabbed his wrists, lifted her up onto the tall black horse's back—"up you go."

She grabbed the reins and a handful of mane, laughing and jerking her head from side to side to look down at the ground. "He's so tall."

"He is, so perhaps no galloping. We'll keep to a pace Odysseus can handle. At least for now?"

Her brown gaze held his, excitement and happiness and everything else right and good shining from her face. "Does that mean you'll let me ride him again?"

"I think a woman whose husband owns a racing stable should know what it's like to ride a racehorse. It does seem like it would make watching the race that much more enjoyable." He placed a hand on the horse's neck. "Let's build up to that, though."

"We'll keep it slow today." She nodded toward Odysseus. "Particularly since I wouldn't want to leave you behind."

With an answering grin, Hudson mounted up and they rode off, the first of many mornings they would spend establishing a new life together. Several feet behind them, Owen followed on the back of Poseidon.

As they crossed the drive and trotted into the pastures, Hudson envisioned one day taking this ride with their children, a family taking on the world together.

It hadn't been the idea of family he'd grown up with, but it was the one he'd come to know since arriving in England, and he couldn't think of any legacy that would be more right for him to build.

Acknowledgments

When I sat down to write my eleventh book (this one, in case you were wondering), I thought I knew what I was doing. It turns out that just like Hudson and Bianca, my plans weren't God's plans, and the entire book ended up being different from how it started.

The tale you just finished would not have been possible in its current state without the help of a great many people.

Jacob deserves all the awards for listening to me gripe, acting as a sounding board when I had to rework the plot, and being willing to read this book more times than he's read anything since I got published.

Much appreciation to my children, who made the enormous sacrifice (note the sarcasm there) of going on a trail ride with me so that I could remember how wonderful being on the back of a horse was.

For my Voxer Girls, the biggest of hugs. Every day you encourage and inspire me. I can't wait to see what we all do next.

Thank you, Regina, for reminding me that my career wasn't over simply because my book needed a lot of editing in those early stages.

And thank you to the team at Bethany House for the patience and guidance demonstrated during all that editing.

To my horse-loving friends, you were worth every cup of coffee I bought you while you shared your stories with me.

Finally, to my readers, thank you for taking this journey with me. A story is dead without someone to listen to it. Thank you for completing the circle.

Kristi Ann Hunter is the author of the HAWTHORNE HOUSE and HAVEN MANOR series and a 2016 RITA Award winner, an ACFW Genesis contest winner, and a Georgia Romance Writers Maggie Award for Excellence winner. She lives with her husband and three children in Georgia. Find her online at www.kristiannhunter.com.

You May Also Like . . .

In the midst of the Great War, Margot De Wilde spends her days deciphering intercepted messages. But after a sudden loss, her world is turned upside down. Lieutenant Drake Elton returns wounded from the field, followed by a destructive enemy. Immediately smitten with Margot, how can Drake convince a girl who lives entirely in her mind that sometimes life's answers lie in the heart?

The Number of Love by Roseanna M. White, THE CODEBREAKERS #1
roseannamwhite.com

Years of hard work enabled Douglas Shaw to escape a life of desperate poverty—and now he's determined to marry into high society to prevent reliving his old circumstances. But when Alice McNeil, an unconventional telegrapher at his firm, raises the ire of a vindictive co-worker, he must choose between rescuing her reputation and the future he's always planned.

Line by Line by Jennifer Delamere, LOVE ALONG THE WIRES #1
jenniferdelamere.com

Determined to uphold her father's legacy, newly graduated Nora Shipley joins an entomology research expedition to India to prove herself in the field. In this spellbinding new land, Nora is faced with impossible choices—between saving a young Indian girl and saving her career, and between what she's always thought she wanted and the man she's come to love.

A Mosaic of Wings by Kimberly Duffy
kimberlyduffy.com

BETHANYHOUSE

More from Bethany House

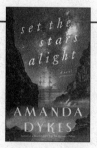

Reeling from the loss of her parents, Lucie Clairmont discovers an artifact under the floorboards of their London flat, leading her to an old seaside estate. Aided by her childhood friend Dashel, a renowned forensic astronomer, they start to unravel a history of heartbreak, sacrifice, and love begun 200 years prior—one that may offer the healing each seeks.

Set the Stars Alight by Amanda Dykes
amandadykes.com

Wanting to do her part in the Civil War effort, Clara McBride goes to work in the cartridge room at the Washington Arsenal. Her supervisor, Lieutenant Joseph Brady, is drawn to Clara but must focus on preventing explosions in the factory. When multiple shipments of cartridges fail to fire and everyone is suspect, can the spark of love between them survive?

A Single Spark by Judith Miller
judithmccoymiller.com

After facing desperate heartache and loss, Mercy agrees to escape a bleak future in London and join a bride ship. Wealthy and titled, Joseph leaves home and takes to the sea as the ship's surgeon to escape the pain of losing his family. He has no intention of settling down, but when Mercy becomes his assistant, they must fight against a forbidden love.

A Reluctant Bride by Jody Hedlund, THE BRIDE SHIPS #1
jodyhedlund.com

◆ BETHANYHOUSE